Praise for Lana Witt's
Stunning Debut Novel,

SLOW DANCING ON
DINOSAUR BONES

"An impressive literary debut, with characters not soon forgotten."
—*Booklist*

"Filled with the humor, pathos, the down-to-earth humanity of the Kentucky mountain people. . . . Lana Witt is a masterful storyteller."
—Florence Gilkeson, *The Pilot* (Southern Pines, NC)

"[An] amiable first novel. . . ."
—Jonathan Bing, *The New York Times Book Review*

"A high-spirited work replete with romance, suspense, and fascinating eccentrics."
—Mary Ellen Elsbernd, *Library Journal*

"A fresh, heart-warming slice of life. . . . Witt's wisecracking, earthy characters. . . . make the novel vibrate with life."
—Kathy Brown, *Lexington Herald-Leader*

"Enchanting, often outrageously funny. . . . Lana Witt's storyteller's voice and lyricism is unmistakable. For me, closing this book brought as much sad contentment for the story's end as it did a teeming desire for another Witt novel."
—Thomas Larson, *San Diego Writers' Monthly*

Slow Dancing on Dinosaur Bones

A NOVEL BY

LANA WITT

WASHINGTON SQUARE PRESS
PUBLISHED BY POCKET BOOKS

New York   London   Toronto   Sydney   Tokyo   Singapore

Selection from "The Visitant" copyright 1950 by Theodore Roethke. From *The Collected Poems of Theodore Roethke* by Theodore Roethke. Used by permission of Doubleday, a division of Bantam Doubleday Dell Publishing Group, Inc. *William Carlos Williams: Collected Poems: 1909-1939, Volume 1.* Copyright 1938 by New Directions Publishing Corp. Reprinted by permission of New Directions Publishing Corp. Quotes from *The Portable Nietzsche,* translated by Walter Kauffman. Published by Viking Penguin, copyright 1954.

A Washington Square Press Publication of
POCKET BOOKS, a division of Simon & Schuster Inc.
1230 Avenue of the Americas, New York, NY 10020

Copyright © 1996 by Lana Witt

All rights reserved, including the right to reproduce
this book or portions thereof in any form whatsoever.
For information address Scribner, 1230 Avenue of the
Americas, New York, NY 10020

ISBN: 0-671-89122-7

First Washington Square Press trade paperback printing September 1997

10 9 8 7 6 5 4 3 2 1

WASHINGTON SQUARE PRESS and colophon are
registered trademarks of Simon & Schuster Inc.

Cover illustration by Wendell Minor

Printed in the U.S.A.

For the storyteller, my father, Ernest Dixon

Acknowledgments

Either through their friendship and support, their invaluable criticism, or their existence on this earth, the following people have inspired and enabled me to write this book. I thank:

- My uncle, Eugene Dixon, for his life and times
- My writing group: Bonnie ZoBell (who was there from the start, opening doors and showing me possibilities), Rhonda Johnson, Patty Santana, Annette Bostrom, John Dacapias, and Kenneth Merrill for all those Sundays at the coffee shop where they helped me stay on track
- Darren Witt for his patience and detailed criticism
- Andrea Witt for listening to me babble on and on
- Kenneth Witt for keeping my computer going
- Ernest and Lucy Dixon for their input during countless Sunday phone calls
- Crystal Goodman for her honest criticism and for the walks by the bay where the idea of the novel began
- Mary Johnson for the chemistry info

- Robert L. Jones for his early encouragement
- Taylor and Gladys Prater for sharing their coal knowledge
- Rhonda Johnson and David Duke for the last go-around
- The entire gang *(past and present)* at the ROV, especially:
  - Caesar *(Ahh-you're-my-best-friend)* Bolchini, cohort in craziness
  - B. Marc *(with a c)* Bradley, who kept shouting, "Words! Give me words!"
  - David Lonsdale for his wonderful suggestion regarding Ten-Twenty
  - Tom and Delores Green for being more like family than bosses
  - Tom Nolan, who went to London, England, and had his picture made with a palace guard while holding the front cover of my manuscript out in front of him
  - Sandy Herndon, Dennis Fiore, Mary Householder, Linda Bunch, Elsie Lawson, and Sylvia Rivinius, to name a few more

I thank Michael Carlisle, Jane Rosenman, Michelle Tessler, Henry Carlisle, and each person who read the manuscript in its varying stages of completion and encouraged me.

Contents

I woke in the first of morning.

Staring at a tree, I felt the pulse of a stone.

Where's she now, I kept saying.

Where's she now, the mountain's downy girl?

But the bright day had no answer.

A wind stirred in a web of appleworms.

The tree, the close willow, swayed.

—Theodore Roethke, "The Visitant"

Part I

1

Chapter

As Gilman Lee stumbles toward his stove to make breakfast, he notices a man sprawled in the recliner asleep. Shrugging, he takes bacon and eggs out of the refrigerator and starts frying. "Sure a tall sonofabitch," he mutters, glancing around at the man. Height is usually the first thing Gilman notices about a person, perhaps because of his own short stature. Even when he was young and backed straight against the wall, he could never stretch himself higher than five feet and six inches.

Though he's past the age for it, Gilman still parties. It's not unusual for him to wake up in the morning and find people sprawled in chairs, but ordinarily he has some idea of who they are. The man in the recliner has black hair, a straight nose, and a cleft in his chin, and doesn't favor any of Gilman's acquaintances. Might be one of them Sizemores, he thinks, one that moved away a long time ago and's moved back. He puts eggs, bacon, and toast in two plates, sets them on the counter, opens the door leading from his apartment to the garage, and strolls through the machine shop, where the hood is raised on a classic 1949 Ford and blackened auto parts are scattered everywhere.

Outside, a light rain is beginning to fall; it's been raining off and on for the past two weeks. He heads for the trailer parked a few yards away and bangs on the door. "Uuuuhh, Ten-Fifteen," he yells. "Have you died in your sleep? Your little woman, out here, has fixed your breakfast, and you know she'll get mad if you don't eat before it gets cold."

Ten-Fifteen parked his trailer by Gilman's place six years ago. He works in the shop and does a good job in spite of his disability. Ten-Fifteen was born with arms that stick out from his sides like the hands of a clock. His real name is Roland, but he hasn't been called that since elementary school. As soon as his second-grade class learned to tell time, they realized that Roland's arms forever told the time of their morning recess. They started calling him Ten-Fifteen, and the name stuck.

Ten-Fifteen opens the door and stands there, smiling like the sun. Because he's always in a good mood, always grinning, constantly up, a lot of people think he's retarded, but he isn't. He just sees the bright side of things.

"It's about time," Gilman says. "I was beginning to think you was cheating on me."

When the two of them march through the machine shop to the apartment in back, Ten-Fifteen says, "God, I feel good today. I'm glad it's raining. I love rain."

The man in the recliner has begun to snore.

"Who is that big, long feller?" Gilman asks, throwing up his hands. "Never seen him before in my life, have you?"

Ten-Fifteen is already sitting sideways on a stool at the kitchen counter. He sits sideways to eat because it's easier for him to get to his food that way. "Come in late last night," he says with his mouth full. "They was so many here I don't guess you seen him. His car broke down, and Joe Carter towed him up here. Didn't you see that Toyota parked behind your truck?"

"I wouldn't looking for a Toyota."

"It's got California plates," Ten-Fifteen adds, cheerfully.

"Well, whoop-dee-doo," Gilman snarls, sitting down to eat.

Gilman and Ten-Fifteen don't know it, but Tom Jett has already been awake once this morning. He woke at the break of day, realizing he was somewhere in eastern Kentucky, but unable to recall the specific location. Then he remembered his car trouble from the night before and remembered being towed to a machine shop. When he had gotten there, the proprietor of the shop, a man who was supposed to be the local king of auto repair, was lying on the floor attempting to make love to an acoustic guitar. "It's curvy like a woman," the man was crooning, "but they's bars over the hole." The other men in the room, about ten of them, kept cheering him on. One of the men yelled, "Play it, Gilman. You can't do no good that way. Play it!" And Gilman began playing the blues, the likes of which Tom Jett had never heard. Tom, who felt as if he'd entered a dream he'd had a long time ago, started drinking the tequila being passed around, sat down in a recliner, and was baited into a conversation about the living habits of cows by a man who not only seemed to be an authority on the subject, but who kept interrupting his own declarations with refrains from a song: "I'm a Long, Tall Texan." Finally, Tom just passed out.

After he remembered how he'd come to be where he was, Tom carefully studied his surroundings. There were two large speakers, an amplifier, and a piano in one end of the room. Against the wall were an electric, a steel, and two acoustic guitars, one of which had been the object of Gilman's affection the night before. Tom's recliner faced an open door that led to a balcony. He heard water running over rocks and figured

there must be a creek behind the house. A kitchen area and a
bathroom were in the other end of the room, and on the wall
behind the couch were hundreds of Polaroid pictures of people in various stages of foolishness. In one of them, a girl sat
on a motorcycle with one breast hanging out of her blouse. A
man nearly twice her age stood beside her grinning like a lot-
tery winner, his arm around her shoulder, his fingers dangling on the prize.

In front of Tom, this same man, whom he recognized as
Gilman Lee, was asleep on the couch with a gun in his hand.
Tom guessed the man to be in his fifties, and he was short and
rather muscular for his age. A scar extended like the trail of a
tear from one of his eyes to the corner of his mouth, causing
him to appear sentimental on just one side of his face.

Gilman stood up suddenly and, gun in hand, marched
straight to the balcony and peed off the railing to the creek below. Then he marched back into the room, unaware of Tom's
presence, and resumed his sleep.

It's real, Tom thought, and dozed off again, too.

W hen Gilman Lee and Ten-Fifteen go outside to have a
look at the Toyota, Gilman hot-wires it and says, "That feller
in there's got a serious problem."

"What's wrong?" Ten-Fifteen asks, peering under the
hood.

"Everything."

Leaving Ten-Fifteen to inspect the car for himself, Gilman
walks out to his mailbox, which he just checks every four or
five days. Absentmindedly skimming through the advertisements and bills, he finds a letter from the Conroy Coal Company. "What have we here?" he growls, stuffing the letter,
unopened, into his shirt pocket.

On the road a horn blares, and he glances up to see Gemma Collet, one of the few women in the area who is successful at ignoring his attentions. Gemma's long white hair hangs out of her car window as she tries to see around a coal truck that has slowed to a crawl in front of her. Gilman chuckles and yells out, "Learn to relax, Gemma. Stop by sometime, and I'll teach you a few techniques."

Her black eyes flash like gunfire as she gives him the finger, peels rubber past the truck, and disappears around the curve.

He takes the rest of the mail inside his apartment, tosses it on top of the piano, and walks back outside where Ten-Fifteen is still studying the inside of Tom Jett's car. "Ten-Fifteen, let's take that feller's Toy apart," he says.

When Tom wakes for the second time, Gilman and Ten-Fifteen have already dismantled the engine.

"I hope you wouldn't in a hurry to get somewhere," Gilman says, as Tom wanders near them, rubbing his eyes. "This engine needs a overhaul."

"That's too bad," Tom says. "I don't have much money."

"That *is* too bad," Gilman agrees.

"Is there any work around here?" Tom asks.

Gilman and Ten-Fifteen look at each other and laugh.

2
Chapter

Tom Jett left San Diego three months ago with a hundred dollars in his pocket and no particular destination in mind. All he knew was that he wanted to go to the mountains. Sitting on the beach one day, he looked out at the ocean, and it suddenly dawned on him that he had been sitting there for a long time.

He had begun his beach-sitting not long after graduating from Stanford with a degree in philosophy. The plan had been to go on to graduate school, but instead he decided to do nothing, absolutely nothing, for as long as he could do it. This decision was carefully thought out and philosophically based. He determined to spend numerous days on the beach being nonexistent outside the roar of ocean waves. He would let the roar go through one ear and come out the other, washing away everything in its wake because, to Tom, doing nothing made more sense than doing something, since something (he'd learned after years of hard study) was the same thing as nothing, anyway.

Tom's parents failed to understand the finer points of his

philosophical change of heart. They had harbored hopes that their son would have a better life than they'd had, that he would be highly respected in the community, a professional. They often glared at him with profound disgust when he returned in the evenings from the seashore. "Sell any seashells today?" they'd ask him. "Find any sand dollars?"

Tom tolerated their disgust, ate his dinner, and went to bed. Sometimes he felt guilty for being a disappointment to them, but usually he felt nothing except low-grade irritation that they had based their relationship with him on the good grades he made at school, on the conventional success they wanted him to be. He resented them for not realizing that a philosophy major would more than likely fall short of economic prosperity. Sometimes at night he frequented bars near the beach, places like The Silver Fox and The Texas Teahouse, where blues spoke its low language as he drank beer at dark tables and made uncouth, transient friends.

Then Tom unintentionally began to make a living. One day as he sat on the beach with the taste of saltwater on his lips and kelp tangled about his feet, he distractedly picked up a piece of deadwood, took a pocket knife out of his pocket, began whittling, and found it pleasurable. The next day he went out to the desert and collected a pile of deadwood. He took this to the beach and started contentedly whittling the interiors of things. From the parched, dry wood, he whittled gastrointestinal tracts; car, truck, and motor home engines; heart valves on a stick. When tourists, seeing him carve these intricately suspect shapes, began trying to buy his art, he looked up at them like a child startled from sleep and shooed them away. The would-be buyers were so persistent that finally he sold one of his figures, then another and another.

In the meantime, his parents got ideas of their own, discovering what was to become the greatest passion of their lives: square dancing. They began adding square dance calls into their everyday conversation. They'd say, " 'Circle up' here at the table and let's eat," and "It was so funny, I laughed 'all the way home and halfway back.' " One evening when Tom came home from the beach, his parents announced they were moving near Sacramento to the Do Si Do Retirement Estates, which, instead of featuring golf, tennis, and shuffleboard, offered all manner of folk dancing along with accordion and fiddle lessons. They hoped he would be able to survive without them.

After they left, Tom was forced to supplement his deadwood-figurine income by occasionally working for a company that built room additions, and discovered he had a natural talent for carpentry. Finally, restlessness came to him from the ocean itself, from the spray, the constant rise and fall of waves, causing his beliefs about nothingness to erode like the beach he was sitting on.

He became obsessed with the opposite of his experience, with elevations instead of sea levels, with dirt rather than sand. He found himself imagining the offshore fog was taking on the shape of mountains, tall mountains, thick with green life. He had dreams of becoming wedged in the crevices of rocks, of existing like marrow in hollow trees, of growing rich with moss as the banks of a mountain stream. Tom began yearning for tension, though not the fast-paced tension one finds in large cities. The tension he sought was slow and dark, booby-trapped with caverns and hollows. He wanted to peer through a camouflage of dense vegetation and find a heart beating.

When he couldn't ignore his restlessness any longer, he decided to go as far as his hundred dollars would take him. If he ran out of funds, he would stop in the nearest town and get a job. When he had saved enough money to continue his trip, he would quit the job, throw his belongings into the trunk of his car, and depart, always heading for the hills. He would sample several mountain ranges and when he found the right one he would stay there and seep into the earth.

Three months later Tom rolled into Lexington, Kentucky, just as it was getting dark and stopped at a gas station to ask an attendant for pointers.

"I'm going to the hills south of here," he said, trying to sound folksy. "Is there a place down there you'd recommend I not miss?"

The attendant finished checking Tom's oil and told him he was a quart low. "You a long way from home, ain't you, buddy?" he asked, spotting the California license plate. "Ever been in the hills before? Got any family down there?"

"No," Tom said.

Shaking his head, the attendant looked up at a star, then at a competing gas station across the street. Tom looked at the star and the station, too, while he waited for the advice. Finally, the attendant turned his eyes on Tom and sized him up. "To me," he said, "you look like someone that orta go to Berea. It's about forty miles down the road. That's where the college is. You've heard of Berea College, ain't you?"

Tom said he hadn't.

"Berea is a real nice town. Got little craft shops everywhere. One of them frozen yogurt places. Health food stores for the nutrition conscious. Restaurants galore. I got a cousin lives in Berea. She said they was even goin to put a Thai restaurant down there. Maybe they already have. Did you ever eat Thai food?"

Tom, having had his fill of yogurt and Thai food, sighed at the star and at the competing gas station across the street. He took out his road atlas and discovered a way to bypass the town entirely.

Abandoning the turnpike for an old state highway, he kept following the yellow line around one curve after another through silhouetted mountains that stood like walls lining either side of the road. Sometimes his headlights fell on rusted cars that had been left in ditches where small animals scurried out from under them and weeds grew out of their open doors. The farther he went, the more closed in he began to feel, with the air coming through his rolled-down windows warm and damp. He felt as if he were traveling inside a living thing, a dinosaur maybe or some other prehistoric animal that had evolved into a geographical area for reasons of self-preservation.

About a hundred miles south of Lexington his car broke down. He looked out of his window and saw that he had come to rest in a three-street town that appeared to be closed up for the night. A lone man, who took an immediate interest in Tom's car having sputtered to a stop, stood under a streetlight on the corner. Tom got out of his car and walked the length of two of the three streets, noticing the gas station was closed and there were no craft shops, yogurt huts, Thai or fast-food restaurants.

He was, however, chased down by the man from the corner, an earnest-looking fellow who ran up to him saying, "Is that yore car broke down back thare? Yon't me ta hep ye git toa garage?"

Tom was pleased.

3

Chapter

The mail Gilman found in his mailbox yesterday kept him up most of the night. This morning he sits on a stool with two letters lying open on the kitchen counter.

In one of the letters, the Conroy Coal Company announced they are sending a land agent to talk to him about leasing land on the mountain where he grew up. For years Gilman has watched people around him sign coal leases that yield them enough money to buy a new car or to put a down payment on a new house or, if they're lucky, both. In either case, the money is usually gone in a couple of years, and all they are ultimately left with is scarred land that is partially stripped of trees and polluted with refuse from the mining operations.

Gilman owns thirty acres of land located about three miles down the road. It is the land he grew up on, the land he inherited after his father's death, the land his father inherited from his grandfather. Gilman's property line begins at the edge of the road and extends across the creek and over half of one side of the hill where, according to the speculators from the Conroy Coal Company, there exists more than a million tons of coal. The company is contacting everyone who owns property on the mountain to obtain leases for mining. Gilman wonders if they've contacted June Collet regarding the proposed mining. June Collet and her daughter, Gemma, own property adjoining his.

He picks up the phone and dials June's number. "Hello, June. This is Gilman Lee. Has anyone from Conroy Coal contacted you?"

There is a momentary silence on the phone, then she answers, "I got a letter from them."

"Are you goin to sign the lease?"

"Sure am. Except Gemma's gotta sign, too. She owns this property same as me."

"How does she feel about it?"

June sighs. "Actually, I ain't told her about the letter yet. You know how Gemma is. She might decide not to sign out of pure stubbornness. I'm trying to find the right time to tell her about it. Did you hear from them, Gilman?"

"Yeah, I did. Well, gotta go. Take care of yourself, June."

Gilman hangs up the phone with a smile on his face. June is right, he thinks. Gemma is definitely stubborn enough not to sign. He gets a clear picture of her in his mind, her coal-black eyes shining out of her porcelain face. He figures she's easily the most striking woman for miles around.

An early morning breeze, cool and clear, wafts through the open door leading to his balcony, where birds perch on the railing and sing. Gilman pours himself another cup of coffee and picks up the other letter that has been bothering him.

Last night just before turning in, he remembered to go through the rest of the mail he had put on the piano earlier that day. Rummaging through the pile, he found a letter from a woman who used to love him in his wilder days. Her name is Rosalee. Dirty blond hair and green eyes, she used to hang around his machine shop trying to get him to love her back.

Sometimes they stayed up three nights in a row while she matched him drink for drink. Rosalee made love as if she were competing for top prize in a lovemaking contest. Other times she sang to him in such a sexy voice that lovemaking wasn't necessary. "You ought to marry me, Gilman," she'd say. "I'd make sure your doors are locked at night. I'd cook too. I'm a real good cook. Not to mention that my name would be Rosa*lee Lee*."

She used to help him work on cars. She'd get right down under them—grease all over her—trying to impress him with her mechanical skills. When that failed, the idea came to her that heavy machinery would do the trick, and she got a job operating a bulldozer while the interstate highway was being built. Gilman took her new profession more or less in stride. Then one day she came to his shop with a mining garb on and coal dust all over her face, holding up a paycheck. "I got a job in the mines, Gilman. What do you think of that?"

"I hope you don't get black lung," was all he said.

Finally Rosalee quit trying—stopped coming around. She had a brief affair with Wade Miller, the manager of the bank in town, a man as unlike Gilman as she could find. Wade was married, couldn't carry a tune, and made love like a mosquito. Then quite unexpectedly, Rosalee, who was born and raised at the head of a hollow and had never been out of the state of Kentucky, packed her clothes and moved to Florida. She's been gone for five years. Sometimes she sends Gilman postcards from Miami, Fort Lauderdale, and West Palm Beach, causing him to wonder what line of work she's in now. Usually her postcards pose questions like, "How's it hanging, Gilman?" and are signed, "Love, Rosalee." This time she wrote a three-page letter.

Last night he dreamed about her several times, and in these dreams, she was behind him asking irritating questions. He looked around at her and she was beautiful; but when he reached out to touch her hair, she faded like poor TV reception.

Rosalee is twenty years younger than Gilman. His friends have always kidded him about his knack for luring pretty young women. She'd be thirty-four by now, Gilman thinks, not so young anymore. "If I'd a married her, I'd probably hate her guts by now," he mutters. The truth is he's never quite known what he wants when it comes to women. Although he loved Rosalee, she just wasn't the one.

Gilman can't get over how much trouble she's apparently landed in. He scans down the first page of the letter once more:

> *Dear Gilman,*
>   *Don't tell anyone about this letter!!! I hope things are going good with you back there. I'm not so hot right now to tell you the truth. I believe a man is following me. I'll tell you all about him if I ever get up with you. I'm in Daytona Beach, but by the time you get this I won't be here.*
>   *I thought I had more sense than to get myself into so much trouble. This man is mean, Gilman, through and through. I'm heading toward Pick, but I don't know how long it will take me to get there. I'm not traveling in any kind of straight line that he can follow. I'm zigzagging. . . .*

The rest of the letter is hard to understand—she doesn't mention the man's name or why she thinks he's following her. All she talks about is how hard it is for a person to cover her tracks. She talks about the color of the sky and gives a weather report—tells how much it's rained, how fierce the wind is blowing.

"Well, that's just fine, Rosalee," Gilman grumbles to himself. "Write me and let me know you're in trouble, but don't tell me where you are. And by all means don't leave any kind of hint of how I can help you out."

Gilman puts the letters away, walks over to the stove, and stands in front of it, trying to decide what to do about breakfast. Ten-Fifteen agreed to let Tom Jett stay with him in the trailer for a while. Tom intends to look for a job so he can make enough money to get his car fixed. The problem is that since Ten-Fifteen has a hard time preparing meals—burning himself on the stove more often than not—Gilman usually cooks for them both. But now that Tom Jett is staying over there, what's he supposed to do? He wonders if they think he's going to fry eggs for three. "What am I? A friggin gourmet?" he asks, looking straight at the stove.

4

Chapter

About five miles north of Gilman Lee's place lies the three-street town of Pick, Kentucky. Pick consists mostly of small businesses—clothing stores, groceries, a beauty and barber shop, and the usual hardware, appliance, and auto parts stores. There are only a few residences in town. Most people live outside of Pick proper.

Ten-Fifteen waits on the sidewalk while Tom Jett tacks a flyer on the bulletin board inside the IGA grocery. It is a flyer advertising the newcomer's carpentry skills. Since Tom hasn't had any luck finding a job, he has decided to create some work for himself. Ten-Fifteen doesn't drive or own an automobile, so this morning they had to borrow one of Gilman's old cars to get down here to Pick.

They've been putting the advertisements all over town. Ten-Fifteen hopes the flyers will help Tom get some business, but if it does, it will have to be inside work because of the weather forecast for continuing rainstorms. Maybe he can build some kitchen cabinets for someone, Ten-Fifteen thinks.

Tom comes out of the IGA and says, "Where to now?"

"Across the street there," Ten-Fifteen says.

They walk into the Pick Citizens' Bank and lay some flyers on a table. It's Saturday, and the Pick Citizens' is busy, it being the only bank in the county. The town of Pick has a population of nine hundred, but Burr County has fifteen thousand residents, about twenty of whom are at this moment in the bank.

Tom spots a bulletin board on the wall and starts to tack up a flyer when he is approached by a woman of about fifty whose head is adorned with blond bouffant hair, whose face and neck are coated with powder, and who is swathed from head to toe in dusty pink.

"And just what do you think you're doing?" she asks, holding up one of the flyers she confiscated from the table.

"I'm, uh . . ." Tom isn't exactly sure what he's doing. The twenty customers in the bank turn around and look at him as if they're trying to spot a gun in his hand.

"This is not for private advertising," the woman continues. "This is for town things, you know, like Coon-on-the-Log on the Fourth of July, or book sales at the library."

Tom turns to Ten-Fifteen. "Coon-on-the-Log?"

One of the customers coughs and another chuckles. The woman glares at the chuckler, then she addresses Ten-Fifteen. "Is this man with you? I'd expect as much from a stranger like him, but I'd have thought you would've known better."

From behind the teller counter emerges another woman, who is much younger than the first and the whitest person Tom has ever seen. Her skin and hair, the color of a porcelain tub, make her eyes, brows, and lashes appear blacker than black. Tom guesses her to be about thirty, his age. Holding up one of the flyers, the white woman reads:

LOW COST CARPENTRY
If you've got the hammer, nails, saw, and wood, I've got the time.
TOM JETT, A Different Kind of Carpenter
749-3243

"You don't have any tools, do you?" the white woman asks Tom. She is wearing an army-green dress with a wide belt girded tight around her remarkably small waist. Tom can't take his eyes off her as she continues the interrogation. "And what does this mean: 'A Different Kind of Carpenter'? Just what is it you do that's so unusual? Do you hold your hammer different?"

Tom scrutinizes her high cheekbones and aquiline nose. "If I had one, maybe I would. And just what the hell is Coon-on-the-Log?" He fears some horrific Southern-mountain racial ritual.

"Well," his first assailant, the woman in pink, interrupts, "if you must know, it is a event that is put on every Fourth of July by the Pick Wildlife Club."

Tom cranes his neck to read the name plate on the white woman's desk: "Gemma Collet/Loan Officer."

Gemma nudges her pink cohort with an elbow. "Go back to your seat, Marcy," whereupon Marcy looks toward the teller counter as if searching for a witness to the fact that Gemma insulted her. Finding none, she stalks back to her desk in a cloud of dusty pink.

Gemma turns to Tom. "They anchor a log in the river and chain a raccoon to it. People bring their coon dogs and whichever dog is able to swim out and yank the coon off the log wins."

"Does the dog kill the raccoon?" Tom asks.

"Just about always," she says, smiling savagely.

"Sounds like a worthwhile cause, Gemma," he says, pronouncing her name with a hard *G*. "Much more noble than, say . . . private advertising."

"My name is pronounced *Jeh* like in *genuine* or *genius*. *Gemmmaah* is how you say it. Where are you from?"

"California."

"Figures." Gemma Collet's black eyes squirm as if they are going to shoot out of their sockets and bounce off his head like racquet balls. She hands him the flyer. "Just take these things out of here and put them somewhere else." She marches behind the teller counter and sits down at the desk, her eyes still pulsing as she waits for the two men to leave.

"In San Diego, bank personnel smile and tell you to have a nice day," Tom says when he and Ten-Fifteen walk out of the Pick Citizens'.

Ten-Fifteen doesn't speak until they are in the car on their way back home. "I didn't know Gemma'd be at the bank. I thought she was still on vacation in South Carolina. She goes to Myrtle Beach every summer to try and get some sun. You have to overlook Gemma. She's been mad ever since she turned white."

"Turned white?"

"Turned."

"I'm afraid to ask what color she was before," Tom says, thinking she must have been a hellish devil red.

"She was, you know, the regular. Well, actually, she was darker than most people around here."

"What happened to her?"

"Skin disease of some kind. Twelve years ago, she was eighteen and the prettiest girl in Burr County. She had dark reddish-brown hair and the same black eyes she's got right now."

"Well, she still looks damned good to me," Tom says.

"Yeah, but when you seen her while ago, she was all the way white. She ain't been that way long, and it took her twelve years to get there. Gemma was ready to go to a modeling school in Chicago when it happened. She started getting big white blotches all on her face, arms, and legs. She was in the same grade as me when we was in school. I used to always like Gemma."

Tom tries to put the woman out of his mind, but her black eyes keep lurking in the corners. He turns on the windshield wipers as another downpour begins. In San Diego, rain usually comes in a drizzle and one spots precipitation by noticing the ground is damp, but here rain pounds down in large sheets and streams, and beside the road the creek is yellow with mud and swollen to the size of a river.

"I like it when the water rises like this," Ten-Fifteen tells him. "It reminds me of that movie, *The River of No Return.* Ever see it? It starred Robert Mitchum and Marilyn Monroe."

*A*t the bank, Gemma Collet drums her fingers on the desk and looks out the window, hoping Ten-Fifteen and his friend return so she'll have an excuse to throw someone out. A fracas would take her mind off the fact that nothing much changed while she was on vacation in Myrtle Beach. The town of Pick and its citizens are still muddling along like turtles in shells, and the only thing different at all is the presence of the carpenter from California. She walks over to the bulletin board, yanks down the old Coon-on-the-Log flyer, and throws it in a waste can. The Fourth of July hoopla took place weeks ago, anyway.

When Gemma gets home that evening, she has dinner with her mother, June, goes to her bedroom, and starts to pace, catching a glimpse of herself in the mirror. "Still whiter than a milk shake," she notes as if one day she expects her old complexion to return.

On the dresser sits an eight-by-ten portrait of her taken the summer after she graduated from high school. In the picture, she has auburn hair and a dark complexion. She wears a green silk blouse, and her smiling face is tilted to one side, dimples flashing in her cheeks. Gemma takes the portrait in her hands and looks down at it, tilting her head to one side now, trying to feel the green silk of the blouse on her skin, not just remembering the way she felt that day sitting in front of the photographer, but trying to be there now. When you're beautiful, she remembers, you walk into a room and men sink, almost fall toward you. Their lips part, and their eyes glaze over. You walk down the road, and they hang their bodies out of truck windows and howl like tormented dogs who can't control what comes out of their mouths. Smile. They always smile.

She raises the portrait in her hands, as if she intends to throw it to the floor. Instead, she turns it facedown on the dresser. "Beautiful people don't have a clue," she says.

Gemma has not been touched in a long time. Or kissed. She has not lain soft in a man's arms. A man has not held her face in his hands and looked at her with lust in his eyes, or love. He has not run his fingers over her breasts or slipped his tongue inside her ear or fucked her, and Gemma has not wanted him to. She would have kicked him in the nuts had he tried.

Before the disease struck, she had a lover who was tall and lanky, beautiful and without a clue. He used to feel her up in a dark car at the Pick Drive-in Theatre. He used to put it in all the way. Sometimes they picnicked beside the creek, eating hot dogs and drinking beer they had bought at Gilman Lee's. Gemma and her lover made plans. He was going to Chicago, where his uncle owned a business, to make money; she was going to Chicago, also, to attend modeling school and become famous. After the fame and fortune, they would be married, live in the suburbs, and have their own towels, pots and pans, and sheets. They planned to buy dogs and have children, and frequently they argued over what kind of alarm clock they'd own. He wanted one that chimed a tune; she wanted an old-fashioned alarm clock with brass bells. Fostering the most ordinary intentions, Gemma and her lover lay cupped together on the creek bank, surrounded by running water, goldenrod, and dark green hills.

It was after her lover had gone to Chicago and a few months before she was to join him that she discovered the first white spot. It was on her knee. When she found a larger place on her back and a few white streaks in her hair, she drove to Lexington to see a dermatologist. She was losing pigment, the doctor said, and called her condition vitiligo.

Gemma looked down at the white spot on her knee. "You mean I'm going to be like this? I'll be *this* white?" she asked the doctor, who sat behind an oak desk with his legs crossed, yawning as if he had not had a good night's sleep. "Will I be spotted for the rest of my life, or will I finally turn white all over?"

"It's hard to say," the doctor told her. "Since you've already experienced rapid pigment loss, I think you may eventually lose all of it."

"If that's the case, how long will it take?"

"It could take as little as six months or as long as twenty years. You may never lose all of your pigment, and in the meantime you will have these white patches over much of your body, including your face. I've only treated two cases. One of the patients had the disease fifteen years, and at that point enough of his skin was depigmented that we took the remaining pigment out."

"There's nothing you can do to stop it from happening?" Gemma asked.

"We could try injections to replace the pigment. A lot of patients improve, but very few regain all their color." He showed Gemma a picture of a patient as he appeared before and after the treatment. She could detect hardly any improvement. "It's most successful when there is very little pigment loss to begin with. Also, some patients with mild cases use makeup to hide the blotches."

"My case isn't mild, though, is it?"

"In my estimation, no, not considering how much pigment you've lost already. When you've reached about seventy percent loss, you might consider contacting me again, and we'll see about prescribing a cream that will take out the remaining pigment. I'm sorry I can't give you a better prognosis."

Gemma returned home and looked at her reflection in the mirror, ran a brush through her auburn hair that was doomed to turn prematurely white. For as long as she could remember, she had always been the center of attention. When she was a small child, people had stopped her mother on the streets of Pick to get a better look at her. "You'll have to fight the boys off with a stick once she gets older," people had said, and, "How did someone as ugly as you have a child as pretty as this?" her father's friends had often joked. Her father, who was killed in a car accident when Gemma was ten years old, had always grinned at these comments.

Gemma kept staring at her reflection in the mirror, trying to memorize her unblemished face, and leaned forward, kissing her image good-bye. She wrote a letter to her lover. "I'm going to turn white," she said. "For years I'll be motley, as spotted as a jersey. Marry someone else. Sincerely yours, Gemma."

Her lover came back to Pick a few months later, but Gemma refused to see him. "I want to marry you," he said on the phone. "I don't care what you look like."

By now the disease had spread over a third of her body, and suddenly she wasn't sure if he had ever liked her for any reason other than her flawless appearance. "That's easy for you to say," she told him. "You've not seen me. You don't realize what I look like or how much worse I'll get."

The next day her lover barged into the house and entered her bedroom. Gemma turned her back and covered her face, stood there for a minute, then pulled off her clothes, and spun around to show him. In addition to those on her legs, back, and stomach, two large irregular-shaped white blotches were on her face. Contrasting with her dark complexion, these white intrusions appeared to have never seen the light of day, their texture baby-soft, their color bleached as the skin of a dungeon dweller. Her lover smiled. It was the kind of smile a person manufactures when he would rather cry. Gemma inched near, put her head on his chest, and heard his heart beating like footsteps running.

"I'm going to take you back to Chicago with me," he said. "I can't stay long this evening. I've got some things to do, but I'll be back tomorrow to get you."

The next day Gemma waited on the front porch with her suitcases, and when her lover didn't come, she ran up the mountain behind her house, went all the way to the top, and stood there screaming wild, mad screams. "I'll never get over this," she screamed. "I don't mean him. I'm already over him. I mean I'll never get used to this!" And she rubbed at the white patches on her face. "I hate well-adjusted people. People who accept things. I hate them," she screamed. "Good attitudes make me want to puke. Strike me dead if I ever from this day on have a good fucking attitude!"

Gemma's mother, June, is breathing deeply—nearly snoring in front of the TV—her lips fluttering like moths under her nose. Gemma walks past her to the kitchen to wash dishes, and she is wiping off the counter when she finds the letter from the Conroy Coal Company stuck between the bread box and a canister of flour. The envelope, addressed to June, has already been opened. She wonders why the coal company is writing her mother and is about to pull the letter out to read when she is interrupted by a phone call from her boss at the bank. When Wade Miller works late, he usually calls Gemma to ask where some file is located. By the time she gets off the phone she is so irritated she no longer remembers the letter.

5

Chapter

Burr County is a dry county, but every Saturday Gilman Lee drives to an adjoining county, which is wet, and buys enough bootleg whiskey to sell to his friends.

Gilman did not set out to be a bootlegger. He became one because people were always showing up at his place to hear him play music. He never had enough whiskey to serve them, and they never brought enough with them to last through the night. On Saturdays, he buys five cases of beer, four or five bottles of bourbon, some vodka, gin, and tequila, and sells it for a profit.

Men, for the most part in their forties and fifties, come to the apartment in back of the machine shop, a few just to buy whiskey, but the majority of them come for the night. Every now and then they are accompanied by their wives or girl-friends, and sometimes they bring their teenage and adult children, indoctrinating a second generation into the Machine Shop Society. They come because there is no place else to gather, because they like to hear good music, and because something worth remembering always happens at Gilman

Lee's. They are an unlikely crew. By day the men work in coal mines and gas stations, own hardware stores and food marts, teach school, sell insurance, and drive trucks. By night they are insane on a rotating basis.

About eight o'clock Tom and Ten-Fifteen go over to Gilman's place, where a crowd is already gathering. Tonight Gilman, in a quiet mood, is playing the guitar along with another man who is picking a banjo. Tom recognizes the banjo picker as the same man who towed him to the machine shop on his first night in Pick. Occasionally, Gilman glances up at his audience. Most of the men are listening; some are talking.

It has stopped raining for the time being, and Ten-Fifteen goes out to the balcony, stares up at the night clouds, and watches the creek, noticing that the posts supporting the balcony are standing in two feet of water. The creek is rising by the minute and flowing fast. He wishes he were on a raft with a beautiful woman and they were riding the rapids like Robert Mitchum and Marilyn Monroe.

Tom Jett, trying to get used to the men's heavy accents, understands only half of what he hears, but he is able to decipher the most prevalent conversation, which concerns the rain. Burr County has one river and an abundance of creeks, all of which are flooded at the moment. The men reminisce about past floods—washed-away houses and drowned farm animals. Eventually, the discussion leads to other natural disasters, and earthquakes come up.

"One of these days California is goin to slide into the ocean. Is that why you left?" one of the men asks Tom.

Tom has been asked this question numerous times in the recent past and can't bring himself to say more than "No."

Gilman Lee sets his guitar down. "I was stationed in San Diego when I was in the Navy. You want to know what I didn't like about California? You couldn't be a wild man out there. I mean, you could be wild as long as it fit in with everyone else's idea of wild. But you couldn't get down-in-the-dirt wild without getting put in jail. Know what I mean?" Gilman grips his eyes on Tom's and doesn't let go.

"Don't people get put in jail around here?" Tom asks.

"If they get caught, they do. But you can lose yourself pretty quick in these hills." Gilman laughs and starts playing "Salty Dog." The banjo picker follows.

As if he's heard his cue, Kelly Coots, a high school teacher in his midthirties and a cousin to one of the regulars, walks over and sits down beside Gilman Lee. He smiles, raises his arm, cups his other hand over his armpit, and brings the arm down in a sudden swift motion, producing a noise that sounds very much like a fart. In this way, he begins to keep a lively rhythm with Gilman Lee and the banjo picker.

"Go, Kelly!" the men shout.

Kelly smiles.

Gilman finishes the number and walks over to the refrigerator to get a beer, and the banjo picker leans his banjo against the wall. Outside, the creek still roars over rocks and around bends, and the moon is covered by thick, dark clouds. Kelly Coots continues to smile and make the farting sounds.

"By God, you can really do that right," one of the men says, while the others beam with pride at Kelly's antics.

Kelly, the high school teacher, continues.

Tom looks about the room, while the men drink their whiskey and throw their burning cigarette butts on the wooden floor. He expects a fire to start up any minute, but it doesn't. Standing by the kitchen counter, Gilman Lee and the banjo picker, whose name Tom has learned is Joe Carter, have become immersed in a conversation about coal.

Gilman draws a letter out of his pocket and slams it on the counter, his placid mood having stormed up considerably. "I'd like to take the president of the Conroy Coal Company and sign my name on his ass—sign it with a red-hot poker. That's about the only signing they'll get out of me," he says.

"But if it wasn't for coal mines, nobody around here would

have any work. People couldn't live," Joe Carter argues. "Not unless they growed that loco weed. And what kind of life is that—always afraid you're goin to get caught, can't even spend your money for being afraid you'll draw attention to yourself?"

"Yeah? Well, at least marijuana don't do any damage to the land. Maybe people ought to pull together and make it legal. That way no one would have to worry about getting caught. But back to coal mining, you seem to think that's the only legal work anyone can do around here. Well, what about people in Iowa? They ain't got no coal mines. Ask Tom Jett over there if they's any coal mines in California. How does people make it out there? They's a shitpot full of people all over the world that's never set foot inside a coal mine."

"People in Iowa grow corn," Joe says. "What would happen if you took the corn out of Iowa? Them people wouldn't know what to do. And people in California . . . well, they do all kinds of things, I guess, but the point is they's certain ways to make a living in every place you go."

Gilman raises an eyebrow and curls his upper lip. "If people was out of work for a while, they'd come up with other ways to make a living."

The two men look at each other long and hard, a lifetime of opposing viewpoints walled between them. Finally, the crisis passes, and they begin to laugh and talk about their last fishing trip, about how many fish they caught, how drunk they got.

After an hour, Kelly Coots is still keeping a beat with his muscular arm, made muscular by a daily regime of lifting weights. Ten-Fifteen comes in from the balcony and pulls up a chair close by the performer, whose arm is moving up and down like a machine. Tom Jett stands in a corner, trying to act as if this kind of behavior is something he's seen all his life.

Some of the men give Kelly sideways glances, and it is obvious they are beginning to get irritated by the noise. Finally, a voice calls out, "Hey, Kelly, the music's over. You can stop with the rhythm section just any time."

But he doesn't stop. Kelly Coots is on the fourth day of a drinking binge. He stares straight ahead with an unwavering smile, sweat beading up and veins popping out on his face.

Two of the regulars walk over to Gilman Lee. "Gilman," whispers one of the men, who goes by the name of Jink, "I believe we've got a problem here. I believe something's wrong with Kelly. Does he seem right to you?"

Gilman Lee turns to look at Kelly. "Kelly's just trying to tell us something, boys. It's something he can't put into words, and he's come up with this way to try and get it across. It may not be the route me or you would've took, but Kelly seems dead set on it." Gilman goes back to his conversation with the banjo picker.

Gradually, the other men in the room stop talking and stare at Kelly. The man called Jink says, "Boys, I believe I'll go home," and one by one the other men leave, too.

Kelly still continues to make his strange music.

Now, the only people left are Gilman Lee, Ten-Fifteen, and Tom. Gilman nudges Ten-Fifteen, and they walk out to the balcony, where the rain is starting up again. "You and your buddy in there go home," Gilman tells him. "I'll keep a eye on Kelly."

"He'll prob'ly quit come daylight, won't he?" Ten-Fifteen asks, peeping inside to look again at the flailing arm.

Gilman shrugs. "Tomorrow, I'll send for his wife and children. I'll stand them right there in front of him where he can't help but see them. Maybe that'll stop him."

When Tom and Ten-Fifteen leave, Gilman turns the light off and lies down on the couch with his face toward Kelly. As his eyes adjust to darkness, he sees the movement of Kelly's arm. The steady rhythm reminds him of the sad swinging of a pendulum, or the steel arm of one of the gas wells that are hidden in the surrounding mountains, an unseen arm driving relentlessly into the earth. He strains to see in the dim light and is finally able to make out more subtle outlines. He finds it is still there, the macabre smile on Kelly's face.

*B*urr County is coal country. Coal is shoveled, augered, stripped, and deep-mined; it is brought out of the hills any way it can be brought out when there is a market for it. The market for coal has been on the downswing for quite some time now.

That is why an abandoned coal truck can sometimes be seen on a dirt road near a creek crossing that leads to a ramshackle house where an out-of-work coal-truck driver sits glumly on the porch, staring down at his fingernails as if they are the bastards who put him out of work.

Sometimes one of these drivers in his rage will have vengeful daydreams in which he dismantles his truck piece by piece. In his imaginings, he solicits the help of his wife and children, and they scatter truck parts all over the ground—the engine here, the steering wheel there, and (with the help of levers and pulleys) the heavy steel truck bed yonder. On rare occasions, a person's daydreams come true.

That's what happens in the case of the coal-truck bed in question, the one that is laboriously removed from a coal truck and left near the creek when the creek begins to rise, the one that after weeks of resting undisturbed in the water, rises up, too, and begins to float. For a few moments, like a disoriented bear rudely awakened from sleep, the truck bed lumbers in the water. Then it takes off with the current, grumpily bumping into rocks in its path. Picking up speed, it goes faster and faster until it's tearing downstream, knocking alder bushes flat, cartwheeling against the creek's shrinking banks.

*I*t is just breaking daylight on the morning after the Kelly Coots situation. Ten-Fifteen wakes up early, wondering if Kelly is still moving his arm and making that sound. He looks out of the trailer window for signs of weird goings-on at Gilman's place. None are evident. Kelly prob'ly wore himself down, Ten-Fifteen thinks.

But Ten-Fifteen is not entirely correct. Kelly is still at it, albeit with not as much fervor. He has moved out to the balcony and is smiling at the trees across the creek. Kelly Coots teaches high school English and hates it. He has always wanted to do something magnificent—crackle like electricity through power lines, chisel a new face on Mount Rushmore, run for the roses at the Kentucky Derby. He wants to be a writer. He wants to wake up one morning and find himself famous like Byron, to write like William Faulkner, to live and die like Dylan Thomas. He wants to be a legend, but he has a wife and two children. Big mistake. In the evenings after school, his children are noisy, and his wife, who is also a teacher, wants him to talk to her. He doesn't have time to write. He can't do it in the summer, either, because with each passing day the fall school term draws nearer. It is the pressure. Kelly smiles at the trees across the creek and still moves his arm, but the movement has slowed, the sound has diminished, the smile waned.

Gilman, lulled by Kelly's arm, is snoozing.

Back in the trailer, Ten-Fifteen looks at Tom Jett asleep on his couch. He wonders what it would be like to drive a Toyota to Kentucky from San Diego. He wonders how it would feel to be a carpenter from California, and he begins to consider the fact that Gilman Lee is skeptical of Tom. When Ten-Fifteen confronted him about it, Gilman said, "I feel about Tom Jett just like I feel about a yijit box."

"How in the world is Tom Jett like a TV?" Ten-Fifteen asked, knowing that Gilman seldom comes within viewing distance of one.

"Figure it out," Gilman said.

That's what Ten-Fifteen is trying to do right now. He's trying to figure it out, and then he hears the noise. He jumps from his chair and looks upstream out of his window, and there it is! big, black, and dirty. The coal-truck bed is bouncing from one side of the creek to the other, cutting down trees midtrunk, glancing off rocks and ricocheting into the air. Ten-Fifteen turns as white as Gemma Collet, runs to the phone, gets down on his knees, and manages to dial Gilman's number with his awkward hands.

The phone rings once . . . twice . . . four times. Finally, Gilman picks it up and answers softly, "Hello, whoever you are. You asshole. This had better be good."

"Gilman, it's me, Ten-Fifteen. Go to your balcony fast! Look at what's coming, then run!"

Gilman slams down the phone. He can hear it now. He runs to the balcony, and here it comes, end over end. Then he sees Kelly Coots standing there limply moving his arm up and down, no sound coming from him, now. Gilman grabs him by the arm. "Come on, Kelly! We've got to go!"

Kelly, the weight lifter, suddenly resumes his strength-of-three-men and doesn't budge.

The truck bed is getting closer.

"Goddamn it, Kelly, *MOVE!*" Gilman Lee curses, raves, and pulls at Kelly, but the man won't even shift his feet. Gilman sees the truck bed hit the cliff on the other side of the creek, and here it comes! right for the balcony. Gilman shouts at Kelly, "OKAY, YOU GODDAMNED SONOFABITCH, DIE!" and runs. Gilman runs through his apartment and on through the machine shop, making it outside just as the truck bed hits the balcony.

The last thing Kelly Coots sees before he becomes a legend is coal-black steel.

The balcony goes, the whole back side of the building goes, and the truck bed slides right inside the machine shop, coming to a stop beside the classic 1949 Ford that Gilman has been working on for the past two weeks.

6
Chapter

Three days after the catastrophe, the rain has stopped and the sun is out. The coal-truck bed has been dragged from the shop and is sitting outside. Gilman says he may keep it around as a reminder of what can land on a person at six o'clock in the morning. The partial remains of Kelly Coots have been removed from the machine shop floor, and the rest of his body was found lodged on a rock four miles downstream. His funeral is tomorrow.

Tom and Ten-Fifteen stand inside the battered structure, surveying the damage. Not only are the balcony and back wall of the building gone, the ceiling is sagging, and the wall that separated Gilman's apartment from the machine shop is knocked down, too.

Ten-Fifteen props his foot on a pile of debris. "I guess you'll finally get to use a hammer. They's already been ten men offered to be here Saturday morning. We'll have this place built back before the weekend is out. And Jink Roberts—you may've seen him here—is goin to donate the lumber. Jink owns a lumber yard just outside of Pick."

Tom kicks at some pieces of wood from a broken chair. He wonders if it is the same chair Kelly Coots was sitting in the other night. "Why do you think Kelly was acting so strange?" he asks.

"Beats me. Course I've seen people act like that plenty times before. One time I seen a ol' boy laugh for two days straight. Laughed hard, too, wheezing and slapping his knees."

"Why was he laughing?"

"Thought something was funny, best I could tell," Ten-Fifteen says, staring down at his shoelaces. "At least Kelly won't have to teach no more. He'd be glad about that."

Gilman Lee steps into the shop, and when he sees the two men standing there, goes back outside and sits down on a truck tire to avoid their sympathetic words and smiles. He moved into the trailer with Ten-Fifteen and Tom just after the accident, and the trailer, a small one-bedroom, is bulging at the seams. Insisting that Gilman take the couch, Tom has been sleeping on the floor in a sleeping bag. Before the debacle Gilman managed to disregard the newcomer, but it's hard to block out someone who's sleeping a few feet away and snores. The dramatic events of the past week have put Gilman in a foul mood. He walks away from the shop, gets into his truck, and drives down the road to his property on the mountain.

He parks his truck in Gemma Collet's driveway, noticing her mother, June, part the curtains at their living room window, look out at him, and wave. He wonders how June can be so sweet and her daughter, Gemma, so sour. He is just getting out of his truck when Gemma pulls into the driveway, parks beside him, and takes two bags of groceries out of her car. She starts to walk past, then wheels around and glares at him. "Come for a visit?"

"Just parking," Gilman says, remembering a day a few years back when he kissed her. "I'm goin to take a little walk up the hill. Has June talked to you about the letter yet?"

"About what?"

"Never mind."

"Well, feel free to park here anytime," Gemma snaps, remembering that same kiss and feeling a pain in the pit of her stomach. "Don't bother asking for the privilege."

"Why, thank ye," Gilman says sweetly.

Gemma wheels back around, and Gilman watches her stomp through her yard and go inside the house, her long, white hair swaying with every step. "Now, there's a woman. Too bad she don't know it. If she knew it, she might not be so scary," he mutters, as he walks onto his property and begins crossing the swinging bridge. He stops halfway across and stares down at the swollen creek, remembering the hours he spent playing on the bridge when he was a kid—tossing stones in the water, watching ripples spread. A sunfish, no more than three inches long, jumps above the water line. Gilman smiles, continues to the other side of the creek, and heads up the mountain.

The house on the hill is gray, decaying wood and torn-away brick siding; the inside is dirty wallpaper and cracked linoleum. There are beech, sycamore, and hickory trees beside the house, and one of the hickory trees is home to a family of flying squirrels. He spots a squirrel glide from a tree branch, land on a rock, and sit there jerking its head around.

The surrounding field was once his playground, but now it is grown up with bull nettle and thistle and a personal supply of marijuana he planted in the spring. Standing at the edge of the field is a small shack that was once a smokehouse. A few years ago, Gilman turned the smokehouse into a sanctuary, and when he needs to think on things undisturbed, he goes inside it and doesn't come out for hours. Allowing no one but himself to enter, he keeps the door locked and chained. A sign carved over the door warns, "Anyone who breaks this chain and enters uninvited will lose his or her genitals." Gilman calls the shack his prayer chamber because it has an atmosphere that he believes a church should have—it is quiet, dark, and it seduces a person into introspection. He hasn't been to church since he was a kid and has no intention of resuming the habit. He figures the prayer chamber is better than religion anyway. When asked what he prays for, Gilman says, "Good times." No one knows about the chamber's other occupant, the skeleton of his dead friend, Zack, who sits at a table with a cigarette in his hand, listening.

Gemma Collet is the only person who ever came close to finding out about Zack. Four years ago, when she was returning home from one of her summer vacations at Myrtle Beach, she decided to stop at Washburn Creek before going on home. Washburn Creek is located about fifty miles from Pick and has always been a special place for Gemma, not for a particular reason other than the fact that it is beautiful and quiet. Gemma turned off the main highway and drove down the narrow dirt road. It was close to midnight, the moon was full, and she didn't want to go home at all.

Gemma sat in the car awhile, thinking about the ocean she left behind in Myrtle Beach. Most everyone in Pick assumes she vacations at the beach in a futile attempt to tan, but that isn't the case. Her sensitive skin can't tolerate the sun for long periods of time. She goes to Myrtle Beach because she loves to walk by the ocean at night, and when she's on her vacations, she has the sleep patterns of a vampire, going to bed at daybreak and strolling the beaches at night.

Finally, she got out of the car and stepped to the edge of the creek bank, hoping to locate an easy way down. Instead, she found bushes, briars, and stickweeds blocking every access, while under her feet overripe soil had the smell of sex. Turning back, she walked down the road, letting the night soak into her skin, occasionally scanning the bank for a path leading to water. She was so preoccupied with her last night alone that she walked nearly a mile, lost in the sounds around her—owls hooting, a wildcat screaming, and insects buzzing

in the undergrowth. Then another sound pierced the night—
a man singing and cursing loudly.

He was drunk; she could tell by his slurred half-sentences
and tone of voice that made him sound wild enough to kill
anyone who might innocently interrupt his jumbled speech.
Gemma stepped off the road into a grove of trees, realizing
that she was standing at the edge of the old Washburn Creek
graveyard. She hadn't thought she'd come that far down the
road.

"Get out of there, you bucktoothed sonofabitch!" the voice
yelled.

Gemma crouched behind a tombstone, thinking the man,
whom she still couldn't see, was talking to her until he roared
again.

"You can't be dead, asshole! Assholes never die!"

The voice sounded familiar to her, like an enemy's voice she
couldn't place.

"We gotta make some plans, here! They's things to be
done!"

Still crouching behind the tombstone, Gemma felt anger
spread over her like fire in a high wind. All she had wanted
was to sit for a moment by Washburn Creek before going on
to Pick where her mother would be awakened by her arrival
and demand the details of her vacation. Tonight, she had
wanted to listen to water gurgle over rocks and fish slide by—
to look into the creek and see the night sky mirrored in it, but
here this loudmouthed heathen on a raging drunk was wal-
lowing all over the place and yelling.

"Typical," Gemma grunted. "Yeah, I guess I must be close
to home."

She stood up and walked in the direction of the man's voice
with full intentions of clobbering him with a tree branch or a
rock, but she stopped dead in her tracks when the gun went off.

"I said to come out of that grave, Zack." The man yelled
and fired the gun again.

She turned, running from the grove of trees to the road and on to her car, the wind blowing her long white hair behind her and tears of hot anger spilling down her face. Gemma had recognized the man's voice—it was Gilman Lee's.

"He's crazy. This whole fucking place is crazy," she shouted as she drove toward home, not caring whether her mother was awakened by her late arrival or not. In fact, she hoped her mother wouldn't go back to sleep for a week.

Gemma never knew the full details of the situation she left behind that night, of how Gilman Lee emptied his gun into the grave and sat down beside it, holding his head in one hand and a bottle in the other. He was remembering how when they were children, Zack had swum out in the middle of the river and saved him from drowning. From that day forward the two of them became like brothers, and they remained close friends until Zack was killed by a jealous husband. He had been dead for two years, and Gilman hadn't grieved until now.

Earlier in the evening, Gilman was sitting on his balcony doing nothing in particular when he noticed the silence of the creek, crickets, and birds, mute as rocks, circling him doggedly. After a moment the realization of Zack's death hit like a blow from behind.

Gilman stared at the grave. "Come on, admit it, Zack. You're bored down there. Six feet under is as boring as it gets. But a friend beyond the end, I'm willing to help you out."

He chuckled as he walked back to his truck, retrieved a pick and shovel, and started digging. It took him nearly three hours to hit the narrow pine box that held his friend, who had been buried without the benefit of embalming fluid. He dusted off Zack's cold bones and said, "I swear, Zack, it's good to see you. I feel like I'm everyone's stranger. The only person knows me is you."

He put the skeleton in the bed of his truck and drove toward the town of Pick. It was dawn when he walked across the swinging bridge to his father's abandoned house on the side of the mountain, carrying Zack's skeleton zipped in a sleeping bag.

He cleaned out the old smokehouse standing in a field near the homestead, set Zack in a chair at a table, put a cigarette between his friend's bony fingers, patted him on the clavicle, and left. Later that day, he chained and padlocked the door and carved the sign above it. He unlocked the door and paid a visit to Zack, poured them both a glass of Jim Beam, and told Zack about his latest problems with women.

"Rosalee quit me about a year ago, Zack. Women used to never quit me. She took up with Wade Miller of all people. Then she left the state. Can you beat that?"

Zack didn't say a word.

*T*onight Gilman steps inside the chamber, sits down at the table opposite Zack, and says, "Zack, what do you see outta them hollow eyes? Do you see what's happening around here? Of course you do. You always know what's happening. Besides, this place was changing way before you died. We used to talk about it, remember? You take one item away from a place, and it changes the color of things, but the change is so gradual hardly no one notices. When you died, the color of this place turned a lighter shade than it used to be. The other day a coal-truck bed crashed into my apartment and washed out the color even more. The boys'll build me a new place, but it won't be the same, it'll be different."

Gilman leans back in his chair and closes his eyes, bringing to mind images from his childhood. There was a time when he memorized the name of every tree in the hills, learned what to call the weeds and wildflowers, and painted himself with red clay and danced for rain during dry spells.

He opens his eyes and says to Zack, "I'm not against all

changes; I'm just against the ones that take a place and turn it into something that ain't as good. They's a new man showed up by the name of Tom Jett, and I wonder about the effect he's having on people. When they look at him they see beaches and white sand. They smell wine and marinated mushrooms. Tom may've never eat a marinated mushroom in his whole life, but he carries around the smell of them—he can't help it."

Gilman reaches inside his pocket and takes out the letter from the Conroy Coal Company. He reads it for the third time today, looks Zack straight in the eye, and howls like a dog. Outside, birds stop chirping, and the flying squirrel sits still as a painting. "Now they want to cut the top off this mountain and turn it into mud.

"And Rosalee's in trouble," Gilman says, noticing Zack's unlit cigarette and full glass of whiskey. "You're not drinking enough, Zack. Let's party."

When he returns home a few hours later, Tom and Ten-Fifteen are back in the trailer. He walks into the machine shop, gets inside the 1949 Ford, and starts it up. The car has been repaired for over a week, but he hasn't told the owner. He smells the seats and dashboard—old cars have a smell of their own. He turns the steering wheel in his hands and switches on the headlights. Zack used to own a 1949 Ford. Being five years older than Gilman, he got his license first, and when the car came into Zack's possession, he drove Gilman, who was just thirteen and a virgin at the time, all the way to Lexington and bought him an evening with a redheaded woman. Gilman backs the car out of the shop, parks it beside the truck bed, and reckons he'll call the owner tomorrow.

*I*t is the day of Kelly Coots's funeral, and Tom Jett is parked beside the road in front of the church. Tom wouldn't be here if not for Ten-Fifteen, who wanted to go and needed a ride. Gilman used to be the one who did the chauffeuring, but now that Tom is around Gilman is off the hook. No other members of the Machine Shop Society have come to the funeral. They will mourn Kelly's death some other day by getting drunk.

Tom wouldn't go inside the church with Ten-Fifteen, and while he sits in the car waiting for the service to end, he hears the hymns being sung—"Rock of Ages," "The Old Rugged Cross," and "Nearer My God to Thee." Hoping to escape the sad, suffocating mood the hymns induce, he gets out of the car and walks down to the water, where the creek is returning to its normal size. He notes the high-water mark on trees and craggy rocks near the stream and stands there for a moment, thinking that people are always a little disappointed when a crisis ends, when the excitement is over and normality sets in. It means they have to get up in the morning and resume their daily activities as if nothing much happened. Tom backsteps up the bank and walks beside the parked cars that line the side of the road. That's when he sees Gemma Collet, sitting in a car, drumming her fingers on the dash. He approaches her cautiously. "Hello, you may remember me. I'm the Different Kind of Carpenter."

Gemma grunts.

"Kelly a friend of yours?" he asks, nodding toward the church.

"Didn't know him," she says.

"I hardly knew him, either," Tom admits.

"But I knew all I wanted to know," Gemma adds.

"Well, a lot of people must have liked him, judging from the number of cars here."

"That doesn't mean a thing," Gemma retorts. "They're afraid if they don't go to funerals, no one will come to theirs. The only people who really regret his dying are his family. I guess some of the bunch that hang around Gilman Lee's feel bad about it, but that's because they're reminded of their own deaths, which are bound to be as ugly as Kelly's."

"You have a wonderful outlook on life," Tom says, glancing around at the church. "Why did you come?"

"I brought my mother. She likes to go to funerals."

"Likes to?"

"Yeah, she's peculiar that way. Momma's had a couple of heart attacks and can't drive herself, so I have to do it."

"Sorry she's not well."

Gemma glares. "You don't even know her. I doubt you're real shook up about it."

Tom smiles. Gemma's response reminds him of how seldom he encounters honesty.

The pallbearers and mourners come out of the church. Gemma waves to her mother, who has stopped to chat with a group of women who are all shaking their heads and looking sad.

"Nice talking to you," Tom says, winking at Gemma.

"Glad you liked it."

"Tell me something. I'm surprised a smart woman like you isn't in a big city somewhere, carrying a briefcase and rushing off to a business luncheon. Why do you stay here?"

Gemma looks away from him and motions for her mother to come on. "I don't like joining crowds," she says.

7
Chapter

Gemma Collet's mother, June, has had two heart attacks in the past four years, causing her to seem older than her age of fifty. June goes to funerals regularly to get ideas for her own, which she is sure won't be long in coming. She has decided on an oak casket with brass handles and a white satin interior; her dress will be lavender silk with long, flimsy sleeves. She'll wear white gloves, a pearl necklace, and a little rouge to color her cheeks. June's hair will be in a bun. Her body is going to lie in state at the Pick Funeral Home, and at the church the choir will sing "Love Lifted Me." June Collet will be buried in the new cemetery that is easy to reach. She doesn't want people carrying her up the hill to the old cemetery lest they drop her casket the way they dropped Cassie Lawson's. Each funeral June attends gives her ideas of what she does and does not want.

"I don't like mums," June tells Gemma. They are sitting on the porch after Kelly Coots's funeral. "They's nothing uglier than a big, round, yellow mum. I don't want mums at my funeral."

"What kind of flowers do you want?" Gemma asks, already knowing what kind of flowers her mother wants. She wants roses. Gemma fans the skirt of her dress against her legs to stir the air. Not a breeze is blowing, and in the yard the sun is sizzling on the rain-soaked grass.

"I want roses," June says. "Pink, red, white, beige—any kind of roses except silk. I don't want no silk flowers at my funeral. People can't wait for burials to end so they can snatch the silk flowers for their coffee tables. I want real ones at my funeral." June Collet settles back on the settee and closes her eyes. In a minute's time she is asleep.

Gemma looks out at the road and sees Ten-Fifteen and Tom Jett driving by in one of Gilman Lee's old cars. Suddenly the car's engine dies, and Ten-Fifteen gets out and tries to push the car with his gawky hands, which keep bouncing back to their permanent time. Finally, he positions his backside against the trunk and starts pushing, his arms waving out from his sides like weather vanes. Some people have a harder time than others, Gemma thinks. She is about to get up and yell at him to see if she can help when the car starts up again. To her mind, Ten-Fifteen is the only one of Gilman's crowd who acts like a human being, and Gilman affects her so adversely that every time she sees him her stomach starts to ache. "Funny how the Californian took to that bunch like a bee to honey," she mutters, as an image of Tom Jett pops into her mind, his tanned skin flashing like a neon sign. What irritates her most right now is that his tan is the same color her own skin used to be.

She goes to her room and lies down on the bed, recalling her conversation with Tom in front of the church. Something about him, not just his tan but something else—his manner of speaking, his questioning eyes, attitude?—stubbornly hangs on to the tail end of her thoughts; but determined to shake free the nuisance, she stares up at the ceiling until all she sees is the color white.

There is nothing to do. There are some towels to fold; that's all there is. Gemma is tired of this room, this house, and her job. She loathes the people who bank at the Pick Citizens'— the rich ones who accrue land by paying off banknotes owed by the poor, then lease the land to coal companies who milk it dry; and she hates the poor for being so worried about being poor. She detests funerals, her mother's heart attacks, mums and roses, too. She abhors all floral arrangements, especially those with baby's breath.

When Gemma came down from the mountaintop that day twelve years ago, the same day her lover returned to Chicago without her, she carried a set of commandments chiseled before her eyes, mind, and heart.

> **The American Dream shalt not be mine.**
> **I shalt not hide myself.**
> **I shalt stare at people harder than they shalt dare to stare at me.**
> **I shalt flaunt mine ugliness before those who shrink away.**
> **I shalt not trust.**
> **Normal people shalt be mine enemies.**
> **People with afflictions shalt be mine friends.**
> **I shalt work for the enemy and eat at them from the inside out.**
> **I shalt be a bitch.**
> **I shalt be the *biggest* bitch in the world!**

Those were the commandments Gemma gave herself when she descended from the top of the mountain across the creek from her house and entered her mother's kitchen a new person. June soon began to realize that her daughter was living by a different code. Gemma, who had usually cast a positive attitude, made good grades in high school, and believed most of what people told her, now kept a scowl on her face. She made fun of everybody and everything that came within her view. She said people were idiots except for men, who she said hadn't come that far. "Men suck," she often spouted out.

Actually, Gemma had always, even during her normal years in high school, leaned toward skepticism about the politics of things—the politics of high school, of being a daughter and girlfriend, of being pretty. But she had kept her skepticism well hidden because that was easier to do than trying to understand it. Now, though, she had taken that aggravating burr in her side out into the sunlight, inspected it carefully, and found some truth among its needles.

She got a job at the bank, and it was her new cynical image that she presented, not only to the bank customers, but to the entire world of Pick. It served her well, helping her to get through many an otherwise dull day.

At home, Gemma became absorbed in solitude. Sometimes, she climbed the mountain behind her house and picked wildflowers, sassafras, and mint leaves. She loved the wildness of the mountain that allowed her to laugh and cry among its trees.

In Pick, children pointed, stared, laughed, and name-called. Some of them became frightened at the sight of her and ran away screaming. Others looked up at her as if she were Santa Claus, their mouths hung open, their eyes stretched wide in awe, and inquired of their mothers, "What's that on her face, Mommy? Is her skin coming off?"

But more than the looks she received from people, it was the disease itself, the white, colorless presence splattering her body—leaving her as void of green as mountains during winter, as an eternity of snow—that gave Gemma Collet her own special demeanor, an attitude that became famous in and around Pick.

8
Chapter

*I*t is Saturday, and Gilman Lee is standing in a corner of the shop watching the men work. He has never seen such camaraderie. Twelve men showed up to help with the rebuilding. Sawdust is flying, two-by-fours are being knocked into place, and Tom Jett, who hasn't had a hammer in his hand in four months, is running around driving nails through wood with single blows. Gilman's friend, the Texan, known as the Texan because he always sings "I'm a Long, Tall Texan," is singing the song for which he was named. The rest of the men, who are keeping a respectful distance from Tex because he is said to have once killed five men for negligible reasons, are frolicking like elves. Glad to see my bad luck has made everyone so happy, Gilman thinks. Maybe when they get the apartment built back, I ought to hire someone to crash a coal truck through it again just to keep these here happy workers supplied with a goal.

Gilman can't keep his mind on the reconstruction of his place; he's thinking of other things. Yesterday he received more news from Rosalee. In a sketchy letter, she said:

Dear Gilman,

For the past week I've been in this rooming house in Atlanta. It's an old three-story white house with a porch that goes all the way around it and has flowers growing all over the yard. My room is on the third floor and looks out on the street. It's got an old-fashion canopy bed that I truly love, and the tub in the bathroom is seven-foot long and has legs. The woman that runs this house is a widow. She's as sweet as she can be and serves a hot meal every evening.

I'm almost afraid to walk out of this yard, afraid I'll see him. I'm scared he's waiting for me just down the street. The man I told you about has a heart like a snake. Sometimes at night I think I see him standing in a corner of my bedroom. He'll kill me, Gilman. I know he will. It's hard to say when or if I'll ever get to Pick. . . .

This doesn't sound like the Rosalee he knows. She was always laughing and singing. Sometimes she would sit for hours in the bathtub singing songs, her feet propped on the rim, her toes wiggling. "Hey, Gilman," she'd yell. "Would you come in here and wash my back? They's a spot back here I can't reach."

He has dreamed about her almost every night since he received her first letter. If he knew she'd be there when he arrived, he'd take off for Atlanta right now.

Ten-Fifteen runs up to him, interfering with his thoughts. "Jink Roberts is goin to give us some knotty pine, and Tom is goin to panel your whole apartment in it. He's goin to make your counter out of it and your kitchen cabinets, too. Maybe we can even git some of them porcelain tiles for the countertop. How'd that be?"

"My, ain't we getting fancy," Gilman scoffs. "Maybe I ought to go all out and hire me a interior decorator. Maybe Tom could send to California for one."

Ten-Fifteen goes back to sawing wood undeterred from his enthusiasm.

Gilman replaces his worry for Rosalee with his anger at the Conroy Coal Company. Their land agent will arrive on Monday to talk to him about the coal lease.

Last night he dreamed he bit the man's ears off.

*B*y Sunday evening, except for the balcony and the inside paneling, the men have completed rebuilding Gilman's apartment. Tom Jett is going to do the rest of the work himself, and to repay him Gilman will overhaul his car engine. After the men have gone home, Gilman wastes no time in moving back to the apartment. He dusts off his couch, which is only slightly damaged, sweeps the floor, and goes to bed.

Back in the trailer, Tom Jett is wide awake. It is a hot night and too quiet for comfort. Even the frogs and crickets aren't talking. Tom has worked hard the past two days, and tonight he's too tired to sleep. Since he has been here, one of the hardest things he's had to adjust to has been the night. In San Diego, the drone of traffic and the noise of planes are constant, and there is always the knowledge that no matter how late the hour thousands of people are coming and going, fighting or making love. Even when voices can't be heard, their messages sneak into a sleeper's dreams and leave faint, nebulous traces. Here, there are none of those sounds. Here, Tom has heard water roar in a flooded creek and rain pound on a trailer's roof. He's listened to frogs and crickets sing. Some nights like tonight there is a stillness so complete, it is as if the entire population has vanished from the earth and been replaced by mute, startled ghosts. Occasionally, this stillness is interrupted by a speeding car on the road, its tires screaming like rare birds that are hell-bent on extinction.

Finally he gets out of bed and walks outside. It occurs to him that he could leave this place as soon as Gilman repairs his car. He could move on, maybe try out a mountain range in Maine. There is something about these hills and their warm, damp nights that suffocates him. "There is no reason why I should stay here," Tom says to the still, dark air. He wonders if the way he feels could be reduced, as has almost every other human dilemma, to a topic for a TV talk show. He doubts it.

Ten-Fifteen comes out of the trailer and walks up behind him. "Tom, are you thinking about California?" he asks.

"Not exactly."

"How about your family? Are you thinking about them?"

Tom yawns. "My mother and father are so happy there is no need to think about them for long."

Ten-Fifteen walks around beside him. "You said you left the beach because you wanted to go to the mountains. They's a lot of mountains between California and here. They's the Rockies and the Ozarks. Why didn't you pick them?"

"I tried the Rockies," Tom says. "They weren't for me. Everybody I saw there wore those quilted jackets with no sleeves. I don't like quilted jackets with no sleeves. The women were so fresh-faced they reminded me of Colgate commercials, and the men all had neatly trimmed beards." Tom stops talking and listens for a sound other than his own voice. "Perhaps I didn't find the real Rockies. Perhaps I was on the wrong side of the mountain."

"Did you find the Ozarks?" Ten-Fifteen asks him.

"No, I missed them."

"Are you goin to leave here when Gilman fixes your car?"

Tom takes the deep breath of a person who anticipates trouble. "I think I'm going to stay for a while."

"I'm glad," Ten-Fifteen says.

*I*t is Monday, and Gilman is in the machine shop, getting ready to talk business with the man from Conroy Coal.

"I would've asked you into my apartment, but, as you might can hear, I got a carpenter in there putting up paneling," Gilman tells his visitor.

"No matter," the man says, spreading his papers on a greasy work bench.

"What did you say your name was?" Gilman asks in a voice loud enough to be heard over Tom Jett's hammering and sawing.

"Toothacre," the man replies. "Ed Toothacre." He pauses and gives Gilman the once-over with his businessman's eye. "You stand to make a lot of money out of this, Mr. Lee."

"If they's one thing I like, it's money," Gilman says, "and you can call me Gilman."

"That mountain's got more than a million tons of coal, just begging to be mined." Ed beams. "That translates into a lot of green."

Ed, fresh from Conroy's administrative office in Lexington, is eager to make a deal. He is up for promotion to vice-president sometime next year, and in order to get on the good side of the president, who believes candidates for vice-president should have at least some experience in all areas of mining, Ed has been working various jobs well beneath his qualifications. Last month he worked in a deep mine, this month he's a land agent, next month who knows?

"Yeah, but I don't own the whole mountain," Gilman says. "I just own thirty acres. How many tons you reckon's on my land?"

"At least two hundred thousand. We'll pay you fifty cents for every ton we mine from your property. That adds up to a hundred thousand dollars. With that kind of money, you could buy a lot of improvements to your place and have plenty money left over."

"Whoop-dee-doo," Gilman says, licking his lips. "Just think how much I'd make if I owned the mineral rights. How much is the people that owns the mineral rights going to make?"

"I'm not at liberty to say."

"Well, I heard they got about two dollars and fifty cents a ton. That'd be five hundred thousand for them. And how much will you people make? Coal's going for about nineteen dollars a ton on the market, ain't it? That's what I heard."

"The market varies, Mr. Lee."

"Yeah," Gilman says. "Well, either way there's several million dollars to be made off that mountain."

Ed narrows his eyes. "Wait a minute. You haven't considered the mining expenses—fuel, dynamite, machinery, wages. We don't get that much free and clear. We have a hard time just making it."

"Yeah," Gilman says, "I feel real sorry for you. I'm surprised you don't forget the whole thing." He leans close to Ed and bares his teeth, two of which have cavities. "Got any dentists in your family, Mr. Toothacre?"

"Dentists?"

"Yeah, you know, them people you go to when you got a toothache."

"Well, actually, no," Ed says, flinching. He hasn't been kidded about his name since high school. Ed, who has a nononsense disposition, is often disgusted by what he has observed as the tendency of locals to "yuk it up."

"Do you ever have tooth pain, yourself?" Gilman persists.

Ed bats his eyes and laughs irritably. "Not recently. Why do you ask?" He waits for what he is sure will be a hokey punch line. Yuk, he thinks, yuk yuk.

Gilman grabs hold of Ed's jaw. "Cause if you ain't gone from here by the time I count to ten, I'm going to pull your teeth, so you can live up to your name. One . . . two . . ."

Startled, Ed jerks away and gets his papers together. "You mean you're not agreeable to this?"

"Did I tell you I dreamed about your ears the other night?"

"My what?" Ed gasps.

". . . three . . . four . . ." Gilman responds.

Ed, who has heard numerous stories about the unpredictable violence of mountain men, leaves in a hurry.

Gilman picks up the phone and calls June Collet.

"Hello, June. Has that man from Conroy been around to see you yet?"

"No, but he's supposed to be here in a little while."

"Has Gemma decided what she's goin to do about it?"

June sighs. "I've still not told her. But I'm goin to after I talk to that man from Conroy. What are you goin to do about the lease, Gilman?"

"Prob'ly not the same thing as you, June."

After Gilman hangs up, he opens the door to his apartment where Tom Jett has already paneled the end wall and is in the process of measuring some knotty pine. Watching him for a while, Gilman decides that Tom is perfect for the plan he has recently begun to formulate, a plan that concerns coal mines, land leases, and his old friend the Texan. As plans go, it is a last resort. But still, he thinks, Californians are supposed to get all worked up over health, conservation, and saving whales—things like that—and besides, Ten-Fifteen says the boy's looking for adventure. Gilman goes to the refrigerator and gets a couple of beers. "Hey, Tom," he yells, "come over here and have a beer."

Tom puts down his tape measure.

"Ten-Fifteen said you was thinking about staying in this part of the country awhile. How long you planning on staying?"

Tom takes a drink of beer and sets it on the counter. "I'm not planning on anything. I'd like to stay for a while, but it depends on whether I can find work."

"Well, I've got a proposition for you. I own a house on some land down the road. You can stay in it rent free if you'll keep a lookout for certain goings-on. The house is in pretty bad shape, but being's you're a carpenter, that oughten shy you away. You're doing a good job on my apartment here, and when I put the word out, you'll get other jobs."

"What are these goings-on you're interested in?" Tom asks.

"A man was here a minute ago that wants to lease my land so he can work the coal. He tells me they's a chance I'd make around a hundred thousand dollars, but I've turned him down."

"Why?"

"I don't like strip mines. Of course they're not as bad now as they used to be, but I still don't like 'em." Gilman finishes off his beer and gets another. "They's more to it than just the stripping—way more. I might feel better inclined to coal mining if people around here owned the mineral rights to their land, but they don't. Way back when my daddy was just a boy, Grandpa sold the mineral rights to our property—sold it for fifty cents a acre. The man who bought 'em told him that the coal wouldn't ever do him no good anyway, that you had to be rich to mine coal. Then he told Grandpa the company he represented wouldn't be mining the coal for years to come. He said, 'You'll be long dead before we ever start in.' I guess Grandpa figured that none of his children or grandchildren would ever be rich enough to mine coal, either. So he sold the rights for fifteen dollars, total. That same thing happened all over this part of the country. Almost everybody sold their coal, oil, and gas rights for fifty cents and less a acre. These companies usually didn't buy the land itself cause they didn't want to pay the taxes on it. They decided to leave that for the poor folks."

Gilman looks out the back door at a broken TV, a victim of the flood that is wedged between two rocks in the creek. He turns back to Tom, continuing his story. "Companies like Conroy been working the coal for as long as I can remember. They make all kinds of money, especially if they own the mineral rights. Course if they don't have the rights, they have to lease 'em from whoever does, and they lease the land from us. They tell people around here they're goin to get rich, but I've never seen it happen. People get cheated left and right. More coal gets mined than gets reported. No one except the companies get rich off a coal lease."

Tom stares at Gilman; he doesn't know what to say. "I still don't understand why you want me to keep an eye on your property. What do you think is going to happen?"

"Everybody else that owns land on the mountain will prob'ly sign agreements. No doubt, I'll be the only one that holds out. I want to make sure the assholes at Conroy don't step their feet on my land."

"If they were to get on your land, what would you expect me to do about it?" Tom asks.

"To get your butt down the hill and tell me. I'll take over from there."

"I would have thought you'd want someone else to do this for you. I'm surprised you picked me."

"I'm surprised, too," Gilman says.

Tom sets his empty beer can on the counter. "I used to sit on the beach and listen to waves," he says. "Waves are good teachers. They teach you that when people are bent on destroying things the best revenge is to let them do it. If idiots level every mountain in order to gouge out coal and oil and gas, that's fine with waves. Waves don't even get overly excited about offshore drilling. Occasionally, they may wash a little blood and dead fish on the beach, just as a reminder of how things really are. But, primarily, waves are cynics biding time."

Gilman stares at a knot on the knotty pine paneling and grins. "Buddy, all I want you to do is watch my land. Are you goin to do it?"

"Sure," Tom says. "Why not?"

9
Chapter

June Collet hasn't had one thought of funerals since Ed Toothacre walked out of her house at one o'clock this afternoon. Instead, she's been thinking about palaces and plastic surgeons.

She holds a secret desire to stand in front of the palace gates in London, England, and have her picture made with a palace guard. June, who loves the guards' red uniforms and tall, black, woolly hats, figures she'll wear blue when she has her picture made—blue to offset the red. Prior to going to England, she wants to make an appointment with a plastic surgeon. That's the shocker. No one would ever suspect her of desiring such a thing. June doesn't seem the type.

She first became aware of face-lifts when she saw a movie called *Mondo Cane*, about twenty-five years ago. She learned a lot of things from seeing that movie. She learned that some people eat ants and snakes, that there are cemeteries just for pets, and that rich people have face-lifts to keep from looking old. Right then at the drive-in theater with her husband, Bob, sitting beside her and five-year-old Gemma in the backseat asleep, June swore that when she started getting old she'd go to a plastic surgeon for a face-lift. As things turned out, she never had the promise of enough money for one until now.

June and Gemma own fifty acres of land on the mountain behind their house. Ed Toothacre said there were three hundred thousand tons of coal on their property. At fifty cents a ton, they'd come out with one hundred and fifty thousand dollars— enough to go to England two times and have a whole body lift.

June walks into the bedroom and stands in front of the full-length mirror, her clear blue eyes assessing the damage of fifty years and two heart attacks. Deep lines groove her pale face, and pepper-gray hair hangs in a loose bun at the back of her neck. The smock she wears is shapeless and of a faded color that could have once been blue or green or gray. Her skinny knees glare at her below the hemline. June takes the pins out of her hair, grabs her brush, draws her hair into a high bun, and goes back into the kitchen.

When she sees her daughter pull into the driveway, she starts setting the table, trying to act natural. She fears that when she tells Gemma about the Conroy Coal Company wanting to lease their land, her obstinate daughter will somehow stop it cold. After June's talk with Ed Toothacre today, she realizes she can't delay telling her any longer. All afternoon she's been trying to decide how to broach the subject. She doesn't want to blurt out the news of their prospective coal riches on the spot; she's decided to let it slip out during the dinner conversation.

Gemma walks in, kicks her shoes off, and goes to the bathroom. June finishes placing the food on the table and is trying to hold down a smile when Gemma comes back into the room and drops into a chair.

"Have some potatoes," June says to her daughter, who is eyeing a drumstick on the platter.

Gemma doesn't hear her. She's thinking about a film she saw the other night on PBS. It was a film about a medieval king who, when he wasn't waging wars, would throw banquets and devour huge amounts of food, grease running like water off his chin. There was a purity and beauty to the way he ate his food. He was a person who, if he was hungry, you knew it.

Gemma is hungry, too, hungry as a third-world country. She thinks it's her job at the bank that has brought her to this state, that it's the numbers—the debits and credits. The thing about numbers is that they add up, Gemma thinks, and if they don't add up it's because some are missing. What she would like is for all the numbers to be there and still not add up. She wants to be surprised by the incalculable, but she knows this will never happen. She knows that everything was figured out a long time ago, and that all people do is look up answers in the back of a book. Gemma would like to come up with some answers of her own.

"How about some slaw?" June asks.

Gemma responds by seizing the drumstick and wrestling it into her mouth. "I'm hungry," she grunts, grasping a biscuit while reaching for the mashed potatoes.

"Yeah, I can see that," June says. She becomes so transfixed by the consumption in front of her that she opens and closes her mouth with every bite Gemma takes. "I've been thinking about buying a new suitcase," June announces, trying to sound casual.

Gemma continues to eat.

"My old suitcase is too old," June explains.

"Um hum," Gemma says, cracking open a chicken bone and sucking out the marrow. She wants to get to the core of things; marrow is what she needs.

"I'm buying a new one," June says. She is used to her daughter behaving oddly, but this devastation of poultry is disgusting. "What in the world is wrong with you?"

"A new what?"

"Suitcase. You need a new one, too."

"Why?"

"Because we won't want to carry our old ones when we go to England," June says.

Gemma stares into her mother's eyes as if they are clusters of numbers that momentarily don't add up.

"I hope you don't eat like that when we go to England," June adds.

Gemma stops eating and listens while her mother explains about the coal, about the hundred and fifty thousand dollars, the palace guards, and face-lift. She listens politely, sometimes nodding her head and smiling. Perfect, she thinks to herself, this is perfect. When June finally finishes, Gemma walks into the living room and sits down. June follows her.

"Well, how about that? We're goin to be rich!" June giggles.

"That's nice," Gemma says.

"We're goin to England!"

"Wow."

"Well, ain't you excited?"

"I'm fit to be tied," Gemma says.

"Maybe you can quit your job at the bank!"

Gemma walks out of the house and stares at the creek. June follows her. "I used to swim right down there in that hole of water," Gemma says. "Now it's never more than six inches deep unless there's a flood. Why do you reckon that is? I'll tell you why. It's filled up with silt. Where do you think that silt came from? It came sliding down the mountains from strip mines. You realize that, don't you?"

"Why, honey, they ain't nothing wrong with that old creek. It was here before we was born, and it'll be here after we're gone." June clutches her chest and thinks about funerals for the first time since Ed Toothacre left her house at one o'clock this afternoon. "Besides, they're doing a lot better with strip mines. They've passed laws."

"Laws, smaws," Gemma says.

"Does that mean you're not goin to sign the lease?" June asks, breathing hard.

"On the contrary, I'm dying to sign it," Gemma says.

June looks at her daughter as if she expects her face to

break out in measles. "But you sounded like you was against it."

"I am against it."

June squints her eyes. "You mean you're dying to sign something you're against?"

"Yes."

"Why would you do a thing like that?"

"Because I'm hungry," Gemma says, taking a look at her mother's pale face and wondering how she can explain that she has given herself a new commandment: *Be For What You're Against.*

Finally, she tries to explain herself to her mother. "There are two normal ways of looking at this: If you're against the mining, you don't sign the agreement. If you're for it, you do. Maybe I'd like to see what would happen if someone were to sign an agreement even though she's against it. And I'm not talking about someone that is pressured into signing. I'm talking about a person who wholeheartedly agrees to something that she hates beyond description."

June takes a few steps back. "That don't make sense, Gemma."

"Good. If there's one thing in this world I'm tired of doing, it's making sense," Gemma says, staring straight into her mother's eyes.

June looks away and tries to rub the chill bumps off her arms. "You're trying to scare me. That's what you're trying to do. Now, I want to know what you're talking about."

"What I'm talking about," Gemma says, "is that maybe I want to see everything destroyed—and the sooner the better."

June's voice begins to shake. "Well, what if *I* don't sign it?" she says. "Since you say it's such a bad thing, maybe I'll just change my mind."

Gemma smiles. "You won't change your mind because you've already got your heart set on a new face and a trip to England. You'll lie to yourself—tell yourself that strip mining adds nutrients to soil, that it purifies creeks, that it causes small animals to sing to children. You'll sign."

"Why do you always do this? I get excited about something, and you take the fun out of it," June says, clutching her chest again. "A person that wants to do something they despise is crazy, Gemma. A person like that is sick. You've got just as much mud in you as that creek has."

That night June paces the floor, unable to sleep. She opens the door to Gemma's bedroom and stands there in the dark, hoping the moonlight coming through the window will calm her nerves. She makes out the shape of her daughter's body on the bed and becomes aware that Gemma is awake, too, that she is lying there with her eyes open, staring at the ceiling.

"You can be thankful you've never had children," June says. "You used to be a happy child, Gemma. When you was about four years old, you stuffed a bean up your nose, and your nose swelled the size of a pear. I tried to get the bean out, but it wouldn't budge. Your daddy was gone on a fishing trip, I didn't have a car, and the phone wasn't working, either. Finally, I just grabbed you up and started walking toward town. I run into old Leonard Woods on the road. He turned me right back toward the house and said he could fix you in no time. He dusted out a handful of pepper and told you to sniff it in. You sneezed, and that bean shot out of your nose like a bullet—bounced against the wall so hard it tore a hole in the wallpaper. You didn't even hardly cry. You laughed about it. You was a happy child back then.

"But you sure ain't happy no more. I guess it was that disease. You think you're ugly. Have you took a good look at yourself lately, Gemma? You've got pretty skin that's white as a china doll's.

"I can't tell you how it hurts me to see you so hateful all the time," June emphasizes. "Just be thankful you don't have children."

"I am thankful, Momma," Gemma says.

10

Chapter

Gilman stands on his new balcony, thinking about the fact that Tom Jett agreed to live in his old house on the hill and keep an eye on his property. He figures a man who not only agreed to that thankless deal, but who is good at carpentry, too, deserves attention. Maybe it's time I got better acquainted with Tom Cat, Gilman decides.

He picks up the phone and calls a couple of his friends, the Texan and Joe Carter.

"Come on over," he tells them, "and let's bore right into this fine afternoon and make a hole right smack dab in the middle of it."

Joe Carter, who is temporarily laid off from his job, is all for the idea, and as for the Texan, he says, "I'm on my way." The Texan doesn't have a job, and people are afraid to ask him how he makes a living. All they know is that he doesn't work.

In twenty minutes, the Texan and Joe Carter are in the apartment, and Gilman is standing in the shop door, yelling for Ten-Fifteen and Tom to join the crowd. Soon a music session is in the works with Gilman on guitar and Joe on banjo.

The Texan, Ten-Fifteen, and Tom sing and tap their feet.

A few songs and drinks later, the music is more spirited, and the men more in tune. They're riding now, flying in and around lyrics and notes, knowing deep down they're too good at this point for radio, TV, or the Opry. Finally, they get so good they can't stand it anymore and take a break.

Gilman says, "Boys, let's have a shooting match."

"Cans or rats?" the Texan asks.

"Belts," replies Gilman.

"Belts?" Tom asks.

"Yeah, the leather strap that runs through your loops," explains the Texan.

"Let's step down by the creek, boys," Gilman says, sticking his .38 in his pants pocket. The men follow him outside and down the bank to a level area near the creek. Handing the Texan his gun, Gilman walks seventy paces from him, draws the end of his belt out of the buckle so that it's sticking four inches from his stomach, and says, "Take your best shot."

The Texan aims and fires, taking an inch off the end of Gilman's belt.

Joe Carter and Ten-Fifteen whoop with delight.

In an attempt to stop himself from shaking, Tom sits down on a rock and takes a drink from the bottle he brought. "You guys realize, of course, that you've been drinking for a while and your reflexes aren't what they should be," he says, trying a low-pressure style of dissuasion.

"Your turn," Gilman says to the Texan. The two men trade places and Gilman shoots a half inch off the Texan's belt.

Tom can't look.

"How about you, Tom?" the Texan says.

"Me? I can't shoot."

"That's disappointing," Gilman says.

"You can say that again," the Texan adds. "I figured a boy like you from the Wild West (It's still wild, ain't it?) would be itching to try this out."

Tom glances around at Ten-Fifteen, who is looking in the other direction. He reflects for a few seconds on the ease and accuracy with which Gilman fired on the Texan's belt, snipping off the end at a safe distance from his friend's stomach. "But I can stand," Tom says, feeling a burst of bravado. "Go ahead, Gilman."

While searching his memory for a moment when he put his life so completely in another's hands, Tom walks out to where the Texan is still standing, draws his belt out, and waits. There is no memory of such a moment, he realizes, just as Gilman fires the gun, taking the tip off his belt. Joe Carter and Ten-Fifteen howl like dogs, the Texan smiles, Tom Jett breathes.

"I think it's time you learned to shoot, Tom." Gilman hands him the gun, walks about thirty feet away, and says, "Shoot the rest of it off."

Tom turns cold as an iceberg. "I've never shot a gun."

"That don't matter. Just look at my belt and see the leather. All I want you to be concerned with in this whole world is the end of my leather belt, your hand, and the gun in it. They's nothing else, Tom, just your hand, the gun, and my belt. The leather looks bigger, now, don't it? It's big as the side of a barn. Now, you wouldn't miss the side of a barn, would you?"

Tom holds the gun in his hand and looks around at the Texan, who is eyeing him with a fierce killer instinct. He is apt to kill me here and now if I don't do this, Tom decides, staring at the three inches of leather sticking out from Gilman's stomach. He holds the gun in front of him, puts his finger on the trigger, and aims at a green leaf drooping down from a tree branch that is situated at least a foot away from Gilman's belt, taking care to hold the gun in such a way (he hopes) that the men won't notice he isn't aiming for the belt.

"Go on, Tom, squeeze that trigger. Squeeze it, Tom—that's all you've got to do," Gilman says.

Tom concentrates on the leaf, pulls the trigger, and fires.

Gilman doesn't bat an eye as the bullet cuts off the end of the drawn-out belt so it's even with the buckle.

Tom sags to the ground as though he's had the breath knocked out of him. "But I didn't ai . . . ai . . . aim at . . ." he sputters incoherently.

Ten-Fifteen and Joe Carter let out sighs of relief, and Gilman walks over to Tom, smiling. "Goddamn, this boy can shoot! Did you see that?"

"I could have killed you," Tom gasps.

"But you didn't, and now I reckon I can trust you to watch my property."

The men return to the apartment and continue playing music with renewed vigor, except for Tom, who sits on a stool at the counter, gulping down drinks, feeling as though his heart is running away.

Gilman Lee parks in June and Gemma's driveway and takes Tom Jett up the mountain, giving him a tour of the property he'll soon be calling home. First he leads him to the old abandoned house, where broken beer bottles lie on the floor and dried-up animal droppings are deposited in the corners. Graffiti scrawled by drunken doodlers grace every wall. "Kids come up here to carry on," Gilman explains.

Tom scans the debris and decides someone had a lot of fun creating it. He likes the place. Gilman takes him outside and shows him the field and the flying squirrels.

"What's this?" Tom asks when he sees the prayer chamber.

"Used to be a smokehouse. My daddy and grandpa both used it to cure meat in, but I've turned it into a prayer chamber. Don't allow no one in it but me."

Tom reads the curse over the door. "That's some pretty serious consequences," he says.

"Yes, it is. That's why no one ever breaks in. And when you move up here, you ain't to go in it, either. This is my place. I'll be coming up here from time to time to visit it, and you ain't to pay me no mind."

Tom glances curiously from the prayer chamber to Gilman. "Whatever you say."

Gilman proudly shows him the marijuana patch.

"Aren't you afraid those kids will get into this?" Tom asks, as he stands among the tall green plants.

"Me and them kids got a understanding," Gilman says. "They don't get into my marijuana, and I don't kill 'em. I let 'em carouse in my house cause I remember how it feels to be young and have no place to let go."

Gilman begins to brag that the best pot in the nation is grown right where they're standing. "Kentucky is a place that feeds vices," Gilman tells Tom. "If you're into gambling, drinking, smoking, or doping, we can get you horse races, whiskey, tobacco, and pot. I've not even mentioned the pretty women. Fine state," Gilman says. "Great place to live."

"When do you think they'll start mining?" Tom asks.

"To be honest, I'm not sure. I've always had better things to think about than the maneuverings of coal companies. I think they have to get a permit first." Gilman walks Tom around the steep grade of his property line, around the entire thirty acres, pointing out beech, sycamore, and pine trees that mark the boundary. Leaving Tom near a cave, he tells him to get to know the place for a while, that he has business in the prayer chamber and will see him later.

Tom sits near the cave's entrance and watches Gilman go down the hill to the field, and when he absentmindedly picks up a handful of leaves, he uncovers an arrowhead. "This place is old," he says out loud. "Maybe it's too old." And his voice hangs in the thick air.

In the field, Gilman opens the door to the prayer chamber and steps inside. "You're about to get a new neighbor, Zack.

He's the future—has future written all over him and's about a inch shy of wearing a business suit. He's all right, though—he shot my belt off and didn't hit me. The man's not nearly as bad as I first thought he was."

Gilman dusts a cobweb from Zack's rib cage, says good-bye, and walks back to the cave to get Tom.

It is when they're about halfway down the hill, on their way back to the car, that they see the vision—Gemma through the tree branches. She is standing trancelike in the creek below them, naked except for streaks of mud on her snowy skin. Her eyes are closed and her arms point to the sky. The men stop dead in their tracks and remain silent for a full two minutes.

Tom says, "All I want to know is, is she real?"

"Beats me," Gilman answers.

"What is she doing?"

Gilman shrugs.

"I wish I knew her," Tom stammers. "I wish I knew what she is really like."

Gilman grins. "You're not getting sweet on our Miss Gemma, are you?"

"I wouldn't exactly call it sweet," Tom says. "Tell me what she's like. You must know."

"She's a hard woman; I can tell you that, but I wouldn't say I know her. I tried to get acquainted once and ended up with some bruised balls. It was about five years ago, back when her disease was real bad. Her face looked like it'd been burnt— had big white places all over it. Prob'ly wouldn't have been so noticeable if she hadn't been dark-skinned to start. Real pretty figure though. Small waist, nice hips—built like a Coke bottle. One day, I'd been up here to my house and was wandering around the property when I came upon her leaning against a tree, crying. Being the softhearted man that I am—good to a fault—I inched up and put my arm around her, told her she was pretty, laid a little kiss on her. Hell, she was pretty, blotches or not. I got nothing against blotches. Anyway, she sorta took to me at first, then all at once, she clamped her teeth down on my lower lip and slammed her knee between my legs. It still hurts me to think about it," Gilman says, grimacing. "Course, you know me, I'm a forgiving soul. Till this day, I keep trying to make in with her, but she won't have it."

"You mean she never goes out with anyone?"

"Not since the disease."

"But she's still young, and she's a beautiful woman."

"Shame, ain't it?" Gilman says, shaking his head.

In the creek, Gemma begins to sway slightly, her arms still pointing to the sky.

"I wonder what she's thinking about," Tom says.

Gilman doesn't offer any suggestions; he's too busy remembering the kiss he gave her and wondering why she reacted the way she did.

The two men watch her awhile longer, then walk around the side of the hill. Coming out a half mile down the road, they backtrack to the car and drive home.

Gemma sits quietly in the water and covers her legs in mud. It's been years since she sat in the creek. She wants to get acquainted with the silt that slides, now, across her skin like brown velvet. As an empty milk carton sails past in the cloudy stream, she begins to hum "The Lone Pilgrim," a ballad she learned from her father. Night falls.

11

Chapter

Since there is no road leading to Gilman's house on the hill, he came to an agreement with June to allow Tom the use of her driveway as a parking place. Tom moved in around the middle of August—carried his belongings across the swinging bridge and up the hill. When he got there, he scraped off the torn wallpaper, swept the place out, drew water from a well in the yard, and scoured both the wood-burning stove in the kitchen and the fireplace in the living room. He scrubbed the floors and washed the windows inside and out.

After the cleaning was done, he walked outside feeling like Henry David Thoreau and perused the ground for ant fights. Sitting down on some pine needles, he contemplated beans he might plant in the field and wondered if people ever planted beans in August. Perhaps it was too late in the summer to plant them, he thought, then remembering that Ten-Fifteen had fed him some fall beans one night for supper, he reasoned that perhaps it wasn't too late to plant fall beans.

That evening as he walked down the hill to make sure his car was locked, he saw her again—Gemma in the creek, her face lifted toward the sky. He settled down under a tree and watched her. Dipping her hands in the creek bottom, she filled them with mud, rose out of the water, and smeared the brown silt over her entire body. She sat back in the creek Indian-style and stayed still for about an hour before washing the mud off. Then, after putting her clothes back on, she walked up the bank toward her house. By then Tom was bewitched, so lost in thoughts of her—wondering if this creek sitting was something she did routinely, speculating about its nature—that he no longer cared if his car was locked, and he meandered around the hill awhile before returning home.

On his first night in the house, he spread his sleeping bag in an empty bedroom and listened for speeding cars on the road, but he could hear nothing except the heavy hum of darkness and the songs of owls and whippoorwills. Tom thought about where he was and how he'd come to be there. He tried to summon carefree memories of his childhood, but all he could muster were scenes that featured his parents' enthusiasm for his IQ. He thought about his straight-A report cards and scholarship to Stanford—the years of study, his youthful adoration of Nietzsche, Schopenhauer, Kierkegaard, and anyone else who had ever managed to stare into space without coming away empty-minded. He thought about the transformation of his eager convictions into hard-core cynicism and his days on the beach where waves rolled in and out like the rhythm of slow sex. He remembered the exact moment he had decided to leave the beach and look for trouble, this decision coming from his belief that something and nothing are the same thing.

Tom looked around the dark room, where the only light coming through the window was from the moon, and wondered why Gilman had chosen him for the vigil ahead. Perhaps he sees me as being a sucker, Tom reflected. Or maybe he gets a kick out of giving people what they want.

G ilman, true to his word, spread the news of Tom's carpentry skills, and a few days after moving to the hill, he landed

a job. He is building a porch for a man who recently retired to
the area from Dayton, Ohio. Tom's days are occupied with the
construction, but he spends his evenings peeping at Gemma's
naked body through the tree branches.

Today he sits in his usual spot and watches her as he once
watched waves. Her skin turns statue-gray in evening light,
and as she sits there, Tom imagines that she begins to disperse
into the water and flow around the curve of the hill. He starts
to panic, to feel like a sinner at a revival meeting who fears his
soul will be lost forever if he doesn't step forward. Finally, he
can stand it no longer and starts down the hill toward her.

Gemma knows he's coming, feels his eyes on her. She has
felt him watching her for the past two weeks while she has
baptized herself in water and silt every evening—a ritual that
is nourishing after her long, hungry days at the bank. The
first time she engaged in this activity, it was on a lark. Two
mud-filled entities ought to get to know each other, she
thought. Now it has become a kind of religious experience—
she sings ballads in the water, and it soaks parables through
her skin while she sits naked, stripped of all her masks, ab-
sorbing history from each molecule of water.

She knows he's been watching her. One day she saw a flash
of his white shirt, a turn of his head, and felt his presence traveling across the space between them. She believes he has had
or is having a similar experience to hers, that maybe even now
as he approaches her, a knowledge of mountains and creeks is
coming to him.

The sensation that he has risen from his perch and is walking down the hill toward her gets stronger with each step he
takes in her direction. It is a feeling akin to fear or anger, a
feeling suggesting she should do something—move—and in
ordinary circumstances she would do just that, but here in this
creek where she has become part of something else, the water
won't let her. She wants to shift her position, wants to cover
her breasts, walk toward him or away. She looks downstream,

trying to find something, some object that will draw her attention away from him. He is standing at the edge of the water now, wearing jeans, no shirt. He's stepping in, wading closer. She wants to stand up and scream.

"Hello," Tom says.

Gemma turns to look at him. He's smiling. Men always smile. "Hi," she states flatly.

"Nice evening," he remarks.

"It'll do."

Tom wants to touch her hair and feel it tangled in his hands. "I've been watching you," he says.

"I know."

"Pretty creek," he comments, looking down at the muddy stream.

"It's ugly, but it's mine."

"I used to sit on the beach listening to waves."

"I used to swim here."

Gemma stands up awkwardly and almost brushes against him. Her breasts are a hairsbreadth from his bare skin; she can feel his warmth. For a moment that seems like hours, Tom and Gemma stand close enough to kiss, but they remain apart. Finally the moment ends, and she steps out of the water.

"Yesterday, I signed a lease with a coal company," she tells him as she gets dressed. "They're going to work the coal right up there. I'm not sure when they'll start mining."

"I'm aware of that lease," Tom says. "Gilman didn't sign it, but I guess you know that."

Gemma didn't know. She starts to walk away, looking down at her feet as she goes, feeling as if someone just gave her a swift kick in the stomach. *Gilman Lee didn't sign.*

"Maybe I can come over sometime, borrow a cup of sugar," Tom calls after her as she walks up the bank.

"Sugar is bad for you," she mutters, and goes back inside her house, where her worried mother sits on the couch looking up names of psychiatrists in a Lexington phone book.

June is worried. Seeing her daughter walk down the bank every evening and strip her clothes off, she hasn't been able to object with more than a few words because the behavior is so bizarre, so alien to June's view of the world, that she can't acknowledge it's truly happening except when Gemma is actually down there in the water, and even then it seems more like a nightmare than anything else.

June has begun to think about psychology, nonstop. She watches *Oprah* every day, listening to pop psychologists spout out words of wisdom to people who haven't even begun to think about going naked. June wonders whether Gemma's strange behavior results from a mistake she made as a mother or whether it is something her daughter might have inherited from generations past. With the possible exception of her uncle Jake, none of June's kin has ever gone completely crazy. As she recalls, most of her family didn't think Jake was actually crazy; they just thought he was mean.

"Someone'll see you," she says, when Gemma walks in, smelling like algae.

"Good," Gemma says. Gemma gives short responses like *good* and *yes* to nearly every comment June makes lately.

"You're likely to get put away—arrested. You might even get raped," June continues. "A man might come along and see you sitting down there naked as a jaybird. Think you're asking for it. They's a lot of beady-eyed men in this world that's just waiting to find a woman sitting in a creek bed without her clothes on. What if our new neighbor on the hill sees you? What's he goin to think? He'll go back to California and tell everyone that women around here sit in creeks every evening naked. Is that what you want?"

"Yes," Gemma says.

June throws up her hands and stalks toward her bedroom, then turns around and makes an announcement. "Conroy called today. They'll start building the road in a month or so."

"Did you know Gilman didn't sign?" Gemma asks.

"Yeah, I knew."

"Why didn't you tell me?"

"You're not usually interested in what Gilman does. It would've sure made things easier if he'd signed. Conroy'll have to build a bridge across the creek. It would've been better if they could've tore down Gilman's old swinging bridge and built it there."

Although Gemma is on the outs with Gilman, she feels differently about his bridge, which has swung across the creek for longer than she can remember. Having been refurbished at various times, it dates back to the 1800s. Gilman's grandfather replaced its heavy ropes with steel cables back in 1927, and new boards have been substituted as needed. From each bank of the creek, kudzu vines trail out of control along its handrails and join together midway across. As a person walks over the bridge, it sways like a lover taking a slow stroll down a country road on the morning after. Gemma thinks her mother must have never sat in the middle of the bridge with kudzu dangling about her head and watched minnows swim in circles in the creek below. "How many swinging bridges do you reckon's left in this county, Momma?" she asks.

"I don't know. Not many, I guess."

"And you wouldn't have minded them tearing his down?"

June sighs. "I'm just saying it would have been handier if they could've built their bridge where his old one is."

"Good point. Why keep something around that you can't drive a coal truck across? Too bad Conroy couldn't have destroyed it," Gemma says, rolling her eyes.

June starts to say something, but she doesn't. Silence descends on her like a fainting spell. She wonders why every word her daughter says slaps her in the face. She picks up the Lexington phone book and goes to her bedroom, thinking that Gemma has never needed help like she needs it now.

12
Chapter

No one is sure how the town of Pick, founded in 1801
by a man named Bob Burr, who claimed to be a distant relative of Aaron Burr, got its name, but there are
several theories, all of which involve Bob Burr. The simplest
theory is that when Bob came upon the site nestled by the
river with enough flatland to room a building or two and said,
"This is my pick," no one including Bob could ever think of
anything else to call the site but that, Pick.

The most popular theory among the youngsters of Pick is
that the town was so named because Bob Burr had a discon-
certing habit of picking his nose. He is reported to have
picked it vigorously everywhere and all the time, in front of
friends and strangers alike; but it is assumed his energy was
wasted, since nothing could have been left in his nose to pick
except a few stubborn hairs.

A variation on this theory holds that the manner of Bob's
death prompted the town's name. Not long after settling the
town, he was killed with a pickax. Since Bob had an appetite
for sexual adventures, some think he was murdered by a jeal-

ous husband. Whatever the reason, he was pickaxed beyond recognition, and the murder weapon was left sticking in his face very near the nose. The location of the fatal blow led many to believe that Bob's nose picking was finally more than someone could take. The townsmen in an attempt to commemorate the tragic event named the town Pick.

Gilman has been in Pick all morning, going first to the courthouse to look up the land deeds of the two families who own property on the other side of the mountain. The Whiteheads and the Simpsons, in addition to June and Gemma Collet, have signed surface agreements to allow the Conroy Coal Company to mine coal on their land. As Gilman suspected, he is the only one not to sign.

Next he stops by the office of Harvey Watson, the least corrupt of Burr County's four lawyers. Harvey assures him that since he didn't sign the agreement, there is no legal way Conroy Coal can get on his property.

"Yesterday, I got a call from June Collet, and she said Conroy would prob'ly start working the coal in a couple of months. How're they getting their permit so fast?" Gilman asks Harvey.

"Maybe this is a special case," Harvey says.

"It's special all right. Someone's getting paid off," Gilman mutters, and leaves Harvey's office, thinking that every lawyer he has ever seen has eyes like a lizard's.

On his way to his car, he passes the manager of the Pick Citizens' Bank, Wade Miller, the man Rosalee took a fancy to shortly before she left town. Wade smiles at Gilman as if he would like to let bygones be bygones.

"Hello, Okra Dick," Gilman responds, and gets into his truck, slamming the door shut.

He drives down the river road toward the Texan's house. It is a pretty drive—the air is clear and the sky, the trees, everything, is exploding with color. The river even looks a little cleaner today, soft green and still. When he gets to his destination, he finds his friend near the fenced area where he keeps his cows.

"How's it goin, Tex?" he says.

"All right."

Gilman leans against a wooden fence post and watches cows swat flies off their backs with their tails.

The Texan scrapes the bottom of his boots on a rock to remove some cow dung.

"I've heard that stuff'll explode," Gilman says.

"What stuff?"

"That stuff you're scraping off your boots."

The Texan smiles. "It will."

"Wonder if a man could blow up a strip mine with it."

"Prob'ly, if you collected a few tons and let it set long enough."

"A few tons?"

"I reckon so."

"Too bad," Gilman says. "That puts a damper on my plans."

"You're not goin to blow up that strip mine, are you, Gilman?"

"Maybe, if worse comes to worse."

"I reckon I could get you some dynamite easy enough."

"How?"

"Don't ask."

"You're a good man to know, Tex. I still might want you to save me a bag or two of that shit. Maybe I could use it somehow for effect."

The Texan smiles.

When Gilman returns to his newly paneled apartment, he stands in the doorway looking into the machine shop at nuts and bolts and wrenches lying scattered on the floor. Still thinking about the Texan, shit bombs, lawyers, and the law, he goes back outside and picks up some lumber from a stack by the door. He grabs his power saw and starts sawing. He isn't exactly sure what he's doing yet, but he thinks he's building a storage shelf for his tools. When he has sawed enough wood, he gets his hammer and strolls to the other side of the room, takes a nail out of a paper bag, saunters back across the room to the wood, and starts hammering. As he walks across the room, taking a nail at a time out of the bag, ideas coiling like snakes in his mind, he hears a voice that sounds like Rosalee's, but it is distant as if in a dream. She's behind him, saying his name, her voice persistent and irritating. "Gilman," she's saying, "why don't you take the whole bag of nails with you, so you don't have to keep walking back and forth across the room?"

I've started dreaming about her right in the day, Gilman thinks. She's nagging me in broad daylight. He turns around and sees her standing there. Thinking her image will soon evaporate, he reaches out to touch her hair, but this time her reflection doesn't fade. Her hair feels as if it was spun on a spindle in a fairy tale, but it's real.

"Hello, Gilman," a bona fide Rosalee says. "It'd cut down on your walking, if you was to pick up more than one nail at a time."

Gilman grins from ear to ear. "What makes you think I want to cut down on my walking?"

"That's what any normal person'd want to do."

"What makes you think I'd want to do something a normal person'd do? I figured you knew me better than that." Gilman takes a closer look at Rosalee. She appears skinny and tired, and her eyes are circled and dark. "How's it hangin, Rosalee?" he asks.

"Prob'ly not as far as yours." Rosalee chuckles.

Walking slowly across the room, Gilman gets a nail out of the bag, moseys back to his cabinet, and hammers it in. Then he throws down his hammer, runs over to Rosalee, and gives her a bear hug. They go out on the balcony, sit down in chairs, and stare at each other head-on. "I heard you had a flood," Rosalee says.

"Where did you hear that?"

"Mom told me."

"How long you been back?"

"A couple days."

"I guess it took you that long to remember to stop by."

"I've been laying low. Don't want many people to know I'm here."

Gilman stares into Rosalee's eyes. There's a different look in them. She lights a cigarette and begins smoking fast, glancing around, as if she's looking for someone. On the road, a car backfires, and she jumps. "I got your letters, Rosalee. Are you goin to tell me about it?" Gilman asks.

"I don't know if I'd make much sense. I ain't slept in about three days."

"Well, Lordy mercy, go in there and lay down. Sleep your eyes out. I won't make a sound, won't let anyone in. Put that cigarette out and go to sleep."

"I don't know if I can."

Gilman walks her to the couch and spreads a sheet over her. Outside the creek trickles and spills over rocks, birds chirp in alder bushes, and bees hang like voyeurs around the window. Picking up his guitar, Gilman plays "Greensleeves" softly. When Rosalee goes to sleep, he straightens the apartment, sweeps the floor, washes the countertop, sprays Lysol disinfectant in the air, and watches her as she sleeps, the dark circles under her eyes reminding him of the trouble she's in.

Ten-Fifteen knocks on the door a couple of times, but Gilman doesn't answer. Rosalee wants to keep her return a secret, and he intends to help her do it. Ten-Fifteen prob'ly saw her when she drove up, Gilman considers, and decides to check it out.

"Yeah, I seen her. I ain't blind," Ten-Fifteen admits when Gilman knocks on his door.

"Don't go spreading it around," Gilman warns him. "She

don't want no one to know, and if anyone drives up for business, shoo 'em off."

He goes back to the apartment, passes the couch where Rosalee sleeps, and takes his guitar out to the balcony. "I wandered today to the hill, Maggie—to watch the scene below—the creek and the rusty old mill, Maggie—where we wandered in the long, long ago," Gilman sings, thinking of how things might have been if he had loved Rosalee the way she wanted. He feels as though something beautiful got away from him when he wasn't paying attention, and he continues singing the old songs as evening comes on. Then he becomes aware that she's behind him again, asking a question. "Been getting any nookie lately, Gilman?"

She looks rested.

"Here and there," he says, curling his upper lip and arching his eyebrow. "Wanta go for a round?"

"Just one?"

He carries her back to the couch. "One is enough, if it's done right," he says.

"For you, maybe."

"I'd watch that smart mouth, if I was you," he mumbles, unsnapping Rosalee's jeans. "A smart mouth'll get you in trouble ever' time."

Rosalee laughs. "You're nothing but a dirty old man, Gilman Lee."

He kisses her closed eyes and finishes undressing her. She runs her finger down the scar on his face and smiles. With them, sex is slow and easy, their bodies slick with beads of sweat, their motions fluid and graceful. They laugh as they make love, occasionally pausing to talk about the old days, behaving more like friends than lovers.

"I went crazy over that man I told you about in the letter, the one that's after me," Rosalee says the next morning after a meal of bacon, eggs, and toast.

"You mean you fell for someone besides me?" he asks, winking.

"Yeah."

"And just how was this man so alluring, if I may be so bold?" Gilman asks in an upper-crust accent.

"He's trying to find me, Gilman. I'm afraid he wants to kill me."

"That's what you said in your letter. But why would he want to do that?"

"He's strange."

"What's wrong with strange?"

"There's good strange, and there's bad strange. His is bad."

It's coming back to Gilman that Rosalee could never tell a story in a day's time. "Just spit it out," he says.

"Well . . ."

Gilman walks out to the machine shop and shuts the doors, hangs his Closed sign in the window. When he comes back out to the balcony, he's carrying two cups of coffee, and making sure Rosalee has her cigarettes within easy reach, he hands her a cup, tilts his chair against the side of the house, and props his feet on the railing. "Sounds like you've got a tale to tell, Rosalee. If you get started right now, you might finish by the end of the week. Take your time, though. I ain't heard a good tale in a long time."

"Since you put it that way, I don't know as I will," Rosalee says, sipping her coffee.

Gilman looks out across the creek and waits.

"When I left here," she begins about ten minutes later, "I was using coke. Thought I'd go to Florida so I could be closer to a larger supply. Well, that ain't the only reason I went; I just wanted a change. Didn't stay on the coke long. It made me fidgety. Anyway, I got a job singing in a nightclub in West Palm—sang Patsy Cline tunes. Tear-jerking songs."

"You're a good singer," Gilman throws in.

"That's how I met him. He used to come almost every night

and get a table right near the stage. Other people'd be talking and laughing, but he'd be listening. There was a look he had that got to me. In some ways, he kind of reminded me of you."

"Really," Gilman says.

"He never made a move toward me; he just listened to my singing. Then one night, I made a move on him. It was his eyes, you see. They could look right through your skin to your insides.

"We started going out. He was wild, Gilman. He'd do anything that come to his mind. I can't even tell you the crazy things we did, except God we had a ball. And he had money— I don't know where it come from, because he didn't work. He started acting as my manager; I think it was fun for him. He got me jobs all along the coast." Rosalee lights a cigarette.

"If everything was so hunky-dory, why ain't you still with him?" Gilman asks.

"Cause things changed. It was like he was bound and determined to destroy whatever was goin on between us. The man was moody to say the least. One day, I did something; I don't even know what it was. Maybe I didn't get all enthused when he said he was going out to set fires in mailboxes. Maybe I failed to laugh when he hung a kitten by the tail to a clothesline. He'd started playing little pranks like that. Who knows? I might have reminded him of his mother that day—he hated his mother. I don't know what I did, but he never treated me the same again. From then on, I was worried I'd say something he didn't like. One night he drove me down to Miami, parked around the corner from a alley where drunks and addicts hang out; and there they were, either staring into space, vomiting, or sleeping. He ordered me to take my clothes off and walk down between them. He had a gun. Said he intended to shoot the first scum that come after me. I was afraid not to do it. It was hot and muggy that night; and the smell of the ocean was in every breath you took—that and a pee smell from the men. They started walking toward me like they'd just crawled out of graves. I'll not go into details, but it was bad. A few days later, I run away and hid. That's when I sent you the letter. He's looking for me; I'm pretty sure he is."

"Does he know you're from here?"

"He knows I'm from Kentucky. I didn't tell him what part, at least I don't think I did. That's why I'm not letting people know I'm back. I'll just stay up in the holler with Mom for a while. Took a chance coming down here to your place, but somehow I didn't think anyone would recognize me. So much has happened, how could I look the same?"

Gilman goes inside the apartment and comes back with a couple of beers. "As soon as it gets dark, go home. If I was you, I'd stick pretty close to my house for at least a month—see how things go. You'd better not come down here anymore. This place is like Grand Central Station."

Rosalee pops open her beer. "He's loaded, Gilman. People with money can find out just about anything they want to know."

That night when Rosalee gets into her mother's car to drive home, Gilman says, "Odds are that feller's already forgot you and's on to someone else. But if you need anything, just give me a call. In the meantime, I'll be right down here acting just like I always do." He watches her drive off until the taillights are out of view, wondering how a pretty woman like her could have such bad luck with men. First me, then Wade Miller, and now this other asshole. He goes back into his shop and continues building his storage cabinet, trying to hold himself down, trying not to jump into his truck and head to Florida in search of a man he's never seen.

13
Chapter

At the Pick Citizens', Gemma stares without pause at Marcy and their coworker, Jo Ellen. Marcy, with her dyed blond hair and Mary Kay makeup, is always the most perfectly groomed. Every summer, she dresses in pastels—powder pink is her first choice with baby blue running a close second. Before the change of each season, she goes to Lexington and buys her spring, summer, fall, or winter wardrobes. She stocks up on perfumes, too. Passion and Poison are her favorites.

"I don't feel good," says Jo Ellen. Jo Ellen is forty years old and has three children. She is married to a coal miner who makes twenty-one dollars an hour (she likes to let people know). Money is important to Jo Ellen. One of her beefs is that people look down on coal miners. When she thinks she's being slighted by a woman such as Marcy, whose husband doesn't work in the mines, she says to her, "My husband makes twenty-one dollars a hour. How much does yours make?" A few months ago, Jo Ellen's oldest son injured his back in the mines and was awarded ninety thousand dollars. He recently bought a stock car that he intends to race in Daytona Beach, Florida. She likes to tell people about this, too.

Gemma prefers Jo Ellen to Marcy, but she wouldn't pick either of her coworkers out of a crowd to be a bosom buddy. She is tired of looking at them both, and because of this she stares at them incessantly. It gives her a perverse satisfaction. This morning, Marcy is dressed like a bowl of Neapolitan ice cream. Gemma gazes at her as others might stare at the blood and gore of a gruesome auto accident.

"Did you h-have a nice weekend?" Marcy asks Gemma, as if she's afraid of what the answer will be. Marcy says weekend, but Sunday and Monday are their regular days off. The women always have to work Saturdays, since Saturday is the Pick Citizens' busiest day. Until a couple of years ago, they worked six days a week, permanent mandatory overtime, but finally the manager hired a couple of part-time workers to fill in on Mondays so they can have two days off.

"No," Gemma says, answering her in a way that is meant to end all conversation forever.

"I didn't either," Jo Ellen complains. "I was sick."

"That's too bad." Marcy's voice quavers as Gemma's eyes bore steadily through her shield of pastel. "I went to Lexington. They've got their fall clothes out already. I bought a few things. Can't wait till it gets cold enough to wear them."

Gemma doesn't know how much longer she can stand to hear about Marcy's spending sprees or be in the same room with her Mary Kay face. Gemma is tired, and she is especially tired of the manager, Wade Miller, who blows into the bank every morning like wind from a propeller and stirs things up. "Hello, girls," he says, when he arrives at nine o'clock sharp. "Gemma, come back here. I want to talk to you."

He whirs into his office and slings his briefcase down. "Gemma," he says, when she enters, "I had a little talk with the girls Saturday. They tell me you've been staring at them."

"No kidding."

"They say you sit and stare at them all day long. They say it's getting on their nerves, that it makes them self-conscious. I know how they feel because you've been staring at me, too."

Gemma looks Wade Miller right in the eye. "People had better be glad that's all I'm doing," she says.

He begins to turn red. He would fire her on the spot except he depends on her. Not only is she a loan officer; she is an accountant, teller, and secretary. The other two women do various duties also, but they are not as proficient as Gemma. "I want you to stop," he says. "I don't want you to look at people unless they're talking to you. When they're not talking to you, I want you to look somewhere else."

"Where would you like me to look?"

"Why don't you try looking at your work? You're supposed to have things to do. I don't care where you look as long as you don't look at me and the girls."

"What if I happened to look at you accidentally? I mean, one of you might drop something, you know, make a sudden noise, and I might glance up without thinking."

Wade spins around in his swivel chair and stares at the wall. He takes a deep breath. "Just go back to your desk and write a letter to the McDonald's Corporation. See what the status is."

Wade Miller has been trying to get a McDonald's franchise going. His motto is "If Russia has a McDonald's, so can we." The town of Pick is divided on the issue. Some people contend that a McDonald's would put the Pick Truck Stop, which is considered a community landmark, out of business. They say that if a McDonald's comes to town, children will refuse to eat anything but Happy Meals. Since his main concern is that McDonald's will be a good investment and he takes his money where he can get it, Wade couldn't care less about what kind of meals the local children eat. He doesn't have time to manage the restaurant and is planning for his wife to take on the job, reasoning that she has been sitting at home on her behind long enough. He coerced her into agreeing to put in a joint application, and she's not happy about it, but so what? Wade thinks.

When Gemma finishes composing the McDonald's letter, she takes it in for his approval. She is about to return to her desk when he stops her. "I hear your coal's goin to be worked. Congratulations. I hope you make some money off it. I also hear that Gilman Lee didn't sign. Reckon why not?"

"How should I know?" Gemma snaps. She is overcome by irritation every time she is reminded of the fact that Gilman didn't sign the lease. The irritation results from a nagging suspicion that she may have misjudged him, that underneath Gilman's gruff, uncivilized exterior may stand a man with his heart in the right place.

"Do you think he'd be willing to sell his land? I'd be willing to buy it, if he was."

"Don't ask me," Gemma grunts and stalks out of Wade's office.

Wade would ask Gilman these questions himself, but he is afraid of him because of what they have in common—Rosalee. When Rosalee finally gave up on Gilman and had her short-lived affair with Wade, Gilman's attitude toward the man grew cold; then when Rosalee moved out of state, it grew even colder. The fact that Rosalee, or any woman for that matter, could throw him over for Wade Miller was more than he could take. For five years now, Gilman has glared at Wade when passing him on the street, sometimes making nasty comments about his physical appearance. Once, Gilman gave Wade the finger and said, "Bank this!" Another time as they were both standing in the checkout lane at the grocery store, Gilman asked, "How does it feel to know you bored a woman so bad she left the state?" On several occasions, he has sent Wade written invitations to appear in a deserted cornfield at midnight in order that they might settle their differences. Wade has never responded to his R.S.V.P.s. Wade doesn't really think Gilman would sell him his land, but, enjoying the prospect of anything that involves money, he likes to pretend he would. The only person, place, or thing that has ever come close to the pinnacle of finance in Wade's heart is Rosalee. For her, he would have just about quit the banking business. He would have almost left his wife along with his family-man reputation. Wade would have done nearly anything to keep her around, but try as he might she left. When he saw that Rosalee was getting bored with him, he introduced her to cocaine, a substance he uses occasionally to keep himself whirring around, procuring the drug from a second cousin who distributes it throughout the county. Wade, a silent partner with his cousin, put up the money to start the operation a few years ago.

He thought cocaine would keep Rosalee interested, but he hasn't heard a word from her since she moved to Florida. He takes out a mirror and dusts out a line, rolls up a dollar bill, and snorts, still wondering if there is any way he can get Gilman Lee to sell him his land. Thoughts spin in his head like pinwheels.

Meanwhile at Gemma's desk, computable numbers stare up at her from a sheet of paper. There are moments when she doubts her "Be For What You're Against" theory and thinks that maybe her land-lease decision was the wrong move. She wishes Gilman had told her he wasn't going to sign because, if she had known, she may have held out, too. With two people refusing the terms, the coal company might have thought the mining operation wasn't worth it. She remembers that there are more mountains than one being stripped for coal in Burr County. The rush is on to mine as much coal as possible before the market drops any further. Why have one mountain intact, when all the others' tops are cut off? she thinks. "Let them all go to hell!" Gemma growls out loud.

Marcy and Jo Ellen glance at each other and shake their heads.

Gemma thinks about her evening ritual in the creek, about the language of water and mud swirling over her legs. It is a language she hasn't quite deciphered yet, but she is getting closer. She was getting especially close the evening Tom Jett waded across the creek and said hello. That same evening Tom mentioned that he used to sit on the beach listening to waves. The *sit on the beach* part of this statement doesn't interest Gemma, since it merely confirms what she has been led to believe regarding how Californians spend their days. It is the second part of the statement—the *listening to waves* part—that draws her interest. She knows what he meant, that he wasn't just listening to the roar but to what it said. She wonders what the waves told him, and she remembers the heat coming from Tom's chest while they were standing in the water, how close her breasts were to his bare skin, how she wanted to lean forward and brush against him. The memory of this loosens Gemma. Her pen slides from her fingers, and she becomes loose-jawed and loose-legged.

Then she realizes that she has been staring at Marcy for quite some time, and that Marcy has stood up from her desk and is walking toward Wade Miller's office in a huff.

Gemma waits for the inevitable, and it happens. Wade bursts out of his office and tells her to go home and not come back tomorrow unless her eyes are closed. "Just go home, Gemma!"

She does. She goes home and down to the creek, where she strips, sinks into water, and feels Tom Jett watching her from his lookout point on the hill.

It is after dark when Gemma comes in from the creek. June is waiting for her as usual, except tonight she is covered with chill bumps. Wade Miller called earlier to say that Gemma had been staring at people. Of all the things he could have told June, this was the worst.

Gemma plops down on the couch, her hair damp at the ends with creek water. June watches her anxiously. "I never told you much about my uncle," she says to Gemma.

"And there's no need to start now," Gemma mutters, vaguely remembering an old man who talked about nothing but weather and corn. "I don't want to know about Uncle Herman."

"It's not Herman I'm talking about," June says. "Herman was my daddy's younger brother. I'm talking about Jake, his older brother."

"What about him?"

"Well, I never even seen him, but he was . . . odd, from what I've been told," June says. "He used to stare at people. One time Jake and my daddy and a friend of my daddy's went hunting. They was boys at the time—teenagers. Daddy and his friend, boy by the name of Matt, was walking in front of Jake. Matt was barefoot, and I reckon Jake got to staring at the backs of his feet as he was padding along. Finally Jake tapped him on the shoulder and said, 'I'll give you a quarter if you'll let me shoot you through the heel.' When Matt turned him down, Jake upped the ante, offered him a quarter a day for the next six months. Matt come from a poor family. Back then, a quarter a day was a lotta money to a boy from a poor family. He took the offer, and Jake shot him right through the meaty part of his heel—bullet went through one side and come out the other. When Matt got home that night, he told his mother he'd stepped on a piece of glass. Jake paid him a quarter every day for the next six months, and neither one of the boys told what really happened. My daddy didn't even tell me about it until not long before he died."

"Whatever happened to Jake?" Gemma asks.

"He left home when he was twenty year old. Nobody ever heard from him again."

"What's your point?" Gemma asks.

"Point is I hear you've been staring at people," June answers.

Gemma looks at her mother and laughs.

"I think you ought to see a psychiatrist or a psychologist or a clinical social worker, just in case you take after Jake."

Gemma keeps laughing.

"I mean it," June says, picking up the phone book and shoving it in Gemma's face. "I've been looking them up in this Lexington phone book. I've got one picked out. His name is Sylvester Gast. See?" She points to an ad in the yellow pages. "Sylvester Gast, Clinical Psychologist, The Center for Healing and Enrichment." Also mentioned in the advertisement are the various ills the center treats: anxiety, depression, phobias, work issues, and habit control.

Gemma's laughter increases.

"Nice name, ain't it?" June says. "His name is the reason I picked him. They's some kind of famous person with a name like that—movie star or something, maybe a senator."

Gemma breaks up. "I know who you're thinking of. Sylvester the Cat—you know—the cat in the cartoon, the one that chases that little yellow bird? That's who you're thinking of."

"No, it ain't!" June insists, blushing. "They's someone else with a name like that."

Gemma starts down the hallway, then turns around and looks back at June. "I'm no crazier than anyone else, Momma."

June plans to call Sylvester Gast tomorrow.

Gemma goes to bed, trying to remember any facts she's previously learned about mental illness. Crazy people see and hear things that normal people can't see or hear, she recalls. Do I see things that are not real? I believe I do, because Marcy can't be real. She's an apparition of fabric, powder, and dye. Wade Miller's not real either. He's a leash without a dog. Do I hear things? Yes, I hear voices every day. When I walk in the mountains, I hear the migration of Cherokees—I hear their footsteps when leaves crunch and twigs break. I hear a hundred verses of English, Scottish, and Irish ballads being sung by aproned old women who sit in rockers, spitting tobacco juice into coal-burning fireplaces in winter. I hear trees change color and snow fall. Water speaks to me. I must be crazy.

The next day, June calls Sylvester Gast and tries to persuade him to drive down from Lexington and spend an hour talking to Gemma.

"I just want to know if she's crazy," June explains to him on the phone. "I want to know if she's about to start shooting people's heels."

The psychologist presses the receiver a little closer to his ear and says, "Pardon me? People's heels? Shoot?"

"It's a long story," June admits.

"Well, I don't usually make house calls," he says from the safety of his office. "Especially not house calls that are over a hundred miles away."

"I'm afraid she'll kill someone," June says. "If she sees a person that don't look to suit her, she's likely to shoot 'em. She might even kill herself. What do you charge for your services?"

"My standard fee is eighty-five dollars a session, and the session usually runs fifty minutes, but . . ."

"Well, I'll pay you a hundred dollars for every hour you're out," June says, adding the hours up in her mind. "Let's see, it takes two hours to drive down here; that'd be four hours here and back, and I'd expect you to be here at the house a couple of hours. That's six hours total. I'll pay you six hundred dollars and a dinner. Do you like chicken and dumplings? I'll fix you some chicken and dumplings, green beans, mashed potatoes, buttermilk biscuits, and a mountain-high apple pie. All you have to do is ask her a few questions. Find out if she's crazy."

"Why don't you just bring her up here?"

"She wouldn't come."

Sylvester hesitates. "Mrs. Collet, I . . ."

"If she shoots someone, it'll be on your head. Six hundred dollars, Mr. Gast, and a right pretty drive all the way down."

"My girlfriend does have a brother in the area that we've been meaning to visit."

"I'll send you a check for three hundred right now and another three hundred when you get here," June tells him. She's not concerned about wiping out her savings account, since she figures the coal money is on the way.

"It's a deal," Sylvester Gast says.

Sylvester and his girlfriend drive down the next Saturday, and after he drops her off at her brother's, he goes on to find Mrs. Collet's house. June's directions were explicit. "It's a white house with a porch and a white picket fence. It's near a curve about two miles from Pick and's sitting down the bank toward the creek. They's a big red ceramic rooster standing near the mailbox, and the mailbox is right by the road at the end of the driveway. You can't miss it," she had told him.

When he gets there at three o'clock in the afternoon, June leads him to the kitchen and gives him a cup of coffee while she starts dinner. "Gemma'll be here in half an hour," she says.

Sylvester takes a sip of coffee. "You said on the phone she had been acting odd. In what way, Mrs. Collet?"

"Well, for starters, every evening she sits naked in the creek, and now she's staring at people. They's a . . . well, they's a family history of staring, Mr. Gast. The one that stared shot a boy in the heel and paid him a quarter a day for six months to do it, and then he left town. We don't know where. I've often studied he might've turned into one of them serial killers because it's plain as day he got some kind of enjoyment out of what he did or he wouldn't a paid for it."

"And you think Gemma might turn into the same thing?"

"Well, not exactly. At least a body can hope."

June rolls dough until it is thin as a place mat, then she cuts it, dropping long curling strips one by one into a pot of boiling chicken. "This is the only way to make dumplings, Mr. Gast. I hate the kind that's round and puffy."

When she is finished adding the dumplings, she sits down at the table. "All I know is they're goin to start working the coal on the hill behind the house in a month or two. They's goin to be men here with bulldozers. If Gemma keeps sitting naked in the creek, they're goin to see her, and untelling what'll happen. And she's staring at the people she works with. If she don't stop, she's likely to get fired. You've got to do something, Mr. Gast. You've got to tell her something that'll make her quit."

Sylvester watches as June cuts up a bowl of apples and pours sugar over them. She rolls out pie dough, plops it into a pan, presses it around the edges, and dumps apples in. When she begins to make biscuits, she doesn't cut them out, she rolls them around in her hands until they are perfectly shaped.

"Don't let on you're a psychologist to Gemma. Pretend you work for the Conroy Coal Company," June says, putting her rolling pin back in the cabinet.

"I won't misrepresent myself," Sylvester insists.

"Better to be misrepresented than dead, Mr. Gast."

It's when June goes to the bathroom that Gemma walks in the door and sees a young man in his midtwenties, sitting at the kitchen table. "Hello," she says to him, "I don't believe I know you."

"Sylvester Gast," he says, blinking at her porcelain skin. "I work for the Conroy Coal Company."

Gemma smiles. "Pleasure to meet you, Mr. Gast. I'm Gemma. I bet my mother has told you about me."

"A little," Sylvester says.

When June comes back into the kitchen, Gemma says, "Momma, me and Sylvester have already introduced ourselves. I've not mentioned it to him yet, but I've heard a name like his somewhere before. A movie star maybe, or a senator. Have you ever heard of a name like Sylvester Gast?"

"No," June groans. "Is everyone ready to eat?"

During dinner, Gemma asks Sylvester a lot of technical questions about coal mining. "How do you know when a mountain has coal, Mr. Gast? And how do you know how much it's got? Do you measure it with something? What are the names of the machines you use?"

"Um . . . yes," Sylvester says.

"How much does a mining operation cost?" Gemma asks, winking at June.

"A lot," says Sylvester.

"How many mining operations does Conroy have going in Burr County, Mr. Gast?"

"Now, Gemma," June butts in, "you already know that. They've got about ten goin. You're asking Mr. Gast so many questions he don't have time to answer."

"Just curious, Momma," Gemma says, smiling.

They eat in silence for a few minutes before Sylvester finally takes his turn at questioning. "How do you feel about us mining on your mountain, Gemma?"

"It's just great," Gemma says, winking at June again.

Sylvester looks out the screen door. "That's a lovely creek out there. Do you ever go wading?"

"No, actually I go sitting," Gemma says.

"Sitting in the creek?"

Gemma grins broadly at June. "Yes."

"What do you think about while you're sitting down there?" Sylvester asks.

"I think about the psychologist I shot. Shot him right between the eyes. I think about him a lot."

Sylvester toys with his mustache as a look of sympathy crosses his face. It is obvious to him that Gemma didn't really kill a psychologist, but he is convinced that she is in the throes of a deep depression and is compounding the problem with denial. "Why did you kill him?" he asks.

June looks at Gemma and begins to cry. "You may as well just forget it, Mr. Gast. She knows. She already knows who you are."

"You still haven't answered my question, Gemma. Why did you kill him?" Sylvester asks. "Would you like to share that with me?"

Gemma stands up. "What I'd like to do is take a walk. Nice to have met you, Mr. Gast."

"Just let him talk to you," June pleads. "It ain't goin to hurt for him to just talk to you."

"I don't think you're really upset at psychologists, Gemma. I think it's someone else you would like to shoot," Sylvester says. "Would you like to talk about what really upsets you?"

"A lot of things upset me, Mr. Gast, but that doesn't take away from the fact that you are in a sappy line of work. From what I've been reading and hearing lately, mental illness is not really mental at all; it's physical. Now, where does that leave you? It leaves you treating people with bad nerves, right? Well, I don't have the jitters. If I were you, I'd start thinking about a career change. Maybe you really ought to go to work for Conroy Coal. Have a nice trip back," Gemma says to Sylvester, as she goes out the door.

They watch as she walks through the yard and down the bank to the water. She pulls off her shoes and wades up the creek until she is out of sight.

"I hope she's not goin upstream to pull off her clothes. They's a lot of people lives up there," June sighs.

But Gemma is not heading upstream. As she walked out through the yard, she noticed Tom Jett's car in the driveway. Once she rounds the curve, she cuts up the hill toward his house.

14
Chapter

Gemma climbs the hill, stopping for a moment by a cliff she played under when she was a child. She used to hide there, pretending she was the only white girl within a hundred miles, that she had become lost from her family, and that a hunting party of Indians was stealthily filing past her. She could scarcely hear the rustle of dry, fallen leaves as they passed.

She often hoped they would find her and teach her their ways. She imagined that an Indian's life was more meaningful than hers, that Indians didn't have to go to church and listen to preachers shout about the fires of Hell or go to school to learn how to earn a living. She couldn't envision an Indian girl wanting to grow up to be a stewardess for TWA, which is what her best friend Kathy wanted to do. Indians were beyond settling for such drab ambitions, she thought. Young Gemma would scramble out from the cliff and pray for them to save her from becoming a stewardess or a nurse or a secretary, but they just kept filing past her like ghosts.

Gemma continues on the old road, which is really just a

slight depression curving around the hill. In summer months, it is completely grown over with weeds, but in winter when the trees are bare, a person can look toward the mountain from a distance and make out what was once the only way out of these hills. When Gemma's grandfather was a young boy, he and his father used to ride their mules to Harlan three or four times a year for supplies they couldn't acquire in Pick. Now the road is nothing more than a fading scar, remembered by fewer people as years go by.

When Gemma nears Tom's house, she sees him in the field, wearing a large straw hat and holding a pitcher from which he's watering a single row of beans, the only vegetables in the garden. Gemma smiles and walks up behind him. "You don't have to water them. It'll rain soon enough. People around here don't water their vegetables."

Tom wheels around as if he's heard a shot. "Where did you come from? I didn't hear you."

"I'm a quiet walker," Gemma says. "Trick I learned from some Indian ghosts. It's a little late in the year to be starting a crop of beans, don't you think?"

"That's what they told Thoreau."

"Who?"

"Never mind."

Gemma notes the improvements on the house—the clean-swept porch and washed windows. "Looks like you've been busy."

Tom invites her inside for coffee and shows her the freshly painted walls and patched ceilings. "I had electricity hooked up last week. I don't have a refrigerator yet. I'd never get one up the hill anyway, but I have an ice cooler. Would you like a beer, instead?"

"A beer would be good," Gemma says.

They go back out to the porch and sit down. Gemma looks around at the trees and field. She doesn't know what to say to Tom or even why she's here. Tom doesn't say anything, either.

He is staring down at the wooden floor of the porch. The longer they sit without speaking, the more Gemma becomes aware of the power of silence. Silence is not golden, it's granite, she thinks. Sometimes you want to ask a person something, but it can't be said in words, and you don't know if he would understand it, anyway, so you think of other things to say, except the words won't come out because they are trapped behind the question you want to ask. And you're beginning to wonder why he isn't saying anything. Does he want to ask you a question? *What is he thinking?* Silence takes your clothes off, stands you naked in front of a mirror, and points out your flaws, Gemma decides.

Tom goes into the house and comes back with a tape player. He slips in a blues tape and motions for her to get up, but Gemma continues sitting there. "I've not danced in a long time," she says. "I don't know how to dance."

"I don't either," Tom says. "Not really. But sometimes I like to move when I hear music. It makes me feel as if I'm inside it."

He takes hold of her hand and something in his touch reassures her that it is all right if she's clumsy, if she steps on his feet, if she's out of time. She stands, and they begin moving slowly to the music. Gemma sinks into it, becomes part of the blues and the creaking boards of the porch. Still not speaking, they dance until the song ends, then she looks up at him. "There's a psychologist in my kitchen," she says.

Tom shrugs. "There's a field mouse in mine. As a matter of fact there are several."

"Momma sent all the way to Lexington for him. He looks worried . . . no, pained. He looks like someone who's trying to grieve at his rich uncle's funeral. That's why I came up here."

"Glad you did," Tom says.

"When you used to listen to waves, what did they say to you?" Gemma asks him.

"They told me to see what was happening inland."

"Is that all?"

"Basically."

"Do you think I'm crazy?"

"I think you should have some fun. Stand on your head and put a lamp shade on your feet—something like that. I think you need to help me water my beans. At least have another beer. Let's dance."

He puts on a tape of Brazilian music, and they dance until the sky turns gray with evening. Later, he gets them a couple of beers, and they sit on the porch watching darkness come with its soft yellow glow of lightning bugs flickering around the beech trees.

"Some people would say that sitting naked in a creek is more daring than putting a lamp shade on your feet," Gemma says.

"It is more daring, but is it more fun?"

"Fun's got nothing to do with it."

"Too bad," Tom says, taking Gemma's hand. "Let's go to Gilman Lee's."

Gemma narrows one eye and widens the other. "You've got to be kidding."

Tom winks. "I know about your falling-out with Gilman. He told me about it. All he did was try to kiss you, and that was five years ago. Big deal."

"I wasn't in the mood to be kissed."

"A crowd is probably there right now playing music. The first time I ever saw him, he was trying to make love to a guitar."

Gemma yawns. "I hate to keep bringing this up, but some people would say that sitting naked in a creek is just as noteworthy as making love to a guitar. The only difference is that before Gilman will do something like that, he has to have a crowd cheering him on. I don't need one."

"Oh yeah? Well, I watch you all the time, and you know it.

I even cheer you on. Would you continue going down there every day if I weren't watching you?"

Gemma doesn't bat an eye. "Would you continue watching me every day if I didn't know you were?"

Tom returns her gaze. "I can almost hear the banjo playing. Let's go. Unless you're afraid."

"Of what?"

Tom pulls Gemma out of the chair, and they walk down the hill in the dark and cross the swinging bridge to his car.

"I don't see Sylvester's Geo," she notes. "He's probably safely on his way back to Lexington. I'd better say a word to Momma before we go. She probably thinks I'm wandering all over the county naked."

Gemma runs to the front door and sticks her head in. "Hey, Momma, I'm going to Gilman Lee's with Tom. Bye."

June, sitting on the couch nursing a headache, throws up her hands and flicks on the TV with her remote control.

When Tom and Gemma arrive at the machine shop, they have a hard time finding a place to park, since it is Saturday night and people are tramping in and out of the shop, their cars lining either side of the road. Finally, they squeeze into a spot down past the curve and walk up. Tonight, Gilman is in fine form. He has put the coal and Rosalee troubles out of his mind and is sitting at the piano, playing like Jerry Lee Lewis and singing "You Win Again." He's grinning on the scar side of his face, his brow arched, his lip curled. Gemma and Tom walk in almost unnoticed and stand behind a middle-aged man and his son.

"What do you think of Gilman?" the father asks his son.

"He's all right," the son replies, clearly trying not to sound too impressed.

"First time I ever seen him he was beatin the shit out of six men, all of 'em biggern him," the father adds. "They'd cheated him at cards, I reckon. He took 'em all on. Fought 'em all the way out of the pool hall and down the street. Look at him. See how short he is? Toughest sonofabitch I ever seen. The Man—that right there is The Man. Now, he could teach you a thing or two."

"He's pretty good on the piano," the son admits, his eyes betraying his enthusiasm.

"You-oo-oo win, uh-uh-gin," Gilman sings, ending the song with a love-torching riff on the keys. People whoop and holler as he stands up. "Take it, Joe," he says to Joe Carter, the banjo picker. "Play me some 'Little Maggie.' " As he trips over to the refrigerator for a beer, he spots Tom and Gemma, grabs three beers instead of one, and heads toward them.

"Brace yourself," Tom says.

"For what?"

Gilman moves slowly through the crowd, stopping here and there to jaw with some of the men. He asks one of them when they're going to have a fight again, and for no apparent reason he asks another to open his mouth and let him see his tonsils. The man does, and Gilman nods, seemingly satisfied with their condition. He moves on toward Tom and Gemma.

By the time he is a few feet from them, he's beaming like a glowworm. "Uh-uuuhhh," he says. "Lordy mercy, I want you to hush and look at who's come." He raises his voice to a shout. "I want everybody to stop what they're doing, and above all else looky who's here. It's sweet little Gemma, come to see me. And guess who's with her. It's Tommy, brightest boy this side of the Divide. I'm overcome. Outdone. I'm almost crying." Gilman turns to some men sitting on the couch. "Get your asses off the couch and let this pretty young couple sit down." Gilman cradles the three beers like newborn triplets as he gets behind Tom and Gemma and noses them toward their appointed seats. When the three of them get situated on the couch, he hands them their beers and says to Gemma, "Welcome."

"I didn't know you cared," Gemma says. "If I'd known a visit from me would have done this much for you, I'd have come before now."

"Oh, but it's made my day, changed my life. I'll never be the same. Talk to me because I can't say another word. I'm bum-fuzzled."

"How've you been?" she asks.

"Fine as frog hair," he says, "and you?"

"Dandy."

"Well, now that that's out of the way, why don't you pick us a tune on the banjo? Joe, bring your banjo over here. You didn't know she was a picker, did you, Tom? Back when she was going with that skinny boy—What was his name? Never could remember his name—she come here a couple of times. As I recollect she could play 'Foggy Mountain Dew' and 'Wildwood Flower' pretty good. Pick us one, Gemma."

Joe Carter hands Gemma the banjo, and she holds it in her lap. "It's been twelve years," she remarks, rubbing the polished wood around the base.

"Well, don't think you've forgot how," Gilman says. "Picking a banjo is like making love."

Gemma puts her fingers on the strings and begins "Wildwood Flower" slowly at first, then she picks up the tempo when a man with a fiddle steps beside her and joins in. Nodding their heads approvingly, the men commence milling around the room. Gilman moves to the center of the floor and begins a dance that resembles the Twist.

This is the scene Ten-Fifteen beholds when he enters the shop, finds Tom, and they get into a discussion about old movies. Later, Gilman and Gemma sing as many words as they can think of to "Fraulein." Finally it's over—the night is played out—and the last of the dancers, pickers, and singers stagger out the door.

"I'd like to talk to you sometime about business matters, coal and the like," Gemma says to Gilman as she and Tom and the last of the crowd are leaving.

"Name it," Gilman says. "My time is yours." He fixes his eyes on Gemma until she almost smiles.

As Tom and Gemma drive home on the narrow curvy road, it's three-thirty in the morning, and the moon is lost somewhere behind a mountain or cloud. When they pull into the driveway, Gemma gets out of the car and stands beside it, looking toward the house. A light is on in the kitchen, and she wonders if June is lying in bed, staring out the window with her doll-blue eyes.

"Did you have fun?" Tom asks, walking toward her.

"Maybe."

"Why can't you just admit you had fun?"

Gemma begins to shiver in the warm night air. She feels more naked now than during her evening ritual in the creek. Tom steps close, brushes his lips against hers, and says, "I'm making a Sunday dinner tomorrow and you're invited. It will be served at three o'clock. Wear your dancing shoes."

Gemma goes inside the house and crawls into bed. She feels alive and it's a strange sensation. As she listens to June tossing and turning in the next room, she speculates about the reason for her mother's restless sleep. No telling what's on her mind, Gemma thinks. She's probably worried that I shot someone in the heel, or maybe she imagines I stripped in front of the gang at Gilman Lee's. I need to talk to Momma. Maybe I've been too hard on her, making her feel small for not caring about creeks and swinging bridges. I confused her when I gave her a glimpse of who I really am. Maybe a person should never try to be honest with their parents.

She thinks of Tom, of his seriousness and good humor, and then her thoughts sidle over to an image of Gilman Lee, his short muscular body arced over the piano keys. His face plants itself in front of her closed eyes and won't budge, no matter how hard she tries to shove it away. Even with the scar trailing down his cheek, Gilman Lee's smile would make a stone squirm. Gemma props up her pillows and leans back against them, looking out at the moon until finally Gilman's image fades and she goes to sleep.

The next morning sunlight wakes her at nine o'clock, and she lies there a moment, not really sure of where she is. Like a visitor in a strange house, she raises herself up and looks around, spotting her reflection in the mirror, the long, white hair and snowy complexion, the black eyes, brows, and lashes. I *am* kind of pretty, she thinks for the first time in a long time. She gets up, and opening the door to June's room, sees her mother still in bed with her face to the wall. June often sleeps late on Sunday mornings, especially if there are no funerals to attend. Gemma goes into the kitchen to make breakfast—omelets, biscuits, and sausage. It's a pretty day. She notices the air is cooler than usual and wonders what Tom is going to make for dinner, if he's out of bed yet, if he's watering his beans.

In her bedroom, June Collet is dreaming of being on a ship headed for England with her new youthful face hidden behind a veil. She's sitting at a table on the sun deck with Gemma. A waiter brings them lunch—snake meat sprinkled with ants. Rising to a fever pitch all around them is the sound track from *Mondo Cane*. June screams and wakes up in a cold sweat just as Gemma walks in carrying her breakfast.

"I know I don't do this every day, but I didn't expect you to scream," Gemma says, and sets the tray down on the nightstand.

"I was dreaming," June stammers, gazing suspiciously at the food.

"Well, sit up and eat your breakfast." Gemma goes to the kitchen and brings back her own plate, then plops down on the floor beside June's bed.

"What is that?" June asks, staring at the sausage.

"What do you think it is?"

"It looks like sausage."

"Good guess."

"I wonder what snake meat tastes like," June mutters, sniffing the sausage before taking a bite.

When they finish their breakfast, June starts to get out of bed, but Gemma stops her.

"Stay right where you are. I want to talk to you."

"If I stay where I am, I'll pee in the bed," June retorts and goes to the bathroom. When she comes back into the room, she sits down and says, "Well?"

"I'm not crazy," Gemma begins. "And I don't take after Jake. If I ever shot anybody, it wouldn't be in the heel. I don't want you sending for any more psychologists no matter how much you like their names. The only reason you think I'm in need of one is that when I finally told you how I felt about something, you didn't understand it. If you don't understand what someone says, you think they're crazy."

"Well, why don't you explain it better, then," June says. "All this business about leasing land to a coal company so they can mine coal because you hate coal mining sure sounds crazy to me."

Gemma sighs, realizing that she needs to give June an explanation she can understand. "Do you ever get disgusted, Momma? I do. I'm disgusted right now because you actually believe we're going to make a hundred and fifty thousand dollars. Do you remember how they told Joe Carter he was going to get rich? Did he? They told him he was going to be a millionaire. But is he? Do you know any ordinary families that have made enough money from leasing land to change their lives? I don't."

"But Joe Carter's deal was different. They didn't find as much coal on his land as they thought they was."

"That's what they told him, Momma, and I guess he believed them."

"Well, what about Bob Tyler? He made some money off it."

"Bob went around buying up land from people who couldn't afford to pay their taxes, until he finally got so much land he couldn't help making money from leasing."

"Well, why in the world did you agree to it?"

"Because they'd probably go to court and get the right to mine anyway since they own the mineral rights. Either that or they'd just start mining and buy off the law. I signed because I didn't want to give them the satisfaction of seeing me fight and lose."

June lies back on the bed and closes her eyes. "Why've you been sitting naked in the creek?"

"I don't know the answer to that one, Momma. I guess I'm just waiting for something."

June sits up abruptly. "I can't believe Mr. Toothacre would a lied. He's too homely-looking to lie. You're wrong about this, Gemma. We're goin to be rich, and all you want to do is put a damper on it. Well, I'm goin to have a face-lift anyway. Do you hear me? And I'm goin to England, too."

Gemma stands up and looks at her mother's pepper-gray hair and frowning face. *"Bon voyage,"* she says and turns around to leave.

"Where are you going?" June shouts. "Are you heading somewhere to pull your clothes off?"

"Yes."

"Well, just don't come back!"

Gemma goes into the bathroom, pulls her clothes off, and leisurely takes a bath, spending an hour rubbing lotion on her skin and brushing her hair. For a while she lies on her bed watching the shadows of tree branches sway like hula dancers on the wall across from her window. Later she walks through the kitchen past June, who glares at her from a chair at the table. Then she heads outside to the swinging bridge and stops for a moment halfway across to lean over the rail and watch the swimming minnows.

15

Chapter

This morning, Gilman takes a carburetor apart in his machine shop, preferring to get his Monday work done on Sundays so he can lie in bed Monday mornings, listening to cars drive by taking people with less foresight to their jobs.

Two weeks have passed since Rosalee's surprise visit to his shop. Their lovemaking felt like a good-bye party attended by two old friends clinking glasses and singing "Auld Lang Syne." He wonders what it is that makes one person love another and why he can't muster the right kind of feeling for Rosalee. "Too late now, anyway," he grumbles to himself, "because she's stopped feeling that way about me."

An image of Gemma Collet intrudes on his thoughts; she's playing "Wildwood Flower" and staring into his eyes. "Shee-it," Gilman says, throwing down his wrench, "why do I keep thinking about that woman?" He goes to the bathroom and takes a shower, spruces himself up, and drives in the direction of Rosalee's mother's house.

In a certain light, mountains glow as if they are lit from

within. Every time Gilman takes a good look at a hill in summer, he wants to park his truck and climb it, disappearing into incandescent green. He drives across a low-lying bridge a few miles up the highway and continues onto a dirt road that is marred with potholes. Sweet William and goldenrod wave in a field by the road where, because of the many arrowheads that have been found beneath the surface dirt, people think an Indian campground was once located. The grade of the road gets steeper the farther he goes, small houses jut from the hillside, people stare at him from porches, and children swing in truck tires that hang from tree branches. When he travels up this road, Gilman always feels as if he's driving his truck into the past. Where the road dead-ends at the top of the mountain, he finds Rosalee sitting on the porch of her house and takes the front steps two at a time, grabs her, and kisses her full on the mouth.

"You shoulda married me when I asked you to," Rosalee says. "Now, it's too late."

"I knew you was goin to say that," Gilman says.

"Then again, maybe you shouldn't of married me."

Rosalee's mother comes to the screen door and opens it a crack. "Howdy, Gilman," she says smiling, her cheeks pink as carnival glass.

"How've you been, Mildred?" Gilman responds.

Mildred looks shyly off to one side. "I was just fixing something to eat. I reckon you'll stay to dinner, won't ye?"

"I reckon," Gilman replies.

Most of the living room furniture dates back to the 1950s, but the Mediterranean couch and love seat skip in time to 1968. The floors are wood and painted caramel brown; the walls are aqua blue. In a kitchen that is sunshine yellow with crisscross curtains on the window above the sink, Gilman sits down to a supper of collard greens cooked with fatback.

During the meal, Mildred begins talking about the changing nature of local crimes, recounting the murder of a local woman who was robbed and killed a year ago. "What about cutting a woman's head off! It's them drugs. They's always been people that'd kill ye soon as look at ye, but they wouldn't cut your head off!"

"Mom, tell Gilman about that picture you sent me," Rosalee says, in an attempt to divert her mother to a less bloody tale. "It was when I was down in Florida. She sent me a picture of three feet, all red and swelled and bruised-looking, and each one looked like it belonged to a different person. Awfulest sight you ever seen. Turns out Gladys Moore that lives down the road had sprained her ankle at the same time that her man, Hank, stubbed three of his toes. Well, Mom's ankles are always swelled. I guess they couldn't think of nothing better to do than to get together and prop their feet on a stool and take a picture. Reckon Hank leaned backwards to snap it."

Mildred looks at Gilman and laughs. "Hush, Rosalee. Telling people everything you know."

After dinner, they leave Mildred in the living room watching *Inside Edition* and walk out to the garden behind the house, traipse up and down the rows of corn, beets, and potatoes.

"The older she gets the more she worries," Rosalee says, adding, "What if the man I told you about was to find me? I'd hate to bring any kind of trouble in on Mom."

"He's not even looking for you," Gilman says.

"Prob'ly not. But I feel like he is. When he used to come into that club and listen to me sing, I could a been blindfolded and knowed he was there. I could feel him. This morning I woke up to birds singing in the top of that pine tree. You don't know how I've missed that. I got out of bed and come out here to get a look at them. The wind changed direction all of a sudden, and it was like I could feel him—just the same as I used to feel him listening to me sing."

"You're prob'ly imagining that, Rosalee."

"Could be."

They walk slowly around the garden, inspecting beans growing up cornstalks for fullness. "These can be picked just any time," Rosalee says. "I need to dig up the rest of these potatoes, too. I don't know why Mom thinks she has to raise such a big garden every year."

"All I've ever heard you call him is *he* and *man*. What's this feller's name?" Gilman asks.

"Frank Denton."

"He didn't see that letter Mildred wrote, did he? You know, the three feet? Do you think he saw the address?"

"God, I hope not. I did leave it laying around the house, but I don't think he paid any attention to it. I brought it with me, though. Didn't leave it in the apartment when I left. I really don't think he knows what part of Kentucky I come from, but I did tell him I lived in a small town."

"Are you sure he wants to kill you?"

"I believe he does."

Gilman sighs. "If I was to let you stay with me, everyone in the next three counties would know it in eight hours' time. People can't make it through the day without stopping by to see me at least once. They love my bones. It's a cross I have to bear."

As they walk back toward the house, Gilman says, "Pack your things tonight. I know where you can stay."

"Where?"

"In my old house."

"Is it fit to live in?"

"It is now. Course they's a man'll be living in it with you."

"What man?"

"Name's Tom. He's from California. Good carpenter."

"I'm not about to live with no strange man. I've done that one too many times already."

"He won't bother you. He's got the sweets on Gemma Collet."

"Now that won't do him any good, will it?" Rosalee laughs,

but her smile fades and she says, "I don't trust people like I used to. Do you really know he's all right?"

"I'd stake my life on it. As a matter of fact, I already have." Gilman gets into his truck, starts the engine, and rolls down his window as Rosalee walks toward her house. "Psst! Rosalee! C'mere a minute," he whispers loudly. She strolls back to him.

"It wouldn't hurt for us to have some fun ever' now and then, would it? After all, sex between friends is the best kind. Neither one of us would have to worry that the other would want to get married or anything."

Rosalee puts her hands on her hips, shakes her head, and smiles. "What time'll you be here tomorrow?"

"When you see me coming," he says and drives away.

When Gemma gets to Tom's house for Sunday dinner, he's nowhere around. She forgot to notice if his car was parked in her driveway, so she doesn't know if he is out for a drive or if he's walking in the mountain. Finding the door unlocked, she stands on the porch for a moment contemplating whether she should go inside and wait for him there. Finally, she steps inside, reasoning that he invited her after all, and she can't help it if he isn't here. Besides, she wants to turn on his tape player and listen to some music. In one corner of the living room, his tape player sits within easy reach of a rumpled sleeping bag. An open book lies on a desk in another corner, and more books are stacked in neat piles around the room.

Gemma walks over to the desk, takes the open book in her hands, and notes the title—*Thus Spoke Zarathustra, A Book for All and None*. Scanning down a page, she reads: " 'Like a robber, hunger overtakes me,' said Zarathustra. 'In forests and swamps my hunger overtakes me, and in the deep of night . . .' " Sounds like me, Gemma reflects. Wonder if the guy who wrote this could be a relative. Maybe he started the Jake strain of the family, she thinks, flipping to another page. " 'And I saw a great sadness descend upon mankind. The best grew weary of their works. A doctrine appeared, accompanied by a faith: "All is empty, all is the same, all has been!" ' " She turns page after page, uncovering a multitude of sentences punctuated with question marks and exclamation points.

In a biographical sketch, she finds that the author, Nietzsche, wrote the book while suffering simultaneously from near blindness, indigestion, nervousness, and migraine headaches. All that and hunger too, Gemma thinks. No wonder he seems hyper. She sits down at the desk and continues to read, and when Tom arrives an hour later carrying a basket of deep-fried fish and hush puppies, she is still reading.

"Hi," he says, surprised to find her in his living room. "I was going to pretend I fried this myself."

"Where did you get it?" Gemma asks, looking up at him.

"Harlan. I had to drive thirty miles to find a lousy fast food restaurant. Are you hungry?"

"Yes, just like him," Gemma says, holding up the book. "Is this one of your favorite authors?"

"He's okay."

"Why does he always refer to women as *little* women?"

"He doesn't always. Who knows . . . maybe all of his girl-friends were short? I seem to remember a book by Louisa May Alcott . . ."

"Yeah, but that's not the same thing and you know it. Wonder why he gets so carried away?"

"Getting carried away can be good," Tom says, spreading a plastic tablecloth on the floor. He procures a couple of beers from the ice cooler and places the basket of fish on the table-cloth.

They sit on the floor and eat, Gemma with a hush puppy in one hand and *Thus Spoke Zarathustra* in the other. "Glad to find I'm not the only one," she mutters as she skims more pages.

Then she puts the book down and looks around the sparse room. "I like this. No frills."

"It's easy to keep clean," Tom admits. He gets up, puts on some music, and sits down next to Gemma.

"I got into a fight with my mother this morning. Walked out of the house. She told me not to come back."

"Good," Tom says, winking. "You can stay with me."

Gemma smiles. "Gilman's not just letting you live up here out of the goodness of his heart, is he? No doubt he's got you looking after his land."

"Something like that."

"Could get sticky."

"I know."

"Why did you agree to it?" Gemma asks.

"It was something to do."

Gemma sees her face, elongated and ghost-white, reflected in Tom's eyes. She looks deep, beyond her reflection to where she sees nothing but Tom Jett—sees so much of him in his eyes that she becomes frightened. "What did you do before you started sitting on the beach?" she asks him.

"I went to school," Tom says. "Studied philosophy."

"I didn't know there was still a market for that. What do philosophers do these days?"

"Teach. Not me, though. I decided to think instead."

"What about?"

"Sand, salt, kelp, deadwood, et cetera. Interesting subjects like that."

Gemma lies back on the floor. "Do you have family in San Diego?"

"My mother and father used to live there, but not anymore. They moved near Sacramento to live in a retirement community with a square dance motif."

Gemma laughs. "What do they think about all this thinking you do?"

"Not much." Tom looks out the window and tries to visualize his father swinging his mother to the sound of dueling fiddles in a retirement community rec room. "Dad used to be a longshoreman. Before I started my new way of thinking, he would get me jobs on the docks during breaks from school. Every day, I'd go down, sign up, and wait to be scheduled. Not being in the union, I'd get the dirty jobs. The worst was loading cowhides, which were always churning with maggots. It would be about a hundred ten degrees in the hold of the ship, and the smell was . . ." Tom looks down at Gemma. "People don't think about things like that when they buy a leather coat or a new pair of shoes."

"I sure didn't," Gemma admits. "But, thanks to you, I probably will from here on out."

"It's hard to get into the longshoremen's union," Tom continues, ignoring Gemma's sarcasm. "Union cards can be passed down from father to son. I'll probably inherit my father's membership when he dies."

"Is that what you're going to do someday? Work on the docks?" Gemma asks, as she visualizes Tom swaggering aboard ships with armloads of maggot-ridden hides, showing off his muscles in bars after work, playing pinball and pool, drinking Bud.

"I doubt it. But I won't be a professor, either. That's what my parents wanted me to be. My mother processed claims for an insurance company for twenty years. Naturally, it wasn't her dream job. The only time she came alive was from about two P.M. to eleven P.M. on Saturdays. That's when she played the ukulele and invited friends over for a game of canasta. College was a big thing with my mother. She thought that people with two or more degrees never had to work in boring jobs, that they woke up every morning singing operas in Italian, improved the world's condition from nine to five every day, then fell to sleep like breast-fed babies. My parents wanted that kind of life for me, and they took it hard when I didn't go on to graduate school. But all of that was before square dancing came into their lives." Tom tweaks Gemma's nose and looks into her eyes. "If I kissed you right now, would you bite my lip like you bit Gilman's?"

"Maybe. Maybe not."

Tom inches his face toward Gemma's and rubs his nose against hers Eskimo-style. His lips saunter to the right, find her earlobe, and dally with it like puppies with a lemon drop, then sidestepping over to her mouth, they lay a big kiss on it. Gemma feels as if she's been transplanted into a romance novel of the brand that Marcy reads on her lunch breaks, the kind she wraps in brown paper so no one can see the picture on the front. Words like *surrender, melt, pulsate,* and *throb* slither across Gemma's mind. It's been twelve years since she's been receptive to a kiss, and she dissipates like cotton candy left out in the rain. Then she begins to cry. Tears come out of nowhere, torrential in magnitude, and while Tom holds her, she weeps for all the mornings when she woke up with no feeling but anger. It was as if the disease had seeped inside her heart, bleaching it of every emotion except white-hot rage. She remembers days grayer than tombstones and the pale moon that shone night after night through her bedroom window, covering her body like a shroud.

Finally the tears are gone, and Tom hands her a napkin to wipe her eyes. Gemma looks up at him. "Did I ask you to stop kissing me?"

"No."

"Well, then?"

Tom begins again, nibbling, touching, and unbuttoning, his bare chest rubbing against her breasts. He kisses her shoulders, stomach, and thighs, and he enters her slowly, purposefully, Gemma notes, staring up at his determined jawline. She feels her surroundings disappear—outside, the trees are gone, the squirrels, the field, the row of beans, the old road to Harlan, gone. There is just Tom Jett above her looking down into her eyes.

Later, she lies still beside him, and while his hand rests in her hair, she savors the moment, recalling small details of their lovemaking, feelings she thought were lost to her forever. "I didn't think I could still do it," she says in a whisper. "I've never thought of it as being like swimming or playing a banjo—something you never lose the hang of. I've always thought of it as an accident that a person is lucky to repeat, that there is a secret door leading to it. I never thought I'd find it again."

"Well, consider yourself a homing pigeon, Gemma," Tom says, smiling. They lie there for perhaps an hour before he puts on another tape, and they dance nude until late in the night.

Gilman waits until after dark Monday to pick Rosalee up. After she says good-bye to her mother, they're on their way.

June is looking out her window when they pull into her driveway. "Who is that with Gilman?" she asks Gemma, as she watches the two of them make their way down the bank to the swinging bridge. Gemma glances up from the copy of *Thus Spoke Zarathustra* she borrowed from Tom. "Don't know and don't care," she says.

Tom began a new job today, putting aluminum siding on a trailer so it will look like a house. He's exhausted and half asleep, and he's just finishing off a can of tomato soup when the knock comes on the door. He opens up, and there stand Gilman and Rosalee, each holding a suitcase. "Hello," Tom says. "What a surprise. Come in."

"Howdy, Tom," Gilman says. "This here is Rosalee."

"Nice to meet you," responds Tom.

"Sit down there somewhere," Gilman says to Rosalee while scanning the room for a chair. "Looks like you've been doing

a lot of work to the place, but I see you don't have much furniture yet," he adds to Tom when he can't spot but one chair
and one desk. "Got any beds?"

Tom clears his throat in an attempt to assess what is obviously a new turn of events. "No, I have a sleeping bag and
plenty of blankets."

"You've slept in a sleeping bag before, ain't you, Rosalee? A
sleeping bag would be all right with Rosalee."

Tom clears his throat again. "Well, that's uh . . . That's
good."

"Rosalee, here, got herself into a little scrape, and she needs
a place to stay. If you wouldn't mind, I thought she might
could lay low with you for a while. Just till things blow over.
She needs to be someplace where no one'd expect she'd be. I
believe right here's the very place. You wouldn't mind helping
a person out, would you?"

"Of course not," Tom says, looking around at Rosalee and
wondering what kind of little scrape she got herself into.
Maybe she killed someone in his sleep, Tom thinks.

"I didn't kill anyone. Nothing like that," Rosalee says
sweetly. "Not on drugs, either. Least not anymore."

"Of course not," Tom repeats.

"Just so you'll know . . . someone *might* be trying to kill her,"
Gilman adds.

"Really?"

"But maybe it's my imagination," Rosalee puts in.

"Then, again, who can say?" Gilman considers philosophically.

"No one, really, I suppose," Tom mutters.

"Well, I guess I'll leave you two here and go home. Busy
day tomorrow," Gilman explains. "Lotta jobs lined up. I'll be
seeing you."

When he leaves, Tom and Rosalee look at each other, then
around the room. "I just ate," Tom says. "Are you hungry?"

"I just ate, too."

Tom's eyes dart toward his stacks of books. "Do you like to read?"

"No."

"I've been sleeping here in the living room," Tom says. "I'll put your bags in the bedroom."

"That's fine," Rosalee says.

Gilman walks down the hill and crosses the swinging bridge to his truck. He stands there for a moment looking toward Gemma Collet's house. He wonders what she does at night. Maybe she's not in her house at all. Maybe she's at the creek, standing naked down there like some goddamned goddess.

He gets into his truck and drives toward home, speculating about how well Tom and Rosalee will adjust to each other and wondering what Gemma will have to say about the situation.

Part II

GOOD STRANGE AND BAD STRANGE

16
Chapter

Driving along I-75, he passes Ocala and Gainsville, Macon and Atlanta. It took Frank Denton almost three months to remember the name of the town scrawled in the upper left-hand corner of the letter Rosalee's mother had written her. For weeks, Rosalee had left the letter lying around their apartment with the picture of the three feet stuffed half in and half out of it. She'd looked at the feet at least once a day. "This is just like Mom," she'd said, shaking up and down with laughter.

When Rosalee left him, Frank lay in bed night after night, conjuring up images of the envelope, but he never saw anything except the illegible scribbling of an erratic hill woman. Then a couple of nights ago he had a dream in which the envelope was all he saw. *Mildred Wilson,* it said in the upper left-hand corner, *Pick, Kentucky.* He awoke, sat straight up in bed, and smiled. Maybe it doesn't mean anything, he thought, once he was fully awake. He took from his nightstand a Kentucky road map he'd gotten from his auto club. There it was, Pick, in the hills as far as you could go.

"Pick, Kentucky, here I come," Frank said and fell into a sound sleep for the first time since Rosalee left.

Now he's on his way, a bottle of Old Bushmills beside him on the car seat and an image of Rosalee reflected in every white line on the highway. Blond hair, green eyes, and an easy laugh that sounded like water running over rocks, that was Rosalee, and she sang torch songs, took them to a higher state than he'd ever heard before. Her laugh was what had attracted him in the first place, and she behaved as if she knew intimately every member in the audience—that's how comfortably she sang her songs. He sat at a table near the stage, pale and brooding, watching the stage lights play across her face and hair.

It was Rosalee who made the first move; he'd wanted it to begin like that. He'd wanted her to be the one to come to him, and so she came one night with her calm manner and haunting songs to his table and said hello. She was hooked, he could tell, he'd drawn her in with his whirlpool eyes. He and Rosalee played that night—flew like birds up and down the Sunshine Parkway.

When Frank reaches Somerset, Kentucky, he pulls off the interstate, fills up at an Exxon station, drives to a Jerry's, and orders their Southern-style breakfast, telling the waitress to bring him a pot of coffee, no cream, no sugar, just black. Sunday morning in Somerset, Frank notes, as the waitress brings him his food. He eats leisurely, sips his coffee, and buys a paper, reads the arts and entertainment section—an interesting story about the Actors Theatre in Louisville. Frank likes good theater, but he hasn't been to a play since he began orchestrating his own drama. In an advertisement for one of the plays, an actress has her head thrown back in laughter, reminding him of Rosalee.

Not only did Rosalee's laugh attract him, it also turned him against her. He grew tired of her never taking things seriously. The whole world was a joke to Rosalee, and even now, when he goes to bed, he can hear her voice in his ear: "Ain't nothing that important, Frank. You oughten to take things to heart the way you do."

He may just have written a poem that had changed his entire view of the world, a poem where each word choice had been agonized over. He didn't know how he wanted her to react, but he didn't want her to say, "That's true, Frank, and I like the way the words go together. Real nice." He didn't want her, at that very moment, to say she was going to send out for pizza.

She meant it, too, when she said she liked the way his words sounded, and that she understood them. It's just that she didn't respond to them in the right way. He hadn't noticed it at first, but everything seemed of equal importance to Rosalee—a pizza was just as meaningful as a poem. She was like his mother in that way.

Frank's maternal grandfather hadn't become a wealthy man from hard work. He had found a sunken pirate ship in the Keys when he was young—treasure chests filled with jewels and Spanish gold. That's where the money came from, and he had invested it wisely. Frank has always thought it was his family's accumulation of wealth through no other means than luck that accounted for their inability to see the importance of things. Frank's mother, Alaine, was the toast of Palm Beach during the fifties. She married seven men in her prime, none of whom she had taken seriously, and one of whom was Frank's father. Alaine hadn't appeared to give her son much thought either, and, to this day, she calls him Fred instead of Frank. Frank assumes she remembers the name she gave him at birth and the only explanation for her use of the *Fred* misnomer is that she wants him to believe he's forgettable.

At Jerry's, Frank looks out the window and watches the northbound traffic—cars with dressed-up families possibly on their way to church, pickups whizzing by with hard-faced men at the wheel. Sunday—Hangover Day. He remembers Rosalee telling him about affairs she'd had with two men back home. One of the men was a musician/mechanic, she had said, and the other a banker. He figures the banker will be the easiest to find, and he visualizes Rosalee in her small-town banker's arms, laughing her soft musical laugh.

He pours another cup of coffee from the pot and glances around the room at the other Jerry's customers—families out for Sunday breakfast. "Let's go to breakfast, honey. Please. We never go anywhere," he imagines the woman with two small children at the next table said to her husband this morning. Now they're here, and the food on her plate is getting cold because her children are crying, and she can't get a chance to eat. Her husband isn't helping because he's looking at a tall, slender redhead who just walked in the door. Frank imagines she realizes that it isn't really breakfast she wants. What she wants, really, is . . . She wants to be rid of them, all of them— the husband, the kids, her parents and friends. She wants to know no one, to be leaping perhaps from a plane, skydiving through clouds, the wind blowing her skin to distortion, alone, to finally land in the San Francisco Bay and swim ashore—to find a lover on the Promenade. How could she want all of those things and only ask for breakfast at Jerry's? Frank doesn't understand married life.

What he understands are extremes and disrepute. He likes the undomesticated part of town, the wrong side of the tracks. He certainly didn't revel in the society of Palm Beach. That's why he went across the bridge to live in an apartment in West Palm and plaster his walls with poetry, why he cruised the back streets of Miami, lost himself for weeks in Key West, and locked on to Rosalee, a nightclub singer, sultry and cheaply dressed. He loved her, truly loved her, until she started not to take him seriously and he knew it.

One night not long after he came to this realization, he marched her into the bathroom, stripped her down, and uri- nated on her bare back. Maybe she'd take that seriously, he thought. But she didn't; she just looked up at him and laughed. Thinking of ways to wipe the smile off her face became his goal in life, and he started doing things to animals (she loved animals), hung them out to dry on clotheslines, tortured them in front of her until she stopped laughing.

Then there was the night in the alley . . .

Rosalee accused him of not having a soul, but she wasn't seeing the truth of the matter. "I have more soul than the average person, and I know what is and is not right. I wouldn't bother doing the things I do unless I believed they were wrong," he mutters to himself as he thumbs through the newspaper and finds nothing noteworthy.

Leaving the waitress a two-dollar tip, he stops by the table of the unhappy young mother and her stray-eyed husband. "Wanta ride?" he asks her. "Next stop, the Promenade." The children cease crying, and the husband says, "What?" But she looks up at him as if she understands. "No, thank you," she says with tears in her eyes.

Frank leaves the restaurant, stops by a used-car dealership, and trades his Acura Legend for a Ford Escort with a Kentucky license plate. He doesn't want to draw undue attention to himself when he arrives in Rosalee's hometown. It isn't until four-thirty in the afternoon that he finds himself on the Daniel Boone Parkway, heading for Pick.

As he drives along, he intently observes the mountains on either side of the parkway. When he was still in Florida trying to remember the name of Rosalee's town, he checked out of the library several books on the history and geography of Kentucky. In one of these books was a picture of Daniel Boone standing on a mountain ledge, leaning against his long rifle and looking out over the Cumberland Valley. The valley was shrouded in mist and covered with a jungle of trees. The expression on Daniel's face was solemn and full of awe.

In his research, Frank discovered that the Indians had few, if any, large permanent settlements in Kentucky, such as they had in Tennessee, and came to the region only to hunt and fight wars. Frank wonders why the Indians decided to set the region aside as a hunting area. Why didn't they live there? Was the hunting *that* good? Frank sure hopes the hunting is good.

With each mile he travels, the mountains get taller and the trees thicker. It is nearly dark when he arrives in Pick and gets a room at the only hotel in town, the Blue Mountain Inn. After he unpacks his clothes and has a greasy hamburger at the hotel diner, he wanders outside, trying to look like any other hick from Pick out for a Sunday night walk. There isn't much to see, just three streets and no bars. He spots the Pick Citizens' Bank and notes their hours on the glass door: Open Monday–Friday: 10:00 A.M. to 4:00 P.M., Saturdays: 10:00 A.M. to 3:30 P.M.

The next morning, he awakes at eight o'clock and looks out the window. He sees a coal truck pass through town, an empty bus go by, and two old men walk toward the bench on the courthouse lawn. He showers, walks down to the restaurant for breakfast, and meanders around town, finding the same three streets and no bars. He goes back to the Blue Mountain Inn and asks the desk clerk, "Where's the bars? I might want a cold one later on."

"Ain't none. You'll have to go to the next county for that. Course there's a few places around here where you could get some, but it'd cost you more."

"Where?"

"Well, Betty Marker that lives down the river. Course she might want to sell you more than a beer. And there's Gilman Lee. He's got a machine shop about five miles up the road. He'd sell you a cold one."

Frank smiles at the desk clerk and turns around to leave. "This Gilman Lee wouldn't happen to play music, would he?"

"Best in the West," the desk clerk says.

Frank gets into his car and drives south until he comes to the bend in the road where Lee's Machine Shop is located. Since Rosalee didn't mention that her ex-lover was a bootlegger, he can't be sure if this Gilman Lee is the right person. Driving slowly by the place, he observes a man with deformed arms walk out of a trailer near the shop and lean against a coal-truck bed. Couldn't be Gilman, Frank surmises. No one could play music with arms like that. His sixth sense kicks in, telling him that this is no place to fool around. He steps on the accelerator and drives back to the Blue Mountain Inn.

"I guess a lot of mechanics around here play music," he says to the desk clerk.

"Hell, almost everyone in these parts can pick and sing."

Still, I bet Gilman is the one, Frank thinks. He asks the clerk for exact directions to Betty Marker's house. As he drives down the narrow dirt road toward her place, he wonders if the local law against alcohol is a holdover from Prohibition or if it has always been this way in Rosalee's hometown. When he arrives at Betty's and knocks on her door, he is led into the living room, where he finds three men watching a movie on the VCR. While Betty, a hefty fortyish woman dressed in a muumuu, steps into the kitchen to get his beer, the men barely acknowledge his presence. Hanging on the walls are several snakes—rattlers and copperheads—that have been stuffed and shellacked to a glossy sheen. In one corner stands a six-foot-high bookshelf filled with video tapes. The men are smoking and talking while the movie plays, arguing, more accurately, about who exactly it was that killed a man named Hank Brock ten years ago. At first Frank thinks they're discussing a character in the film, but then he realizes that they knew the victim personally.

When Betty comes out of the kitchen carrying a case of Bud, she says, "You're not from around here, are you?"

"No," he replies. "I'm from Somerset."

"Didn't think you was from around here. How long you goin to be staying?"

"I'm not sure yet. Nice snakes," Frank says, eyeing Betty's wall.

"Killed 'em in my garden," Betty says, then nods at the case of beer. "Come back any time. They's more where that come from."

He drives away, wondering what it is like at midnight in Betty Marker's house. Were the men in her living room her lovers? Do they fight over who gets to hang on to her muumuu? He decides he likes the woman. She reeks of corruption and decline. It shows in the dead ends of her hair and cavernous pores of her skin.

When Frank arrives back at the Blue Mountain Inn, the desk clerk steps outside and watches him park the car.

"Get your beer?" he asks.

"Yes."

"Are you visiting someone around here?"

"No," Frank says, wondering if everyone in Pick is as inquisitive as Betty Marker and the desk clerk.

"What's your business then?" the desk clerk persists.

"I just got laid off from my job in Somerset, and I'm looking for work."

"Looks like you'd a went north for that."

"I don't like the North," Frank says.

"Don't blame you, but they ain't no work around here that I know of unless you're ready to work in the mines."

"The manager of the bank across the street is a friend of my pap's. I know him pretty good myself. Thought he might help."

"Wade Miller a buddy of yourn? Well now, he might be able to get you something."

Now knowing the name and location of one of Rosalee's lovers, he thinks that perhaps he'll call on Wade Miller tomorrow. Frank goes to his room and lies down on the bed. He assumes he can find out shortly if Gilman Lee is the other boyfriend, but he didn't like the feeling he got when he drove by the machine shop today. The place had an atmosphere, and the man with the funny arms made the hair rise on the back of his neck.

17

Chapter

About 300 million years ago, Pick, Kentucky, was a swamp forest. Seed ferns the size of small trees covered the lowland marshes, where lepidodendron trees with cone-bearing branches stood one hundred feet tall. Every day was warm as the day before in the Paleozoic era. Insects like dragonflies with wingspans of more than two feet glided past ferns and over water lilies, and reptiles and amphibians lolled in the never-changing sun. The forests, when they fell into the boggy waters, partially decomposed, but didn't rot away. From the remains, peat was formed and later coal.

Then came the Appalachian Revolution, a period of world-wide physical disturbance. Seas receded, volcanoes erupted, land warped, and mountain ranges were formed. Coal that had been formed in the marshlands now lay in seams in the mountains of Appalachia, remaining virtually unnoticed until the late 1800s when the coal men arrived with geologists and speculators, unearthing an economy that has lasted a hundred years.

*I*n October they came with a vengeance, the Conroy Coal Company's crew, to build a bridge across the creek down the road from June and Gemma Collet's house. When the construction of the bridge was complete, they set to clearing a road to the top of the mountain. Now they buzz, saw, and bulldoze. They rattle and roar their way to the top. There is a preacher among them and a drug addict, a man who can't write his name and another who has a degree from the University of Louisville. Some are temporary and others career miners. Soon they will be ready to begin the mining operation.

Gemma sits on her back porch and watches them build the road. She sees one-hundred-year-old trees fall and roll down the hill. She hears the drug addict laugh and the preacher pray as they sit by the creek on their lunch breaks, arguing over morality. She reads the lease she signed. It says the Conroy Coal Company has the right to:

> . . . enter and use, move, disturb and destroy so much of the surface and subsurface of the leased premises as lessee deems necessary, convenient, or useful for the exploration, mining, ventilation, drainage, transportation, or removal of the coal; the right to construct, operate, and maintain in and upon the leased premises any and all buildings, structures, and improvements as lessee determines to be necessary, convenient, or useful for such purposes including, but without limitation or restriction thereby, the right to core drill, and make crop openings; the right to use sand, stone, water, and gravel from the leased premises; the right to construct, operate, and maintain roads, ventilation fans, gas, telephone, and other public utility lines, water lines and water drains, mine buildings and

shops, processing and cleaning plants; the right to bore holes; the right to establish refuse and waste disposal areas, and to dump refuse and waste materials thereon.

Gemma is depressed. She is depressed about the coal mining and about Rosalee living with Tom. She is mad enough at Gilman Lee to kill him, but she is too depressed to do it. Tom has tried to tell her that he doesn't like the Rosalee situation, but Gemma won't listen—refuses to speak to him, for that matter. She won't speak to June, either, because deep down she blames her for the fact that she signed the lease. She still works, though—still drags herself to the bank, adds up numbers, and stares at Wade, Marcy, and Jo Ellen. Sometimes she even laughs and makes wisecracks to the customers, but there are moments when she sinks so low that she thinks of calling Sylvester Gast. "Hello, Sly," she imagines herself saying. "Wanta watch me cry? I know you think that when people wail like babies they're lancing a boil, letting that awful emotional pus run out. I cried, Sly, in a man's arms like a baby till I drenched his shirt. It did me a world of good. I felt a whole lot better for about twenty-four hours, because that's how long it took him to start living with another woman. Crying helps, Sly. Maybe I'll do it again in another twelve years."

"Thanks for sharing that with me," Sly replies in her imagination. "I bet you start getting well, now that you've told me that."

She pictures herself as she was that evening when she got home from the bank, still dazed from her Sunday afternoon with Tom, still aglow, remembering the scent of him, his voice in her ear. He wasn't home yet, but she decided to go to his house anyway, thinking she would wait for him. In an attempt to show restraint, she hadn't visited him on Monday, but by Tuesday she could wait no longer. With *Thus Spoke Zarathustra* stuck under her arm, she walked across the swinging bridge and up the hill, singing as she went, wondering what other books she could borrow.

As she approached Tom's house, she saw a woman in his garden pulling weeds from around his scraggly, wilted beans, and she was wearing his hat. Gemma walked up behind her quiet as an Indian ghost and, unable to raise her voice above a whisper, asked, "What are you doing?"

Rosalee turned around. "Pulling weeds."

The two women looked at each other for a full minute, taking each other in, pinpointing identities and personal history—exchanging this information with their eyes. "You're Rosalee Wilson," Gemma said.

"You're right."

"I thought you were in Florida."

"I was."

"Why are you pulling Tom's weeds?"

"Nothing else to do," Rosalee said, and, taking Tom's hat off, she sat down on a rock and lit a cigarette. "I hope you don't tell anyone I'm back. I'm trying to keep it a secret."

Gemma looked around at the house. "Are you staying *here*?"

"Gilman figured this was the best place. They's not but a few people knows I'm here: my mother, Gilman, Tom, Ten-Fifteen, and now you. I'm hiding out. Might be someone trying to find me. I'd really appreciate it if you didn't tell people you seen me."

"You mean this was Gilman's idea?"

"Yeah, he didn't think anyone would dream I'd hole up with this Tom guy."

"I sure wouldn't have," Gemma said, her heart racing. She noticed how pretty Rosalee was, her blond hair and Florida tan. She handed her *Thus Spoke Zarathustra* and added, "Tell Tom I returned his book."

"You won't let on to anyone I'm here, will you?" Rosalee yelled as Gemma walked down the hill.

Gemma didn't answer.

She hasn't told anyone, though, and won't, mainly because she isn't speaking to anyone. The funny thing is, she isn't mad at Rosalee. She doesn't know the woman well, but she's seen her around and heard plenty of talk about her over the years. She's heard that Rosalee is wild, that she'll go anywhere and do anything—sleep with anyone. Rumor has it that Rosalee was on drugs when she went to Florida, either that or pregnant with Wade Miller's baby, or both, or had herpes that she caught from Gilman Lee or someone like him. Tongues will wag. Gemma figures that the next best thing to avoiding human contact altogether is to speak, sleep, and carouse with everyone all the time. She figures there is not much difference between the two ways of living, that it's when you try to get intimate with one person that you get into trouble.

She visualizes Rosalee and Tom in the house on the hill. At first they are polite to each other; maybe they have meals together, say good morning and good night. Gradually they begin to talk and laugh on a regular basis. One evening Rosalee accidentally brushes against Tom as they walk through the living room; this causes them to feel awkward for a day or two. They try to avoid each other, but they can't and start talking and laughing once more. Finally by chance, they brush against each other again, and it happens: they have wild, uncompromising sex. Gemma imagines that Rosalee feels at ease with sinews, muscle, and sweat bending over her, with damp sheets beneath her, that she has no regrets.

"I regret everything, Sly," Gemma imagines herself saying to the psychologist.

"Tell me about it," Sly replies.

When Tom got home from work and Rosalee told him about Gemma returning the book, he ran down the hill to her house and knocked on her door. No one answered, but he could hear June and Gemma arguing in the kitchen.

"Let go of me!" June yelled. "I reckon I'll answer the door to my own house when someone knocks."

"Not this time," Gemma yelled back.

Tom knocked again, louder. "Are you sure you're finished with this book? Would you like to read *Twilight of the Idols*?"

No answer, just the sound of scuffling in the kitchen.

"How about some Plato?"

"If you cause me to have a heart attack, I'll die!" June hollered at Gemma.

"If you'd keep still you wouldn't have a heart attack," Gemma replied.

"Kant? Camus? Sartre?" Tom asked and tried to open the door, but it was locked.

Gemma finally acknowledged him. "Let Rosalee read them."

"She doesn't like to read," Tom said. "Besides, she won't be staying much longer."

"Rosalee who?" June asked them both.

"A girl in the book I was reading," Gemma answered.

"Open up!" Tom shouted.

"I'm not in the mood. You know what happens when I'm not in the mood: I bite lips and kick balls. If I were you, I'd leave me alone."

Tom lay *Thus Spoke Zarathustra* on the porch and went home, wishing he was back in California listening to waves.

Gemma watches the crew get closer to the top of the mountain. Tom still parks his car in her driveway every evening when he comes home from work. Some evenings he undertakes speaking to her, tries to loan her books, but she goes inside the house. She has put *Thus Spoke Zarathustra* on the mantel in the living room as though it were just another *Reader's Digest*. She tries to settle down to the person she once was, but she isn't that person anymore. She wants to do something—anything. She thinks of sitting naked in the creek, but the water has taken on an autumn chill. She decides to do it anyway—cold water or not, men-on-the-hill-staring-at-her or not. The men are too far up the mountain now to see me, she decides, as she walks down the bank and undresses. Cold creek water awakens her, makes her keenly aware of what she feels, and what she feels is pain.

Gemma's speculation about Tom and Rosalee having wild, uncompromising sex has not happened. For the first week they were together in the house, they were uncomfortable in each other's presence to say the least. Tom didn't know what to say to Rosalee, who seemed always to be looking out the window as if expecting some horrible entity to approach the house. She smoked constantly, and Tom, who doesn't smoke, found her habit difficult to adjust to. She dusted ashes in dinner plates, in glasses, in the fireplace, on top of the wood-burning stove, and sometimes she would not ash at all, holding the cigarette gently between her fingers, allowing the gray, dying ember to burn down to the filter until there was no fire left and it dropped all in one piece to the floor.

Their first real conversation occurred when she ran out of cigarettes.

"If you pass a store on your way home this evening, I'd appreciate it if you stopped and bought me some cigarettes, Marlboro Reds," she said to him one morning, as they ate toast and jam.

"You mean the cowboy-on-the-billboard brand?"

"That's the ones."

"He's dead now, you know."

"Yeah, but they hired a new one."

"He'll die, too," Tom said.

"So will you," Rosalee countered.

"But not as soon as he."

"How do you know?"

"I just do."

"Prove it."

"I can't. It's a spiritual kind of knowledge, something you have to accept, that can't be demonstrated until it's too late."

Rosalee opened her purse and took out a couple of dollars. "Marlboro Reds," she said.

Tom accepted the money.

That conversation broke the ice, more or less, and they began telling each other things about their lives. Rosalee told Tom about Florida and mentioned some of the milder aspects of Frank Denton's nature. Tom told Rosalee about California and about his attraction for Gemma Collet, about his frustration that she is so angry with him for no good reason.

Now at night, Rosalee goes to bed early, sleeps in the sleeping bag in the bedroom. Tom stays up late and reads, falls to sleep on a pile of blankets on the living room floor.

They learn to adjust.

18
Chapter

It is ten-thirty in the morning, and Gemma has just gotten off the phone to the McDonald's Corporation. The way it looks, Big Mac wrappers will be peppered all over the countryside in six months' time. She is not happy at this prospect, but there is a long line of situations that irk Gemma. She is silently reciting some of the more choice irritants when Frank Denton walks into the bank.

He is tall with medium brown hair and pale skin, and his eyes are so dark blue they're almost black. Something about his manner suggests he's from out of state. Maybe he's a spy from McDonald's come to check things out, she speculates.

"Name's Fred Dudley. I have an appointment to see Mr. Miller," he says to her.

"No, you don't. I'd know about it if you did," Gemma snaps. The man's eyes grip onto hers, and realizing he's trying to stare her down, she almost laughs out loud.

"Nevertheless, I'd like to see him," the man says.

Gemma steps into Wade's office to check the situation out and returns, saying, "I reckon it's all right."

When Frank enters Wade's office, he finds him sitting at his desk, rolling a pen around his fingers. "Hi," Frank says, sitting down in a chair and crossing his legs. "I'm Fred Dudley."

"Have we met somewhere?" Wade asks. The man in front of him is wearing jeans and a work shirt, but somehow the clothes don't agree with the way he carries himself.

"No," Frank says, "but we have a mutual acquaintance."

"Who?"

"Rosalee Wilson."

"Rosalee?" Wade's heart begins to speed up a bit.

"I knew her in Florida, and from what she's told me you knew her pretty well, too."

"We were acquainted," Wade says. "How's she doing these days?"

"That's what I was going to ask you. Have you seen her lately?"

"Not since she left."

"What I'm asking is, has she come back?"

"Not that I know of."

Frank studies the expression on Wade's narrow face, a face that most probably was formed during infancy by a mother who habitually left her baby lying on the side of his head for hours at a time. Frank decides, however, that Wade Miller, whether he was neglected as a child or not, is telling the truth.

"But Rosalee could have come back without you knowing it," Frank says to him. "She had another friend around here. I believe she said he was a mechanic."

"Gilman Lee? I doubt that she'd have got in touch with Gilman, but even if she did, it would pay you to stay away from him."

Frank smiles. "Why?"

"Because he's a snake in the grass, and he wouldn't tell you anything about Rosalee no matter what you said or did." Wade eyes Frank suspiciously. "Why are you trying to find her, anyway?"

"I want to marry her."

As they often do, Wade's thoughts are doing pirouettes, the first and foremost thought being to locate Rosalee and, if she has returned home, to find out why she's keeping her return a secret. Who wants her the worst, Fred or Gilman? Does Wade want her for himself? No, he decides, he's almost gotten her out of his system. Is there a profit to be made from this thing?

"I wish I could help you," Wade says, "but I don't know anything about her coming back. Tell you what, though, I'll try to find out about it."

"That's great," Frank says. "But I'd like you to keep it quiet. You see, me and Rosalee had a little spat before she left, and she might not be too eager to see me. But I know if I find her I can change her mind."

Wade's ideas twirl like batons. He takes a closer look at the man in front of him, takes in his pale face and blue-black eyes. He can see Rosalee being attracted to a man like him in a pinch, that part fits. But something else doesn't. The clothes? Wade isn't sure what it is.

"I wonder if you could help me out with something else," Frank says. "I'm staying at the Blue Mountain Inn until I find her. But in the meantime, I need a job of some kind. I can't stay at the hotel for long and not be working or everyone in town will start wondering why I'm here. Won't be able to keep anything a secret."

"There's no work around here except mining," Wade says, his suspicion growing. He can't believe this man would go to so much trouble just to find Rosalee and marry her. Besides, if Rosalee is so mad at him, she probably wouldn't marry him anyway. In other words, Wade asks himself, why is Fred Dudley looking for Rosalee?

"If mining's all there is, I'll take it," Frank says. "You realize that I'd just be working temporary. I mean it's not like I'd be doing it for the money. As soon as I get Rosalee, we'll be heading back to Florida."

"It might be kind of hard finding you a temporary job. Usually people want a man that'll stay," Wade says, his eyes narrowing into slits.

"I'd really appreciate it if you could help me out. In fact, I'd give you five hundred dollars for it," Frank says. "You know where I'm staying. Let me know if you find something."

Frank leaves, and Wade leans back in his chair, forcing himself to calm down so he can think clearly. If Rosalee told Fred about their affair, she may have told him about the cocaine, but for the time being there is no other choice than for him to go along with the man. He already stands to make five hundred dollars just for getting him a job, and he wonders how much Fred would pay to know the whereabouts of Rosalee.

The strip mine that will soon be in operation on the mountain behind Gemma's house—that'd be a perfect job for Fred, Wade decides. It appeals to him that Rosalee's Florida boyfriend would be working next door to Gilman's property. He paces the floor in front of his desk, drawing up plans in his mind.

*T*en-Fifteen sits in his trailer thinking about Rosalee. In his heart, she is like Marilyn Monroe, except tougher. He has loved her since he first moved his trailer near the machine shop six years ago. Rosalee and Gilman were a hot and heavy item at the time; but Rosalee started pressuring Gilman to marry her, he wouldn't, and they broke up. Being unselfish with his love, Ten-Fifteen was all for the marriage and wanted to know why Gilman turned her down.

Back then, Gilman said, "Rosalee and me are like a wildfire, but, if you was to put us together every day, we'd go out like someone doused us with water. I love a lot of people, but I don't want 'em to move in with me."

"But you care more about Rosalee than you do most other people, right?"

"What's that got to do with anything? Besides, why on earth would she want to live with me? They's always a crowd here, playing loud music and carrying on. What if she got tired of that? I couldn't make it without my parties, we'd fight, and that'd be the end of it. Or maybe she'd start flirting with one of the gang that comes here, and being's we was married, I'd feel like I had to stop her. When you love someone, you want more and more of 'em. You try to get inside 'em and never come out. Why can't we just keep it like it is? I don't want to hinder Rosalee from any notion she might take, and I sure don't want to put a damper on myself."

"Well, then, you don't love her, at least not the way you ought to."

Tired of reliving those old arguments, Ten-Fifteen watches *Days of Our Lives* until he can't watch it anymore, then he goes over to the shop to help Gilman flush out a radiator, hoping at the same time to learn more about the trouble Rosalee's in. She's been back for a month, and he still hasn't talked to her once. When he gets to the shop, Gilman says he'd rather work by himself today. Ten-Fifteen leaves, but instead of returning to the trailer, he walks down the road toward Gilman's old house on the hill.

When Rosalee hears him knocking, she runs to the door and hugs him. "Is word getting out that I'm back?" she asks.

"Not that I know of," Ten-Fifteen says, glancing around at the bare living room. "Tom is a pretty good feller, ain't he? Don't ever bother anyone, does he?"

"No, he don't."

"Gilman says you're in trouble, but he won't say much about it."

"That's because he don't know much about it."

"He said a man might be after you."

"Might be."

"Why?"

Rosalee shrugs.

Crisp air rattles the leaves as it passes the house, and the sound of bulldozers moving up the mountain can be heard in the distance. Rosalee shivers and puts some coffee on. She asks Ten-Fifteen how he's been, if he's seen any good movies lately. He tells her about one he saw on the late show called *Lonely Are the Brave*. "Best movie Kirk Douglas ever made," he says.

Sipping their coffee, they sit on the floor and talk about old times.

"Gilman seems different somehow," Rosalee says.

"Different?"

"Yeah, he seems . . . I don't know . . . not as full of piss and vinegar."

"Well, he don't seem that way to me, and anyway we're all getting older, you know."

"It's not just age, Ten-Fifteen."

Ten-Fifteen looks away from her.

Rosalee smiles. "It's probably nothing. Anyway, I've got my own problems. I didn't report the full story to Gilman . . . I mean, about Frank Denton, the man that's following me. Maybe I'll fill you in on the gory details, if you don't mind. I've got to tell someone. Couldn't tell Gilman because I didn't know what he'd do."

"I reckon you can tell me anything," Ten-Fifteen says.

"Frank made me strip off naked late at night and walk down a alley between some bums. It's what happened next that I ain't told no one."

Ten-Fifteen looks down at the linoleum, tracing its floral pattern with his eyes, and imagines himself becoming small as a bean bug, walking underneath the petals and stems in order to give Rosalee privacy while she talks.

"They started coming toward me, all of them drunk or drugged. Did you ever see that movie, *Night of the Living*

Dead? That's what they looked like. This big guy took over and said, 'She's mine. I get her first.' The others must of been too out of it to complain, because they started moving away in slow motion and lined themselves up on either side of the alley, watching me all the time, their eyes dull as marbles. Frank opened the car door and got out, but the men was too busy watching me to hear him. The big guy, I guess you could call him the ring-tailed leader, come up close, unbuckled his belt, and let his pants drop. He pulled his shirt off and stood there stark naked, his pecker standing straight up against his belly, which (I found out later) gave Frank a clear shot at his balls. The gun went off, and the man dropped to the ground. I'm positive he died. When I got my bearings, the other men in the alley was gone—no one was there except Frank. I ran back to the car and got in, but Frank stayed there in the alley for a few seconds inspecting his handiwork. A few days later, I managed to get away."

"Didn't you have no idea beforehand that he'd do something like that?"

"He had a hold over me, Ten-Fifteen. Didn't just tell me when to breathe, but how and where to. And they was things he did to me."

"What things?"

"Kind of like what I just told you about, but without the gun." Rosalee turns her face to the wall. "I can't tell you about it right now. It's never out of my mind, though."

"Is Frank crazy?" he asks her.

"Crazy is too easy," Rosalee says. "You know how in them scary shows someone'll start glaring their eyes and say that someone else (usually a vampire or a werewolf) is *eeee-veee-il*? Well, that's what Frank is; he's *eeee-veee-il*."

"*Eeee-veee-il* or not," Ten-Fifteen says, "most people're too lazy to go looking for someone out-of-state."

"Frank ain't most people."

"We won't let this feller bother you, Rosalee."

Rosalee nods her head and stares out the window.

Later, as Ten-Fifteen walks down the hill to the bridge, he turns to look back at the house and sees her still at the window, searching the field with her eyes.

19

Chapter

Gilman sits on his balcony, pondering situations and twists of fate. Since Rosalee moved in with Tom, he hasn't paid one visit to Zack, and he misses their conversations. Looking back inside his apartment at the silent piano and guitars, he considers the whiled-away nights of his life—the ragers, the music, the fair-weather friends. It occurs to him that all of his life he's kept the party going, delivered laughs, and rolled out good times like red carpets for himself and his friends to walk on. "It's not a bad life," he says to himself. "It's better than selling encyclopedias."

Lately, though, he's been wondering what his life would have been like had he married when he was young. He would have children, possibly even grandchildren by now; and they would sit on his knee, pull his earlobes, and beg to be carried around the room on his shoulders. He wonders how it would feel to wake up beside the same woman every morning. An uninvited vision of Gemma Collet drifts across his mind, and he pushes it away, replacing it with an image of Rosalee. Neither one of them women would work out for me, he decides. They'd ex-

pect me to do things I don't want to do—may even ask me to go
to a barber and have my hair styled or join the Better Business
Bureau. Stepping inside his paneled apartment, he notices how
perfectly the wood is installed and wonders if Tom courts a
woman like he panels a wall and whether the Californian and
Rosalee are well acquainted by now. He opens a beer and picks
up his guitar, intending to sing "Pour Me Another Tequila,
Sheila," but the words get lost in his imaginings.

He forces himself to think about something else: the coal.
One thing he's found out is that his property may have more
coal than the company led him to believe. He's asked several
people's opinions on the subject and been told that Conroy
will, no doubt, set up a neat little operation just across June
Collet's property line and auger his coal out, signed lease or
not. Since they own the mineral rights such an action would
not be illegal as long as they don't get on his property.

Every evening Tom Jett stops by the shop and gives him a
report on the road builders' progress. He assures Gilman that
the workers never come near his land, but Gilman still worries
about Rosalee's close proximity to the crew. He puts his guitar
down and sits for a while deep in thought, trying to trace
down the reason he is so perturbed by this coal situation in the
first place. He's known about the corruption of coal companies for years, and he's griped about it to friends during lulls
at gatherings, but he never considered doing anything about
it till now. Granted, the companies never threatened to get on
his property till now, but a few years back that wouldn't have
bothered him. He would have been too busy playing or listening to music. Gilman stands up abruptly, slicks back his
hair, gets into his truck, and takes off down the road, not
knowing what he intends to do exactly. All he knows is that he
has to get in his truck and go; he has to put a bug in someone's
ear, pluck a few wild hairs.

Parking in his usual spot, he climbs the mountain to where
the men are building the road. They are almost to the top of

the mountain now. The air smells of exhaust fumes mixed with freshly dug earth. The men are busy as bees—grading, chopping, coughing, and spitting.

"Howdy," Gilman says to the preacher, who is driving a bulldozer. "I don't know you, buddy. Who are you?"

"Wallace Couch," the preacher says. "From over on Kettle Creek."

"The Kettle Creek Couches?"

"That's right."

"Well, then, I *do* know you. Heard of the Kettle Creek Couches all my life. What kin are you to Landon Couch?"

"First cousins."

"First cousins to a sonofabitch," Gilman says. "Landon killed a buddy of mine, Zack Morley. Ever hear of him? Landon run him up against a tree with his truck. Yeah, I know the Kettle Creek Couches."

"I remember that," the preacher says, "but the way I heard it, Zack and Landon's wife were fooling around. Landon was out of his mind over it."

Gilman gives Wallace Couch a look that chills him to the bone. "You'd better tread a little softer, buddy. I'm pretty touchy when it comes to the subject of Zack."

"Well, I ain't got nothing to do with that business," Wallace says. "I'm a preacher."

"That don't cut no ice with me. What kind of preacher?"

"Church of God."

"Ever handled snakes?"

"A few times."

"Good," Gilman says. "The practice might come in handy. Where's your boss?"

"Up the hill, there."

The boss has his back turned, looking toward Gilman's property. Gilman comes up behind him and says, "Like to get your hands on it, wouldn't you?"

The boss wheels around, and Gilman finds himself staring

into the face of Ed Toothacre. "How's your teeth, buddy?" he asks.

"They're still okay," Ed says, reaching his hand out for a shake, but changing his mind midway.

"I thought you was a land agent," Gilman says. "What're you doing overseeing this deal?"

"Getting experience," Ed says. "It always pays to get experience."

"Hope it's not a bad'un, Ed."

"What brings you up here?"

"To say that if you get on my property, heads are goin to roll. To tell you that if your men go anywhere near my house around there behind them trees, I'll put their balls in a pickled baloney jar and start me a roadside attraction."

"We have no intentions of getting on your property, Mr. Lee."

"That's comforting to know. Have a happy day," Gilman says and, leaving Ed, walks through the sycamore trees to his old house. He doesn't knock on the door—just walks in. Rosalee is sitting on the floor, listening to the radio through earphones, tapping her toes to the beat. She doesn't hear him until he eases up behind her and whispers, "Rosalee?"

She jumps up and starts to run, but he manages to grab her before she gets out the door. He puts his arm around her waist and his hand over her mouth. When she opens her eyes and sees him, they kiss. "That's real cute, Gilman. Sneaking up on me when I'm scared of my shadow, anyhow," Rosalee says, pulling away.

"Sorry, I wouldn't thinking about that."

Shaking her head, Rosalee looks at him as if he's a lost cause. "Have you heard from Mom?"

"Yeah, I called her just before I left the house. She's doing okay, and told me to fill her in on how you was doing as soon as I could. Which I'll do, of course, since I've turned into such a good little go-between."

Rosalee smiles. "Want something to drink?"

"Gotta beer?"

She gets them each one, and they sit at a table in the kitchen. It isn't a regular table, it's a picnic table Tom recently built from pine. "Handy with his hands, ain't he?" Gilman says, admiring the construction.

"I reckon so."

"What else can he do with his hands?"

"He can open a book and close it pretty good."

"Is that all he does in his spare time? Read?"

"That and stare into space and listen to blues, classical, and Brazilian music."

Gilman arches his eyebrow. "What else is his hands good for?"

"How would I know?"

"I thought maybe he'd been twiddling his thumbs on you."

"Not hardly."

"What do you two talk about up here at night?"

"We don't talk much."

"When you do talk . . . ?"

"About California and Florida. We compare the good and bad points of the Atlantic and Pacific oceans. You know, about how the Atlantic is warm and has white beaches with hardly any kelp, but don't have much surf. And how the Pacific has surf, but is cold and has kelp all over the sand . . . things like that."

"Fascinating," Gilman says.

"Are you goin through some kind of midlife crisis? Why are you acting like you're jealous? You know you're not interested in me for the long term. You just can't stand for any woman you ever went with to get her eye on somebody else."

Gilman drains his beer and rubs his hand over the wood grain of the picnic table. "To tell you the truth, I don't know anything anymore. My mind's on too many things at once, I reckon."

"Why did you even move me up here in the first place, if you're so worried me and Tom might get together? I can tell you right now that this whole situation is pretty uncomfortable, and it's completely destroyed any chance for Tom and Gemma. I'm figuring on carting my little butt back to Mom's house any day now."

"That might be a good idea. I wouldn't thinking of the side effects when I brought you up here. I just thought it would be a safe place. In the meantime, you better be careful during the day or them men out there'll see you," he says, nodding his head toward the sound of bulldozers. "Do you still feel like Frank Denton's looking for you?"

"Yeah, sometimes."

"Don't just take off to your mom's house in broad daylight. Let me know when you want to go, and I'll take you after dark."

Rosalee scoots up close to Gilman and kisses him on the scar side of his face. "Don't ever get old, Gilman. I couldn't stand it."

"Who said I was getting old?"

"Ten-Fifteen said we was all getting older."

"Ten-Fifteen needs to learn to speak for himself."

Rosalee kisses Gilman on the mouth and the atmosphere in the old house heats up substantially. They wander into the living room, where Rosalee pulls her clothes off, lies down on some blankets, and props her feet against the wall. One at a time, she brings her legs down to touch her shoulders, as if she's doing warm-ups for an aerobics class. She looks around at Gilman and winks.

This time, when they make love, it's like the old days—they have a marathon.

When Gilman leaves, he stops in at the prayer chamber for a chat with Zack. "I almost killed me a preacher today, Zack. Landon Couch's cousin. But I took a gander at him, and he looked like meal. His face looked like a big dish of cornmeal—

all yellowish and gritty. He's already dead, Zack. I'd of been wasting my time.

"Anyway, Ten-Fifteen thinks I'm getting old. What do you think? Personally, I feel like I'm aging as fine as a bottle of Kentucky bourbon."

From the window, Rosalee watches Gilman walk out of the chamber and down the hill toward the swinging bridge. "He sure don't make love like a old man," she mutters. But he still seems different to her. He almost seems like a man who is on the verge of taking off somewhere, leaving the whole country.

Rosalee sweeps the floor and tosses the beer cans in the garbage. She opens a can of tuna and chops some onions, takes out a frying pan and sets it on the hot plate, thinking about how Tom Jett oohs and aahs as if she'd fried porterhouse steaks when she fries tuna cakes. Rosalee doesn't know what to make of Tom. She figures he must have the hots real bad for Gemma Collet because he's the first man she ever met who has managed to be alone with her and not get her into bed. She's not used to platonic relationships, but she decides she sort of likes them. She tries to imagine being platonic with Gilman Lee and smiles as she stirs her tuna, eggs, and onions.

This evening Tom Jett, who is almost finished with his current job, began the preliminary discussions for his next. Betty Marker hired him to construct a large room at the rear of her house, in which she will set up card tables. She also wants a covered patio to be added to the back of the room, complete with a Jacuzzi and hand-crafted planters. It is a major project that will keep Tom employed for quite some time. Since he and Betty spent a couple of hours planning the details, he is late getting home.

"Gilman came by today," Rosalee says when they finally sit down to eat.

"Any particular reason?"

"I think he's worried that them workers out there'll see me."

"Does he think it's safe for you to go back to your mom's yet?"

"He thinks it might be a good idea."

Tom cuts his tuna cakes into bite-size pieces.

"I know I've kind of messed things up between you and Gemma. I didn't mean to," Rosalee says.

Tom stabs a bite-size tuna crumb with his fork. "She's jealous."

"Do you want me to talk to her?"

"She wouldn't listen."

Rosalee stares down at her plate and says, "I've been nosing through some of your books. It seems like they're all about the way people think and feel. Like they're trying to explain the way people act."

Tom looks at Rosalee as if she just stepped into the room. "I didn't think you liked to read."

"Not much else to do up here. Anyway, I was just wondering if you ever run into a person in one of them books that thought they'd figured everything out? That's the way Frank is sometimes. It's like he could kiss you and kill you in the same breath because nothing matters to him. I started to say he hates people, but that's not it. I don't think there's a word for how he feels. Did you ever run into anyone like that in any of your books?"

"One or two," Tom says.

"Is there a chance of him changing?"

"I don't know."

Rosalee gets up from the table and walks outside to the porch, where the dark blue of the evening sky is the color of Frank Denton's eyes. A memory of how good they once were together presses against her like a kiss; in the memory it is dawn and they're on the beach with its warm sand of mid-summer, after having held each other, had sex, and talked all night. Frank takes her face in his hands and says, "You're like that glow there around the sun, red-orange and warm, the way it looks before it pops above the horizon. Your smile is like that, your voice, and see how brilliant the color becomes? Sex with you is like that."

He was a drug more addictive than cocaine, and in spite of everything, Rosalee loves him, even now. In an attempt to shake her hunger for him, she grips the porch railing until her knuckles turn white, and finally the hunger subsides. She looks out at the view in front of her. The road builders are gone for the day, and except for a lone whippoorwill and the rustle of leaves it is quiet. Dew is settling on the ground, and the faint scent of apple pie is drifting up the hill. Everything around her denotes home and protection, but she knows Frank is out there trying to find her. She feels him grabbing on to her in his dreams.

20
Chapter

Gemma and June glare at each other from opposite sides of the living room with neither the TV nor the radio on. They are not reading newspapers or magazines, not talking or laughing. The house smells like an apple pie. June has been baking all day—six apple pies, one after the other. Gemma is used to eyeing Wade, Marcy, and Jo Ellen, but they don't stare back the way June does. She remembers playing this game as a child—gazing at a playmate until the playmate broke into laughter—and considers how hard it is to look into a person's eyes for a ten-minute stint. Noses, lips, and foreheads are easy; Adam's apples are good, too, but stare into someone's eyes, and don't smile, don't cry, don't go insane. It's a challenge.

Gemma wonders if her mother played this game as a child, and for that matter, if she played hopscotch, hide-and-seek, and ring-around-the-rosy. She tries to imagine June as a youngster—eight years old with tangled hair and a red face from climbing mountains and trees, carrying with her that wild, out-of-doors smell that children have. She has heard stories that in high school June was captain of the girls' softball team. Gemma tries to picture her mother hitting home runs and striking people out. What was she like when she fell in love?

When Gemma's father died, June was thirty years old, the same age Gemma is now. She remembers her mother grieving for about a year before she finally relented and started dating. After the dating began, June's cousin, Marlene, would stay with Gemma while June went to a dance club in the next county every Saturday night. Sometimes men would come to dinner on Sunday, funny-acting men who brought coloring books or bobjacks for Gemma and candy or wildflowers for June, and who always wanted to take the two of them on Sunday drives to picnic spots by the river or to the Pine Mountain lookout tower in Harlan County. This went on for about two years, and then it stopped. Gemma opens her mouth to ask June why she quit going out on dates, but she remembers she isn't speaking to her. It occurs to Gemma that she is bored with this ogling episode, and she goes into the kitchen, where six apple pies covered with tea towels sit on the table. Picking out the coolest of the six, she cuts two pieces and puts them on saucers, returns to the living room, hands June a piece, and the mother and daughter sit opposite from each other, eating pie.

"You put cloves in this one, didn't you?" Gemma says, breaking the silence.

"What if I did?"

"I don't like cloves. Your apple pies baked with red-hot candy are better."

"I don't like them with red-hots," June says, blowing a spoonful of pie before putting it in her mouth.

"Why did you stop dating?" Gemma asks.

"What?"

"You used to go out with men a long time ago. What made you stop?"

"You're a fine one to talk about someone not going out with men," June says.

"Why did you stop?"

"Why did you?"

"I stopped because I figured they were all the same."

"So did I," June says. "They're prob'ly not *all* the same, though, are they?"

"Probably not," Gemma says. "Some of them wear jockey shorts, and others wear boxers. Some don't wear any shorts at all, and they are the ones you really have to look out for."

June takes their empty saucers into the kitchen and returns. "You like that man from California, don't you?"

"He already has a girlfriend," Gemma says.

"That's too bad. He's sorta good-looking." June gets up from the chair and yawns. "I guess I'll lay down early tonight." As she walks through the hall to her bedroom, she says, "I'm glad you started talking again. I can't figure out why you stopped in the first place. Did someone do something to you?"

"No more than usual."

June goes on to bed, and Gemma sits alone in the living room, watching the empty fireplace as though it has a fire in it burning out of control. She was nine years old when she moved with her mother and father into this house. It used to belong to her grandparents, but it was passed on to June after their deaths. Gemma remembers her grandparents sitting like bookends on either side of the fire, shucking corn, stringing beans, and spitting tobacco juice that sizzled like bacon when it hit the flames. She wonders what they would think about the activity on the mountain—the coal, the Californian, and Rosalee.

Pondering why Gilman chose to move Rosalee in with Tom, she finally decides to just ask him. Gemma has never gone to see Gilman without being in the company of someone else. Before the vitiligo, she used to go to his shop with her young lover, and, more recently, she has gone with Tom, but Gemma is wary of calling on Gilman alone and remembers the day when she stood on the hill by a tree crying, her face marked like cowhide, white and brown. Gilman Lee came up behind her and tapped her on the shoulder, and when she turned around, he looked straight at her and said, "You're one of the prettiest women I've ever seen." His face about an inch from hers, she saw in his eyes the Indian ghosts from her childhood. A history of the ground where they stood, a past rooted in the bogs and marshlands of shaggy whorled plants and slithery creatures, drifted around them like fog. It was as though, having emerged from the same dark, humid soil, she and Gilman were just one person. He kissed her on the mouth, and for an instant she sank into his kiss as if she were immersing herself in a prehistoric swamp. She began losing control, a condition she didn't like, so she bit his lip and kicked his balls. Gemma figures that Gilman put Rosalee in the house with Tom because he is still holding a grudge.

The next morning she is awakened by a detonation of dynamite that breaks apart the cool, clear morning like a warning of the end of the world. She looks out the window half expecting to see a mushroom cloud, until she remembers the strip miners on the hill. Everywhere, trees are myriad variations of gold and red. Listening to the lingering resonance of the explosion, she lies in bed while, on the mountain, power shovels have already begun to dig through the rubble for coal.

By the time she pulls in front of Gilman's machine shop, it is noon. Still stationed by the door like a monument to an act of God is the truck bed that caused so much damage during the flood. She walks past it into the shop, knocks on the apartment door, and hears a shuffling of feet and something being knocked to the floor. When Gilman finally opens up, it is apparent that he is hungover and semi-alive.

"Have a party last night?" she asks him.

"Have one every night," he responds, fingering the stubble on his cheeks.

"Can I come in?"

"Of course," he says, ushering her into an odor of stale smoke and spilled whiskey. "Have a seat. I usually fry me and Ten-Fifteen some eggs about now. Want some?"

"No thanks, but you go ahead and eat." Gemma looks around at the Polaroid pictures on the wall, remembering the night she came here with Tom and played the banjo. Gilman steps into the kitchen area and begins to fix breakfast. She imagines he goes through this ritual every morning, that he fries a quarter pound of bacon, puts toast in the toaster, fries eggs sunny-side up, and that all the while he has a headache and is sick at his stomach. "Why do you drink?" she asks him.

"It keeps me honest. People that don't drink ain't honest."

"I hardly ever drink," Gemma says.

"Then you ain't hardly honest."

"I think you're an asshole for moving Rosalee in with Tom. Is that honest enough for you?"

"Pretty much, considering you don't drink."

"Why would you move a girlfriend or even an ex-girlfriend in with another man?"

"Beats me."

"You wouldn't have been trying to get back at me for kicking you in the balls, would you?"

"Why, Miss Gemma, I'm surprised you'd think such a thing of me."

"One of these mornings you'll have a heart attack and die," she says as Gilman heaps two plates with bacon and eggs. He grunts and walks out the door with one of the plates, and she can hear him banging on Ten-Fifteen's trailer door.

"Then I'll die happy," he says when he gets back to the apartment, sits down on a stool by the counter, and begins to eat.

"They started the mining this morning," she says. "I woke to a blast of dynamite."

"I wonder why Tom didn't let me know," Gilman mutters, sprinkling his eggs with Tabasco sauce.

"Maybe he'd already gone to work when they started, or maybe he didn't hear it because he was too busy with Rosalee."

Gilman scowls and stuffs a piece of bacon into his mouth. "Conroy's aching to get my part of the coal. I figure they'll try to auger it out from your side of the line."

"Can't you stop them from that? I'd at least try to get me a lawyer."

"As far as I can tell, it's not against the law, but I don't intend to sit by twiddling my thumbs while they auger it out."

"What are you going to do?"

"Well, now, I don't guess I'd tell you since you so eagerly signed the lease."

"Maybe I signed the lease just so I could stop them some other way, a more interesting way, maybe even one that's illegal."

Gilman offers her a bite of toast, and she refuses. "Don't tell me you'd perform a unlawful act, Gemma Collet. They might be hope for you yet."

Ten-Fifteen walks into the apartment carrying his empty plate. He looks at the two of them as if he can't believe they're just sitting around talking and not arguing.

Gilman says, "We're trying to think up ways to stop the Conroy Coal Company from getting on my land. You didn't know Gemma was a outlaw, did you, Ten-Fifteen?"

"Sure didn't," he responds.

"What are some things we could do?" Gemma asks, nodding a hello to Ten-Fifteen.

"I reckon we could dynamite some of their machinery, or we could remove some essential parts from some of it. A mechanic like me oughten have much trouble along that line."

"I want to be in on it," Gemma says.

"We're not to that point yet, but when we get there you're welcome to help if you still want to."

"I'd like to help too," Ten-Fifteen says. "What'll my job be?"

"Don't worry about it. I'll figure out something real crucial for you to do."

The three walk out to the balcony and watch the creek flow around the bend. "I don't know how it happened that I came here with no intentions except to give you a piece of my mind and ended up plotting sabotage," Gemma says to Gilman.

A smile spreads slowly across his face. "You're not the first that's got sidetracked in this shop."

"Could you tell me something that I'm curious about? Just who is it that is looking for Rosalee? Is she really in trouble?"

"Could be," Gilman says, staring into Gemma's eyes, "but then it seems like everyone's in trouble."

Gemma feels the same discomfort that she felt when he kissed her years ago and decides to leave before the feeling gets stronger. "Well, I, for one, am not in trouble."

"Not yet, but the potential is there."

On the drive back home, she puts him out of her mind, not wanting to think about Gilman because when she does her head tightens and her heart starts to pound. Instead, she thinks of Tom Jett and Rosalee. Maybe it's just like Tom says and nothing's going on with them. It's not as if Tom asked Rosalee to move in with him. Gemma decides that the next time he parks in her driveway and tries to get her attention he can have it.

21
Chapter

Tom Jett began laying the foundation for the room addition at Betty Marker's house a few days ago. Today as he drives slowly home from work he looks on either side of the road at the foliage in full sway on the hillsides. A couple of miles from Betty's place, he is gazing at the red and gold trees when he spots a cabin positioned near the top of the mountain. He pulls to the side of the road and sits for a moment, looking toward it. The house appears to be abandoned. Marveling at how many places around here look like rustic scenes that belong on a postcard, he gets out of the car, crosses the road, and climbs the hill to get a better view.

Approaching the house, he notes that it appears to have been unoccupied for years; many of its logs are crumbling and the roof is shot. Tom tentatively steps inside and finds a living room, kitchen, and bedroom. In the yard are the remnants of an outdoor toilet and a chicken house. There are four pines, two on either side of the cabin, and the wind when it blows through them leaves a fresh piney scent. Tom sits down on the front steps and breathes deeply, feeling as though he's sat on these steps before—lived here in this house in some previous lifetime. It is with hesitance that he finally walks back down the hill to his car and drives home.

Gemma is sitting on the porch that evening waiting for Tom Jett to pull into her driveway, hoping he will speak or wave. Just one nod in her direction, that's all it would take for her to jump out of her chair and run to him. Finally he arrives, gets out of his car, and locks the door; she believes he sees her out of the corner of his eye. But instead of speaking, he turns and walks across the bridge and up the hill.

"What do you make of that, Sly?" she asks Sylvester Gast, in her thoughts. "Do you guess he's lost interest?"

"It's hard to say," the psychologist replies. "But that's not the point. What really matters is that you're reaching out."

"You sound like a phone ad," Gemma notes. "Who says that reaching out to another person is a good thing? When you touch someone else, you're really just trying to touch yourself. The difference being that you're going about it the long way around."

"Is it easier being alone, Gemma?"

"Nothing is easy, Sly."

*T*om Jett did see Gemma on the porch, sitting like a statue, white and cold as marble, and wanted to step a few feet in her direction, to wave at her, maybe call out her name, but he didn't because he's tired of rejection. Her dismal expression and stone-cold gaze exhaust him, and as he walks up the hill toward his house, he considers the mixed feelings he has developed for her. On the one hand, he would like to hold her in his arms again, while on the other, he would like to wring her stiff white neck. She doesn't blink, move, or budge. She just sits there on the porch, as if by her solemnity she can ruin in slow, torturous degrees whatever it is that brought her into this world.

When he nears his house, he hears Rosalee stirring in the kitchen. She has begun waiting until he gets home to start dinner in case the miners should smell her cooking. Tom supposes she gets lonelier than a fifties housewife, sitting in the house all day, no one to talk to, no TV. She is unable to step outside once during the day for fear of being seen, and Rosalee, who says that singing is her biggest love in life, now doesn't even listen to the radio without wearing earphones.

"Hi," Tom says, when he steps inside.

Rosalee drops spaghetti into a pot to boil, spreads butter on two slices of bread, and pops them into the toaster oven. Outside, the miners are rattling down the hill. Work is over for the day. Every evening after they leave, Rosalee runs outside and circles the house, singing to the top of her lungs.

"You must get awfully bored, having to sit in here all the time," Tom says during dinner. He says this to her almost every evening.

"I do," Rosalee admits. "And you know what I miss the most? I miss the smoky nightclubs, the singing and dancing. I miss the rattle of ice cubes and drunks talking loud enough to be heard over music." Rosalee wraps spaghetti around her fork and takes a bite. "I guess you think I'm crazy."

"Women always think I think that," Tom says.

After dinner, Rosalee steps out into the cool October evening, the sharp air and violet-blue sky. Almost behind the mountain now, sunlight has colored clouds shades of abalone shells, and trees stand partially silhouetted, as though waiting for darkness to hide them. Frank is getting closer; she feels him breathing beside her.

What Rosalee still hasn't told anyone are the events occurring after the incident in the alley—how she sat naked in the car amid stifling heat and heavy air while Frank, who only moments before had shot the man, marched like a soldier back to her, got behind the wheel, and started the engine. It wasn't until they were halfway back to West Palm that he began to laugh, snicker, really, at first.

"Talk about a rush," he said, between chortles. "Whooo!" He began to laugh more boisterously, glancing around at Rosalee as if to gauge her reaction to the recent event.

She, by then having pulled her pants back on, was attempting to button her blouse, but her hands shook so hard she couldn't manage even one button. Frank, beside her, tittered as if he were enjoying a private joke, and even with the air-conditioning turned on high, she perspired until her blouse was wet.

"Say something," he said.

She couldn't.

A cloud passed over his face as he drove on in silence; and when they arrived at their apartment in a run-down part of town, a cheap duplex flanked on either side by shaggy palms, he opened the car door, got out, saw her not making a motion, and dragged her rigid body over the stick shift and out the driver's side, dragged her inside the apartment and dropped her on the floor.

He raped her.

Rosalee was numb, unable to feel him on her.

"Let's play poker, Rosalee," he said a few minutes later. "I come from a lucky family. Luck runs in my blood."

She couldn't move.

He hit her. She couldn't feel.

He drank for two days, and when he finally passed out, she raised her head, got up from the couch where she had lain as if in a coma, picked her clothes out of the closet and dresser drawers, put them along with all her belongings into a suitcase, took money out of his wallet, and, before she left, stood over him with a knife for five minutes. She took a bus up the coast, stayed for a while in Daytona Beach, and gradually meandered back to Pick.

And even after all that, she still remembers the other Frank, the one who held her face in his hands and made her feel like the deep orange glow of sun rising over the hazy line of ocean. She still loves that Frank.

When Rosalee returns to the house an hour later, Tom is sitting at his desk, his tape player buzzing with Brazilian music while he reads. She sits down on the floor and leans her head against the wall. "I'm afraid," she says.

Tom puts down his reading material and turns around, noticing that Rosalee looks fragile enough to be blown over in a strong wind. "Don't tell me the woman who worked in a coal mine and drove a bulldozer is afraid."

"It don't take guts to work in a mine or drive a bulldozer. That's nothing. But it takes a lot of nerve to sit and wait for an asshole to find you, especially when that asshole is Frank Denton."

"I'm sorry," Tom says, getting up from his chair and sitting on the floor beside Rosalee. He puts his hands on top of hers, noticing how small they are, and cold, and for a moment, the two of them sit without speaking while outside wind clatters in trees like gossips in the aisle of a country church.

"I don't want to sleep alone tonight," Rosalee says.

Tom glances around the dimly lit room, where flames flicker in the fireplace, and he feels it, too—whatever it is that put Rosalee in this mood. In the white coals near the flames, he sees a perfect white image of Gemma, immovable as a statue and unwilling to be touched.

"I don't either," he says, and puts his arm around Rosalee.

*T*hat night, Gemma lies in bed, watching tree branches sway in the breeze outside her window, and, remembering how Tom hadn't even acknowledged her presence on the porch, she hardly sleeps at all. At the bank today, she goes through the motions as usual; nothing awful happens, but nothing wonderful happens either. Now it is evening again, and she stands in the driveway, holding *Thus Spoke Zarathustra* in her hands, stroking the leather on its binding as if it is the skin on Tom's chest, not knowing what she wants from Tom. Maybe it is his knowledge of books that she wants or maybe she only wants him to hold her while she cries. He is unfamiliar, from a coast of sand and sea spray, and she feels light when she is around him, not heavy and steeped in fog and dark soil, which is the way she feels around Gilman.

When Tom pulls into the driveway, it will be impossible for him to avoid me, she thinks, as she listens for the sound of his engine and turns to check out every car that passes the house.

But Tom is late getting home this evening. At Betty Marker's he ran out of cement blocks and had to order more. Since he couldn't get them delivered until tomorrow, he took off from work early. On his way home, he stopped by the abandoned cabin again, drawn there as if by a magnet. He climbed the hill and walked around inspecting the yard and chicken lot. It was when he meandered behind the house that he noticed the opening in the side of the hill. It was no more than two feet in height and ran about ten feet in width. Jagged rocks jutted down from the top, and briars and bushes almost hid it from view. Tom lay on the ground and peered inside, seeing nothing but darkness. "Hey!" he yelled, sticking his head all the way inside the opening. An echo resounded back. Tom ran down the hill to his car and rummaged through his tool chests until he found a flashlight. Scrambling back to the opening, he shined his light inside.

It was a cave. A rather huge room was what it looked like, with a smooth, powdery floor and gray rock walls. Tom slithered inside, crawled at a slightly downward angle for about fifteen feet, and stood up straight. There was still a variance of five to ten feet above his head. It suddenly occurred to him that this would probably be a fine place for snakes to live, and he couldn't remember whether snakes were active this time of year. He began shining his light all around the floor and walls of the cave just in case.

It was then that he saw the lettering on the rock wall to his right, but it was a language he was not familiar with. It wasn't Spanish, French, or German, and neither was it Latin, Greek, or Russian. All he knew for certain was that it was a sentence, not painted on, but chiseled into the gray rock. Tom sat down on the floor of the cave, mesmerized.

Gemma is about to give up on Tom ever coming home. She has been waiting in the driveway for an hour when he finally shows up.

"I'm through reading this," she says, handing him the book when he gets out of the car. "I really liked it. What was that other one you mentioned? *Twilight of the Idols*? I'd like to borrow it, if you don't mind."

Tom wonders what made her decide to give in. Maybe she didn't decide anything at all, but walked out here to the driveway like a robot. He thinks back to that Sunday when he held her while she cried. A feeling passed between them that has now vanished into thin air. Perhaps it will come back or be replaced by some other feeling, one that is even stronger. All Tom knows for sure is that last night he made love to Rosalee, and now Gemma is standing in front of him wanting to borrow a book.

"I'll bring it to you tomorrow evening," he says, glancing up the hill toward his house, still somewhat dazed from his discovery of the writing in the cave.

"Bring me what?" Gemma asks.

"*Twilight of the Idols.*"

"I thought maybe I'd walk up the hill with you and pick it up this evening."

"Rosalee might be too busy to visit," Tom says, uncomfortable with the prospect of Gemma, Rosalee, and himself all in the same room. "She usually starts dinner the minute I get home."

"Well, now ain't that domestic," Gemma says, eyeing Tom closely.

Tom starts walking down the bank toward the bridge.

Gemma follows him, not caring that she is obviously intruding where she is not particularly wanted. Maybe they need me to intrude on them, she thinks. That's what everyone needs, intruders—outsiders who barge in unannounced. People are too polite, Gemma thinks. They are too worried that they may be saying or doing something that their neighbors won't like.

"Rosalee will probably be glad to see you. She gets lonesome by herself all day," Tom finally says, as if he's trying to be polite.

"I thought she wasn't going to stay with you much longer. Has she had a change of plans?" Gemma has decided that from now on she will ask lots of nosy questions, too.

"I don't know how long she'll be staying."

On their way to the house, they meet the strip miners coming down the hill, their work finished for the day. They are a scraggly crew, sullen and sweaty, engaging in mundane arguments as they go downhill.

When Gemma and Tom reach the house, Tom unlocks his front door and whispers through the screen to Rosalee, "We've got company," and quietly ushers Gemma into the house.

Rosalee is sitting in one corner of the living room with her head on her knees. As the door opens, she looks up like an animal caught in a trap. "I'm tired of this," she blurts out, as if she is not speaking to Gemma and Tom, but to an invisible someone else who is standing right behind them, someone for whom she has been saving a speech. "I'm tired of hunkering down in corners afraid to breathe. Every little sound I hear, I think it's him, except it's turned into more than him. It's bigger now—on top of, underneath, and on every side of this house, trying to get in."

"Rosalee?" Tom says, glancing from her to Gemma.

"I don't even know what it is anymore," she continues. "I go to the window and pull open the curtains so it can see me because I'm tired of hiding from it, but nothing is there except the sun shining, the wind blowing, and squirrels running around. It's like they've been playing a trick on me and are laughing at the look I have on my face."

"Are you all right?" Tom asks.

"Just now when I heard you on the porch, I thought it was him, even though I knew it was time for you to get home from work. I still thought it was him, hoped it was so he could do whatever he intends to do and get it over with. But when the door opened, it was just you and Gemma."

Gemma nods, unable to speak. Suddenly everything seems trivial next to the fear and anger in Rosalee. All Gemma wants at this point is to be somewhere else. "Reach out," she hears Sly Gast say in her imagination. "Go to hell," she responds.

"I just came to borrow a book," Gemma says, looking around at Tom. "Except it doesn't really matter that I borrow it this minute. I can get it some other time."

"No, I want you to have it right now," Tom says, and begins rummaging through the various piles of books in the room, coming up empty. "I must have left it in the car," he adds. "I've tried to loan it to you several times. Remember? Stay here with Rosalee while I get it."

"It doesn't matter," Gemma whispers, tears forming at the corners of her eyes.

"Stay here," Tom insists, "I'll be back in a minute," and before she can object again, he's out the door. Gemma sits

down on the floor, and the two women turn their faces in opposite directions, the air between them clumsy and full. The
sound of crickets and frogs hum around them. Gemma
glances at Rosalee. She can tell by the weighty atmosphere in
the room that Tom and Rosalee have already experienced
that night of wild, uncompromising sex she thought would
happen. "So, are you and Tom going to get married or
what?" she asks.

Rosalee sighs. "I got tired of being alone, and I was afraid.
That's all it was. It won't happen again. It's not like I'm trying
to take him away from you or anything."

"I don't have him for you to take," Gemma says, "and I
don't want him. It doesn't matter." She hates tears that come
when she doesn't want them to and her voice being stuck in
her throat.

Outside on the porch, Tom stands at the door with the book
in his hands. He hears the women's voices low and urgent.
Oh, God, he thinks, they're bonding. He walks back down the
porch steps and decides to take refuge at Gilman Lee's.

"Just what is your problem, anyway? Who are you so afraid
of? Why are you here?" Gemma asks Rosalee.

Rosalee's story sneaks from her lips like an old-fashioned
fable. She tells Gemma about the beauty of doomed love,
about Frank with his whirlpool eyes, the excitement and danger that hang around him like yes-men. She tells Gemma
about how it started to go bad, how it was destined to do so.
She tells her all the details, except for the rape and beating
that took place after he shot the man. She can't bring herself
to tell that. "I was never afraid of anything until now. He's
made me into someone I don't even know."

Gemma sighs and leans her back against the wall. "Men,"
she says.

Rosalee lights a cigarette. "I promise you it won't happen
again between Tom and me."

The two women are still talking when Tom returns with a

six-pack of beer and *Twilight of the Idols.* "Made a little trip to Gilman's. Want one?" he says to Gemma.

"No, I've got to be going," she mutters and, when he hands her the book, she leaves abruptly and walks down the hill in the dark.

22

Chapter

Zipping up his jacket as a cool blast of wind whips him in the face, Ed Toothacre stands at the top of the mountain, watching his crew load the coal onto a truck. Winter is definitely around the corner, he thinks, glancing in the direction of Gilman's property, where a major seam of coal lies. After trying to determine a good location for augering out Gilman's coal, he's pretty much decided not to position the auger on June Collet's land, especially since Tom Jett, Gilman's new renter, walks the property line every morning looking for anything out of the ordinary. Ed can't figure a man like Gilman. Why wouldn't he want to get what he can out of his land? It's not doing him a bit of good otherwise, and when the operation is over, the top of the mountain will be leveled except for one corner. How is that going to look?

Ed has been considering placing the augering operation on Dwight Simpson's land, which joins Gilman's from the other side of the mountain, figuring it is as good a way as any to siphon out Gilman's coal. Ed has already spoken to Dwight about it, and on the condition that he receives compensation

Dwight is agreeable, not that Conroy needs his approval. According to the surface agreement, the company is allowed to drill holes anywhere they like. Ed looks down the mountain toward Gilman's old house and wonders why Tom Jett agreed to spy for Gilman Lee. Mulling this over, he turns to see Wade Miller driving up the hill in his Cherokee. It occurs to him that there might be a problem with the account he opened at the Pick Citizens' several weeks ago.

Wade brings his vehicle to a stop and jumps out. "How's it going?" he asks as he walks briskly toward Ed.

"Just fine. How's it going with you?"

"Great. I've not been around a strip mining operation in a long time. Just thought I'd visit."

"Glad you came by," Ed says, grinning.

Wade glances out toward Gilman's land. "I hear there's a lot of coal on his property. But he didn't sign the agreement, did he?"

"There's not as much as all that," Ed says, narrowing his eyes. "Wish he'd signed though."

"Have you got enough help up here?"

"What do you mean?"

"I mean, do you need to hire anyone else?"

Ed laughs. "You're not looking for work, are you, Wade?"

"It's not for me. It's for a buddy of mine."

"Actually, we don't need anyone right now."

"I bet you didn't realize that Dwight Simpson and me are buddies, did you?"

Ed stares at Wade long and hard. "What're you getting at, Wade?"

"I'm just saying that me and the guy who owns the property on the other side of this mountain go way back. Raised up together almost. He came to see me just the other day, and we talked a long time."

"What did you talk about?"

"Well, he asked my advice on something about mining—

augering in particular. But I didn't mean to get off the subject like that. I really came here to ask if you could hire this buddy of mine. Name's Fred Dudley. He's from Somerset and could sure use the work."

Ed sighs and looks back toward Gilman's property. "Tell him to come by tomorrow morning about seven o'clock, and I'll see what I can do."

The next morning, Frank drives his Escort up the hill to the strip mine. He isn't sure what they'll have him doing, but he soon finds out that they have assigned him to the washing operation. As he works he notices that much of the coal is etched with fossils of ferns and other plants and wonders how far the fossils date back. He listens to the man beside him talk about his Sunday job—preaching. It doesn't take the man long to ask Frank if he's a Christian. To keep the preacher, who has by now introduced himself as Wallace Couch, from trying to save his soul, Frank says yes, he is. One of the other workers, a man named Bige Barnes, has a college degree and talks about education as though it is more sacred than religion, says the world can be saved only through education, and makes knowledge sound like a radical concept, advocating it in such a way that a listener might think that Bige himself was the first person to think of it.

Wallace, the preacher, wonders aloud why, if education is the savior of the world, it didn't save Bige from working at a strip mine. Bige responds by questioning why God didn't save Wallace from the same fate, and adds, "Personally, I've got a teaching job lined up for next semester."

Wallace looks up at the sky and says, "Lord, forgive Bige."

Another worker named Duke Moore, who takes a break every hour on the hour to smoke a toke behind a pine tree, says, "Chill out, men, you're making twenty dollars a hour in a state where the cost of living is cheap. Maybe God and Education didn't think they was a need to save you'uns."

Frank doesn't say a word; he just listens.

At noon, the men wander down the mountain to have their lunch by the creek. "Did you say you was from Somerset?" Wallace asks Frank.

"Yes."

"Used to go fishing over there," Wallace says. "You don't talk like you're from Somerset."

"I lived in Louisville for a while. Guess I lost some of my accent."

"You don't talk like people in Louisville, either," Bige says. "That's where I went to college. Maybe you're talking a mix between the two."

"Maybe so," Frank says.

As they near the creek, Duke, the pot smoker, says to Frank, "I seen a nekked woman in this creek one day. It was that woman lives by the road over there, that real fair-skinned woman."

"Don't pay attention to Duke," Wallace instructs Frank. "He's said that before and ain't none of us fool enough to believe him." Wallace turns to Duke. "You've been smoking too many of them funny cigarettes. That's Gemma Collet you're talking about, and she works in a bank. Ain't no woman works in a bank'd do a thing like that."

"You wanta bet?" Duke says.

"It's against my religion," Wallace replies.

The men sit down and eat lunch with Duke, Bige, and Wallace still bickering and Frank listening. When they finish their meal, they start back up the mountain, passing close enough to Gilman's property to see his house through the trees.

"Speaking of odd actions, that feller from California's sure got 'em," Wallace says.

"What fellow from California?" Frank asks.

"The one that lives in that house right there."

Frank peers through the tree branches at the small weathered house, and the men walk closer, within several yards of it, as if drawn by their curiosity.

"How is he odd?" Frank asks.

"Can't put my finger on it," Wallace says, "but he's odd, I can tell."

"Wonder why a man from California moved to this particular mountain. Does he have family around here?" Frank asks.

"Not that I know of. Course you don't have any family around here either, and you moved here. I guess sometimes people do things that don't make sense," Bige says.

Inside the house, Rosalee lies on the floor, browsing through Tom's books. It is a cold day, and she has pulled out the small electric heater that Tom brought her yesterday. He doesn't want her starting a fire during the day, afraid someone might see the smoke and get suspicious. Tom is such a worrywart. She wishes Gilman would come to see her again and sing her a song.

"Did he buy this property?" Frank asks.

"No, he rents the place from Gilman Lee."

"The same Gilman that owns the machine shop?"

"That's right, and he's a tough customer," Bige says. "He's already come up here and threatened us not to get on his property. And his renter, Tom Jett's his name, comes out every morning and walks all along the line, making sure we haven't."

"Is there a need for him to be worried?" Frank asks.

"Maybe. Maybe not."

Tom Jett don't sing, Rosalee marvels. What must it be like not to ever sing? She starts humming a tune . . .

Duke cups his hand over his ear. "Shhh, Bige!" he whispers loudly. "I hear something."

"What?"

"Someone singing."

... but she stops when chill bumps cover her arms and legs, and the skin on her neck crawls back and forth. What would I see if I opened the curtains and looked out? Would the sun still be shining? Would squirrels be running around? She rolls over on the sleeping bag and closes her eyes.

The men stand still and listen attentively, but hear nothing.

"If you didn't smoke that loco weed, you wouldn't see and hear so many things," Wallace Couch says.

The men continue bickering as they walk away from the house and on up the hill to continue work.

That night at the Blue Mountain Inn, Frank goes straight to his room, takes a shower, grabs a beer from the ice cooler, and lies back on the bed. Things are shaping up nicely, he thinks, and wonders what his mother, Alaine, would say if she knew he was working at a strip mine. He wonders how she would react to any of the things he does, his mother with her good luck and laughter.

"It is not by some fluke that I'm here at the Blue Mountain Inn in Pick, Kentucky, Mother," Frank says aloud. "I did not happen upon this place like Grandfather happened upon those treasure chests. I'm here because I located Pick on a map and drove here on purpose. Have another mint julep, Alaine. Sit back and watch." Frank smiles and finishes his beer, proud of how easily he blended in with the workers at the mine today. "They think I'm a good ol' boy from Somerset, Mother."

He considers Wade Miller, the bank manager. It is hard to believe that Rosalee ever went out with him, but he guesses she did. He decides to talk to Wade soon about giving him directions to Rosalee's mother's house. Then Gilman Lee pops into his mind, the man he has heard about but not seen. Maybe I need to meet this musician/bootlegger/mechanic, he concludes, but he remembers the eerie feeling he got when he drove by the shop that day. I've still got a long way to go, he thinks, and closing his eyes he conjures up images of Rosalee. He begins doubting that she even returned to this part of the country. Then he stops wondering about anything at all and goes downstairs for dinner.

*T*om is unable to get the writing in the cave off his mind. At work today, he asks Betty Marker if she knows who owns the property where the abandoned cabin is located. She says she isn't sure but she thinks it belongs to a man named Daniel Sparks. She is also able to give Tom directions to the man's present address. After work Tom stops his car by the road in front of the location Betty described to him. He walks up a path and knocks on the door. Daniel Sparks turns out to be in his eighties, wearing a heavy flannel shirt and gray pants that are held up by suspenders.

"What de ye want?" Mr. Sparks says in a none too friendly tone of voice.

"Betty Marker referred me to you," Tom says, trying to see around the man to the inside. "She said you owned that log house about a mile down the road. The one that sits close to the top of the mountain. Is it yours?"

"Might be," Daniel says. "What de ye wanta know for?"

"Do you think I could come in for a minute? I'd like to ask you some questions."

"What kind of questions?"

"Just some questions about the house. I'd really like to come in."

"I said what kind of questions?"

"Well, I don't really want to ask that much. I just want to talk . . . about the house."

Daniel Sparks eyes Tom suspiciously but lets him in.

They sit down in birch-back chairs by a heating stove. "You

have a really fine place up there, Mr. Sparks. How old is that cabin?"

"Pretty damn old," Daniel says loudly as if he's afraid Tom can't hear. "I was borned in it. Growed up in it. Couldn't wait to git out of it. Where're you from, anyway?"

"California."

"That's a long ways off, ain't it? Never was out there, but I've heard a lot about it. Some good. Some not so good."

"Like a lot of other places," Tom says, hoping the man is warming up to him.

"Is that all you wanted to talk to me about?" Daniel shouts.

Tom smiles. "Well, I also wanted to ask you about the cave behind the house."

"You mean you've been up there? Seen the cave?"

"Yes, I took a walk up there. I hope you don't mind. I wonder if you could tell me about the writing in it. Do you know the writing I'm talking about?"

"Sure do. I used to play in that cave when I was a little feller. I allus wondered about that. I figured it was something the Indians wrote a long time ago."

"So it's been there as long as you can remember?"

"It was there when my pap built that house around nineteen hunnert."

"Do you mind if I go up there from time to time?"

"Well, it depends on what you're goin to do up there."

"I just like the place—that's all. I like sitting around up there . . . you know . . . to clear my head."

Daniel Sparks narrows his eyes. "Ye don't wanta drag a lot of other people up there with ye, do ye? I wouldn't want a whole crowd up there milling around, hemming and hawing over that cave."

"No way," Tom says.

Daniel Sparks shrugs. "Well, I reckon it's all right."

"Thanks for letting me talk to you, Mr. Sparks," Tom says and stands up to go. He takes a long look at the man sitting straight and alert in his birch-back chair. "Do you live here alone?"

"Hell, yeah," Daniel says. "My woman died ten years ago last month, and my children are scattered all over the place. If Mattie was still alive, she'd have you sitting in there at the table eating a meal. Never would let anyone walk out of here afore she fed 'em."

"I'd like to stop by again sometime and shoot the breeze with you if it's okay."

"I reckon that'd be all right," Daniel says, "if you was to quit calling me Mr. Sparks. Makes me feel like a deacon."

Tom is still thinking about his visit with Daniel when he steps in the door of his house and finds Rosalee pacing the floor. "Take me to Mom's," she says.

"Right now?"

"As soon as it gets dark."

"I thought Gilman wanted to take you."

"Gilman don't have to do everything for me."

Tom studies Rosalee's face. "Are you leaving because of what happened between us the other night?"

"Not exactly. I just want to see Mom."

Later that night, Rosalee packs a few things, and they drive to Mildred's house. Tom drops her off at the front door and asks her to keep in touch. On his way back home, he stops by Gilman's shop and tells him about Rosalee's change of address.

Gilman says, "Good. Mildred could prob'ly use her company, and you could prob'ly do without it."

That night, Rosalee and Mildred sit up late and watch a talk show on which one of the guests brings out a dog that is supposed to have a talent for singing. The man sits down at a piano and starts playing, the dog howls, and the host, who acts a lot like Johnny Carson, taps his pencil on the desk and says, "That's wild."

"Why don't you get a pet, Mom?" Rosalee asks. "Seems like a dog would be company to you."

"I don't need one. A dog is like a child, Rosalee. I've already got a child—you."

"I'm not a child anymore."

"The hell you ain't. A child is a child until you stop worrying over them. I ain't stopped yet."

"No need to worry over me, Mom."

"Oh, no? What am I supposed to do when I know they's a man after you that's prob'ly trying to kill you?" Mildred draws her legs on the couch and pulls her nightgown over her feet. "Why on earth do you take up with such shit-asses? "

"I don't know, Mom. You tell me. Daddy was a shit-ass, too, wouldn't he? I mean, he did leave the country right after he found out you was pregnant with me. Right?"

"Yeah, but that learned me a lesson. It appears to me that you don't learn."

"It's just that I don't like men unless they're wild or dangerous."

"Looks like you'd turn against a man that's trying to kill you. Ain't you worried about saving your skin?"

"Of course I'm worried. Why do you think I ran away from him and came here? I *am* trying to save my skin; and I do hate him, Mom, but it's like they's two of him, and one of the two I still love."

Mildred goes to her bedroom, and when she returns, she's carrying a guitar. "Look what I found in the closet yesterday. I didn't know it was still here. I thought you'd carried it off someplace and lost it."

Rosalee smiles, picks up the guitar, and starts playing a tune.

23
Chapter

It is early Saturday morning, and Gilman wakes with a start and sits straight up, pointing his gun around. Day is just breaking, and the room is still nearly dark. He feels as if he has forgotten to do something that he should have done, and he sits there aiming his gun at shadows, his heart beating like a buzzard's wings. Maybe I'm goin to have that heart attack Gemma warned me about, he thinks, and tries to remember what it is he has forgotten to do, finally realizing that he hasn't gone fishing this summer. Here it is, near the end of October. I can't believe I've let a whole summer slip by without goin fishing once. Must be getting old, he thinks, twirling the snub-nosed .38 around his fingers. Then he rethinks: Nope, must be something else. He jumps up and runs over to Ten-Fifteen's trailer. "Hey, buddy," he yells, banging on the door, "we're goin fishing."

Ten-Fifteen stumbles to the door and opens it. The first thing he sees in the dim morning light is Gilman's smile spread all over his face. "Grab your tackle box, buddy," Gilman tells him.

"Ain't you goin to eat breakfast first?"

"It's best to go fishing on a empty stomach," Gilman says. "That way a person's more interested in catching something."

"I thought we had a job to do today. What about Ned Begley's van?"

"They's more important things in this world, Ten-Fifteen, than Ned Begley's van. Now get your ass in gear. Winter's about to set in any minute."

"Where you got a mind to go?"

"Washburn Creek."

Ten-Fifteen begins to smile, remembering the last time they went fishing on Washburn Creek. "Good a place as any," he says. "Why don't we stop by Tom Jett's and see if he wants to go? I bet he's just laying around with nothing to do."

"The more the merrier," Gilman says.

While Ten-Fifteen drags out the tent and camping utensils, Gilman walks down the bank to the creek and starts digging for worms. He uncovers whole clumps knotted together and drops them wriggling and squirming into a bucket of dirt. He has a closet full of rods and reels that he's collected over the years, and when he gets back to his apartment he chooses three, checks their lines, and puts them in the truck bed. He prepares two ice coolers: one for beer, and the other for hot dogs and pickled bologna, just in case the fish aren't biting. He and Ten-Fifteen pack the coolers and a guitar out to the truck and take off for Tom Jett's house.

It is a cool, damp morning, and the sky is lavender-blue. The mountains are still sprinkled with autumn colors, but most of the leaves have begun to turn brown and fall from the trees. Ten-Fifteen knows every curve and rough spot on this road, every house and trailer that is parked beside it. He knows exactly when Gilman will put his foot on the brake, or step harder on the gas pedal, or turn the steering wheel to the right or left. Ten-Fifteen likes knowing what will happen next, although it is seldom easy knowing the next sequence of events when Gilman is in the picture.

Tom Jett got up early this morning, walking over fallen dew-covered leaves, traversing the entire property line, looking for signs of trespassing. He paid close attention to the area around June Collet's boundary, but he found nothing that suggested an augering operation. Tom didn't sleep well last night for thinking about Gemma and Rosalee and his own presence in this quagmire of a place on earth. Although Rosalee has been gone for a week, he and Gemma still haven't bridged their differences. He has visited her, though. The other evening as he returned from work, he noticed her raking leaves in the yard. He walked down the sloping path to her house and unlatched the gate.

"Rosalee went back to her mother's house," he told her.

Gemma turned to him. "What am I supposed to do? Applaud?"

Tom sat down his lunch box. "Don't you think you've overreacted a little to this whole thing? Let's go over what happened. Rosalee is either in danger or perceives herself to be. She told Gilman about it and he tried to hide her where she would be safe. She stayed with me for a while, and for that you threw a conniption fit. I repeat, don't you think you overreacted?"

"Maybe, but then you did go to bed with her, didn't you? A man usually lives up to a woman's expectations."

Tom glared at her. "I still don't know why you got so upset. It's not like we pledged vows to each other."

Gemma threw down her rake. "Well, I guess maybe I misread what happened, but I'm probably not as experienced in the ways of the world as you are—especially since I've not dated anyone in twelve years. Looks like I put a little more significance on what happened between us than you did. My mistake. It won't happen again."

He reached out his hand and placed it on Gemma's shoulder, realizing how fragile she is under her rough exterior.

"I'm sorry you feel that way." He leaned forward as if to kiss her, but she stepped back and marched into the house.

He hasn't been to see her since, but he imagines himself doing so even now as he finishes this morning's inspection of Gilman's property.

As he steps onto his porch, he spots Gilman and Ten-Fifteen walking up the hill. Gilman is humming a tune. Now what? Tom asks himself. Maybe they need some other friend to move in with me, a friend who is either on the lam from the law or being chased by some perverse Southern Mafia.

"Find anything interesting out there this morning?" Gilman yells, as he moves in quick, boisterous steps toward him.

"Nothing," Tom says, glancing suspiciously beyond Gilman and Ten-Fifteen for signs of someone else, troubled and weary, lagging behind them.

"In that case, let's go fishing," Gilman says.

"Fishing?"

"Yeah, fishing. You've heard of it, ain't you? Put a hook on a line, drop it in the water? Fishing."

"This early?" Tom, who was all set to go back to bed, asks.

"Hell, we're late already. It's daylight," Gilman booms, as if he's trying to wake up the world. "If you need to do anything before we go, now's the time. Why don't you bring that tape player of yours in case you get edgy for some of that shitty music you listen to?"

Later, as the men are piling into the truck, Tom Jett notices a light come on in Gemma's house. She probably gets up this early every morning, he theorizes, so she'll have time to consider all her disagreements with the world before she leaves for work. He turns to Gilman and Ten-Fifteen. "I'll be back in a minute." He runs down the driveway to her house, knocks on the door, and, when she answers, stands there for a moment, taking in her cool, pale image, not knowing how to phrase the question he wants to ask. "I'm going fishing with Gilman."

"So?" she says, not batting an eye.

"So I don't think we'll be coming back tonight, and if Rosa-lee were to have any trouble neither me nor Gilman would be around. Would you call her at her mother's tonight just to see if everything is okay?"

Gemma shakes her head and looks up at the porch light as if to say, "Why me?"

Instead she says, "If you're so worried about her, why are you going?"

"Forget it, then," Tom says, and starts to walk away.

"Okay, I'll call her," Gemma says.

Tom turns around, smiles, walks back to where she is stand-ing, takes her face in his hands, and kisses her. "I need to talk to you as soon as I get back."

Gemma is so flustered that all she can think to say is, "Have fun."

In a few minutes, the men are on their way to Washburn Creek. It is a fifty-mile drive, and Tom puts in a tape of Schu-mann sonatas as they cruise along. Gilman listens carefully through most of two movements, then remarks, "That feller can't decide if he's relaxed or not. Makes me jittery. Let's lis-ten to something else." When Tom puts in a Wagner tape, Gilman says, "This one's out of his mind, but I like him." The truck sails down the highway amid ever heightening crescendos.

About an hour later, they turn onto a narrow dirt road that runs near Washburn Creek. The road is so constricted that when a truck comes toward them from the opposite direction, they have to pull over to the side to let it pass. Tom notices that Gilman and the driver of the other truck tip their hats as their trucks meet, yet fail to smile in recognition. "Do you know him?" Tom asks.

"Not from Adam," Gilman says, "but when you're out in this neck of the woods and meet up with a stranger, you tip your hat so he'll know you're harmless—not that I am."

They drive about two miles farther and park by the road. A grove of trees stands beside their parking place, and beyond the trees Washburn Creek flows toward the Kentucky River. The three men get out and tote their supplies toward the water. As Tom meanders through the trees, he begins to notice that he is walking among graves and that paths that have been cleared off and tended lead from one grave to another. Forgetting about Gilman and Ten-Fifteen, he sets down his bundle, walks along the trails, and soon discovers that there are fifty or sixty graves scattered among the trees.

"This is a cemetery!" he exclaims to Ten-Fifteen, who appears out of nowhere and marches past him with another load of supplies.

"Sure is," Ten-Fifteen says, "a old one at that."

"Are you goin to help us get this stuff down to the water or are you goin to stand there all day?" Gilman says, walking by.

"Why would someone put a cemetery in a grove of trees?" Tom asks, picking up his bundle and following Gilman to the campsite.

"They prob'ly wouldn't no trees here at one time. Did you notice how old them graves are? The kin of the dead back there must have moved off or died themselves. Either way, the graveyard was forgot, and trees grew up, as trees will. Now people have started taking care of the graves again, just because they're old. Every time I come here, I tidy up a bit."

Tom wanders back into the grove of trees and inspects the tombstones. Some of them are just flat rocks sticking out of the ground, their lettering worn away by wind and rain. Others show names and dates: William Johnson, BORN 1743 / DIED 1795; Sarah Johnson, BORN 1750 / DIED 1797. Most of the tombstones date back to the late 1700s and early 1800s. He finds two small stones belonging to twin boys, who were not only born the same day, June 5, 1865, but died the same day, March 1, 1866. The most recent stones are dated 1918—five of them belonging to children.

"Must have been the flu," Gilman says, walking up behind Tom. "My pap used to tell me they was a bad flu around nineteen eighteen that took a lot of people."

Gilman leads Tom around the paths, pointing out graves of special interest, and says, "C'mere, I bet you didn't see this one." They step off the trail into a thick clump of trees, where a tombstone stands apart from all the rest. The epitaph says, Zack Morley, BORN 1935 / DIED 1985. In front of the stone, the ground is sunken and poison ivy covers the depression.

"Zack ain't there anymore. Someone dug him up about four years ago," Gilman says. "One day I come out here to go fishing with some buddies, and found him gone. Must have just happened because the dirt was still fresh, laying in piles around the grave. I don't know who would a done it, or why. Maybe they was something about Zack Morley they wanted to get closer to. Right now Zack is prob'ly hanging in someone's closet with their old clothes and other secrets."

"Who was Zack Morley?" Tom asks.

"A friend of mine," Gilman says. "A real good friend."

After Gilman has gone back to the campsite by the creek, Tom still stands in front of the tombstone, looking at the poison ivy. The evergreens about him are so thick that their branches could provide shelter were it to rain. He feels as if he's in a time warp and that Zack Morley might step out from behind a pine tree at any moment and shake his hand.

When he returns to the campsite, he baits his hook, casts out, and the three fishermen retire their rods to forked branches that Gilman has stuck in the ground, not particularly concerned at the moment whether the fish are biting. They pop open beers, sit back, and relax. Across Washburn Creek, the land turns into low-lying hills—grassy, with few trees. A white church that looks as if it were transplanted from Vermont rests on one of the knolls; a red barn sits on another. The air is still and quiet except for the cawing of crows as Washburn Creek coasts by like a silver mountain trout.

"This is the closest creek to where we live that ain't been destroyed by strip mines," Gilman says. "I could stay here from now on. Right here." He leans back and closes his eyes as if eavesdropping on an inside conversation.

Ten-Fifteen falls asleep beside Gilman; but Tom Jett remains wide awake, listening for ghosts from the graveyard to come waltzing down to the water, occasionally glancing around at his sleeping partners as he keeps vigil over the fishing poles. Tom wonders what makes Gilman tick. The man seems to have no motive for living other than playing music and having good times. Is that what drives him? How can he party nightly and still have enough energy to instigate early-morning fishing trips such as this? He's fifty-four years old. Why isn't he tired?

Beside Gilman, Ten-Fifteen dozes peacefully, his arms spread in their quarter-past pose. It is obvious that he dressed in a hurry this morning. A baseball cap is askance on his head, his tennis shoes are unlaced, and his flannel shirt is stuffed half in, half out of partially zipped corduroy pants. Ten-Fifteen smiles even in sleep.

Tom wanders back to the graveyard, sits down by Zack Morley's stone, and speculates about where the body is now. He wonders what kind of man Zack was, if he had problems with women. Every now and then, Tom considers moving on to someplace new—perhaps to Tennessee or Virginia. On the other hand, this place is a border region—not quite North, South, East, West, or even Midwest. Like Tom, it doesn't fit. He feels as though he has known the people here all of his life, especially Gemma—pure white, standing in the mire of her desecrated creek, unbending as a statue. She is not an easy person to care for, but she is all he can think about. He intends to meet with her when he gets back from this fishing trip and walk beside her up a mountain.

Tom's thoughts drift to the writing in the cave. Daniel Sparks had said he thought the writing was left by the Indians. But it wasn't. Tom knows the Indian languages, not well enough to speak, but he recognizes them when he sees them. Tom wonders if this mysterious language that he stumbled on one evening as he drove home from work is what he came to this part of the country to find. He decides not to tell Gilman about it, or anyone else for that matter—not yet. He thinks that for the time being the words are meant for him alone, that they will tell him something he needs to know.

When Tom recalls his family and California, the remembrance seems to be of a people and place that exist only in his imagination. He sees his mother and father in sand and mists of rain, twirling like toy dancers, and considers calling them. He'd like to tell them about the graveyard and Washburn Creek, about Gilman, Ten-Fifteen, and Gemma.

Tom's thoughts are interrupted by a yell and scuffle coming from the campsite. He runs through the graveyard toward the creek and finds Ten-Fifteen and Gilman standing side by side—Ten-Fifteen holding the rod and Gilman reeling. The two men work together well, as if they have had lots of practice. Finally a fair-sized bass appears near the edge of the stream, and Gilman steps aside while Ten-Fifteen flips it onto the bank.

Gilman hooks the fish on a chain and drops it into water.

"Next time I want to see if I can reel it in myself," Ten-Fifteen says.

A smile spreads across Gilman's face. "Sure thing," he says.

Beside Washburn Creek, the day slows to a crawl. Tom catches a couple of bluegill and a catfish. Gilman pulls in three bass. Tom listens to Ten-Fifteen and Gilman tell stories about gunfights and people breaking other people out of jail. He dozes while they reminisce about a man who died from drinking rubbing alcohol and about another who fell drunk in a ditch and drowned. They talk about the stupidity of the county law against selling alcohol. "If it was legal, people wouldn't be so attracted to it," Ten-Fifteen says.

"If it was legal, I'd be out of the bootleg business," Gilman says, "but that'd be all right." Gilman plucks a dry weed out of the ground and picks at his teeth as Ten-Fifteen turns his attention to his fishing line.

"Me and my buddy, Zack, used to come here to fish," Gilman says, as if he needs to proclaim from time to time the significance of Washburn Creek.

"How did Zack die?" Tom asks.

"Got killed by a man named Landon Couch. Landon run him up against a tree with a truck. They was fighting over a woman, a pretty woman. Funny thing was, I was dating her too, but neither one of 'em knew that."

"Who was the woman—not Rosalee?"

"No, not Rosalee. There's more pretty women than Rosalee. Actually she was Landon's wife."

"Where's Landon now?"

"Dead. Got killed in a mining accident. How are you and Gemma getting along?"

"Could be better." Tom opens another beer and decides to shift the conversation away from Gemma, finding it impossible to discuss her with anyone. "Sometimes I wonder if Rosalee is just imagining this whole thing about Frank Denton. Do you think that's possible?" he asks Gilman.

"In my opinion, she's overestimating him, but I don't reckon she's imagining him."

"I feel better now that she's staying with her mother," Tom says.

"It's improving things with you and Gemma, I bet."

Tom sighs. "I don't know about that. Speaking of Gemma, this morning I asked her to call Rosalee to make sure she's all right, since both of us are out here away from a phone."

Gilman laughs. "Let's hope poor old Frank Denton don't mess with Rosalee tonight then. We wouldn't want anyone to have to answer to Gemma Collet."

Tom grunts in agreement, and realizing with some surprise

that he doesn't like to hear Gilman even say Gemma's name, he switches the conversation again. "Is there any chance you and Rosalee will take up where you left off a few years ago?"

"Me and Rosalee don't think in terms like that. We don't like to shut out other possibilities."

"Sounds like you might be interested in someone else."

"I'm interested in a lot of things. Take for example this coal thing. I'm interested in that. I've just about decided not to do anything about it, though, unless they try to auger out my coal. If they do, I'll have to drag some tricks out of my bag. Gemma's offered to help out, and Ten-Fifteen's in on it, too."

"What tricks?" Tom asks, a little surprised to learn that Gemma is in cahoots with Gilman.

"Still ain't thought it out."

"Maybe I'd like to help," Tom says.

"It's not your battle."

"Everything is my battle," Tom says.

Engrossed in their conversation, the two men don't immediately notice Ten-Fifteen grab hold of his fishing line, which has been stretched taut by a huge fish, but their attention is aroused when he starts trying to reel it in, holding the rod in his ten hand, the line spinning wildly as the fish swims downstream. He tries to bring his fifteen hand close enough to the reel to grab hold, laboring until veins are popped out on his face. But his hand trembles and shakes, moving an inch or two closer to the handle but not close enough. Finally, with the rod still in his ten hand, he clinches the handle in his teeth, and slowly starts reeling, the fish remaining precariously hooked for about five minutes before the line becomes taut again. Ten-Fifteen continues to hold the rod in one hand and reel with his clenched teeth. He starts walking backward up the bank and into the graveyard, still reeling until finally the bass is dragged onto the bank, flopping and slippery and nearly two feet long.

Gilman gets up and takes the bass off the hook, puts him on

a chain, and hangs the chain in the water. He turns to his buddy, looks him in the eye, and lets out a yell. Ten-Fifteen and Tom join in, and the three men holler as though they're falling off skyscrapers. Then the music begins, and the fish-frying, and the serious drinking. It isn't until a couple of hours later, while Tom is cleaning up the camp area and Ten-Fifteen is standing straight as a sentinel listening to Gilman spin another tale of his youthful misadventures, that the change is noted.

Gilman stops midsentence and eyes Ten-Fifteen left to right. "Fo' my God, buddy," he says to him, "you've gained five minutes."

Ten-Fifteen looks around as though Gilman is talking to someone else. "I've what?"

"You ain't ten-fifteen anymore, Ten-Fifteen. You're ten-twenty."

Ten-Fifteen turns his attention to his arm, and Tom looks up from his cleaning to study the change. Sure enough, Ten-Fifteen's arm is hanging about five minutes lower than it was before. "This may give me a whole new outlook," Ten-Fifteen says. "You reckon it'll stay? Wonder what caused it to move. Reckon it was when I was trying to reel in? You ain't goin to start calling me Ten-Twenty, are you?"

Gilman yelps like a hound and runs to his truck, bringing back a fifth of mescal. "This calls for a celebration," he says. And the men look at the bottle with a momentary silence, respect, and dread. Night settles, and the mescal, beer, and fish rest in the men's stomachs as uneasily as common household objects in surreal landscapes. The moon and stars spread an eerie light around the graveyard, bullfrogs croak in the reeds, and a huge fish swims by, causing ripples to wash like waves against the banks of Washburn Creek.

The men tell stories in hushed voices as if the words they speak are too profound to be understood when spoken in normal tones. At one point Gilman says he's going for a drive be-

cause if he sits still much longer, he'll never be able to move
again. When he gets to the truck he discovers that he has lost
his keys, and for the remainder of the night all events are cat-
egorized according to whether they took place before or after
his keys were lost. Gilman wanders through the graveyard
and by the water playing the guitar and singing songs. Tom
requests "Blue Eyes Crying in the Rain." Gilman says, "The
last time I sang that song, I had my keys. Now they are gone,"
and he performs a particularly mournful rendition of the
song. Thus the night progresses and finally ends, the keys remaining lost until the morning when Ten-Fifteen discovers
them lying on top of Zack Morley's tombstone. None of the
men quite remember the night as it really was. They come
away with only an impression of something strange and beautiful and a little scary.

24
Chapter

hree mornings in a row Mildred has made pancakes.
"I'm goin to get fat," Rosalee says, cutting off a large
bite and swirling it in syrup.

"That'll be the day. You've never had a ounce of fat on you."
Mildred yawns and toys with her food. "I got the big eye last
night and couldn't go to sleep."

"Why?"

"Things running through my mind—every old thing in the
world."

"Like what?"

"Like the man that's after you, for one thing. And then I got
to thinking about the woman thats head was cut off. Why do
you reckon them fools did that to her? I mean, they'd just
come to rob her store. They wouldn't no need to go that far.
What was on their minds?"

Rosalee sighs. "Nothing was on their minds, Mom, except
a craving to do damage. I don't know why you keep talking
about it. It happened a long time ago. You didn't even know
the woman. She was just someone who had a store and got

robbed, and one of the worst things in the world happened to her. I wish you wouldn't think about it so much."

Mildred stares down at her plate. "Why do you reckon I do?"

"I don't know, but you're not the only one. A lot of people want to know what it's like to be that afraid, that close to death, to be that alive. They want to read about it in the paper, hear it on the radio, and see it on TV—to get as close as they can without actually being the one that gets hurt or killed."

Tears come to Mildred's eyes as she gazes out the window over the kitchen sink. "I'm afraid something bad's goin to happen to you."

"Nothing's goin to happen to me," Rosalee says and walks over behind Mildred's chair and starts massaging her shoulders. She follows her mother's eyes out the kitchen window. "Remember how I used to collect fall leaves and press them in the Bible? I think I'll go out this morning and bring us back some pretty ones before they all turn brown."

Later she pulls on her jeans and a pair of boots and walks through the harvested garden to a thicket of oak, maple, and poplar trees to search for the remaining deep red and gold leaves. She sits on a rock and looks back toward the house, realizing that Gilman, Tom, Gemma, and Ten-Fifteen probably think she's blowing the Frank Denton situation out of proportion. That's really why she came back up here to her mother's house; she wanted to prove to herself that she wasn't in danger and that she wasn't putting her mother in danger, either. But it's not working. Just my being here makes Mom dwell on mutilated bodies. I was wrong to come up here. I am putting her in danger because he *is* coming for me. I've got to go back to Tom's for a while, and then maybe I'll take off for parts unknown.

When Rosalee returns to the house, she spreads her collection on the kitchen table, takes out the Bible, and presses the leaves between the pages. Mildred watches her daughter closely. "You're leaving again, ain't you?"

"Yeah, I am. It's safer at Tom's. If Frank was to come to Pick, he could easily find out where you live. This would be the first place he'd look for me. He wouldn't look for me at Tom's. I shouldn't have come back up here."

Rosalee dials Gilman's number. There is no answer. She dials Ten-Fifteen's number—no answer there, either. She waits an hour and calls them again, but they are not at home. They are at Washburn Creek, and Ten-Fifteen is reeling in the fish that will change his time to ten-twenty.

She decides to wait until dark and call them again, since Gilman wouldn't want to pick her up until after dark, anyway. She and Mildred sit on the porch and sing songs, and as they sing, Rosalee looks out at the mountain beside the house and spots a trail through a grove of leafless trees. She points to it. "Do you see that old trail up there? They's one just like it that goes around the mountain from Tom's house."

"It's the same trail," Mildred says. "It goes all the way to Harlan."

"You mean it would lead me back to Tom's house?"

"Sure would."

"Well, that's what I'll do then."

"Walk? Why, I could drive you down there."

"I'd rather walk," Rosalee says. She packs the few things she brought into a pillowcase, hooks a strap to her guitar, slings it over her back, and takes off.

*B*y the time Gemma gets off work Saturday evening, she has almost changed her mind about calling Rosalee. Does Tom think she can raise Rosalee's spirits? Is she supposed to tell her not to give in to her fear? Gemma isn't so sure that there is nothing to be afraid of. This world is crawling with weird people, she considers, remembering what her mother told her about Uncle Jake, who was definitely left-from-center. According to the book she borrowed from Tom, Nietzsche wasn't exactly the boy next door, and she even thinks of herself as pretty strange. Why shouldn't Frank Denton be crazy enough to come looking for Rosalee?

When she gets home and steps inside her kitchen, June has dinner ready as usual. Gemma sits down and props her elbows on the table, still thinking about the situation at hand.

"What's on your mind?" June asks.

"Nothing."

"Good, because I want to talk to you about something." June looks up at the ceiling and down at the floor. "That coal money is liable to start rolling in any minute. Did you ever think any more about going to England with me?"

Gemma sighs. "Yeah, I think about it all the time. Personally, I can't wait to see Big Ben and the Tower of London. Figure just seeing them'll change my life. How about you?"

"Why don't you stop your smart mouth and talk straight for a change?" June snaps.

"Okay, I've not thought about it, but if you get any money I hope you *do* go to England. That'd be better than buying new furniture or getting a new roof put on the house. I hope you get some fun out of it."

"I will," June says, "because I'm going."

"Good for you. Bring me back a souvenir."

When June is busy washing the dishes, Gemma goes into the living room and makes the phone call.

"Can I speak to Rosalee?" she asks Mildred.

"Rosalee's not here."

"Yes, she is. I know all about it. I know she was staying at Tom's. I know she's in trouble with some man and that she went back to your house. Can I talk to her?"

There is a momentary pause on the other end of the line. "Well, she's still not here."

"What do you mean?"

"I mean she left for Tom's house a couple of hours ago. Walked there on that old road."

Gemma hangs up and goes back into the kitchen. "I'm going out," she tells June.

"Fine," June says.

As Gemma approaches Tom's house, she hears Rosalee playing the guitar and singing "Hello, Walls."

"Hello, Gemma," Rosalee sings, not missing a beat when Gemma steps inside the door. "Do you play the guitar?"

"No, I play the banjo."

"Do you have one?"

"Yeah, I guess it's still in the attic."

"Why don't you go get it, and we'll play some music."

"I'm not very good at it."

"All I care is that you play," Rosalee says. "Besides, I bet you're good enough to be on the Opry."

"Not hardly, but I'll go down and get it. In case you're wondering where Tom is, he went fishing with Gilman Lee."

"Really? Well, I'm glad. That boy needs to have more fun."

Gemma stands there, a little embarrassed to ask Rosalee the thing she wants to know. "So you're going to be staying here, now? Why did you leave your mom's house?"

"It was doing her more harm than good for me to be there."

She starts to ask her why, but changes her mind. "Well, I'll go get the banjo."

As Gemma walks back to her mother's house, she regards the change in Rosalee. She seems different than the person she and Tom found crouching in the corner the other day— less afraid. When she gets home, Gemma lets down the trap door to the attic.

June gets up from the couch and stands by the ladder as Gemma steps up. "What're you looking for?"

"Mice," Gemma says.

June shakes her head. Now that the weather is getting

chilly, she guesses her daughter has thought up a new activity to replace the old one of sitting naked in the creek. First water, now mice, June notifies the worrying side of her brain.

Gemma finds the banjo leaning against the wall, spiderwebs spun between the strings, dust layered over the frets. She picks it up and holds it in her hands. It was her father's. She can picture him now, sitting at the table wearing a T-shirt and jeans, plucking a ditty, and never cracking a smile. Always, his face became like stone when he played. It was as if he forced all of his feelings, facial expressions, and thoughts into his fingers, and all other bodily activities shut themselves down for the duration of the tune he was picking.

She finds a rag lying in a corner, shakes out the dust, and wipes the banjo clean. It is badly out of tune, and she's afraid the strings will break if she tightens them much. She decides it will have to do and goes back down the ladder into the living room.

"Where're you goin with that?" June asks.

"Back on my walk."

"You're goin for a walk, carrying your daddy's banjo?"

"That's right."

"Okay. Go ahead. See if I care. Maybe you ought to take it down to the creek and set it in the water. Make sure you pull its strings off first, though, so it can float downstream naked."

"I'll be back late unless I decide to stay out all night," Gemma says.

"With the banjo?"

"You got it," Gemma says, walking out the door.

On her way back to Tom's house, she notices a white Escort driving slowly up the gravel road toward the strip mine. The man in the car looks around at her, and for an instant she thinks she recognizes him, but then he drives on toward the strip mine before she can connect a name to the face. Gemma wonders if the miners have started working on Saturday nights. As she nears Tom's porch, she hears Rosalee playing the guitar and singing. She plays well and has a voice that is a mix between Peggy Lee and Patsy Cline. Gemma stands there for a moment, listening before she goes inside.

"There she is," Rosalee says, when Gemma opens the door. "And with her banjo, too. Do you smoke?"

"No."

"I harvested me some of Gilman's pot. He'll prob'ly kill me if he finds out. I guess if you don't smoke you never smoked pot."

Gemma shakes her head, no.

"You wanta try some?"

"No, but you go ahead," Gemma says. "Are we going to play music or what?" she adds and sits down.

Rosalee begins playing the "Tennessee Waltz."

"That's a pretty slow song for a banjo," Gemma says.

"I know," Rosalee agrees, "but I like it." She stands up and walks around the room singing while Gemma concentrates on playing the banjo.

When Rosalee finishes the song, she starts in on "A Fool Such as I."

"That one's slow, too," Gemma remarks. "I don't think I ever heard a banjo with either one of those songs."

"Me either," Rosalee says and keeps on singing.

The women continue to play music—they play slow songs, fast songs, songs they can't remember the words to. They remember hints and suggestions of songs that they puzzle over for minutes at a time. It grows dark outside and late in the night.

*F*rank Denton is not in his room at the Blue Mountain Inn. He is on top of the mountain, walking around the mining site. Earlier today, Ed Toothacre phoned and asked him if he could

fill in for the regular night watchman who called in sick. Frank
knows the watchman is not really ill. From what he has heard,
the man has a romance going with Popov vodka. This isn't the
first night he has been asked to fill in for him, and he doesn't
mind these nights alone on the mountain. His eyes have ad-
justed to the darkness around him, and he takes in a deep
breath of cool air, lets it fill his lungs with the scent of dry
leaves and pine.

Frank imagines he hears Rosalee singing somewhere in the
distance. This is not an uncommon occurrence since he often
imagines her voice, her laughter, her songs, but tonight the
music seems clearer than usual. He hears not only her voice,
but her guitar and a banjo. Then he remembers the woman
he saw this evening as he was driving up the mountain, the
white woman that Duke, the pot smoker, claimed had a habit
of sitting naked in the creek. She was walking up the path to
the house on the hill, and she was carrying a banjo. This is not
just something I'm imagining, he realizes. It must be the white
woman's voice that I hear. Perhaps these hills breed the same
silky-sounding voice in every woman. It must be the man from
California accompanying her on the guitar. Several times
when Frank has gone to Betty Marker's to buy beer, he has
seen Tom Jett walking around her house carrying a hammer
or saw. But he's never been introduced. Strange, though, that
he would have a playing style like Rosalee's, Frank thinks, as
he sits on the ground and leans against the side of a small
shed, listening.

Rosalee stops playing and relights her cigarette. "How
have you managed it?" she asks Gemma. "To be alone all these
years?"

Gemma lays the banjo in her lap. "How have you managed

being around people all these years? Personally, I can't stand them. Besides, I'm not really alone. I work at the bank every day. People are always coming into a bank, you know; I see them at their worst—when they are borrowing, withdrawing, and depositing money. Then there's the people I work with. I'm so tired of them, I can't even stand to tell you about them, and finally there's my mother when I come home in the evening. I'm never alone. I wish I was."

"What I meant was, you don't socialize much."

"You got that right. I'd rather have a dream at night than go to a party. Dreams are more interesting because you never know how they'll end. Usually when people tell their dreams, they're not quite honest about what happened, because what takes place in them is so strange and unheard of that they don't want to own up."

Rosalee looks down at the floor. "Had you rather go home right now than to be having this conversation?"

"No."

"I hate to get real crude, here," Rosalee says, "but what about M-E-N?"

Gemma fidgets with the banjo strings. "What about them?"

"Well, I mean, keeping yourself good company, thinking, and dreaming are all fine things to do, but that don't stand up to men . . . at least in my opinion, it don't."

"That's your opinion," Gemma says, adding, "I think maybe I *will* take a puff off one of your cigarettes."

The women walk outside and sit on the porch. As an owl spreads its wings and glides from one tree to another, Rosalee puts her finger to her lips, signaling Gemma to be quiet. "When I was little," Rosalee whispers, "I used to think owls were ghosts hiding in trees, talking to each other. I wish I could still believe things like that."

"I used to believe in ghosts, too—Indian ghosts. I still do."

Rosalee and Gemma listen to the subtle music just beneath the birdsongs—the rustle of leaves and the rattle of tree branches.

"If Frank Denton is so bad, why were you ever attracted to him?" Gemma asks.

"It was the danger. I'm always attracted to it. I like people who surprise me. Gilman Lee used to surprise me; that's why I liked him. Then I met Frank. I never knew what he might do."

"What kind of things did he do?"

"Well, take, for example, this. He knew how much I always liked Willie Nelson, right? One night—don't ask me how he did it—he got hold of Willie's phone number and called him up. Said, 'I got a little lady, here, who is just dying to say hello to you.' Willie got on the phone and talked to me for forty-five minutes. Anyway, Frank always managed to do things that other people just think about doing. One time he took me up in a hot-air balloon, and we got drunk and made love in it. It's a wonder we ever come down. He wrote poetry, too. Can you believe it? Pretty poetry. Well, all of it wouldn't pretty, but it made a person think, you know. And he was a good lover. I know this is going to sound strange in light of how evil I've claimed he is, but Frank was good-hearted, too. Remember that movie *Sophie's Choice*? One night we rented that movie, and he cried like a baby, sat around depressed for a week. He got mad at me cause I wouldn't as depressed as he was. Frank is a good feller until he gets turned off on you, then look out."

"What made him turn against you?"

"I'm not sure, but I think it was a combination of things, like the fact that I didn't get as depressed as him over *Sophie's Choice* and the fact that I didn't get excited over a sunrise he'd woke me up after a night of hard drinking to see. Things just kept piling up, I guess. I know I should have left him way before I did, but I couldn't."

Gemma takes another puff off the cigarette, looks around at the darkness, and for the first time in a long time she feels afraid, not of anything in particular. It is a loss of control that she feels, a general notion that something is amiss—she feels as if a copperhead is crawling up the porch steps, getting ready to strike, and she can't move. Maybe it's the pot, Gemma thinks, and remembers having heard that pot makes some people paranoid. She turns to look at Rosalee.

"He'll kill me, you know," Rosalee says quietly, "and he'll smile, too, while he's doing it. At least I've lived a full life. They's not much I've missed out on." Rosalee looks up at the stars. "Maybe he won't kill me. Maybe he'll just take me with him and never let me out of his sight." She laughs. "Gilman tells me I ought to stop worrying about things so much. I think I'm going to take him up on it. To hell with being afraid. Who knows? Maybe I'll be the one to kill Frank."

Gemma grins. "Let me know if you need help doing it. I've already agreed to help Gilman Lee with some sabotage against this coal deal. I don't guess it'd hurt to throw a little killing on top of the crime heap."

Rosalee eyes Gemma with renewed interest. "I didn't know you and Gilman were so buddy-buddy. He told me you turned him down once a long time ago. I reckon it was a shock to his system. You're the only woman ever did that."

Gemma laughs. "Do you really think so?" She takes a deep breath and leans against the side of the house. "We've not exactly turned into pals. It's just that I hate that coal company as much as he does."

Rosalee takes another toke, thinking, *Uh huh.*

Gemma says, "Speaking of Gilman, I'd like to know something. You may think I'm trying to be insulting, but that's not it. I just want to know."

"Know what?"

"Well, I just wonder how you go from one man to another the way you do. I mean, you and Gilman were almost married or something, weren't you? And then you went straight from him to Wade, and on to Frank Denton. I just wonder how you get rid of your feelings for one man and start concentrating on another right away. Believe me, I'm not putting you down for it. The subject just interests me, that's all."

"I don't get rid of my feelings. I still care about Gilman. And I never cared about Wade. I just went with him to spite Gilman. As far as Frank goes, my feelings for him are hard to describe. I hate him, the things he does, how cold he can be, but there is still a part of him that I love."

"If you say so," Gemma says, "but I sure don't understand why."

"Mom said almost the same thing this morning. I don't know why, either, unless it's because I know where he's coming from. I know he's mad at the world and wants to get back at it any way he can. He's mad because nothing in this world is as good as it ought to be. His mother sure wouldn't as good as she ought to have been. So he killed a addict in a alley. Well, that's real bad—I know it is—and he hurt me, made me feel like I wasn't even a person anymore. I hate him for that, but there were times when he made me feel like I was the only person in the world worth knowing."

Gemma nods her head. "So you hold all of these feelings for Gilman and Frank and maybe even other men inside you?"

"Yes, I do."

"Just wondered," Gemma says, "because I've sort of been feeling that way lately. I mean, I've not admitted it to myself, I don't guess, until right now, but . . ."

"Who've you been feeling that way about?"

"Let's just change the subject," Gemma says, handing Rosalee the cigarette. "This shit makes a person talk too much. I'm getting sleepy. Think I'll lay down in there and go to sleep."

Gemma goes inside the house and crawls onto the pile of blankets in the corner of the room, wondering briefly why Tom hasn't bought himself a bed yet, or at least built himself one. She closes her eyes, thinking about some of the comments she made to Rosalee, wondering if she was altogether truthful when she told Rosalee that she hated people. Maybe I just feel sorry for people, myself included. No, she decides,

I don't feel a bit sorry for myself or anyone else. We all ought to know better, and we ought to do better than we do.

Outside on the porch, Rosalee sits awhile longer, still trying to believe that the singing owls perched high in the sycamore trees are something other than what they are.

At the top of the mountain, Frank Denton stands up and walks around the mining site again. He listens for the music he heard earlier, but it's gone—evaporated into the night. He wonders if Tom Jett and the white woman are having sex.

25

Chapter

*B*ecause it is good for his public image, Wade Miller usually goes to church with his wife on Sunday, and after church they go on to her parents' house for dinner. But today Wade has other fish to fry. Begging off with the excuse of having a headache, he sits back in a recliner until he hears her drive away.

His other fish is Mildred Wilson. He's going to her house to find out if she's heard from her daughter, Rosalee. He hasn't informed Mildred of the visit, hoping to catch her off guard. If he is really lucky, Rosalee will be there, making no further investigation necessary, and if she isn't there maybe he can persuade Mildred to tell him her whereabouts.

Last night he stopped by the Pick Flower Shop, bought a half dozen roses, and stored them in an ice cooler in the backseat of his Cherokee, reasoning that every woman likes roses, even Mildred Wilson. He intends to turn on the charm, but if Rosalee is there, he will give the flowers to her instead. He decides to dress down for the occasion. No point in rubbing Mildred's nose in the fact that he has more money than she. Wade puts on old sneakers, slacks, and a pullover sweater, messes up his hair a bit, and takes off, thanking God that life still supplies a few challenges.

Driving through Pick, he slows down as he passes the bank, enjoying the spectacle of the vacant bank on Sunday, situated as it is in the center of town, the culmination of his success. Wade brought himself out of a tar-paper shack to get where he is today, made A's all the way through high school and college to do it, and when a subject was not to his liking, he wrote answers in ink on his pants legs. Whatever it took to make the grade, Wade did.

He spots his wife's car parked in front of the First Baptist Church and drives on. After the service, she will have dinner with her parents as usual, affording Wade plenty of time to spend with Mildred Wilson. As he glances over at the Blue Mountain Inn, wondering what Mr. Dudley is up to today, he considers stopping by and telling Fred where he's going, but afraid the man will want to come with him, he discards the idea.

On Wade travels toward the hollow where Mildred lives. He passes Lee's Machine Shop as Gilman and Ten-Fifteen, having just returned from the fishing trip, stagger out of the truck, looking more than a little worse for wear. Probably got drunk last night as usual, Wade considers, still amazed that Rosalee ever had anything to do with such a man. She was too pretty for the likes of him.

When he finally arrives at Mildred's house, he sees a curtain part on a front window and thinks that she is no doubt peering out to see who's come and that she has probably been waiting on him for the past ten minutes. People who live in the heads of hollows can hear a car coming a mile away. Wade takes the roses out of the cooler and walks up the porch steps. After three knocks, Mildred opens the door.

"Howdy, Wade," she says. "Long time no see."

"How're you doing, Mildred?"

"Come on in," she says.

Wade walks in carrying the flowers. "Thought maybe you'd like these."

"Sure," Mildred says, and, taking them, goes into the kitchen to put them in a vase. When she comes back into the living room, she sets them on the TV. "They sure are pretty," she says. "Course I like to see roses growing wild, don't you? I usually don't raise flowers. I'd much rather see them rambling around the ground—flowers that ain't been planted. That just come up on their own."

Wade forces a smile.

"But they sure are pretty," Mildred says.

Wade's smile endures.

"I just put on a pot of coffee. Would you like a cup of coffee?"

"Yes, thank you," Wade says.

Mildred pours them each a cup. "You know, flowers from a florist don't hardly look real, do they? They look too perfect like maybe they was made out of plastic," Mildred continues. "Not that I'm saying they ain't pretty . . . because they are."

Wade sips his coffee.

Mildred sits down in a chair opposite Wade and places her coffee cup on a coaster. "I've not seen you around since you and Rosalee stopped dating."

"Now, Mildred, I've told you and told you that me and Rosalee weren't really dating. We were just friends. I'm a married man, Mildred."

"Well, then, let me put it this way. I've not seen you around since you and Rosalee stopped being such close friends that when you drove her home late at night you'd stand on the porch and kiss her until I'd think you'd both lost your breath. You've not been around since she went to Florida."

Forget the charm, Wade thinks. "Have you heard from Rosalee lately?"

"Not a word."

Wade studies Mildred's face carefully for signs of nervousness. He spots a little shyness and a lot of mulish pride but nothing he can pin down as a lie. "I was hoping you had," he said. "I wanted to give her some money I owe her."

Now it's Mildred's turn to study Wade's face. Like Frank Denton, she notices how narrow it is, and long. She wonders if the doctor stretched it somehow when he was pulling Wade out of the womb. She also wonders how her daughter, even if she were desperate to make Gilman Lee jealous, could sink to going with Wade. She wonders this not because of his narrow face, but because of everything else about him. "How come you owe her money?" she asks.

"She did a favor for me once and . . . well, I just owe her some money."

"A lot of money?"

"A lot."

"How much?"

"Well, not a whole lot, but I do owe her about a thousand dollars."

"I doubt that she needs it," Mildred says. "From what I hear she's took up with a rich man down there."

"Is that so?"

"That's what I hear."

"I didn't think you'd heard from her lately."

Mildred blushes. "Well, I ain't . . . lately. It's been a while ago."

"If it's been a while ago, she may not be with the rich man anymore and might need the money. Can you give me her address?"

"I don't know where she is right now. Her and that man are traveling. They travel all the time."

"Is that so?" Wade says and stands up to go. "Well, I hope you enjoy the roses."

Mildred watches him walk down her porch steps to his Cherokee. It seems odd to her that during the whole five years Rosalee has been gone, Wade has not once come by asking for her until now. Why now? Mildred wonders, shaking her head as he drives away. She goes back inside and dials Gilman Lee's number. The line is busy.

Wade drives down the narrow dirt road leading from Mildred's house at a steady speed. The man is rich, he thinks. Fred Dudley is rich. When he arrives in Pick, he decides to stop by the Blue Mountain Inn for a little chat with old Fred. Glancing over at the First Baptist Church, he notices that the service is over and guesses that his wife is, no doubt, at her parents' house by now. He walks up to Fred Dudley's door and knocks.

"I've got some news for you," he says when Frank opens up.

"Great," Frank says, and motions him in.

Wade sits down in a chair and leans forward. "I paid a visit to Rosalee's mother today. Didn't find Rosalee, but I wouldn't say the trip was a waste."

Frank Denton stretches out on the bed, props his head up with his arm, and smiles. "What did you learn?" he asks.

"Well, all I know is that Mildred was most likely lying when she said she hadn't heard from Rosalee. She said Rosalee had taken up with a rich man and that they were traveling. The only thing I'm not sure about is whether that rich man she was talking about is you. If it is, then we know Rosalee's not traveling with you. That'd make what she told me a lie."

Frank smiles.

"Well, are you? I mean, are you the rich man Rosalee told her mother she was living with?"

Frank laughs. "I don't know why that should concern you, Wade. I'm the one trying to find Rosalee. All that matters is that *I* know whether I'm the rich man in question."

Wade realizes that he is becoming increasingly irritated by Fred's smile. "Well, then, I don't guess I can be of any further help to you."

"Actually you can," Fred says. "You can tell me where Rosalee's mother lives. That would be a big help."

Wade narrows his eyes. "What'd be the profit in me doing
that?"

"There wouldn't be a profit in it."

"I won't tell you where she lives, then."

"Yes, you will, Wade." Frank lights a cigarette and takes a
deep, long puff.

Wade looks down at the shit-brown carpet, having always
hated hotel rooms because so many of them are carpeted in
this same shit-brown color. "She told you, didn't she? About
the cocaine. I guess you think you've got something on me.
But you don't—not really. No one would believe you. I'm well
thought of around here."

Frank grins and shakes his head. "I didn't know about it,
Wade. Rosalee didn't really talk about you, except to say she
couldn't stand you. I didn't know about the cocaine." He
laughs. "But I do now. Thanks for the information." Frank
stretches his arms over his head and yawns. "No, Wade, the
truth is, if you don't give me directions to Rosalee's mother's
house, I'll blow your head off with a shotgun."

"Why do you want to know where Mildred lives?" Wade
asks.

"That's none of your business, Wade," Frank says quietly.

"Why do you want to find Rosalee?"

Frank gets up from the bed and walks over to where his visitor sits. He slowly leans down, puts his hands on Wade's
shoulders, and looks deep into his eyes. Frank stands in this
position for a full minute, during which time his previous
statement, "I'll blow your head off with a shotgun," registers
in Wade's mind, and Wade becomes paralyzed with fear and
begins to hyperventilate. "I'll tell you where she lives," he says.

After Wade leaves the hotel room, Frank Denton lies back
on the bed and closes his eyes. Not having slept since he got

home this morning, he hopes the regular night watchman shows up for work tonight. He lies there thinking about Rosalee—hears her laughter almost as clearly as he imagined her singing last night—and reflects on certain aspects of her character. She used to accuse him of the very things that she was guilty of, telling him that he didn't care about anything, when it was she who didn't care. In the very next breath she'd beg him not to take things so seriously and seemed uncertain of what she wanted to accuse him of, contradicting herself at every turn. Poor baffled Rosalee, he thinks, and drops into a sound sleep.

26
Chapter

The men didn't say a word on the return drive from Washburn Creek Sunday morning. They were spent— tired as soldiers returning from a war. Gilman told Tom and Ten-Fifteen that when he got home he intended to take the phone off the hook and sleep for two days.

When they dropped Tom off at June Collet's driveway, he made it partway across the swinging bridge and sat down. He sat there for half an hour before he remembered that he had intended to talk to Gemma when he got back. Now he looks around at her house and sees the kitchen door open. Why not? he thinks, and manages to stand up. He even manages to walk the length of her driveway and up the steps to her porch. Knocks on her door. With these feats accomplished, he waits in a sort of stupor for a response.

Gemma appears behind the screen door and shakes her head at the sight of Tom's muddy, wrinkled, motley self.

"Have fun, did you?" she asks.

Tom engineers a half smile.

"Do you want something?"

Tom opens his mouth. "I want to talk to you."

"You don't look able to do anything but crawl off somewhere and suffer," she says.

"I want to . . ."

Gemma feels a surge of emotion sweep over her, a feeling that teeters between sadness and love. She imagines Tom in California, riding a bicycle and wearing those funny-looking stretch pants that bicycle riders wear. Although she knows there was more to his old life than that, she sees him on a sunny, sandy beach, innocently throwing a Frisbee and playing volleyball with people that resemble actors in a gum commercial. She beholds Tom as he is today—here on her porch, dirty and somewhat deranged, hungover from a weekend fishing trip with Gilman Lee. "God only knows what you've been through," she mutters.

"If all I can do is suffer, I'll need to make a phone call to let Betty Marker know I won't be working tomorrow," Tom says. "Can I use your phone?"

Gemma motions him into the house and sits at the table while he makes the call. She observes what appears to be fish guts on the seat of his Levi's. A dead tick, perhaps poisoned from the alcoholic content of Tom's blood, swings from the tangled hair over his ears. Gemma is grateful that June is still asleep.

"Pull your clothes off," she orders, when he hangs up the phone.

In hopes of rising to what he perceives as an occasion, Tom starts clutching at his shirt, trying to unbutton it. But it is impossible for him to perform such an intricate maneuver in his present state, so he gives up and stands there looking forlorn.

"You're taking a bath," Gemma says, "and I'll get you some clean clothes to put on."

She leads him into the bathroom, runs water in the tub, and proceeds to undress him. Tom, still unclear as to what is going on, grins bashfully and tries to put his arm around Gemma.

"Get in the tub," she orders.

He obliges and is thinking, Tub-love with Gemma Collet, when he realizes with harsh surprise that she has begun scrubbing his head with something akin to a wire brush. She hands him a washcloth and says, "Wash yourself."

"Why don't you wash me?" he pleads.

"Men," Gemma says and leaves the room.

She climbs to the attic and opens the trunk that holds her father's clothes. She picks out a pair of jeans and a plaid shirt and takes them to Tom. "Here, put these on," she says, but Tom, still soaking in the warm, sudsy water, is already asleep.

She goes into the kitchen and brings back a pot of ice-cold water that she pours over his head.

"Dry yourself off and put these on," she orders, holding up the clothes.

Tom shivers. "You like this, I suppose. You like taking advantage of a man when he's down."

Gemma smiles. "I do kind of enjoy it."

She returns to the living room, and when Tom comes out a few minutes later he is wearing her father's clothes. The jeans fit him around the waist, but they are about six inches too short with the pants legs reaching midcalf.

"Get over there," Gemma says, ignoring Tom's ridiculous appearance. "Lay down on the couch and go to sleep."

Tom lies down. "What if I can't go to sleep?"

"But you can," Gemma says, and she watches him until he does. She is still there when June finally wakes up and comes into the room.

"What's he doing here?" she asks.

"Sleeping," Gemma says.

June looks closely at the slumbering figure. "Why, he's got on your daddy's clothes! I'd recognize that shirt anywhere, and them's his pants, too."

Gemma grunts. "I reckon Daddy's been dead long

enough that he wouldn't mind me lending them out."

June eyes Tom from head to foot. "They're too short on him."

"Shh!" Gemma says. "You're going to wake him up. Let's go in the kitchen."

The two women leave him on the couch, and since June can't watch TV for disturbing Tom, she insists that Gemma play a game of Sorry with her at the kitchen table.

When Tom wakes at eleven o'clock that night, he is still suffering from a hangover, the worst he's ever had. Every pulse pounds in his head. June has retired for the night, and Gemma is sitting in a chair beside the couch reading a newspaper. She crosses and uncrosses her legs, looks up at the ceiling, and rolls her eyes. "Oh, God" and "Idiots" and "Assholes," she grumbles as she reads.

"What are you reading?" he asks.

Gemma looks at him and sighs. "The newspaper. You'd be surprised at what you can find in a newspaper. I'm reading about a new regulation that is going into effect in a couple of weeks."

Tom yawns and sits up. "What regulation?"

"Have you recovered?" Gemma asks him.

"Almost, but my head is killing me."

She goes into the kitchen and brings back a plate of leftovers, a glass of milk, and two aspirin. "Here, eat something."

Tom takes the aspirin and begins to nibble the food. "What regulation?" he asks again.

"Are you sure you're up to hearing about a regulation?"

"It can't make me feel any worse."

"I wouldn't count on it. The government is changing their policy so coal companies can strip-mine in national parks and forests if they want to. The regulation is supposed to become final in mid-November."

Tom rubs his head. "They won't strip-mine in a park. The

public would go ape if they did something like that."

"You're right. That's what this guy here says. But he also says that these companies will pretend they're going to mine, and that the government will buy up the mineral rights from the owners, who are, of course, usually coal and oil companies. In other words, the government could end up paying millions of dollars to buy mineral rights which there wouldn't be a need to buy if they hadn't made a regulation allowing strip mining in the parks to begin with. Now does that make sense?"

"Maybe someone is trying to do their friends in the oil companies a favor."

Gemma sighs. "They already paid a hundred fifty million dollars to some company in Wyoming to keep them from mining on protected land. I can't stand to think about it."

"Well, maybe if a new president is elected he'll do away with this regulation," Tom says.

"Maybe so," she says, adding, "Did you know Rosalee's back at your house?"

"What?"

"She's back at your house. I stayed with her last night. She seems different. I started to say she doesn't seem so afraid anymore, but she is. It's just that she's somehow in a better mood."

"Why did she come back?"

"Something about her mother."

Tom stares long and hard at Gemma. "Well, you don't seem to be upset about it."

"I'm not. She's just trying to keep her mother out of danger, I reckon. Anyway, I stayed up there last night and we played music. She brought her guitar back with her. It was kind of fun."

"Good," he says. "I mean, I'm glad you had fun."

Tom suddenly grabs his head, and Gemma walks over to the couch and sits down beside him. "Is your head still hurting?"

"It comes and goes." In addition to the headache, Tom feels sexually aroused. He always feels starved for sex during a hangover. Gemma is wearing a wine-colored gown that sets off her white hair and black eyes. She has never looked more beautiful to him.

"Is there anything else I can get you?" she asks.

"Yes, there is, but you probably wouldn't."

"How about another aspirin?"

"How about a kiss, instead?"

Gemma scoots away from Tom. "I thought you felt awful."

"I do, but it's nothing a kiss wouldn't cure."

Gemma decides to humor Tom. Obviously he is not used to consuming so much alcohol and is going through a major withdrawal. She leans over and kisses him on the cheek.

"That's nice," Tom says, "but it would be a lot nicer if you were to scoot a little closer and kiss me a little longer."

Gemma scoots closer.

Tom puts his arm around her and kisses her, long and soft and slurpy. "Now what's wrong with that?" he asks when he releases her.

"Nothing, I guess."

"Was there anything good about it?"

"Yeah."

"Well, then why don't we do it more often?"

"Because you never come to see me."

Tom kisses her again. "I'd like to spend the night down here."

"No."

"Why not?"

"Momma would have a heart attack and die."

"Not if I leave before she gets up in the morning." He kisses Gemma again, and she feels herself becoming foamy as an ocean wave.

"I thought you wanted to talk to me," she mumbles.

"We'll talk later," he says, and they go down the hall to Gemma's bedroom.

Tom slips out of Gemma's bed at four o'clock in the morning and heads for the house on the hill. He never got around to talking to her last night, but he figures he got his point across. Gemma got a few points across, too. The morning is heavy with dew and quiet except for his own footsteps and the occasional call of birds. He doesn't walk up the hill on the road built by the miners, but on the path worn into existence by Gilman's grandfather and his brood of Lees. When he comes in sight of the house, he stops for a moment, seeing it as the old man must have seen it years ago on his return trips from Pick and points beyond. Then he thinks of Daniel Sparks's cabin, the cave, and the history standing around it thick as trees. Tom realizes that he has come to think of this part of the country as home.

When he steps inside the house, Rosalee isn't there. He runs back out to the porch, thinking that while he was making love to Gemma last night, Frank Denton decided to drop in. He is about to take off running wildly through the mountains in search of her when he sees her approaching the house from the direction of the field.

"You scared the shit out of me," he says when she steps on the porch. "Gemma told me you came back, but when you weren't here, I . . ."

"I was just taking a morning constitutional," she says.

"I'm glad you're back. You didn't get too close to the top of the mountain, did you? Those miners have a watchman that keeps an eye on their equipment at night."

Rosalee laughs. "I didn't go up there. I was just out in the field, sitting on a rock, thinking about breaking into Gilman's prayer chamber. God, you're getting worse than my mom at worrying." Rosalee points at Tom's jeans. "Nice pants you got on."

He looks down at his bare shins sticking out from the jeans legs. He had forgotten about putting them on again this morning. "Beauties, aren't they?"

"Where were you last night? Still fishing?"

"No, I spent the night down the hill there."

"Oh?" Rosalee says, winking. "Well, I'm glad to hear it."

They go inside the house, and Tom sits at the table while Rosalee puts on a pot of coffee. "You seem to be in a good mood this morning," he says.

"Well, I've just decided I'm tired of being in a bad mood. You're kind of chipper yourself, if you don't mind my saying so," Rosalee says.

Tom smiles and gets up from the table. "I think I'll walk around the property while the coffee perks."

He steps outside and goes to the edge of June Collet's land and, following the line all the way to the top of the mountain, begins his inspection. Off to his right he sees the strip-mining equipment—the graders, bulldozers, and high lift—silently waiting for the day's action to begin. He moves closer to the night watchman's shed and looks in the window at the man asleep on a cot. Beside him is an alarm clock, which Tom supposes he sets to wake himself before the miners arrive.

He steps back onto Gilman's property and keeps going until he comes to where it borders with the land on the other side of the mountain. It is there that he sees down the hill through the trees a glint of shining metal. He goes farther and finds the auger hidden behind a grove of trees. Nearby, a hole surrounded by upturned earth leads straight to Gilman's vein of coal. Tom hurries back up the hill and runs down the other side toward the house.

"It's starting," he says, when he opens the door and finds

Rosalee pouring her first cup of coffee. "I've found the auger."

Rosalee yawns. "Sit down a minute. They's no point in you breaking your neck to tell Gilman. If I was you I'd take my time about it, and when you do tell him, speak in a calm voice. Maybe that way he won't get so excited he'll bring a shotgun up here and kill everyone, us included."

Tom stands there. "I didn't think they'd do it. I mean, they know the reason I'm here in this house is to watch for that very thing. They don't care, do they? They think no one can stop them."

"No one prob'ly can," Rosalee says.

*W*hat in the hell are you doing here this early in the morning?" Gilman asks when he opens the door and sees Tom standing there. "I told you I was goin to sleep for two days."

"I just thought I'd stop by and tell you I found the auger. I would guess that it's been in operation for about a week. It's sitting down the other side of the mountain. I hadn't looked down there until this morning."

Gilman breaks into a smile. "I knew you'd come through. Get in here and let's mull this over."

Tom enters the apartment and plops down in the recliner. Gilman goes to the stove and heats coffee. "The other side of the hill?"

"Yes."

"That'd be Dwight Simpson's land," Gilman says.

"It's hidden behind a thick grove of trees."

Gilman laughs. "They're smart, but not smart enough."

"Well, I guess it's up to you now."

"You're right about that." Gilman sips his coffee and smiles. He feels twenty years younger already. He can't remember the last time he had such a lively prospect of raising hell. Maybe it was at the age of sixteen when he planned a break for the entire clientele of the Burr County Jail.

"What are you going to do?" Tom asks.

"Several things."

Gilman walks over to the piano and starts playing a tune. "I'm goin to start out small by playing around with some of their bulldozers and shovels, and if that don't work I'll try something else." He gets up from the piano. "What kind of deal they got goin up there at night?"

"They've got a watchman," Tom says. "Usually when I've gone around the mine early in the morning, he's been asleep in a shed. I don't think he does much watching."

"Interesting," Gilman says. "Do you still wanta help out on this deal?"

"Yes, I do."

"Well, if you'd find out exactly what this watchman's habits are, I'd be grateful. Spot-check him for a while and report back."

"Be glad to," Tom says.

After Tom has gone, Gilman takes a shower and shaves. He puts on the newest of his old clothes and cleans up his apartment. He opens the door to the garage, looks in at the car he's supposed to be working on, walks back to sit in his recliner, and just thinks. He feels as if he is on the verge of something that could change his life, and as he thinks about his plans, he decides that he is pissed, not only because his land is being trespassed and its coal pilfered, but because of the whole world in general. "It's time someone around here started acting foolish," he mutters, "and I'm tailor-made for it."

He figures he'll start with the pranks in a couple of weeks and tries to think of exactly how Gemma and Ten-Fifteen can help out. He recalls that every time he gets around Gemma he feels as if he has been away on a long trip and has just come home—but the house is on fire, and he is forced to start right in fighting flames. He can't remember a woman ever making him feel quite that way. Gilman comes to the realization that there is nothing he can do about the coal situation today, and he calls Ten-Fifteen to come over and help him out with the car he's supposed to be working on.

Later in the day while the men are busy at work, Gilman is still thinking about Gemma. He sees her with Tom. They are lolling around on a sleeping bag, eating marinated mushrooms, reading chapters of books aloud to each other between lovemaking bouts. "It's just not right," he mutters. "How could she do that when she could have me on a platter?"

"What?" Ten-Fifteen asks.

Gilman pictures himself making love to Gemma, a slight shudder passes over him, and he says, "Lord, what a woman!"

"What?" Ten-Fifteen asks again.

Gilman sighs and motions for Ten-Fifteen to hand him a wrench.

27
Chapter

*T*om sits on the floor of the cave and stares at the words on the wall, wondering what they mean. He recollects an article he read somewhere that quoted lines from a two-thousand-year-old Egyptian poem. "To whom can I speak today?" the ancient poet had written. Tom wonders if the line on the wall says something similar.

"To whom can I speak today?" Tom could have easily written those words himself. He has always found language to be inadequate and has trouble conveying what he really means—not that he has difficulty with the functional language of day-to-day. It is when he is trying to wrench forth a concept, some idea or emotion important to him, that language fails. Sometimes his words come out sounding stiff and unnatural because of his deliberation of each one.

He remembers a sociology class at Stanford, in which his professor spoke about a study of primitive islanders who didn't have a word for *work* in their language; the result was that they never thought of their daily activities as a chore.

Tom came close to communicating when he was at Stanford, but mostly what he found there were people like himself who were being seduced into trimming the depth and expanse of what they wanted to express in order to make it fit the dialect of the day.

Sitting on the floor of the cave, staring at the words he can't translate, he understands fully for the first time the real reason he began to think that going on to graduate school was no more important than sitting on the beach doing nothing. Graduate school was a contrived enterprise predestined by the language of the twentieth century. Tom was better able to learn from waves because their mode of exchange comes from presence, not words. He thinks that many of the people in Pick speak with presence also. Gemma certainly does. So do Gilman, Ten-Fifteen, and Rosalee.

The Egyptian poet went on to say, "One's fellows are evil: the land is left to those who do wrong." Well, that is certainly still true. There must be something a person can do when land gets into the wrong hands. Perhaps those words on the wall are trying to tell me how to rectify the situation.

When Tom goes home that evening, he begins to write down words, trying to find the ones that come close to describing what he means. When a suitable word cannot be found, he invents one.

He is still writing as the alarm goes off at 2 A.M. Tom pulls on his boots and steps outside. It is the fifth night of his vigil, and the air is cold and dirty blue as he walks up the hill toward the mining site.

Hiding behind Ed Toothacre's office, Frank Denton watches Tom approach the night watchman's shed. The regular watchman called in sick, and Frank is taking his place. Frank doesn't know what to make of this turn of events. He has seen Tom make his morning inspections several times before; but he has never seen him out this early, and he has certainly never seen him actually trespass on the mining area. Frank stands still as a shadow, taking shallow breaths, his eyes following every step Tom makes.

Tom is bewildered. Since he began the vigil, the night watchman has proven to have a routine of sorts. Tom has seen him sing songs, dance, and stumble into the shed and go to sleep. Twice Tom has heard him make speeches that seem to be modeled on presidential campaign orations. "My fellow Americans," the watchman proclaims passionately and gripes about everything from the Arabs and Israelis to the price of chicken feed. Until now, Tom hasn't given him a second thought, but tonight the guy isn't anywhere around. Perhaps he wandered off somewhere and passed out. Tom decides to stop by Gilman's shop before going to work this morning and update him on the latest events.

Frank watches as Tom stands beside the shed deep in thought. He cocks his gun and aims as Tom walks back down the hill to the old house. He wonders if he should tell Ed Toothacre about Tom Jett's excursion to the mining area, but he comes to the conclusion that he really doesn't care if Ed knows about it or not. The whole mining/augering business is not something he cares about. All he is interested in is finding Rosalee.

"What do you mean he wasn't there?" Gilman asks Tom a few hours later.

"I just didn't see him anywhere. I looked all around. Usually, I can hear him singing or grumbling or something. He wasn't asleep, either, because I checked the shed. Maybe he just didn't come to work last night. Or maybe he came to work and decided to quit."

"Well, this worries me a little," Gilman says. "I mean this night watchman being a drunk is perfect as far as we are concerned, but I'm afraid he's gonna get himself fired. What time does he usually start to work in the evening?"

"Five o'clock."

Gilman squints his eyes in thought. "Well, keep a eye on him for a few more days just to make sure he's still got his job."

At the end of three days, during which time the regular night watchman showed up for work regularly, Tom stops by the shop to tell Gilman the news.

"Three out of three ain't bad," Gilman says. "Maybe he's straightened himself out enough to at least show up for work. I believe we're in business."

When Tom leaves, Gilman decides to call Gemma to set up a meeting. There are schemes to be plotted; he needs to find out what she can or will do.

Gemma has been lost in thoughts of Tom all day, and now, home from the bank, she is still remembering how good it felt the other night to go to sleep beside him. All she needs is to be with him for an instant and she forgets the sentiments she's been having for Gilman, feelings she has experienced no matter how hard she has tried not to. They began stabbing her with their pointy little heads the night that Tom took her to Gilman's shop and she played the banjo. Since then, she dwells on the music session with regularity, recalls the kiss he gave her on the hill years ago, and feels the fire that touched her the other day when they were talking sabotage. Every time these memories come to her, she pushes them down and buries them under layers of defenses.

So Gemma is thinking only of Tom when the phone rings, and it is Gilman wanting to talk to her immediately about the coal situation.

"Now?" she asks, feeling a pang in her stomach.

"Now," he says.

She gets into her car and drives to the shop, wondering what exactly it is that has hit the fan. When she gets there,

Gilman greets her with a grin. He is dressed in a black turtle-neck sweater and jeans, and he's wearing a green beret, not a poet's beret, but a green beret from the Vietnam War. The whole apartment smells like Old Spice.

"Where'd you get that?" she asks, pointing to the hat.

"Somebody left it here one time."

"What did you want to talk to me about?"

"There's plans to be made," he says.

She looks around the room. "Where's Ten-Fifteen? I thought he was in on this."

Gilman clears his throat and shuffles his feet. "I wanted to talk to you first. We'll all three get together later."

She notices a tape of soft country music playing on the stereo. She sits on the couch, and Gilman brings her a glass of dark red wine.

"Wine? That's pretty cultural stuff for you, ain't it?" she asks, eyeing his turtleneck sweater suspiciously.

"Sometimes I get a penchant for refinement," he says. "It only happens every now and then and never lasts long."

Gemma laughs. "So what are these plans that need to be made?"

He shakes his head. "You always wanta get down to business, don't you?"

"I thought a business meeting was what this was."

"Well, it is," Gilman says. "But let's not wade into it before checking out the temperature. How's the wine?"

"Fine," Gemma says.

"Do you wanta dance?"

"Dance?"

"Yeah, I thought maybe you'd wanta dance."

"Well, I don't." Gemma smooths her skirt, making sure the hem covers her knees. Gilman walks over to his counter and brings back a dish containing cheese, grapes, and French bread, and sets it on an end table beside the couch.

Gemma stares from the food to Gilman's sweater and green beret. "Are you trying to be artsy?"

"I don't have to try. I'm artsy as they come," Gilman says.

"Where did you get that bread?"

"At the Kroger's in Hazard."

"My, my," Gemma says. "I guess you got the wine there, too. What kind is it? Ernest and Julio Gallo?"

"No, it's Martini something or other. Are you sure you don't wanta dance?"

"I don't think Tom would appreciate me dancing with another man. We're back together, you know."

"And a fine couple you make," Gilman says, undeterred. "Tom seems like a pretty liberal guy to me. I bet he wouldn't mind a bit if you danced with me."

"I thought you and Tom were friends. Is that the way you treat your buddies? Try to make it with their girlfriends?"

"Not usually, but I don't happen to believe that you and Tom Cat belong together. You're not cut from the same mold. Me and you are. I'm just trying to prevent a mismatch."

Gemma notices that the "Tennessee Waltz" is playing in the background. "I was just picking that on the banjo the other night," she says.

Gilman stands up and walks over to the couch. He bends over and takes her hand, kisses it, and asks her if he can have this dance. Hesitantly, she stands up, and they begin moving slowly to the music. A hundred pointy-headed Gilman emotions pierce Gemma like needles.

"I've got to get out of here. I can't breathe," she finally says and heads for the balcony.

Gilman follows her. "Okay," he whispers. "I won't bother you anymore. If you don't want to dance, so be it."

They stand there in the dark, listening to the water run over the rocks, listening to the frogs and the birds and to a car whiz by on the road.

"It's cold out here. Let's go back in," Gemma says.

They go back inside and sit down on the couch.

"So what is this coal business you wanted to talk about?" she asks.

Gilman clears his throat. "I've been trying to decide what part you'd play in the coup."

"The coup?"

"Yeah, we're taking over." Gilman inches a little closer to her. "I thought maybe the first thing I'd do is tamper with some of their equipment, but they've got a night watchman—one that rants and raves and drinks too much. I wouldn't want him to think he has to defend the place and get hurt."

Gilman puts his arm over the back of the couch so that it's almost touching her shoulder. "That's where you come in," he says.

"How so?"

"While I'm tampering with the machinery, I thought maybe you could distract the watchman."

"How?"

"Well, like I said, he's a drunk. Tom says that by three o'clock in the morning he's pretty wet down. They's a little shed up there that he goes to sleep in, and I wouldn't start the business until he's in the shed laying down. What I'd like you to do is sneak up there and listen. If you hear him rolling around like he's waking up, I want you to go right in and get in the bed with him. I'll guarantee that'll keep him out of my hair."

Gemma gets up from the couch and walks to the other side of the room. "You're an asshole, you know that?"

Gilman stands up. "Why?"

"Because all you can think of for a woman to do in a case like this is use her sex. Well, just maybe I can do more than that. Maybe I want to be the one to take apart their machinery!" Gemma walks right up to within an inch of Gilman. "And if you decide to blow up the place, maybe I want to light the fuse!"

"I didn't mean to insult you, Gemma. The fact is that if someone is goin to be messing around with their equipment, someone else needs to be looking after the watchman."

Gemma laughs. "And the next day after it's discovered that their equipment has been tampered with, the night watchman is going to put two and two together, right? I mean he's going to know that the woman who came into his shed had something to do with it. And he's going to talk, right? And the woman—me, if you have your way—is going to be in trouble."

"Not if he can't identify her. Not if she wears a mask."

Gemma laughs a little louder. "What kind of mask is she going to wear?"

"A ski mask."

"Oh, God!" she says. "Would you let a strange woman wearing a ski mask come into your shed in the middle of the night and get in bed with you?"

"Yes, I would," Gilman says.

Gemma folds her arms across her waist and glares at him. "I won't do it. I don't want to."

Gilman moves a few steps toward her. "What *do* you want to do?"

"Nothing," she says. "I don't want anything."

"Except me," Gilman says, arching his eyebrow in a ludicrous pose and moving close enough to touch her.

"You? Why in the world would I want you?"

"I don't know. Must be my charm."

"Get away from me!" Gemma shouts.

Gilman moves closer, so close that his face is almost touching hers. "If you really want me to get away, I will."

Gemma doesn't say anything. She can't because she is lost in a time warp with fog so thick around her that she breathes it in and out like smoke. She feels as though she is returning to someone she has mistakenly rejected for years. Gilman moves close to her, his lips brush her face, and the room takes on the warmth of a greenhouse. As if they have a mind

of their own, her lips reach for his. Gemma sinks into a kiss
even more remarkable than the infamous kiss of a few years
back. Like ancient amphibians lolling to and fro, Gemma
and Gilman do a dance of sorts, a great thundering dance,
their lips squishing in a swamp, their feet suctioning the
marshland of Paleozoic bliss. In a magnificent slow-motion
ballet, they kiss each other's nose, ears, and eyes and fall on
the couch in a heap of tangled arms and legs. *One,* Gemma
keeps saying to herself repeatedly, *one,* because that is what
she and Gilman have become. And they spend hours in this
separate reality of high sex and sweaty prehistory before losing themselves in sleep.

When Gemma wakes the next morning, she lies still for a
long time with her eyes closed, realizing that at some point
during the night Gilman must have let down the sofa bed because they're in it, lying between rumpled sheets. The previous night seems like a dream, like what she imagines an LSD
trip to be, a close encounter of a strange kind. Trying to remember what happened, she sees only flashes of seed ferns
and dinosaurs before her closed eyes.

She sits straight up. "Oh, God!" she proclaims. "I've made
love to two different men in two weeks—a man a week. I'm
going to the dogs."

Gilman props his hand under his head. "It happens to the
best of people," he says.

Gemma looks around at him—his hair is sticking straight
out from his head, his eyes slowly traveling the length of her
scantily covered body. "Don't you care?" she asks.

"I care a lot," Gilman says, "about you."

"Shut up!" Gemma hisses. "You don't understand. I don't
know what I'm doing."

"That happens to people, too."

"Just be quiet and let me think."

Gilman lies back on the pillow and closes his eyes.

"I don't know why I did this," Gemma says. "I can't stand

you—I've never been able to stand you even years ago when I was a teenager and used to come to your shop to buy beer."

"Yeah, I remember you back then. You were cute as a button."

Gemma's eyes slice into him like cleavers.

"Anyway," Gilman says, "I know you couldn't stand me then, but you can sure stand me now, can't you?"

Gemma looks around at his flashing eyes, studies his face like a road map. "How did you get that scar?"

"Well, I wish I could say I got it fighting in a war—something brave like that. But it was a car accident. My head went through a windshield."

Gemma reaches out, touches his face, and the desire from the night before takes control. She stares at him unabashedly. "What happened with us last night?" she asks.

Gilman weathers her gaze—wears it as comfortably as an old shoe. "I'm not exactly sure what happened. Nothing like that ever happened to me before so I don't have anything to compare it with. All I know is that it was mighty powerful."

"I don't believe it's love, though. It's something else," Gemma says.

"Good, I don't like the term *love*. It sounds too wishy-washy. I'd like to think what I feel for you and what you feel for me is something stronger than *love*."

"But you don't understand. I care about Tom, too. He makes me feel lighter, somehow. I like that feeling. I love it."

Gilman grins. "From the way you acted last night, I must make you feel pretty light, too."

Gemma can't help smiling. "I thought I told you to be quiet."

"I'd say you've got a situation on your hands," Gilman says, chuckling. "Maybe it's just that you need two men in order to tango."

She lies back down. "I didn't go to work today. Didn't even call in. I'll probably be fired."

Gilman leans over and kisses her, and they make love again.

Gemma doesn't even think about going home until two
o'clock that afternoon. Just before she leaves, Gilman says,
"Just a minute. I almost forgot." He picks up a scrap of paper
from the top of the piano. "Would you give this to Rosalee?"

"What is it?"

Gilman becomes flustered and looks down at the floor.
"Mildred called and gave it to me over the phone. It's a
recipe."

"A recipe?"

"Yeah, it's a recipe for divinity—some kind of candy. She
wanted me to give it to Rosalee. Are you goin to take it to her
or not? I reckon I got it all wrote down. She said the main
thing was to let it cook to the hard ball stage."

"The hard ball stage?"

"Yeah, whatever the fuck that means. Why are you looking
at me like that?"

Gemma gives him another big kiss and leaves.

When she gets home, she says to June, "Momma, I need
psychiatric help."

June looks up from the TV program she's watching. "What
do you mean?"

"Nothing. I'm going to bed."

Gemma goes into her room and lies down. Five minutes
later, June comes in. "What do you mean, you need psychiatric help?"

"I don't want to talk about it. Just leave me alone. I mean
it; I just want to be left alone."

June shrugs her shoulders and walks out. Gemma stares at
the ceiling. I've finally gone over the edge, she thinks. Can a
person feel this way about two men at the same time and not
be crazy? How can I want Gilman, anyway, when I get mad
every time I see him? It's not ordinary anger that I feel, either.
It's like I've got a score to settle with him, like I've known him
sometime before when we were different people, like I can't
get away from him no matter what I do. Maybe I really ought

to go to some kind of therapist just to see what he'd say. Maybe I ought to call Sylvester Gast.

She remembers the look of the good psychologist as he sat at her kitchen table a few months ago. He was a gentle-looking man with a soft smile, a man who thought talking about problems solved them. *Be For What You're Against,* she proclaims silently to her ceiling. Maybe if I could just pretend I'm someone else, someone who believes in therapy, it would do me some good. Besides, I need to get out of town, if only for a day.

Gemma goes into the living room. "Momma, I've got to make a phone call, and I'd like some privacy. Would you mind leaving the room?"

June looks at Gemma and starts to object, but there is something in her daughter's eyes that keeps her from it. She stands up and goes to her room without a word. Gemma searches under one of the end tables and drags out the phone book. She looks in the yellow pages until she finds Sylvester Gast.

"I'm sorry," the receptionist says when Gemma dials the number, "Mr. Gast is with a client."

"Well, I'm his client, too," Gemma says, "and I'm going to kill myself right now unless you let me talk to him."

"What's your name?"

"None of your business. Just get Sylvester."

"Hello," Sylvester Gast says, a few minutes later. "How can I help you?"

"This is Gemma Collet. Maybe you remember me."

"The young lady from Pick?"

"No, it's the woman from Pick. I'd like to make an appointment to see you, if you're agreeable."

There is a momentary silence on the other end of the line. "My receptionist tells me you threatened suicide."

"I did, but that was just to make sure you got on the phone. I do have a couple of immediate problems, though; but I'd rather tell you about them in person, and I can't wait a month for an appointment."

"Miss Collet, after our last meeting, I checked into the availability of doctors in Pick. There is at least one very reputable psychiatrist at the hospital down there. Now, I would like to treat you, but if you need to see someone immediately, you could get an appointment sooner down there."

Gemma laughs. "Do you think for one minute I'd tell my personal problems to a doctor from Pick? Why, the news would be all over town in a week!"

"You're wrong about that, Gemma."

"I want an appointment with you, Mr. Gast, and maybe I wasn't kidding about doing myself in."

Sylvester sighs. "I'll put my secretary back on, and she'll schedule you. And Gemma, you may have to wait a couple of weeks for your appointment because that's just the way it is."

After the appointment is set for the first of December, Gemma hangs up the phone and yells to June, "I've made an appointment to see Sylvester."

June walks slowly back into the living room and stands in front of Gemma. "Does this have anything to do with the fact that you stayed out all night? I guess you know I didn't sleep a wink."

"It has something to do with it, but I'd rather not say what. I just wanted you to know I'm going to see Mr. Gast."

June sits down in the rocking chair and looks off to one side. "I'm glad you are, Gemma."

28
Chapter

*F*rank Denton parks his car in the field that was once an
Indian campground. Avoiding the road and smattering
of homes that are located beside it, he walks up the
mountain to Mildred Wilson's house. Hers is the last house at
the head of the hollow, Wade has told him. As Frank ambles
among the bare trees and naked undergrowth of late Novem-
ber, he wonders if Daniel Boone ever walked the same
ground. He contemplates the irony that the explorations of
wild-eyed trailblazers like Daniel (men who believed that the
neighborhood was overcrowded when their closest neighbors
lived twenty miles away) led to the establishment of forts and
settlements that defiled the virgin wilderness the men had
sought in the first place.

He sits down under a pine tree near the edge of the clearing. Through the trees the small white house is visible. It has
a front porch, as do most of the older homes in the area, and
no fence. Off to one side are the remnants of a garden—
squash, dried corn stalks, a scarecrow. Parked in front of the
house is a 1963 Chrysler. It is quiet here at the head of the hol-

low, except for wind moaning through the tree branches.
Leaning against the trunk of a pine, he listens for sounds beneath the wind and hears dishes rattling and Mildred humming in as pretty a voice as Rosalee's.

He wonders what she does when she isn't washing dishes or
performing other mundane chores. Does she watch TV? Live
in her past? Perhaps she has a part-time job, Frank speculates.
No, he decides not. He believes that Rosalee said her mother
receives welfare. The front door opens and Mildred steps outside with a broom in her hand. She begins to sweep the weathered floor of the porch. She appears to be about fifty-five and is
wearing a robe and slippers. Perhaps she never gets dressed
during the day, he considers. Mildred stops sweeping and, almost as though she senses his presence, leans against the broom
handle and gazes toward the mountain where he is sitting.

If he walked down the hill right now and questioned her
about Rosalee, she would refuse to tell him anything. He
knows this. He would have to get rough with her, and she
would still refuse to talk—wouldn't say a word. He can tell this
just by looking at her. He'd have to ram the broom handle
down her throat and stir her insides with it as steadily as a
cook stirs soup with a spoon. And then what? Rosalee would
eventually come out of hiding, but she'd be pointing her finger at him. Frank doesn't think that wasting Mildred is a practical idea at present. He doesn't know what his next move will
be. Perhaps he'll just bide his time.

When Mildred ceases to gaze in his direction and resumes
her work, he stands up to walk back down the mountain to his
car. Suddenly, he hears a yell. "I see you up there! What're
you doin?"

Frank looks back at the woman, who is shaking her broom
with one hand and pointing her finger with the other. A look
of anticipation sweeps over him. If he keeps going without acknowledging her, she'll alert everyone in the county that a
stranger has been snooping around. Frank retraces his steps

and walks down the side of the hill to her house; he smiles as he approaches her, his hand extended for a friendly shake.

When he leaves her an hour later, Mildred is lying in bed, covered by her favorite quilt, a wedding-ring design in yellow and white. Her eyes are closed (Frank closed them), and her face is still flushed from the struggle she made when he dragged her, kicking and screaming, into the bedroom and smothered her with the pillow. Before he left, Frank took her phone off the hook and banked the coal in her fireplace. He sliced a piece of peach pie he found in the refrigerator, washed the saucer he ate it in, and put it back in the cupboard.

Wind blows in circles around the house at the end of the road. Mildred, never one to receive many visitors, lies still as a sleeping bride under her wedding-ring quilt.

*T*his morning Gilman called Gemma and requested that she meet him and Ten-Fifteen at lunch for another conference regarding the mine.

"Are you sure Ten-Fifteen will be there?" she asked.

"Of course he'll be there."

"Well, I don't know . . ."

"I thought you wanted to help out."

"I do."

"Well?"

Gemma hung up the phone, told June she'd be back by evening, and drove to the shop. Now she is in the apartment with Ten-Fifteen and Gilman, drinking beer and eating peanuts. Gilman is sitting close to her, giving her meaningful sideways glances, and Gemma, determined to ignore his attentions until after her appointment with Sylvester Gast, is trying very hard not to acknowledge him. Ten-Fifteen doesn't know what to make of Gilman's eyeing

Gemma, but for the moment he is taking it in stride.

"I've decided to sweeten them up," Gilman says. "I bought several five-pound bags of sugar last night."

Gemma looks bewildered. "What are you talking about?"

"I'm talking about sugar, Sugar. We're goin to pour some in their gas tanks. It's a old trick, tried and true."

Ten-Fifteen smiles.

"What good's sugar going to do?" she asks.

"It's goin to put every machine they've got out of commission for a while."

"Sugar will cause that?"

"Yes, darlin, it will. The minute it gets in the gas tank it gums things up. The next morning their vehicles will start all right, but as soon as that sugar flows through the fuel line to the cylinders, it'll be repair time."

Gemma leans back and sips her beer. "What time will we do it?"

"If all goes well, we'll do it late tonight, or I should say early tomorrow morning. We'll meet at Tom's at ten o'clock, and each of us'll take a bag of sugar apiece and head up to the mine about three A.M. The watchman should be asleep by then. We'll each pick out our machinery and start pouring in the cane. They've got trucks up there, dozers, graders, and a high lift, not to mention the engine that operates the auger. We'll dump sugar in every one of them." Gilman looks at Gemma. "Of course it would be better if you kept a lookout for the watchman instead of pouring sugar, but that's up to you."

"I'll think about it," Gemma says.

"Don't take too long."

Gilman walks to the corner of the room and picks up his guitar. He starts playing "Blue Moon Over Kentucky," while Gemma and Ten-Fifteen tap their toes to the beat. When he finishes, Gilman says, "I figure we'll have a little party sometime shortly after our gig. Temporarily rename this place

the Sugar Shack, and ask everyone to bring something sweet.
Are you goin to come, Honeybunch?" he asks Gemma.

"I'll let you know later," Gemma says. "By the way, if you
really need me to watch the watchman, I'll do it."

Gilman smiles. "I do."

Gemma glances around at Ten-Fifteen. "Ten-Fifteen, you
look different somehow. Did you get your hair cut or something?"

"No."

"Well, something's different. I just can't decide what it is."

Gilman winks at Gemma. "It's his arm. It's fell down to ten-
twenty."

Gemma takes a closer look. "You're right. Well, what about
that!"

Ten-Fifteen blushes. "Yeah, I kind of like it."

"I do too," Gemma says.

"Well, I reckon I'd better get back to the house. I'll see you
fellers later."

After he leaves, Gemma turns to Gilman. "You won't let on
to Tom about what happened the other day, will you?"

"I don't think that's a topic we'd naturally hit on," he says.

Gemma sighs. "Well, just make sure you don't. I want to tell
him about it myself. Not that I'm sure yet there's anything to
tell. I won't know until later."

Gilman chuckles. "When's later?"

"In the near future."

"People who think all their questions are goin to be answered at a specific time are usually disappointed."

"For your information, I don't really think I'll find any answers at a specific time; it just suits me right now to say I will."
She gets up to leave.

Gilman stares at her in dismay. "Are you really goin to leave
without saying good-bye?"

"Good-bye," Gemma says.

"That's not what I meant." He walks over to her, and they

grab hold of each other like lovers who get to see each other only once a year.

"I've got to go," she persists.

"Not quite yet," Gilman says, and they stumble awkwardly toward the couch for another go-around.

*W*hen Gemma arrives at Tom's house that night, Gilman and Ten-Fifteen are already there. Everyone is sitting around the picnic table in the kitchen, drinking strong black coffee. Gilman is telling a story about his uncle Bob, who was a hobo during the Depression.

"He sang on the radio once in New Orleans," Gilman says. "He worked as a cowboy in Colorado, begged food from nuns at Catholic churches. Uncle Bob must have spent time in jail in every state in the union."

Tom and Ten-Fifteen, spellbound by Gilman's tale, don't notice her entrance. Even Rosalee barely acknowledges Gemma, she is so caught up in the web he is spinning. Gilman always captivates an audience in this way—makes them lose themselves in his words.

"What did he do to get put in jail?" Tom asks.

"Some of the time, it was for being drunk, but mostly it was for disturbing the peace. Uncle Bob had this knack for disturbing people. He'd just walk into a room, and people would get all agitated."

"Why?" Tom asks.

"I don't know, but I think it was because of the way he looked at them."

"I had an uncle like that," Gemma interrupts. "His name was Jake."

Gilman hasn't been aware of Gemma's presence until now. "I'm not surprised to hear that," he says, winking at her.

Gemma looks down at the floor.

"But getting back to my particular uncle, at some point in his travels he got hooked on heroin. One day he was out trying to fix his car all doped up, and the car fell on him. So much for Bob. Hand me another cup of coffee, Rosalee."

Rosalee starts to get up, but Gemma stops her. "Looks like you'd get your own coffee, Gilman," she says.

Gilman looks around at her. "You're absolutely right. A man ought to get his own damned coffee. Thanks for setting me straight, Gemma." He winks at her again and pours his own.

"Oh, by the way, Gilman," Rosalee says. "Next time you call Mom, tell her the candy turned out real good."

Gemma goes into the living room and starts thumbing through some of Tom's books. Tom follows her. "Hi," he says and kisses her on the cheek. She moves away.

"Is something wrong?"

"I really can't talk about it right now."

"What do you mean?"

"I mean I'm keeping my mind on the business at hand, that's all."

"Okay, fine." Tom shrugs his shoulders and goes back into the kitchen. "I'd like to go with you tonight," he says to Gilman.

"I'd like to go, too," Rosalee says.

"I figured you would, so I brought some extra supplies. Rosalee, maybe you can watch the night watchman so Gemma'll have a chance to pour sugar."

Gemma, still in the living room, hears this bit of conversation and smiles. This little get-together has been harder to handle than she thought it would be. As she sits down and begins reading from a collection of short stories, Gilman walks into the room. "I'm going out to my prayer chamber," he says. "Be back after while."

Rosalee follows him to the door. "I wonder if he really prays when he goes in there," she says, watching him disappear into the shack in the field.

Gemma grunts. "I'd like to hear a prayer that Gilman Lee would say."

Ten-Fifteen and Tom join the women in the living room, and they discuss the job ahead of them. Finally, Rosalee drags out the guitar, and they sing softly. A couple of hours pass and Gilman still hasn't returned.

"Surely he can't still be praying," Tom says, and he looks out of the window toward the shack in the field.

Finally at 2 A.M., Gilman bursts in the door. "Let's go," he orders. "I checked out the situation. The old boy on the hill is already asleep."

Everyone springs into action, donning their ski masks and grabbing their sugar.

On top of the mountain, the regular night watchman has been drinking all night and is passed out cold. The five vandals, masked beyond recognition, file up the hill toward the mining equipment and vehicles. Rosalee positions herself by the shed while the others go about their business. She looks in the window at the watchman asleep on a cot and spots an empty bottle lying on the floor. A wave of nausea sweeps over her, and she feels as if someone is standing behind her. Turning around, she finds only a stack of cable and several oil drums stationed in the shadows. She turns back to the sleeping figure in the shed, who is clearly visible in the light from a lantern by the cot. For an instant, he looks familiar—his stubbled face and oily hair turn into the face of someone she knows. Then the image recedes into a corner of her imagination, leaving her with chill bumps running up her arms and the back of her neck.

Take this, Gemma declares, silently, as she pours the sugar. She's speaking to the faceless people who for years have polluted every creek in Burr County. Take this, you sonsof-bitches, she reiterates, as she screws the cap back on and heads for another grader. She curses the coal companies, their lawyers, their land agents, and smooth talkers. She goes from the second grader to the high lift, trailing sugar behind her, pouring it like polluted silt into every tank she can find.

Gilman works close by her. He watches the way she moves in the pale light. He loves this woman—ogles her like a goofball-eyed teenager gaping at a cheerleader in a short skirt. He loves her because she's out here in the middle of the night becoming a different person than she has ever been before.

Tom watches Gemma, too, as she makes her way from one piece of equipment to another, fortitude emanating from her in waves of electricity, and remembers how every evening this past summer she sat naked in the creek. It occurs to him that she was preparing for the work she is doing tonight. Tom's thoughts are interrupted when Ten-Fifteen taps him on the shoulder. Together, they head down the other side of the mountain to contaminate the auger.

With everyone hard at work, it doesn't take but twenty minutes to poison every machine on the site. When the deed is done, Gilman gathers everyone up and herds them down the hill. The night watchman doesn't so much as roll over.

*E*d Toothacre and his crew arrive at 7 A.M., and the watchman, who has somehow roused himself from sleep, is standing outside the shed trying to look alert.

"How'd it go last night?" Ed asks him.

"Fine. Got a little chilly, though." The watchman picks up his lunch box containing the empty pint of vodka and takes off for home.

Ed stands around with the men for a minute, jawing and joking, knowing that these little morning chitchats keep them happy. Ed looks around at Fred Dudley. Except for Fred, he

thinks. Fred doesn't seem to need mollycoddling. Ed passes
around a thermos of coffee and some doughnuts, which he
buys from a bakery in Harlan every Saturday and stores in his
freezer, enough doughnuts to last his crew a week.

When the last one is downed, he says, "All right, men, get
to work."

The men go to their stations and start up their equipment.
All the engines start, and then they stop—every last motor.
Puzzled expressions leap like bullfrogs to the men's faces. They
try to restart their engines, with no luck. Exclamations pour
from their mouths. "Shit," they say. "Fuck! Damn it all to hell."

Ed Toothacre gives the night watchman time to get home,
then calls him. "Are you sure you didn't see anything strange
last night?" he asks.

"No," says the night watchman.

"Hear anything?"

"Not a sound. Nothing ever happens. There's times I almost wish something would."

"Is that right?" Ed says. "Well, this is your lucky day, because something is going to happen right now. You're fired,
asshole!"

Ed hangs up the phone. He should have fired the man
weeks ago, the minute he suspected him of drinking on the
job. He didn't though, he screwed up, and the brass at Conroy will know it.

Ed calls a tow truck, calls several. They haul away the dozers,
graders, high lift, and coal trucks to be repaired. "It was Gilman
Lee," Ed shouts at the sheriff, whom he also called. "No, I can't
prove it, but I know it! Arrest his ass, do you hear me!"

"I can't arrest him without proof," the sheriff says.

Ed stands there for a moment, trembling slightly. He feels
as though a minor earthquake is erupting in his stomach. He
runs to a portable toilet, and emerging a few minutes later,
walks sadly back to his makeshift office and calls his boss at
Conroy Coal.

29
Chapter

It is early morning, and Gemma is getting ready for the drive to Lexington. Occasionally she glances out the window into the darkness of 4 A.M. Since the parts needed for repair haven't arrived, the mining operation on the hill has been at a standstill for over a week; and she has enjoyed the quietness, not to mention the fact that she helped to bring it about. Her appointment with Mr. Gast isn't until two o'clock this afternoon, but she likes getting early starts on trips. Instead of taking the Daniel Boone Parkway, she intends to drive the old road and stop in Berea at a roadside diner for breakfast.

It is still dark as she drives through Pick. Lights are on in some of the apartments above the hardware and jewelry stores. The town, never crowded except on Saturdays, is dead. Five miles out of town, daylight spreads its fluorescent glow behind the charcoal sky. In houses beside the road, people are beginning to get up for work—breakfast is being made and children are turning over in their beds. A rooster flies up on a fence rail and crows, tries to strut on the frosty wood, falls. A man stands on his porch smoking a cigarette as he looks out toward a far mountain. He's probably still in a dream he was having an hour ago, Gemma speculates, as she picks up speed and makes her way around the curvy road to Berea.

Every year when she has left Pick to go on her vacations, she has noticed one thing: A place looks different when you're leaving it. Especially if you're leaving a place early in the morning. You pass by a house where a man is walking down the driveway to his pickup, and you find his actions mysterious and intriguing. Suddenly you want to know where he's going, but you wouldn't even notice him if you were on your way to work instead of heading out of town. Gemma loves taking a trip, even if her destination is no farther away than Lexington and her plans include seeing a therapist.

She wonders what Sylvester will suggest she do. Probably nothing helpful. Still, she hopes his reaction will at least be interesting. Since she usually thinks more clearly when she drives, one of the main reasons she is going to see him is for the trip there and back. So far she has managed not to face her dilemma, but she intends to do so today.

It is only 6 A.M. when she arrives in Berca. Having always liked this town in the foothills—the last town before the onslaught of level terrain—she drives through it slowly, noting the nearly empty college campus and the closed shops and restaurants of early morning.

On the other side of town, she stops at a truck stop and orders coffee and a Danish. Three truckers sit at a table next to hers, talking about speed traps and impending layoffs. She wonders if she should ask one of them for advice about her situation. She's heard that many a trucker has more than one woman—sometimes more than one wife. The youngest man keeps trying to flirt with the waitress, who is having nothing to do with him. The waitress wears a dull white uniform and churlish expression as she sets his plate in front of him. Gemma remembers once reading a book written by a man who had traveled around the country with his dog. For about a page this man—she can't remember if it was London or Steinbeck or Hemingway—complained about a waitress in a restaurant he'd stopped in. It wasn't that the waitress, whose mere presence had put him in a down mood, had done anything particularly nasty to him; she just wasn't cracking jokes like a good waitress should, wasn't smiling, didn't respond in the right way to his comments. Well, maybe she didn't feel like it, Gemma growls to herself. Why should anyone have to smile all the time? It isn't natural. Maybe her feet were hurting, asshole! Gemma shouts silently to the writer of the book, who she believes is now dead anyway. Yes!! she screams to him, the waitress you met in your travels hated her job. Why didn't she quit, you ask? Because she had to pay the goddamned rent, sonofabitch!! Gemma slams a tip on the table and leaves.

Near Richmond, she passes an old Union-Confederate battleground—a historical marker stands by the road marking the spot. She parks the car and looks out at the rolling swells of earth covered in frost. She would like to go out there and walk around, to see if the noise of battle can still be heard, but she decides against it. Years ago, the government buried containers filled with nerve gas just beneath the surface of the land. There is talk of unearthing the gas, transporting it to an unpopulated area, and burning it, but so far nothing has been done. Gemma wonders why this particular spot on Earth has always been so connected to war and the weapons of war.

In Lexington, she spends her time visiting tourist attractions—the horse farms and Mary Todd Lincoln's childhood home. Finally, she ends up in a shopping mall eating a taco and drinking a Pepsi, watching shoppers traipse in and out of stores. In spite of her early determination to face her predicament, she is still avoiding thinking about the fact that she loves two men equally, wants them both, craves them so much she can taste them.

Later, in the waiting room at The Center for Healing and Enrichment, which is located in a ten-story glass building with modern art sculptures stationed in front, she flips through magazines and eyes the two other patients in the room, wondering what mental ills brought them here today. The woman sitting next to her also browses through a magazine, and when a smile comes to the woman's lips, perhaps from an amusing anecdote in an article, she glances around to see if Gemma noticed, as though she is guilty for even a moment's happiness.

Gemma gets lost in a daydream. She imagines herself walking into the room where Sylvester awaits her. He is sitting in a chair by a window and motions for her to sit in another chair opposite him. He has a clipboard in his hands and a smile on his face.

"How are you today?" he asks, looking into Gemma's eyes. She can tell that eye contact is not something he comes by naturally, but is something that is a requirement of his job.

"About the same as I am every day," Gemma says.

"How was your drive up?" he asks.

"Fine." Gemma watches while Sylvester jots down notes. "What are you writing?"

"Just notes from our discussion. When we have our next meeting, I'll know what ground we've covered. Are you still sitting in the creek every day?"

"It's December, Mr. Gast. Do you think I'm stupid?"

"Have you thought any more about harming yourself?"

Gemma puts down her magazine and closes her eyes so all she can see before her is the imagined session. Every evening June tells Gemma about what happened on *Oprah*—tells her about the psychologists' latest theories. Feeling like a guest on the show, Gemma leans back in the chair. *Be For What You're Against,* she whispers to herself. Hang your problems out the bedroom window for the whole world to see. "I never intended to harm myself," she tells Sylvester in her daydream. "I just pretended that so I could talk to you on the phone."

"Then you admit you wanted to talk to me."

"Unfortunately, I guess I did. And I am harming myself."

"How?"

"By coming here, probably. But also, I love two men. I first realized that I loved one and hated the other. Then I realized that I loved the one I thought I hated, too." She takes her time describing Gilman and Tom to Sylvester. She tells him how she feels about them both, about the different ways they affect her.

"How have Gilman and Tom reacted to the fact that you feel like this?"

Gemma sighs. "Only Gilman knows. He doesn't seem to mind, which makes me wonder why I care about him at all."

"Are you going to tell Tom?"

"I guess. Look, Mr. Gast, let's get right to the point. Until very recently, I hadn't been with a man in years. It's hard for me to know how to handle one man, let alone two. Actually, I don't figure I really love Gilman; it's probably a lust thing. I thought maybe you could help me figure out just exactly what I do feel."

Sylvester sits back in his chair and puts the tip of his pencil in his ear. She wonders if he knows he's doing this.

"Gemma, I think before we go any farther we need to examine your motivations. Can you think of any reason why you would choose to fall for two men?"

"I didn't choose to fall for them, Mr. Gast. It just happened."

Sylvester takes the pencil tip out of his ear and inspects it carefully, as if hoping to find a dot of wax. "You said you hadn't been with a man in years. Why not?"

"I had a bad experience with one and figured they were all the same. A lot of it has to do with my condition. No doubt, you've noticed how white I am. Well, I look good compared to the way I looked for years. I was brown and white splotched, not exactly anyone's dream girl."

Sylvester writes feverishly in his notes. "When did this condition first occur?"

"I was diagnosed as having vitiligo when I was eighteen."

Sylvester strikes a thoughtful pose. "You must have had problems adjusting."

"Must have," Gemma says.

"Your self-image probably suffered as a result."

"Probably so."

"Is it possible that since you haven't had a relationship in a very long time that the prospect frightens you? That you don't feel you deserve to be happy? And that you have become involved with these two men because you know it creates an impossible situation?"

"I'd say it's just the opposite, Mr. Gast. Because I've deprived myself of men for so long, somewhere deep down inside, I probably think I deserve to have two. But I can't handle it, and I don't think Tom can either."

Sylvester considers this for a moment and says, "Maybe your problem has nothing to do with the vitiligo. Perhaps you're doing this to yourself because of something else, something that happened in your childhood . . . that you have possibly forgotten."

"What do you mean?"

Sylvester smiles like a benevolent teacher. "I'm talking about your inner child, Gemma. We each have one, you know. Often, these inner children are wounded and crying out for help. Right now I want you to sit quietly and try to get in touch with yours."

Gemma narrows her eyes. "Excuse me? My inner child?"

"Yes, Gemma. Try to picture her in your mind. How old is she? Is she crying? Why is she crying?"

Gemma glances over her shoulder, as if she expects to see a kid behind her who is bandaged and wearing an arm sling.

"Wounded?" she asks.

"Yes, Gemma. We all have wounded children. What happened to yours?"

"I don't think I have one."

"Yes, you do, Gemma."

Gemma sighs. "I can't just take the child from the rest of me, look at her as if she's a separate person, and ask her why she's crying. That would be downright silly, Mr. Gast. It's a game that I'm sure is fun for psychologists like yourself to play, and if I were bored and had absolutely nothing else to do, maybe I'd play along. I don't remember anything bad happening to this kid you're talking about unless it was the vitiligo, but I wasn't exactly a child when that happened."

"Just because you can't remember doesn't mean something didn't happen. This coming week, I want you to try to get in touch with the child. I want you to come back next week with stories about her. Will I see you next week?"

Gemma stares at Sylvester, who sits temperate as a Buddha by the window. She imagines he is not alone, that he is surrounded by all his patients' inner children, some crying to sit on his lap, others begging to be told stories. "Sure," she says. "I'll be back."

Sitting up straight and glancing around the waiting room, she notices that the woman who was there earlier is gone. She walks up to the receptionist and plops down eighty-five dollars. "Tell Sylvester it was a good session."

The receptionist looks confused. "But you've not seen him yet. You can wait until after the session to pay if you like."

Gemma turns and walks out the door.

On the drive back home, rain turns into sleet, then snow, the first snow of December, and she is still in a quandary. No matter how much she doesn't want to do so, she loves Gilman, loves the green beret he wore when he seduced her, his messy apartment, his greasy machine shop and the broken-down cars inside it. She loves the way he arches his eyebrow when he smiles, the way life trails behind him with music and laughter. Gemma watches snowflakes dance in front of her windshield like fitful dandelion puffs that can't decide whether to rise or fall or be carried away.

30
Chapter

*T*his morning the local sheriff, Bill Shepherd, paid Gilman a visit and told him that Conroy Coal will have their equipment repaired very shortly, and that they are making sure the man who is taking the old night watchman's place is not a drunk and knows how to shoot. Plans that have been resting quietly in the corners of Gilman's mind step right out into plain view and strut around like peacocks.

Since the sugar attack, Bill Shepherd has questioned him several times. Gilman just smiles and cooperates in every way he can. He tells the sheriff how shitty he thinks it is that someone would have done such awful damage to the mining equipment on the hill. "Sugar ain't always sweet," he confides to the man of law.

As soon as Gilman finishes with the Honda that he has been working on for most of the day, he plans to clean the apartment for tonight's sugar party. Too bad Rosalee can't come, he thinks as he works. Earlier today, he tried to call Mildred Wilson, but her phone was busy. He's tried to call her two or three times over the past week, and her phone has always been busy.

Women, he reflects irritably, always on the phone gossiping. A few minutes ago, he called Gemma, and although she agreed to come to the party, he could tell she wasn't in a good mood.

And she isn't; Gemma feels like a slut. She feels guilty. What is she going to tell Tom? Will she say, "Tom, remember how mad I got about you and Rosalee? Well, I hope you're a better person than I was—more tolerant, being as you're a philosopher—because, you see, I've got this thing for Gilman. I promise not to fool around with him much—probably no more than once a month. I'll just do it when I can't stand it any longer, and you know it doesn't *meeeaaan* anything. No, that's wrong. Actually, it means a hell of a lot, but it won't interfere with us, Tom. With what's going on between us."

Gemma fidgets as she waits for him to pick her up and take her to Gilman's party. She asks herself how she would feel if he announced that he is still rubbing noses with Rosalee and intends to keep on doing it. She would be hurt, she answers herself, cut to the quick, the bone marrow, madder than a wet badger in heat. Why would I be mad, especially knowing as I do that it is possible to hanker after two people at once? she asks herself. Because I want to be the only one, she answers. Maybe Tom would like to be the only one, too. But he's already the only one—he is the only one unless I'm with Gilman, and even then, there is no one like Tom. No one is like Gilman, either.

Standing up, Gemma paces the floor, watching for Tom to walk across the swinging bridge and into her yard.

*F*rom all ends of the county, people have come. They pile into the shop as if it is the last shop they will ever pile into, and have the kind of sneaky expressions on their faces that makes it hard to tell whether they have already gotten themselves into trouble, or if they intend to do so shortly. As some of the more civilized guests eye him suspiciously, the Texan enters singing his song, stakes out a corner of the room, and systematically intoxicates himself. Gilman, nodding at him from time to time while everyone else keeps a safe distance, has a guarded sort of friendship with the Texan that threatens to explode at any given moment.

By the time Tom and Gemma show up, the gathering is abuzz with merriment. Gilman's bathroom, which is receiving an enormous workout, is unable to meet the demands of all who require its services, so people are slipping outside in the snow to relieve themselves of excess alcohol behind the coal-truck bed, where they have deep conversations in the process.

The party progresses nicely until Gilman asks Gemma to dance. As Tom sits in the recliner watching them move across the floor, he notices the way Gilman's arm rests on Gemma's hips, her head on his shoulder, her eyes closed. He feels the thing between them, heavy as a fogbank, thick enough to cut into bite-sized pieces. Everyone else feels it, too, sliding around the room like a reptile. So this is the way it is, Tom thinks. Why do a man's friends always want his woman? Is it curiosity? Or is it just that a man's friends wouldn't be his friends unless they thought they could beat him in whatever game he's playing? Not that I consider Gemma a game. Maybe that's what a friend is—a person who likes you because they feel superior. Gilman probably knows he couldn't pass a college entrance exam with as high a score as mine, but he also knows that's not important. I, on the other hand, know that I've thought of things that have never crossed Gilman's mind, and I feel pretty good about that until I remember what a good musician he is, and that I can't even play one tune. Right now, Gilman probably thinks he knows something about me and Gemma that I don't know. He's wrong.

Tom stands up from the recliner and walks outside, where it is still snowing large, feathery flakes. Ten-Fifteen is out there too. He came outside to get away from the crowd. All night people have been noticing the change in the position of his arm, and he's not used to receiving so much attention. He is standing in front of his trailer with his hand cupped over an ear, as though he's listening for something, when Tom steps up.

"Trying to see if I can hear it fall," he says. "The snow," he explains. "I love the snow."

"How long has it been going on?" Tom asks.

"Ever since yesterday."

"I don't mean the snow. I mean Gilman and Gemma. How long has it been going on?"

Ten-Fifteen turns away from Tom and mutters, "Not long. I don't think it was intended. I figure it was a accident of some kind."

"They're not good for each other."

"That's what Gilman says about *you* and Gemma."

"He's wrong."

Ten-Fifteen reaches down and picks up a handful of snow. "What're you goin to do about it?"

"Maybe I'll go in there and start an old-fashioned fistfight."

"I wouldn't do that if I was you."

"I'm not afraid of Gilman Lee," Tom says, and walks back into the shop. Ten-Fifteen follows him.

Gilman and Gemma are still floating around the room, and everyone is watching. Tom walks up and taps Gilman on the shoulder. "Would you come outside with me? I'd like to talk to you alone," he says.

Gemma jerks her head away from Gilman's shoulder as if she's been caught standing right in the middle of the overall scheme of things.

Gilman grins. "I guess you know it's pretty cold out there."

"I know how cold it is," Tom says.

"I don't think you do, but I'll go out there with you if you're set on it."

The other people in the room try not to notice that things are amiss. Some even attempt, with not much success, to start up conversations about other subjects. The Texan puts his drink down and raises an eyebrow when Tom and Gilman leave Gemma standing in the middle of the room and step outside. Ten-Fifteen is the first to follow them out. Then the others, except for Gemma and the Texan, dawdle out of the apartment and through the shop to the outside, where they find Gilman and Tom standing by the coal-truck bed, staring at each other.

When Gilman sees the crowd gathering, he turns to them: "Everybody go back inside so me and my buddy here can have a private conversation. Y'all start singing and picking; we need some accompaniment." He and Tom stand quietly until the others have gone back inside.

"A fine friend you turned out to be," Tom finally says.

"Glad you appreciate me," Gilman responds.

"What are your intentions?"

"You mean in regard to our Miss Gemma? I always make it a practice not to have intentions. That way I never get disappointed."

"You just can't stand to let even one woman get away from you unscathed, can you?"

"I'm not thinking about it in them terms."

"What terms are you thinking about it in?"

"Thinking has nothing to do with it. I'm just carrying out what is meant to be."

"I don't think anything is *meant* to be, and even if it is, sometimes fate can be altered," Tom informs him, "but philosophy aside for the moment . . ." He takes a swing at Gilman and hits him in the nose.

Blood trickling down his face, Gilman reciprocates, knocking Tom to the ground. Tom reaches his hand out and grabs a fistful of snow. He squeezes it into a small, compact ball of ice and throws, hitting Gilman on the ear. Gilman counters with a snowball of his own. Unable to keep away from the action a minute longer, the crowd emerges from the shop and starts engaging in their own skirmishes, and what later becomes known as the most elaborately performed snowball fight in Pick history ensues.

In the apartment, Gemma pours herself a beer and sits back on the couch. She looks around at the Texan, who is staring at the floor as if he's never seen one until now.

"They're out there fighting over me," she says to him. "I've never been fought over before."

He looks up at her as though he is surprised to see her there. "Shows you how stupid they are," he says.

Gemma narrows her eyes. "Did you really kill five men?"

"That's what they say."

"But is it true?"

"I ain't never knowed anything to be true. They's always a hitch to the truth."

Gemma sighs and curls up with her beer. Outside the fight is still raging; she can hear the thudding snowballs and drunken battle cries. She should have told Tom about her indiscretion before they came to the party. They shouldn't have come to this party at all. She shouldn't have danced with Gilman. Fuck it, Gemma decides, walking over to the Texan. "Wanta dance?" she asks him.

"No, thank you," he grunts.

Gemma remains silent for a moment before laughing. The Texan gets up from his chair. "I'll be goin home now," he says, and strolls out of the shop.

Gemma continues standing there in the empty apartment, empty except for idle musical instruments leaning against walls and opened beer cans sitting on the counter, and she's laughing so hard she's crying. Finally, she puts her coat on and steps outside. Making herself two big snowballs, she hits Tom with one, and Gilman with the other, and slips away from the brawl, walking toward home in the cold, snowy night.

At the shop, the fight begins to break up—people get into their trucks and cars and head home. Gemma has walked about half a mile in the snow before a carload of Gilman's guests picks her up and drives her home.

Finally there is no one in the snow except Tom, Gilman, and Ten-Fifteen. Ten-Fifteen is leaning in the door of the shop, watching the other two aimlessly mill around in small circles.

"Boys, I think you'uns ought to go inside," Ten-Fifteen says. "And I don't think you'uns ought to fight any more tonight."

"Now, ain't that a sensible idea," Gilman mutters. "You're always so sensible, Ten-Fifteen."

Ten-Fifteen walks over to his trailer and opens the door. "Well, I don't know about you fellers, but I'm going to bed."

Tom and Gilman stand there watching him. "Do you feel like anything got settled tonight?" Gilman asks.

"No, but I sure do feel better."

"You're not the right man for her, Tom," Gilman says.

"Vice versa," Tom counters.

"Well, why don't we go inside and see what Gemma has to say on the subject?"

When they step into the apartment, they don't find her because, by now, she is in her own living room watching a late late film noir, starring Lizabeth Scott and Burt Lancaster. She figures she's lost both of her men on this one fateful night, and she's watching this old movie as though she is someone else, someone who needs to get used to being alone again.

31
Chapter

When Tom wakes the next morning, the snow has stopped falling, and from his window, he views the white-covered hillside and listens to the stillness that only a snowfall can bring. Icicles hang like crystal wands from the eaves of the house, and at the bottom of the mountain, the creek is frozen like a snake playing dead. He hears Rosalee moving about in the kitchen, humming a tune in a minor chord. The melody and the snow-muffled day fit well together.

For a while, he contemplates leaving Gemma and Gilman and whatever connects them. He tries to picture himself back home, sitting on the beach, but he can't construct a clear image. No, I am here, he says to himself. I feel as if I've always been here. I'll have to move, though, from this house. I can't stay here in Gilman's house while he plays footsies with Gemma. Perhaps I can persuade Daniel Sparks to let me rent his old house. I'll have to do a lot of repairs, though, before I can move in.

He finally gets up and stumbles into the kitchen, where

Rosalee is making oatmeal and humming her minor-chord melody. She gets herself a bowl and says, "Help yourself."

"I'm not hungry," Tom says.

Rosalee looks closely at Tom's haggard face. "Have fun last night?" she asks.

"Had a ball."

Rosalee taps her spoon on the edge of the bowl. "I've been thinking about leaving," she says.

Tom looks at her as though she's been reading his mind and says, "Oh, you mean you're going back to your mother's."

"No, farther than that. I figure to stay on another couple of weeks, just long enough to figure out where, but I just can't be here much longer. Maybe I'll head out West somewhere. Remember that movie *Alice Doesn't Live Here Anymore*? Maybe I'll go to Arizona like Alice and get a job in a diner."

"What about Frank Denton?"

"What about him? I can't spend the rest of my life worrying about Frank Denton. I mean, I feel like he's here, you know? I can actually feel him. Maybe I'm crazy. I just know that I can't let him stop me dead in my tracks. I've got to move. Know what I'm saying? Moooooove!"

"I'm going to be moving, too," Tom says. "I mean, I'm not leaving the state, just this house. I've got to find another place to live."

"Why?"

"Me and Gilman had a falling-out."

"Over Gemma?"

"How did you know?"

"I saw it coming. I saw it the other night when everyone was sitting around this table. Gilman thinks he's found the woman of his dreams, but he hasn't. There ain't no one love affair can satisfy him. He has to have several going at the same time, with even more prospects for the future. It's just the way he is, and he's too old to change. I wouldn't give up on Gemma if I was you."

"Yes, but I have to know I'm number one. I don't want to run second, not even a close second."

"I guess I don't blame you, but I still say if anyone is barking up the wrong tree, it's Gilman."

"What makes you say that?"

"It's a feeling I have."

Tom gets himself a bowl of oatmeal and begins to eat. "What would you do if you were me?"

"Well, like my mom always says, 'Never let the sun set on a argument.' When I was little, I didn't know exactly what she meant. I'd get in a fight with one of my friends, and I'd be scared to death as I watched the sun, red as a ball of fire, sink past the top of the mountains. I figured that if I didn't patch things up with whoever it was, the sun would never rise again. It would just sit down behind the hills and catch everything on fire. I always used to make up with my friends before sunset. Of course, that little bit of advice don't always apply. It didn't apply to me and Frank, but I think it does to you and Gemma. It may even apply to you and Gilman."

Tom finishes his oatmeal, gets dressed, and walks down the hill and across the swinging bridge toward Gemma's house.

Gemma is sitting opposite June, who has spread a 1,500-piece jigsaw puzzle on the kitchen table. She watches her mother line up the sky pieces.

"Here's a corner," Gemma says.

"That's brown—part of that block there," June says, pointing to the picture on the box. "I'm just interested in sky right now."

"Wouldn't it be better to find your corners first?"

"Who's working this? Me or you? I didn't think you liked

puzzles. Why don't you just go in the living room and leave me be?"

"Just trying to help out," Gemma says. She looks out the window and sees Tom standing on their porch with his collar turned up. He knocks on the door.

"Oh, God," she mutters. "Momma, I've got company. I'm going to take him in the bedroom so we can talk. Don't worry, I'm not going to rape him in there, okay?"

June looks around at Gemma and sighs. "Right now, at this minute, I don't care what you do to him. But you'd better let him in before he freezes to death, fool."

Gemma opens the door and tells Tom to come in.

"Hello, Mrs. Collet," he says to June when he sees her at the table. "How's it going?"

"It's going fine, Mr. Jett. Except I'm getting cabin fever. I always hate it when we get snowed in because Gemma drives me crazy. I wish you'd take her in another room so I can see a minute's peace."

"Glad to," Tom says.

Gemma glares at June and leads Tom into her bedroom.

She takes his coat and hangs it in the closet, and as they sit on the edge of her bed, Tom notices her picture on the dresser.

"Is that you?" he asks.

"Yes, that's me. I bet you wish you'd known me then, don't you?"

"I didn't notice it the other time I was here."

"Sometimes I turn it facedown—get tired of looking at it."

"You're beautiful to me, the way you are right now."

"Just to you? You mean for some strange reason you think I'm beautiful, but no one else in their right mind would?"

"No, Gemma. That's not what I mean. You should know that's not the case. Obviously, Gilman thinks you're beautiful."

"So just you and Gilman could ever possibly think I'm beautiful. Is that it?"

Tom sighs. "Are you trying to start a fight with me so you'll have an excuse to run to Gilman?"

Gemma stares at the floor. "I don't know what I'm trying to do."

They sit quietly for a moment while outside a grader growls past the house, attempting to clear the road of snow. "That's not going to do any good," Gemma says. "It's supposed to snow again tonight."

Tom stands up and walks around the room, glances out the window. "There doesn't seem to be anything for me to say. Maybe I shouldn't have come."

"Where are you going?" Gemma asks as Tom turns to leave.

"I've got to find different living quarters," he says. "I can't stay up there anymore."

Gemma puts her arms around Tom, but he pulls away from her and leaves.

After he is gone, she paces the floor for a while before going over to the dresser and turning her picture facedown.

Tom drives down the river road and stops in to see Daniel Sparks.

They sit by the heating stove in the birch-back chairs. "I need to move from my place," Tom tells him. "I was wondering if I could rent your cabin."

"Rent my cabin?" Daniel says confoundedly. "That old house ain't in any shape to rent."

"Nevertheless, I'd like to rent it. I'm a carpenter. I could repair the roof for you."

"They's more wrong with it than just the roof. It's got airholes all over it. Anybody'd freeze plumb to death in that house."

"I could repair the holes," Tom insists, pleading his case for half an hour before Daniel relents.

"Well, if you'll do that, I'll let you stay in it six months rent free. I never woulda thought anybody'd be living in that old place again."

Tom sits around with Daniel for several hours. Daniel tells him the names of the birds who are the first to fly south in winter and the first to come back in spring. He makes him a pot of sassafras tea and sings him a ballad with twenty-six verses. Later as Tom is driving home, he realizes he has found someone with whom to speak.

Gilman walks outside for a minute to feel the cold, clean air, to let it blow against his chapped face and clear his brain of debris. Last night's fracas in the snow took more out of him than he would ever admit to a living soul. Tom turned out to have a formidable accuracy with snowballs. He tries to imagine what is going through Gemma's mind this morning. He knows she's up and pacing. He imagines he's put a twist in what would otherwise be a straight situation between Tom and her. Won't be the first time I've twisted things up, he thinks, going back inside and looking in the mirror at his face, which appears more haggard than usual.

"Maybe I'm not much of a catch after all," he grumbles to himself and turns away to appraise the damage done to the apartment by the sugar party. There are cans and cigarette butts and pieces of cellophane paper from cigarette packs scattered everywhere. He makes a vow that the next time he throws a measurable party, he won't allow anyone to leave until they've cleaned up the mess. All at once Gilman grabs a broom and a dustpan and attacks the rubble as if it were a representative from the Conroy Coal Company.

As he cleans, he goes over the plan for demolishing the auger on the hill. The auger's days are definitely numbered. For quite some time now, the long, tall Texan, who really did kill five men for negligible reasons, has been collecting cow, horse, and dog manure, along with some of his own bountiful excrement thrown in for good measure. He's been saving the mixture in a heavy-duty plastic bag for his good friend Gilman Lee. He also intends to give him a couple sticks of dynamite. Gilman plans to ignite the dynamite very shortly after the Conroy Coal Company resumes the mining, thereby bringing a fitting end to some of the machinery and to the auger that is boring into his vein of coal. The Texan also has a handy pocket-sized remote control detonator. He's prepared to deliver these instruments of destruction to Gilman as soon as he asks for them.

When Gilman finishes the cleaning, he walks back to the mirror, arches his eyebrow, curls his lips, gives himself a pretend smooch, and starts dancing around the floor, singing "Foggy Mountain Dew." He is in full sway when Ten-Fifteen walks in and wants to know if they're having eggs for breakfast.

"You're damn right," he says. "Eggs and bacon."

Ten-Fifteen smiles and sits down at the counter, waiting. "I've been meaning to ask you something," he remarks casually as Gilman fusses over the stove. Gilman doesn't even acknowledge that his friend has made a remark.

Ten-Fifteen clears his throat. "I've been meaning to ask you about Gemma."

"Go right ahead and ask," Gilman says. "What about her?"

"Well, as everybody knows, Tom really likes Gemma, and I reckon she likes him. She hadn't fooled with anyone in years till he come around. Maybe you ought to just let 'em be. You know?"

Gilman takes his bacon out of the skillet, cracks some eggs in it, and turns around, giving Ten-Fifteen his full attention. "Buddy, did you ever think about becoming a columnist, one like Ann Landers or Dear Abby? Maybe you ought to go down to the *Pick Times* and hire on."

"Never thought about it," Ten-Fifteen says.

Gilman turns the eggs, sets the spatula on the counter, and

puts toast in the toaster. "I guess you think I'm just causing trouble for the fun of it. Well, it's more than that. I've always been interested in that woman."

"Why, though? Ain't it because she wouldn't give you the time of day? Maybe now that she is, you'll lose interest."

"That ain't it, Ten-Fifteen. It's something else—hard to describe. Rosalee used to say she'd keep my doors locked at night, but I wouldn't have let her. Gemma'd come closer to doing something like that. What I'm talking about is a even match. Tom is a young man; he'll get over this. I won't. Besides, he'd let her get away with too much. She'd lead him around by the nose. By God, she won't have any kind of hold on my nose, though." Gilman laughs. "I don't reckon I'll have a hold on hers, either."

"Why bother, then?"

Gilman glares at Ten-Fifteen. "So you think the only reason two people ought to latch on to each other is to hold each other down? I gave you more credit than that. No, buddy, me and her are goin to let each other fly. And we're goin to have a lotta fun letting each other do it."

Gilman puts the eggs, bacon, and toast in two plates, and the men begin their morning feeding ritual. "What about Tom, though?" Ten-Fifteen asks.

"I like Tom Cat a lot. I figure he'll come around in time."

When Ten-Fifteen finishes his eggs, he scoots his plate back and walks outside to the balcony to look at the frozen creek and trees. He wants Gilman to let go of Gemma because deep down he has a feeling his buddy is going to lose her, anyway. A chill runs over Ten-Fifteen that is coming from somewhere other than the weather; he feels as if it is coming from a dark place at the bottom of the world that no one has ever seen.

Part III

GHOSTS

32
Chapter

Mildred Wilson was never very social. Living at the head of a hollow for most of one's life tends to make a person shy. Her closest neighbor, Gladys Moore, whom she does sometimes visit, thinks nothing of the fact that Mildred hasn't been to see her lately. Mildred often hides away like a bear every winter, and Gladys knows that she doesn't like to talk on the phone. Even the man who owns the grocery at the bottom of the hill doesn't think anything is out of the ordinary. Mildred stopped by in mid-November and bought enough groceries to last a few months. The only two people who have given Mildred a second thought are Gilman Lee and Wade Miller. Both men have noticed that when they've tried to call her, the phone has been busy. Gilman isn't too concerned, though; he just figures she's gossiping, and Wade doesn't know what to think. He is, in fact, afraid to think what might be wrong with Mildred. Most of the time, he manages to block out the fact that he gave Fred directions to Mildred Wilson's house. The possible consequences are too horrible to imagine.

Wade has been terrified since the day Fred Dudley threatened to blow his head off. He's tried to avoid crossing his path, but sometimes he sees Fred standing on the corner, watching him go in and out of the bank. If the two men happen to make eye contact, Fred always winks at Wade and smiles, chilling him to the bone. Wade has acquaintances he could hire to do a number on Fred, but deep down he's afraid they'd fail. Fred seems like the kind of character who would make mincemeat out of the most violent men he knows.

At home, Wade paces the floor in his den while his wife watches a Christmas special on TV in the other room. Usually he watches TV with her, but tonight he told her he had some work to do. He looks up at the clock; it is 10 P.M. He glances at the telephone, debating whether to call Mildred tonight, knowing that if he calls her at ten o'clock on a weeknight and the phone is still busy, something is definitely wrong. He stops pacing, picks up the receiver, and dials her number. The line is busy.

Wade sits down in a chair and starts rocking back and forth, mumbling a singsong he learned in the first grade: "ring-around-the-rosy." He goes into the living room and stands behind his wife's chair for a moment, looking at the Christmas tree. It is one that has been sprayed white and adorned with blue ornaments and velvet bows. He bets no one in the entire county has one prettier and wonders if Mildred Wilson has her tree up yet. Of course she doesn't, he says to himself, because she's . . . Wade's face turns gray. "Honey, I'm going for a drive," he tells his wife.

She looks up from her TV program. "You're what?"

"Going for a drive."

"This time of night?"

"I've got something on my mind—a problem at the bank."

"What kind of problem?"

"The auditor is coming next week."

His wife turns back to her TV program. "Oh."

He puts on his coat and walks outside, where the wind is blowing and not a star is in the sky. As he drives his Jeep up the icy road to Mildred's house, his headlights shining on frozen trees beside the road, he thinks of the possibilities. Maybe Mildred is not in the mood to talk to people and has taken her phone off the hook. Or maybe Rosalee is still in Florida, and Mildred took her phone off the hook before she went to visit her for Christmas. Maybe Mildred is dead, Wade thinks.

He parks his Cherokee alongside Mildred's 1963 Chrysler and sits there for a moment, afraid to breathe. Not a light is on in the house, and no smoke is coming from the chimney. He walks up the porch steps, frozen over with snow, and knocks on her door. No answer. Of course there's no answer, Wade thinks. He turns the knob, and finding the door unlocked, walks in. It's as cold inside as out. And, yes, there is an odor. It hangs frozen in the air like a putrid fog and takes his breath away. Wade, who has a low gag level, begins to dry heave, water streaming from his eyes. When he gains a modicum of control, he finds a light switch and flips it. She's not in the living room, and he doesn't see blood. Wade covers his eyes with one hand and walks into the kitchen, gradually peeping between his fingers. There is no blood in the kitchen. Back in the hall, he notices the bedroom door slightly ajar, and can feel her in there, ticking like a bomb. Stepping inside, he flips on the bedroom light, and there she is in bed, her face swollen blue. He vomits on her linoleum floor, then blindly runs out of the house to his Cherokee.

Wade doesn't sleep a wink that night; he tosses and turns, finally getting out of bed and sitting alone in his dark den to wait for daylight. He decides there is nothing he can do about what he has just seen. What would he tell the sheriff? That he just happened to be out riding around at ten o'clock at night and decided to stop by Mildred Wilson's house at the head of the hollow and found her dead?

"I'll blow your head off with a shotgun." That's what Fred

had told him. If ever Wade doubted that he meant it, he
doesn't now. In fact, he realizes that the statement wasn't just
a threat, but a foregone conclusion. "I'm dead," Wade mutters to the dark room, "even if I never say a word. I know too
much." Breathing faster and faster, he goes into the kitchen
and puts a brown paper grocery bag over his head. It occurs
to him that Fred will know he found Mildred. "If he sees me
tomorrow, he'll know. His eyes see right through a person,"
Wade whispers inside the grocery bag.

The Conroy Coal Company's repaired mining equipment
and trucks roll across the bridge downstream from June and
Gemma Collet's house and continue up the mountain to resume work at the mine. Ed Toothacre, who was soundly chas-
tised by his superiors at company headquarters for keeping a
drunk in the ranks, assigned Fred Dudley to the permanent
position of night watchman. He also hired an armed guard to
walk the perimeters of the mining site during the day shift,
just in case Gilman Lee decides to try something in broad daylight.

Gemma hears the graders rumbling up the mountain as
she gets ready for work. Didn't take them long, she thinks, as
she looks out the window at the miners heading up the snow-
covered mountain. Last night three inches of new snow fell,
and she wonders about the condition of the road into town.

Tom is up, too. He's getting ready to go to Pick and rent a
temporary room at the Blue Mountain Inn. He intends to stay
there until he can move into Daniel Sparks's old house. Every
evening after he gets off work at Betty's, he goes up to the
cabin and works until dark.

Rosalee watches him get ready. "You don't have to do this,

you know. Gilman don't mind you living here. He'd let you know if he did."

"I mind," Tom says, looking around at her. "You'll be all right up here, won't you? If Frank Denton were really looking for you, he'd have found you by now. I don't think you have any reason to worry."

Rosalee smiles. "Who says I'm worried? Besides, I'm goin to be leaving here in a week or two myself, remember?"

Tom reaches out and takes hold of her hand. "I'm glad I got to know you," he says. "I'll miss your singing and your attitude."

"Me, too," Rosalee says. "I mean, I'll miss you, too. I never met anyone like you, Tom Jett. I didn't think people like you were real."

"I don't know if that's a compliment or not."

"It is."

Tom puts on his jacket and gloves. "I'll be back tonight to get my things."

*A*t the bank, Gemma glares at Marcy and Jo Ellen. Ever since she got to work this morning, they've been babbling about the McDonald's that will be constructed at the edge of town if Wade has his way. "We can have lunch there every day," Marcy says. "I just love Big Macs."

"I like Quarter Pounders, myself," Jo Ellen admits. "And Chicken McNuggets."

"I like their wrappers," Gemma growls, "especially when they get littered all over the ground and blow along ditches by the road and get scattered up hillsides and down creeks, where they float like boats. Yeah, just give me the wrappers any day."

Wade comes out of his office and hands her a letter to type. For a long time now, he has been in a strange mood—doesn't twirl around half as much as he once did. Gemma has never thought Wade capable of being moody, and watching him walk slowly back to his office, his head down, his eyes darting nervously toward the front doors of the bank, she wonders what put him in this state.

At her desk, Gemma types Wade's letter, assessing his increasingly poor handwriting and misspelled words. Whatever is wrong with him is getting worse. She looks up from her typewriter, reminded of her own problems, and decides to drive by Gilman's shop this evening before going home.

"They're working the mine again," she tells Gilman when she gets to the shop that evening. "The trucks and machinery arrived this morning."

"Too bad. Guess I'll have to do something else."

"Like what?"

"Never mind."

"What do you mean, never mind? I thought we were in this together."

"We were in the sugar attack together. This is something I intend to do alone."

"Why?"

"Because it's a one-person job."

"Why are you bothering to do anything, Gilman? You know they always win. I mean, they've got the jobs, and people need work. Most of the creeks around here are already destroyed anyway."

"I'm doing it for the hell of it," Gilman says. "Why did you help out the other night?"

Gemma smiles. "For the hell of it."

Gilman walks over and kisses her on the cheek. "I never got around to saying how proud I was of you that night on the mountain. You took to sugar like a ant."

Gemma kisses him back, sits down on the couch, and puts

her feet on the coffee table. "Did you know Tom's moving out of your house?"

"No, I didn't," Gilman says, and looks down at his feet. "Where's he goin?"

"He said he was going to look for another house."

"Then he's not leaving the whole country. Well, that's good. I'd hate for him to do that."

"I would too," Gemma says, picturing Tom dressed in her father's clothes. She sees his smile and feels the warmth she experiences every time she's around him. She looks up at Gilman, who is bending down to kiss her again. "I've got to go," she says.

"You just got here."

"There's some things I have to do."

Gilman bends down and kisses her anyway, and noticing her absence from the kiss, considers the fact that she's somewhere else. "You really care about him, don't you?"

"I told you I did."

"You're a fool," Gilman says.

"I'm a what?"

"You heard me."

"I didn't think you minded me liking Tom. You said maybe I needed two men in order to tango."

"Well, maybe I've changed my mind."

"I've got to be going."

"Go then," Gilman says, and walks out to the balcony.

On the way to her car, Gemma runs into Ten-Fifteen and corners him in front of his trailer. "Ten-Fifteen, I need to ask you something."

Ten-Fifteen can see that Gemma is very uncomfortable with whatever it is she wants to say. "What do you want to ask?" he asks.

Gemma looks away toward her car. "Nothing. I've got to go."

"Is it about Gilman?"

"Gilman? Why would I want to ask you anything about him?"

"I don't know."

Gemma shuffles her feet. "Well, what do you think about Gilman?"

Ten-Fifteen smiles. "He's my best friend."

Gemma rolls her eyes. "What do you think about Gilman in . . . in regard to women? I mean, if I said the words *Gilman and women*, what would you have to say about that subject?"

Ten-Fifteen shakes his head. "I'd say Gilman loves every woman he's ever seen."

Gemma glares at Ten-Fifteen. "Would you say he's ever loved any one woman in particular?"

"Well, he seems to have a special hankering for you. He says you're the only woman he knows that could come close to keeping his doors locked at night."

"What does that mean?"

"You can take it different ways, I guess. It might mean keeping people from coming in, but it could also mean keeping him from goin out."

Gemma sighs. "I wouldn't want to spend my time trying to keep somebody in. If he wanted to go out, I'd say, 'There's the door.' "

Ten-Fifteen moves away from Gemma. "Well, I guess that's for you fellers to figure out. Right now, the Tuesday evening movie is coming on Channel Five. Wouldn't miss it for the world."

"Happy viewing," Gemma says, and she gets into her car and drives home.

*T*om checked in at the Blue Mountain Inn this morning before going on to his job. This evening when he got off work, he went back to the house on the hill, got the rest of his things, and is now settling into his room at the old hotel, laying his books on the dresser, selecting one to peruse before bed. There are twelve rooms in the main house and eight more in a recently built wing. Most of the rooms appear to be occupied by miners. Possibly their homes are in neighboring counties, he considers, but they spend their weeknights here.

He goes to the window and looks across the main street of Pick at the bank where Gemma works. Closed down and dark, it reminds him of an abandoned prison, and he wonders how she stands going there every day. When Tom checked in this morning, the desk clerk told him that the Blue Mountain Inn dates back to 1915 and has witnessed much of Pick's history, that a gunfight had taken place in this very room ten years ago. A man was killed. Tom looks down at the floor, wondering why the fight started and where the man fell and why people around here are always telling him stories of killings in awestruck voices. It seems to Tom that for such a small town, Pick has had more than its share of death.

He tries to imagine what Daniel Sparks is doing at this very moment, Daniel who holds so many stories on the tip of his tongue. What was it like to play as a child in that cave with those words staring down at him? Does he tell stories as he sits alone by the heating stove at night?

Tom's thoughts drift back to Gilman and Gemma. He tries to rationalize why Gilman chose to instigate a fling with her in the first place, but it is impossible to associate reason with such an action. "He's just another old man trying to prove he's still young," Tom speaks sadly to the walls in his room. He drags out the typewriter he purchased this evening and begins to write.

33
Chapter

*F*rank Denton warms his hands at the kerosene heater in the shed at the mining site. He's made several rounds tonight, and all is well on the mountain. For the past two weeks, he's expected to hear word of Mildred Wilson's body being found, but so far nothing. That means Rosalee doesn't visit her regularly, he surmises, thinking that perhaps she really isn't anywhere around here. Earlier, while he was on his inspection, he thought he heard her singing again, but then he recalls the evening he saw the white woman walking toward Tom Jett's house, carrying a banjo, and comes to the conclusion that it must have been her voice he heard.

This evening as he was leaving the Inn, he noticed Tom Jett entering one of the rooms. Perhaps he was visiting a friend, Frank considers. But Tom had something in his hand . . . a key. He didn't knock; he opened the door with a key. Maybe he was meeting a woman there, but that would mean he finished with her in record time to already be back here on the mountain playing music with the white woman.

Frank sits on the cot in the shed, thinking that Mr. Tom Jett of California bears closer watching. Perhaps I'll try getting acquainted with him someday when I'm at Betty's. "This is a strange burg with even stranger burgers," he says out loud.

A cold wind creeps through a crack in the door, and he shivers, remembering the warm, balmy breeze on a spring day in Palm Beach with the blue-green sea rolling in front of him. He is a child of perhaps six or seven, watching his mother, Alaine, lie on his grandfather's private beach with her latest indistinct lover. The man rubs tanning lotion on the back of her legs, lets his fingers slide playfully near her crotch. His mother giggles and turns facing the man, and they kiss. Frank grabs his board and runs out to the waves, paddling himself farther away from the beach than he has ever gone before. Alaine's laughter rises buoyantly above the noise of the sea, drifts past when he is caught in an undercurrent, taunts him as he struggles to stay afloat. Her lover accidentally looks up, to see Frank nearly drowning, and swims out to rescue him. When they arrive back on the beach, Frank sputtering and coughing for air, Alaine is no longer there. She has gone inside the house, perhaps from the sheer boredom of the balmy spring day.

Gemma couldn't sleep last night for thinking about Gilman Lee, and this morning she called in sick, unable to imagine herself in the same room all day with Marcy and Jo Ellen while Gilman is so strongly on her mind. She sits at the table, offhandedly fitting together pieces of her mother's jigsaw puzzle, working on the sky because it is more difficult. She has been upset ever since she left Gilman's shop the other day on such a sour note. "Go then," Gilman had said, standing with his back turned. "Go then," and she had left, and he hasn't called her once since.

Finding it impossible to wait in this post-spat limbo an instant longer, she gets dressed, drives to the shop, and bangs on the door until he opens up, disheveled and holding his head.

"Do you always have to get drunk every night?" she asks him.

"Not always," he mumbles, "just on the nights when I know you're goin to bang on my door the next morning and wake me up."

"Well, are you going to invite me in, or are you going to keep me standing out here in the cold?"

"Come in," Gilman says.

Gemma brushes past him, walks straight through the shop and into the apartment, sits down on the couch, and props her feet on the coffee table.

Gilman asks, "Did you come here for a reason?"

"Yes," Gemma replies, "I did. I came to tell you that it's high time you stopped being mad at me because I'm not mad at you. And I don't understand why you're mad, anyway. Why are you mad?"

"I'm not mad," Gilman says. "I'm just giving you a chance to make up with your other boyfriend. Have you made up with him yet?"

"He's not my boyfriend, and no, we've not made up."

"But you want to, don't you? Because he makes you feel . . . what was it you said? Light?"

Gemma stands up, walks over to Gilman, slaps him hard as she can, and says, "That's right, why don't you throw it in my face? Throw some private thing I told you right back in my face. I hate you!"

"No, you don't, Gemma."

"Yes, I do."

"You're not even mad at me," Gilman says, walking over to the kitchen area to begin making breakfast. "You just told me a few minutes ago that you wouldn't mad at me."

"Well, I am." She looks at him in complete frustration while he begins frying bacon. "What are you doing?"

"Fixing me something to eat."

"How can you eat at a time like this?"

"I'm hungry."

Gemma walks over to the stove and stands beside him. "Ten-Fifteen told me that you said I was the only woman in the world that could keep your doors locked at night. Well, I don't want to keep your doors locked. You're free to go anytime you want. Have you got that?"

"I don't want to go anywhere right now. I'm getting ready to eat breakfast."

Gemma picks up the frying pan of sizzling bacon, sticks it under the faucet, and turns on the water. "Goddamn it, I'm talking to you."

Gilman puts his hands on Gemma's shoulders. "Go ahead and talk. I'm listening."

"Well, I . . ."

"Cat got your tongue? How about Tom Cat? Has he got it?"

"Look here, Gilman Lee. I'm not seeing Tom anymore."

"Why not?"

"Because I don't feel about him in the right way."

Gilman's eyes turn soft around the edges. "And what about me, Gemma?" he asks. "How do you feel about me?"

"A few seconds ago, I hated you."

"And now?"

"I don't know. How do you feel about me?"

"You're the damnedest woman I've ever seen, Gemma. I'll say that. You know I don't like the word *love* because it's been so overused, but I do feel something powerfully strong for you. Now are you goin to let me fix some breakfast? I'm starved to death."

After Gilman's usual fare of bacon and eggs, they make love and sit on the couch staring at each other like a nameless entity studying its reflection in a mirror. Later, as Gemma hangs around the shop, handing him wrenches and watching him repair cars, she tells him about the Indian ghosts from her childhood.

"I used to see 'em, too," he says. "I used to play with Indian ghosts when I was a little feller."

When they part company later that evening, they agree to meet again soon and promise not to fight with each other for at least a month.

The next afternoon, Gilman Lee walks outside and heads for his truck. Earlier, it rained some, and the snow on the ground has turned to slush, causing his feet to leave brown, watery prints with each step he takes. He's on his way to the house on the hill to check on Rosalee and find out if Gemma was right about Tom's moving out of the house.

This time he doesn't park in Gemma's driveway, but drives on past her house, crosses the bridge the miners built, and continues up the hill on their road. About halfway up, he pulls his truck off the road and parks just inside his property line. The ever watchful armed guard, recently hired, observes this activity, runs to get Ed Toothacre out of his office, and together they walk down the hill toward the truck where they see Gilman drag a wheelbarrow, a red one, out of his truck bed and struggle to lug out a heavy plastic bag, sealed tighter than a drum, too.

"What're you doin, buddy?" the armed guard asks when they get to the truck.

Gilman looks around and smiles. "I sure hope you boys don't mind me using your road. This bag here is full of fertilizer. Sometimes I don't get paid for my services with money; people pay me with whatever they can get their hands on. I thought I'd store this up here in that little shack that sits out in my field, just in case Tom Jett wants to grow a garden next spring. This would've been awful heavy to drag all the way up the hill on foot."

The guard looks around at Ed Toothacre with questions in

his eyes. Ed doesn't notice because he's glaring at Gilman. "I know you're responsible for what happened up here. And don't you think for a minute that it's over. I'll hire detectives if I have to. Someone's bound to know something about what you did. And I'm sure someone will talk for a price."

Gilman shakes his head. "Ed, Ed," he says, "I don't know how you could think such a sorry thing of me. I'm just a mechanic, Ed. Motors are how I make my living. I love 'em too good to put sugar in 'em. Now, I know I used your road, but after all you're augering my coal and right now you're standing on my land. I promise to take this fertilizer over there to that shack and get out of here as quick as I can because I know I upset you, Ed, and I don't like to upset people, no sir."

Ed grinds his teeth until his jawbone experiences shooting pains. He walks with the guard back to his office at the top of the mountain.

Gilman walks past his house to the field, unlocks his prayer chamber, and says, "Zack, looky here. I've got some goodies for the bastards. Whaddaya think?"

Zack looks straight ahead.

"I'm goin to give it to 'em good, ol' buddy." He sits down at the table and eyes Zack closely. Streaks of moisture mark the bones of Zack's face like drying tears.

"You wouldn't cry on me, would you?" Gilman figures frost must have gathered on Zack that the afternoon temperature is melting. "Ain't nothing to cry about, Zack. Everything is just fine."

For the first time ever, he feels uncomfortable sitting at the table with Zack and hurriedly stores the manure concoction, leaves without another word. Before going back to the truck, he stops by to see Rosalee.

When she opens the door for him, he notices the change right away. It's not just that she is in a better mood (she's been in a better mood for a couple of weeks); she is fueled with some purpose that wasn't in her before.

"What's up?" he asks, as he pulls off his jacket and sits down on a stool in the living room.

"Several things," she says. "What's up with you? What did you put in your chamber?"

"Just something I plan to use some night."

"What is it, Gilman?" Rosalee asks.

"Turds."

Rosalee laughs. "What kind of turds?"

"Cow, horse, dog, and human. Turds explode, you know, after they've set for a while in a airtight container. Turn to methane gas."

"You mean . . . ? Shee-it, Gilman."

"You said it, Rosalee."

Rosalee shakes her head. "Never heard of it exploding. Just let me know when you plan on lighting it up, so I can be gone from this house."

Gilman chuckles. "Well, I don't have enough of it to make a bang. I'm goin to throw in some dynamite. That'll do the trick."

"When?"

"Pretty soon."

Gilman looks around the room, noticing that Tom's books are gone, that his sleeping bag is not rolled up in the corner. "Has your roommate deserted you?"

Rosalee sits down on the floor, Indian style. "He's moved into a room in town."

"Did you and him get in a fight?" Gilman asks.

"No, *you* and him got in a fight."

"Oh."

Rosalee leans against the wall and narrows her eyes, looks at Gilman as though he's scum. "Why did you do it?"

"Do what? Everybody seems to think I did something."

"You did."

Gilman sighs and looks at the desk in the corner. "Is he goin to leave that here?"

Rosalee rolls her eyes. "Oh, don't you want him to leave it here? I guess you expect him to lug a big desk down the mountain. I can't believe you."

"I can't believe you, either. What's the matter? Wake up on the wrong side of the bed?"

Rosalee shrugs. "I was just thinking of how things used to be, how I'd hang around your shop. I had a crush on you that wouldn't quit, ever since the fifth grade. I'd see you always surrounded by your cronies, them looking at you like you was some kind of god, listening to every word you said and marking them down. I guess I'm just wondering why you never felt about me the way you claim to feel about Gemma."

"I've always cared about you, Rosalee. I still do."

"Thanks."

Gilman turns sideways and looks at her out of the corner of his eye. "Besides, you ain't had the hots for me in a long time. Otherwise you wouldn't have gone to Florida and got in so deep with Frank Denton. You're still carrying a torch for him, ain't that right?"

"I'll get over it. I got over you, and if I am still carrying a torch for him, it's a torch I feel like setting him on fire with, because I hate him, Gilman." Rosalee stands up and walks around the room. "I've been thinking about leaving."

Gilman follows her with his eyes. "Why would you want to do a thing like that?"

"Why not?"

Gilman smiles. "Where would you go?"

"Arizona, maybe."

"When?"

"In another week or so. I'd go right now but I'm taking time to let the idea settle in . . . and I'll need some money. You reckon you could lend me some?"

"I reckon."

"Have you called Mom lately? I'd like to talk to her before I go."

"Every time I try, the phone is busy."

Rosalee looks around at Gilman. "Her phone is busy?"

"Yeah . . . what?"

Rosalee stops pacing and looks out the window at the melting snow. "Mom don't like to talk on the phone. Just has one for emergencies."

"Well, she's called me a time or two since you've been back here."

"That's because this is a emergency. There's no other way for her to get word to me."

"Maybe she's changed her mind about phones. Must get pretty lonesome up there. I figure she's took to gossiping."

"Mom don't gossip or get lonesome, either. She'd as soon be alone as not."

"Well, maybe I ought to run up there and check on her."

"Maybe you ought to."

"I'd intended to pay a visit to Tom today, after I found out where he was."

"I wish you'd go to Mom's instead."

Gilman puts on his coat and walks down the mountain, stands on the bridge for a while, listening to ice crack. A few minutes later, he is driving by his shop and on past the field where the Indian campground used to be. He continues up the icy dirt road to Mildred's house. When he pulls into her yard, there's not a puff of smoke coming from her chimney, and he knows something is wrong.

He walks up to her door and opens it, steps inside, and smells the odor. Like Wade, he finds her in the bedroom lying under her wedding-ring quilt. He throws back the cover, and notices that she's wearing her robe and slippers. He figures she must have had a heart attack—died in her sleep.

Gilman stands there for a minute, remembering Mildred's pink complexion and pretty smile, and how much Rosalee cares about her. "Funny she'd get in bed with her slippers on," he says to the empty room. "At least she died a peaceful death," he mutters, then he spots a few bruises around her wrists. Maybe that just happens naturally when a person's been dead for a . . . He tries to remember how long he's been trying to call her only to hear a busy signal and wonders why he's been getting a busy signal at all. He should have been getting rings with no answer—not a busy signal.

On his way to the living room to check out the phone, he steps in Wade Miller's vomit. She must have been sick at her stomach, he thinks. In the living room, he finds the phone off the hook and sits down on Mildred's sofa, trying to assess the situation, considering that possibly she knocked the phone off the hook by accident before she went to bed. Maybe she was trying to call someone, but the pain got so bad she couldn't finish the call. If that's the case, how did she make it to her bed and take the time to fold the cover so neat around her? "Almost like someone tucked her in," Gilman decides, pacing the floor, unsure of what to do next, knowing he ought to call someone and tell them what he's found, but who? The undertaker? Hospital? Sheriff? Rosalee? He can't call Rosalee; she doesn't have a phone. Going back into Mildred's bedroom, he takes a closer look at the discolored marks around her wrists. The bruises are shaped like fingers. He reexamines the vomit on the floor, thinking that maybe he threw up after he did it. He? Who's he? Frank Denton, maybe?

He gently pulls the cover over Mildred, switches off the light, and leaves. Outside, it is completely dark as he drives down the icy dirt road to the highway.

34
Chapter

Gilman opens the door to the house on the hill and finds Rosalee lying in front of the fireplace asleep. He stands silently for a moment, thinking how easy it would be for Frank Denton to enter through the front door and kill her. She looks so peaceful he hates to wake her. Finally he sits down on the floor beside her and, stroking her hair, speaks her name.

Rosalee stirs slightly, but she doesn't open her eyes.

"Rosalee?" Gilman says softly.

Suddenly she is wide awake and grabbing hold of his hand. "What's the matter?"

Gilman lifts her head, positioning it in his lap. "I went up to check on your mother."

Rosalee doesn't say a word. She takes in a deep breath and waits.

"She's dead, Rosalee."

Rosalee abruptly sits up.

"I didn't know any other way to tell you," Gilman mutters.

"That's all right," Rosalee says, feeling herself begin to

float. She darts her eyes around the room as though she is trying to latch on to something that will keep her anchored.
"What happened?"

"I don't know. She was in bed."

Rosalee catches her breath and tears start to come. "When?
I mean . . . how long?"

"I'm not sure. I think she's been gone for a week or two."

Rosalee stands up and grabs her coat. "I've got to go to
her."

Gilman catches her by the arm. "It's pretty bad, honey . . .
because she's been up there a long time and . . ."

"I don't care. Are you goin to take me up there or not?"

"Let's go," Gilman says, and they walk quickly down the
mountain and begin the drive to Mildred's house.

On the way, they hardly speak a word. Rosalee can see
nothing but her mother's face. What was the last thing she said
to her? She can't remember. She doesn't remember the last
words Mildred spoke to her, either. They had spent a few
good days together, though. They'd talked over coffee in the
kitchen, sung ballads in harmony, watched the last of autumn
fall from the trees. At least they hadn't parted on bad terms.
She thinks of her mother living most of her life in that small
house at the head of the hollow. She only had one love affair,
just had sex a few times and got pregnant. Rosalee doesn't
even know what her mother wanted to be when she grew up.
What were her dreams?

When they get to the house, Gilman leads her into the bedroom, and Rosalee stands quietly by the bed, crying. "I did
this to her. It's because of me."

Gilman finally persuades her to go with him back to the living room. "Shhh," he whispers softly as she sits on the sofa still
crying.

"If it hadn't been for me, for my stupid-assed problems,
she'd still be alive."

"That's not true, Rosalee."

"Yeah, it is. It's something I'll have to live with for the rest of my life." Rosalee stands up and starts pacing the floor.

"You don't know Frank Denton had anything to do with this."

"Oh no? I'd stake my life on it."

"She may've just had a heart attack."

"Bullshit, Gilman. He killed her and you know it. She was fine when I was up here staying with her. She didn't have any health problems. All she'd ever had wrong was trouble with her feet."

"Ain't they a kind of heart trouble that makes your feet and legs swell?"

"Yeah, but that wouldn't what was wrong with Mom. He got her. Didn't you see the bruises on her wrists?"

"I ain't so sure they're bruises."

"Well, I am. He got her. He's here. . . . I know he is here. God, I wish he'd got me instead. Goddamn his ass. I'll kill him, Gilman. I'll kill that bastard!"

Gilman puts his arms around Rosalee and leads her back to the couch. "We've got to decide what we're goin to do. I know that's hard to do right now, but we have to."

"What do you mean, that's hard to do right now? I'm thinking clearer than I have in years."

"We're goin to have to bring the law in on this."

"No!" Rosalee shouts. "I mean, don't tell them about Frank. If you do, it'll scare him off."

"Well, we can't just leave things as they are. We've got to do something."

Rosalee puts her hands over her eyes. In the room, the smell from the decaying body is almost overwhelming. "Okay, you can call the sheriff. Who is the sheriff these days, anyway?"

"Bill Shepherd."

"I went to high school with Bill Shepherd. He's okay."

"What am I goin to tell him exactly?" Gilman asks, realizing the decision is Rosalee's.

"Don't tell him about Frank and don't tell him about me either. As far as you know, I'm still in Florida. You just found the body, that's all."

"But he'll want to know why I come up here in the first place."

"You come to ask her about me—to find out my address so you could write me."

Gilman nods. "I guess that makes sense."

They sit there for a moment longer. "Even if Frank did kill her, it still wouldn't your fault. You can't help it if he's crazy," Gilman says.

Rosalee walks back to the bedroom and peeps in again at Mildred, but the body under the quilt isn't really her mother anymore. Her mother is somewhere else humming a tune and smiling her shy smile.

*A*fter Gilman takes Rosalee home and gets her settled in, he goes back to Mildred's house and calls the sheriff. Within half an hour, Bill Shepherd arrives with his deputies in tow. The mortician at the Pick Funeral Home, who also serves as the county coroner, arrives a few minutes later and carts Mildred's body back to Pick for examination.

"I still can't figure out why you were up here," the sheriff manages to say, while vigorously chewing gum.

"I told you I come to find out about Rosalee."

"I'd have figured you already asked about Rosalee a long time ago."

"I did, but she moves around. Don't stay in one place."

"Well, looks like a heart attack to me. I wonder who does

know where Rosalee is. I mean somebody's goin to have to tell her about this."

"I don't know."

"Well, I'll find out," the sheriff says. "Did you notice them bruises on Mildred's wrists?"

Gilman looks off to the side. "Yeah, I noticed, but I don't know what to make of 'em. I'd like to go on home now if you're about through here."

"Yeah, I guess you would," the sheriff says, holding his nose from the lingering odor. "I guess you would, after all this."

Gilman spends the night at the old house with Rosalee, holds her while she cries, watches her silently as she sits in the dark room and stares out the window at nothing. The next morning he has coffee with her before returning to the shop.

"I'd better get to the house. Bill Shepherd is liable to want to ask me some more questions today. Will you be all right?"

"Sure."

"Tell you what I'll do. I'll stop by Gemma's house, if she ain't already left for work, and get her to come up here and stay with you today. Do you want me to?"

Rosalee seems to barely hear him. "Sure."

She's thinking about Frank. She's imagining how he must have looked as he was snuffing the life from her mother. How did he do it? she wonders. Did he choke her to death? Smother her? Did he have a smile on his face?

Gilman leaves and she continues sitting there, lost in thoughts. "He killed her," she tells herself repeatedly, almost as if she never would have thought he could. "But I knew he could kill a person. I've seen him do it before," she mutters, walking from the kitchen to the bedroom and back to the living room. Repeatedly she asks herself how it is possible that she loved so completely a man who is capable of such brutality. Was it just the excitement of not knowing what he'd do? If that's true, I'm just as bad as him—worse. I could have stopped him from killing that man in Florida. I could have run away before we even got to the alley. I knew something was going to happen the minute I woke up that morning. Why did I stay to see it through? If I had turned him in, Mom would be alive. What kind of person does that make me? Exhausted, Rosalee drops to the floor and goes to sleep.

Gemma is sitting at the table, thinking about how much she doesn't want to go to work, when Gilman knocks on the door. She knows something is wrong the minute she sees him. He tells her about Mildred, and they stand in the middle of the kitchen, holding on to each other for dear life. Gemma kisses Gilman so long and hard he finally has to come up for air.

"I do love you, if that's the word for it," he mutters.

"It is."

"Well, then I do. Rosalee is up there by herself. Could you stay home from work today and keep her company? I've got to get back home. The sheriff will prob'ly want to see me again today."

Gemma nods her head. "I'll go right up there." She sees the concern in his eyes. "Do you think Frank Denton had anything to do with this?"

"I don't know. Prob'ly not, but just in case, lock the door to the house when you get up there, and keep a eye out the window."

35
Chapter

When Sheriff Bill Shepherd arrives at the shop late that evening, Gilman is surprised by what the man has found out. While questioning Gladys Moore, Bill discovered that Rosalee is somewhere in the vicinity. It seems Mildred had shared the joy of her daughter's return with her friend and nearest neighbor, Gladys Moore, not long after Rosalee moved into the house with Tom. Luckily, she didn't tell Gladys exactly where Rosalee was staying or mention Frank Denton.

"Rosalee didn't happen to get in contact with you today, did she?" Bill Shepherd asks Gilman.

"Wish she had."

"You mean she's not contacted you at all?"

"Not since she wrote me several months ago."

"Did Rosalee and Mildred get along?"

"Why? You don't think Rosalee had anything to do with her own mother dying? I thought Mildred had a heart attack."

"Maybe she didn't. It'll take a few more days to find out the exact cause."

"Why don't you ask Gladys Moore where Rosalee is staying, since she knows so much?"

"I told you the only thing Gladys knows is that Mildred said Rosalee had come back here. She doesn't know her exact whereabouts."

"If Rosalee's here, why wouldn't she let herself be known?" Gilman asks.

"That's what I'd like to know. It sure seems strange that she has been gone for five years, and now suddenly her name is cropping up all over the place at the same time her mother is found dead."

"Stranger things have happened."

"Probably so. By the way, I wish you'd stick close for the next few days. I might want to ask you some more questions."

"Whatever you say, Bill. You know, you're a lot more talented at this job than I ever gave you credit for."

"It pays sometimes not to brag about what you're good at, Gilman."

"And quite the philosopher, too," Gilman adds, as he walks Bill out to his car.

*F*or most of the day, Rosalee has slept, occasionally waking and staring out the window toward the field beside the house. Gemma has not said much to her; she's just been there. Having set a pot of soup on to cook this afternoon, she considers waking Rosalee, who hasn't eaten a bite all day, but Rosalee is sleeping so peacefully, she leaves her alone. Gemma stares out the window at the trees that are naked except for clumps of old snow scattered here and there on the branches. Her thoughts run back to this morning when Gilman stopped by her house to tell her the news. She remembers the kiss she gave him and feeling the need to reach down inside him and drag out whatever it is she loves so much. She is lost in this reverie when Rosalee opens her eyes and sits up.

"Gemma? Looks like I've slept all day," she mumbles.

"Just about."

"Right now, I don't want to do anything but sleep. I can't stand to think it's my fault . . . my fault. God, I wish I'd never come here, that I'd just stayed down in Florida and let him kill me or do whatever it was he intended. All I've caused is trouble."

"You didn't cause anything, Rosalee. Sometimes things just happen. I never could figure out why people are always so eager to lay blame."

Rosalee sits up and picks at the lint on her blanket. "It was always just me and her when I was growing up. My daddy left the minute he found out she was pregnant. She never went out with another man. All them years alone. She was shy, didn't get around much. Just went to town sometimes on weekends—went to a movie or to church. She seemed to make out pretty good, though—liked living up there in that little house, liked the mountain, the trees, the wildflowers. God, I'll miss her."

Gemma walks over and sits down close by Rosalee.

Rosalee looks around at her. "So, are you and Gilman hard at it?"

"What do you mean?"

"You know what I mean."

"I don't know what Gilman and me are doing."

"He's a good man—I'll say that. I've never knowed anyone that could top him. Once upon a time, I thought I'd met one that could, but that just shows you what a bad judge of character I can be."

"Do you feel like eating some soup?"

Rosalee grins. "It smells good."

*N*ews of the discovery of Mildred's body spreads through Pick like wildfire. Even though Mildred was never a well-known figure in the community, the very circumstances of her death, as it now appears—the fact that she lay dead in her bed for two weeks before her body was discovered—have ignited everyone's curiosity. Wade Miller finds out about it from Marcy and Jo Ellen as soon as he gets to the bank this morning. The first thing he does is to walk over to the courthouse to check out the details with Sheriff Shepherd. The sheriff doesn't mention anything about Fred Dudley, so Wade figures Fred isn't a suspect. He does, however, mention Rosalee, asks Wade if he knows where she is.

"Why should I know where she is?" Wade responds.

"Because you and her had a fling of some kind."

"Who did you hear that from?"

Bill Shepherd laughs. "Wade, the whole town knows you were sneaking around with Rosalee before she left for Florida. Say, you wouldn't happen to know exactly where in Florida she used to live, would you?"

"I told you I didn't."

"Do you know that she's back here, now?"

"Certainly not."

"Yeah, she's back here somewhere."

As Wade turns to leave, Sheriff Shepherd says, "Let me know if you hear from her."

Wade doesn't reply, just keeps walking out the door.

*T*hree days have passed since the discovery of the body, and Frank Denton sits alone in his room at the Blue Mountain

Inn, reading a well-worn copy of the *Pick Times*. On page 2,
the story is captioned MILDRED WILSON FOUND DEAD OF APPAR-
ENT NATURAL CAUSES. In the article, it is clear that the local authorities don't know half the story. No mention is made of foul
play. It is noted, however, that an autopsy is being performed,
with the results to be released in a couple of days, and more
interesting to Frank is the appeal for information regarding
the location of Mildred's daughter, Rosalee. Apparently, rumors have spread that she is in town, but she hasn't stepped
forward, and the authorities have had no luck in verifying
whether the rumors are true. He wonders if he is correct in
his assessment that somewhere between the lines of the article
is a hint that Rosalee is responsible for her mother's death.

Frank smiles. She's here. I knew she was here. "Ain't life
wonderful!" he says, sipping a beer. He closes his eyes in deep
concentration, trying to make himself become Rosalee. Where
would she go? Obviously she didn't go to her mother. He picks
up the newspaper again. The article states that Gilman Lee
found her body at approximately eleven o'clock Wednesday
night.

"Gilman Lee," Frank says aloud. "Why was he visiting the
woman that late at night?" He tries to imagine the look on
Gilman's face when he pushed open the bedroom door and
saw her. Frank wonders if she looked as pretty after two weeks
of lying unattended as she had looked the day he left her. He
remembers how carefully he turned down the covers, how
neatly he folded them around her neck—he remembers the
pink flush in her cheeks.

It is suddenly obvious to him that Gilman Lee would not
have gone to see Mildred at eleven o'clock Wednesday night
unless he had a good reason. "For all I know, Rosalee is staying with him," Frank whispers to the silent room.

Until now, he has determined to keep a respectful distance
from Mr. Lee's machine shop. He hasn't wanted to give Rosalee's old boyfriend the faintest reason to suspect his true iden-

tity. From what he has heard, the local musician/bootleg-
ger/mechanic is smart as a tack and carries the potential for
danger. It is speculated that even if he isn't dangerous himself
he has friends and associates who are. "Maybe it's time I got
to know the good old boy," Frank says, as he reaches for another cold one, noticing that only two beers are left in his
cooler. He smiles, thinking that perhaps he should go to
Gilman's shop for another case, but after careful considera-
tion he decides not to, reasoning that he isn't ready to see
Gilman yet, that he needs to think about the meeting, plan his
strategy. Frank leaves the room at the inn and drives down the
river to Betty Marker's house. Because of the faint aura of
decay that envelops her, he has developed some affection for
the middle-aged, bootlegging Betty.

When he pulls into her driveway, he sees Tom Jett's Toyota
parked alongside her house. He gets out of his car and walks
toward the front porch, noticing the aggravating noise of construction work coming from behind the place. He walks inside
the house and finds her sitting at the table having a drink and
reading the paper.

"Hello there, Betty. I'd like a case of Bud."

Betty looks up and grins. "Well howdy, Fred. How's it
goin?" She puts down the paper, walks into the pantry, and
comes back with a case. "Here you go."

"What's that you're reading?" he asks, noticing the paper
turned to the section about Mildred Wilson.

"Ah, just reading about that Wilson woman they found
dead. I've always been afraid that's the way I'll go. Just be
found dead some morning by someone wanting to buy a case
of beer."

"Yes, I heard about the Wilson woman. What do you think
of that story?"

"Well, I think it's the awfulest thing. I wonder why they
can't find her girl, Rosalee."

"I don't know. Kind of makes you wonder, doesn't it?"

"About what?"

"About the fact that they don't know where she is." He looks at her wrinkled muumuu and tousled hair and feels a surge of emotion. He wonders how different his life would have been if he'd been born to a woman like Betty. I bet she would have spoiled me rotten, Frank thinks. She would have served me cookies and milk every evening when I got home from school. Tacked a basketball net on the oak tree in the front yard so the two of us could play one-on-one. Made her boyfriends take me fishing in exchange for her favors.

"Anyway, I doubt they'll ever find you all alone and dead, Betty. You've usually got someone with you." He looks out the window, listening to Tom Jett's saw. "Sounds like you're keeping that carpenter out there pretty busy. I'm surprised you haven't shown me your new room."

"He's done with it except for nailing on the baseboards. Come in here, and I'll show you."

The two of them walk into the new card room, which is paneled in the same knotty pine that Tom used in Gilman's apartment. A huge fireplace dominates one end of the room and tables are positioned throughout. Betty points out the tiled floor. "Easy to keep clean," she remarks. "Now, I don't want you to be no stranger when I open this up."

When they step out the sliding glass doors to the patio where Tom is working, Frank says, "Hello, there. This is really nice."

Tom, who has been constructing the wooden planters for the patio, turns off his saw and glances around at the man.

"I don't know if you two have been introduced," Betty says. "This here is Fred Dudley, Tom. He's from over at Somerset."

"Hello," Tom says.

Betty grins proudly. "This is Tom Jett from California. He studied philosophy out there. Every time he takes a break, he drags out a book and starts reading. Have you ever been to California, Fred?"

"No," Frank says. "I've always wanted to go, though."

The introduction is interrupted by the sound of the phone ringing. Betty, visibly irritated, goes inside to answer.

"Didn't I see you in the parking lot at the Inn the other day?" Frank asks.

"Probably so. I'm staying down there until I move into my other place."

"Oh?" Frank says, slightly confused. He wonders how long Tom has been staying at the Inn and whether he intends to move back into Gilman's old house on the hill.

Tom decides to be friendly. "So you're from Somerset? I may have passed through there on my way here. I can't remember. Is it a small town like Pick?"

"It's small, but not as small as Pick. Actually, it's different than Pick in a lot of ways." Frank slouches to one side and grins, electing impulsively to bring up Mildred's death in hopes of getting an idea of what someone besides Betty thinks about the subject and perhaps even of planting a suspicion that Rosalee is to blame for Mildred's passing.

"Somerset is a peaceful little town, but this place . . . I don't know," Frank says. "Yesterday I read in the paper that a woman was found dead in her house. I guess she'd been dead for quite some time. Anyway, people are saying she might have been murdered. They're even thinking her daughter might have had something to do with it."

"Perhaps people don't have enough to occupy their minds," Tom says. So that's what the gossips are cooking up, he thinks, imagining conversations on phone lines—"Yeah, that Rosalee was always wild. Was on drugs before she left here. I wouldn't put anything past her."

"It's about time for you to get off work, isn't it?" Frank asks. He senses that Tom is a complicated individual, and Frank craves a stimulating conversation. "Why don't you have a drink with me and Betty?"

"Maybe I'll do that," Tom says as Frank walks away. Tom

heard about Mildred's death yesterday and went to see Rosalee; but he didn't stay long because Gemma was there, and he
found nothing between them but silence. He tried to comfort
Rosalee, but she was hard to reach also. She just kept staring
out the window, talking about how much she hated Frank Denton, seemingly convinced that he killed her mother. Tom sighs
and puts down his saw. From inside the house drifts the sound
of Betty and Fred Dudley laughing. He stores his tools in a
shed in the backyard, thinking he could use a beer about now.
With his book tucked under his arm, he enters the living room.

"What's that you're reading?" Frank asks as Betty hands
Tom a beer.

"*Twilight of the Idols*."

"Really? I went to a community college near Somerset. My
philosophy teacher was a Nietzsche fanatic," Frank says.
"Made us read all of his books."

"What did you think of him?" Tom asks.

"Nietzsche? I agree with him that people are *good* because
they're either afraid or feel guilty. I like what he says about
criminals—that they have the nature of warriors and that under different circumstances they'd be heroes. I like the fact
that Nietzsche was a loner—a true sign of genius. What do you
think?"

"I don't hold myself to one man's beliefs. All philosophies
are true."

Frank laughs.

Betty looks from Frank to Tom and takes a drink.

"Betty, what do you say we put on some music? I brought
my Robert Johnson tape," Frank says.

Tom's eyes light up. "You like Robert Johnson?"

"One of my favorites."

For over an hour, Tom and Frank talk about subjects rang-
ing from philosophy to the Romantic period in English liter-
ature. Betty listens for a while, then curls up on the couch and
goes to sleep.

"Does it seem cold in here to you?" Frank asks Tom. "I'm afraid she'll get cold." He goes into her bedroom and comes back with an afghan. As he gently covers her, he stares down at her aging body—the flabby arms that sag in repose, the lined but peaceful face, the gray hair stringing around her shoulders. Frank is amazed at the depth of feeling he has for Betty at that moment. "I'd better get back to the Inn," he mutters.

"Yeah, it's been a long day," Tom says, noticing the swift downturn in Frank's mood. "I'd better go too."

36
Chapter

Tom reads the latest article regarding Mildred Wilson.
DEATH BY SUFFOCATION the caption says on page 1. He
is convinced that Rosalee is no longer safe staying at
the old house and drives up there to persuade her to find
a better place to stay. When he gets there, he finds Gemma
with her.

"You've got to get out of here," he tells Rosalee. "You
shouldn't be up here by yourself."

"But Gemma has been staying with me."

"Well, Gemma can't stay with you indefinitely. She'll have to
go back to work soon. Maybe this would be a good time for
you to go to Arizona like you planned."

"It's too late to go to Arizona now."

"Why? It might prove better for your health to just leave."

"I'm not budging from here now, not after what he's done.
No, I'm staying for the outcome, and there's nothing you can
say to make me change my mind."

"Well, you could at least stay down at my house with me
and Momma," Gemma offers.

"What would June have to say about that?" Tom asks her.

"She'll keep quiet about it. What do you think, Rosalee?"

"Well, I guess . . ."

"Let's get your things together, and we'll go down there tonight."

When they arrive at Gemma's house, June is sitting in a rocker dozing. "Wake up, Momma, we've got company," Gemma says.

June rubs her eyes and finds herself staring directly into her daughter's face. For the past five nights, Gemma has been staying in the house on the hill. June hasn't had the vaguest idea why. Gemma told her that Tom no longer lived up there, and that she was going to put the empty house to some use. June didn't believe her, though. She figures Tom has been joining her daughter every night for frolicking good times, and that news is bound to break out any minute that Gemma is shacked up with a man.

She looks past Gemma and discovers Tom and Rosalee. She doesn't know who Rosalee is, though, not at first. The face looks familiar, but she can't pin it to a name. June sits up straight. "Company?"

"Hello, Mrs. Collet," Tom says.

"Hello," June replies, still trying to place the other woman.

"Momma, this is Rosalee," Gemma says.

A look of shock and confusion sweeps over June's face. "You mean . . . Rosalee? Mildred's girl?" June has heard the news of Mildred's death, too. She was never really friends with Mildred Wilson, but she has known of her all her life. June has also heard the speculation concerning Rosalee. "Mildred's girl?"

"Yes, Momma, this is Rosalee."

Gemma proceeds to tell June the story of Rosalee—of how long she has been staying in Gilman Lee's old house, the works. "She needs a place to stay, Momma. I thought maybe she could stay here."

June sighs. "I don't know . . ."

"She can't stay up there anymore," Gemma says.

June stands up and walks toward the bedroom. "Come here, Gemma, I want to talk to you in private."

Gemma follows her into the room.

"How could you do this? Bring somebody in here and me asleep and already have it set up that they can stay? This is my house, you know. I grew up in this house. It's mine more than yours, and I decide who stays here or not."

"I know you do, Momma. That's why I'm asking you."

"They think she might of killed Mildred."

"Well, she didn't. I told you a man named Frank Denton probably killed her."

"How do you know Rosalee didn't make all of that up? You've not seen the man, have you? No one has seen him. Maybe that's because they ain't no such man."

"I believe her, and I'm asking you to let her stay."

June sits down on the edge of the bed. "It seems like so much has changed this year. Everything is going haywire." She looks around the room. "And it's cold in here. The heat never did work right in this room." June hugs her arms to her stomach.

"Can she stay or not?"

"Oh, all right."

"And you won't say anything to a living soul?"

"I won't."

Gemma bends down and kisses June on the top of the head.

At the machine shop, Gilman Lee sits on his couch with his head leaned back and his mouth slightly open. His eyes are rolled up in their sockets, and he's so deep in concentration that if anyone saw him at this moment they would think he was dead. Since the coroner's report finding that Mildred was suffocated, murdered to be exact, he has been as convinced as Rosalee that Frank Denton is responsible. What irks him most is that everyone suspects Rosalee of killing her mother. Just because she acted as though she were alive and made a few bad choices in the process—took a few drugs when she was younger—people think she walked into the house she grew up in and took her mother's life. He knows it will be impossible to keep Rosalee's presence a secret much longer. He will have to either get her out of town or somehow find Frank Denton.

The phone rings and he picks it up.

"Hello," he says.

"Gilman, I brought Rosalee down to my house to stay."

It's Gemma, and he's plenty happy to hear her obstinate voice.

"It's good to hear you," he says.

"We brought her here because we are just afraid for her to be staying up there in that house by herself. And I can't keep on staying there. I have to go back to work. Tom came up here today and we all decided that she ought to stay with me and Momma."

"That's good," Gilman replies. "How is Tom, by the way?"

"Fine. Do you think it's okay that we brought her here?"

"It's fine. How did June take it?"

"She's calmed down some, now. She'll be all right."

"So you and Tom are getting along again?"

"This is not about that subject," Gemma says, glancing around at Tom, Rosalee, and June, who are pretending not to listen. "This is about Rosalee."

"Fine. I mean, it *is* really fine. It's a good idea, you taking her down there."

"I'm glad you think so," Gemma says. "Well, I've got to be going. I'll talk to you soon."

"I can't wait," Gilman says.

"Gilman?" Gemma adds, just before hanging up, ". . . I do, too."

"Do what?"

"You know."

"No, I don't. What?"

"I can't tell you right now."

"Oh, you mean because they's people—maybe even Tom, included—all around you listening to every word you say? What did you want to tell me, Gemma?"

"That I love you."

Gilman smiles. "I'll see you later," he says and hangs up.

Gilman keeps the smile on his face for about five minutes longer, completely immersed in thoughts of Gemma. Finally, he drifts back to the Rosalee–Frank Denton problem. It is good that they took her out of his house since she was such an easy target up there, alone. But what now? For a moment, he considers driving Rosalee to Harlan and putting her on a bus heading West, but he doesn't like that idea because it is at least possible that Frank might find out she left and track her down. Gilman asks himself what he knows about the man— he's crazy, about thirty-five years of age, has strange eyes, and is rich. Being rich is the only one of those characteristics that distinguishes Frank from a lot of other men in the county. A person can disguise wealth fairly easily; all he has to do is wear old clothes and not throw money around. What else does Gilman know about him? Nothing. Has anyone new arrived in Pick lately? There are always a few out-of-county men who come to Pick to work the mines. It is not as though the town never receives a stranger in its midst. Since Frank Denton is technically from the South, he could probably adapt to the local accent fairly easily, thereby concealing that he is from as far away as Florida.

As Gilman keeps rolling these thoughts over and over in his mind, he comes back to the one thing that sets Frank apart:

his wealth. What does a rich man do when he first comes to town? Maybe he goes to the bank, Gilman answers himself. He decides to give Gemma another call.

"Hello," he says. "It's me again."

"Yeah?"

"Have you had any new customers at the bank in the past few months? Anyone that might have started a new account, deposited a lot of money?"

"I've had some people start new accounts, but no one who had a lot of money."

"Remember their names?"

"Well, Ed Toothacre, for one."

"Anyone else?"

"Well, you know, men that work in the mines." A memory of the man with the blue-black eyes comes to her mind. "Then there was this other guy, but he didn't start an account."

"What guy?"

"Just this man that came to see Wade one day. Actually, I think he does work in the mines. . . . I don't know. He lives downtown, but like I said, he didn't even start an account. Gilman, why are you asking about this, anyway?"

"Oh, no reason. I'll see you later, Honeybunch."

Gilman hangs up the phone, thinking that, as much as he hates to, he needs to have a talk with Wade Miller.

*W*ade Miller is standing at the window looking out at the alley when Gilman Lee brushes past Marcy and Jo Ellen and casually enters his office.

"How's it goin, Okra Dick?" Gilman asks Wade politely.

Wade stiffens, walks quickly behind his desk, and sits down. "Why are you here? What do you mean coming into my office and calling me names?" Wade asks, getting angrier with each word he says. "You know, it's one thing to call me that out on the street, but it's another to call me that in my own office."

"Yeah? Well, when you get right down to it, they's not much difference," Gilman says.

"I repeat, why are you here?"

"Oh, I just want to ask you some questions, that's all."

Wade turns red as a stop sign. He knows, he's thinking. Somehow the asshole has found out I was at Mildred's. "What questions could you possibly want to ask me? I don't have any business dealings with you, and we certainly are not buddies." Wade stands up. "Leave my office, right now!"

"Cool down," Gilman says. "Have you heard from Rosalee lately, Wade?"

"No I have not! Maybe it's me who ought to be asking you that question."

"I've not heard from her, either. Seems like everyone is looking for our ex-girlfriend. They can't even find any trace of her in Florida. I'll tell you something, though. For a while, she was writing me letters from down there in West Palm. She told me about this man she was seeing."

The color falls from Wade's face.

"Yeah, she was dating this man, this rich man. He was strange, she said. You've not seen anyone like that around here, have you? Someone that might have come into the bank, you know, that was strange-acting and rich? Have you seen anyone like that?"

Wade's heart is beating so hard he can see his starched white shirt move up and down. "I told you to get out of here, and I mean it. If you don't leave right now, I'm going to call the sheriff. Get out!"

Gilman Lee smiles. "Okay, Wade, whatever you say. But I think you know more than you're telling, Wade. And I'm not goin to let up until I find out what it is." Gilman walks quietly out of Wade's office past Marcy and Jo Ellen, who have been straining their ears attentively to hear the gist of the argument. Before leaving the bank lobby, he stands for a moment looking out the plate-glass windows toward the Blue Mountain Inn across the street, thinking about how close Tom Jett's room is to the bank where Gemma works. He knows Gemma hasn't been to work for the past four or five days, but he wonders if, on her return, she will stop by to visit Tom occasionally before going home in the evenings.

Gilman walks quickly out of the bank to his truck. "I can't believe I'm jealous. I never thought I'd see the day I'd be jealous." He drives toward home with all kinds of thoughts dip-diving through his mind, fighting for first place.

G emma stares out the kitchen window toward the mountain behind her house. The miners are still there blasting, scraping, and digging out the coal. Just a reminder that the single death of a woman at the head of a hollow is not an end in itself. The crap still continues. She looks down at the creek still partially frozen over, water gurgling out of breaks in the ice, and a hunger for spring, for dogwoods and redbuds, overwhelms her. Rosalee and June are in the living room talking. They've become friends. Rosalee is telling June about a ride she took one time in a hot-air balloon, how she could see for miles, how it felt to rise like helium in the air. June sits there with her mouth open, taking it in. Gemma supposes her mother is adding a hot-air balloon ride to her list of things to do when she gets the coal money.

Gemma thinks of Tom, of the few times she has seen him of late. As usual, he was polite to her and attentive to Rosalee. In this world, she thinks, as she stares again toward the mountain with its miners hard at work, kind people are scarce. Tom is kind, and he gives me hope, but I don't love him the way I love Gilman. Gilman Lee is like a star that's burning and falling, and when I'm with him, I'm a star, too. It's like we've run into each other somewhere in space, and there's nothing we can do but burst into flames. She thinks this as she stares toward the mountain, occasionally glancing down at the frozen creek.

She decides she needs to talk to Tom, to tell him exactly how things are. She doesn't want him to think there is a chance for them to continue. At least she owes him that. Maybe after the funeral she will have a long talk with him. Mildred's funeral is this afternoon. June, of course, is going, and Gemma is taking her. As a matter of fact, June has been helping Gladys Moore with the funeral arrangements, picking out the casket, reserving the church. June tells Rosalee, who doesn't dare attend, to rest assured Mildred is passing to the next world in style.

As the hours draw nearer to the time Gemma and June will be leaving for the church, Rosalee grows more fidgety. "I wish I could go," she says. "I mean, what difference does it make? They'll find out where I am soon enough."

"Rosalee, honey, I wish you could go, too," June chimes in apologetically.

Gemma looks at the two of them and sighs. "Rosalee, don't you know that they will put you in jail? I know it doesn't make sense. None of it makes sense—this whole thing of them suspecting you, of all people. But they do, and they will put you in jail." Gemma turns to June. "Come on, Momma, it's time to go. Rosalee, we'll be back as soon as we can. Don't you worry about anything. I asked Gilman to come by and keep you company. He should be here pretty soon."

At the church, Gemma and June sit in the front pew, listening to the sermon. Eyeing the flowers like a critic, June whispers, "I'm glad she don't have too many mums."

The pastor is saying that God had a reason for taking Mildred. He says that Mildred has gone to join the angels, that she will know a joy she never knew on Earth. It is a tear-jerking message—handkerchiefs are being dragged out of pockets all over church. People are nodding their heads, almost as though they wish He would take them to heaven, also. Finally, the pastor is finished and opens his hymn book to "Nearer My God to Thee." He motions to the choir to begin, and the singing starts. That's when Rosalee steps quietly into the church, walks slowly up the aisle, stops by the closed casket, and says, "Bye, Mom. I couldn't let them put you in the ground without saying good-bye."

People drop out of the singing, one by one, until there are only two or three voices and a faltering piano. Finally, there is complete silence. Gemma jumps up like a president's bodyguard and zips up to the casket with Rosalee.

"I just had to come," Rosalee says.

"I reckon you did," Gemma whispers, glancing around at the stunned congregation, "but we need to go now."

"Well, let's go then."

The two of them scoot down the aisle of the church and disappear like ghosts. The congregation, which luckily for Rosalee does not include Sheriff Bill Shepherd, murmur and stare, not sure until they corroborate Rosalee's appearance with each other numerous times that what they just saw was real.

37
Chapter

"Don't ask me why I did it," Rosalee says, as she and Gemma are driving home. "Because I don't know."

"Don't worry about it."

Rosalee fidgets in the car seat. "I'm not worried. As a matter of fact, why don't you turn the car around and let's go to the cemetery? Everyone has already seen me. May as well let them get a better look."

"I gather Gilman didn't stop by the house like he was supposed to."

"Must of been held up."

"How did you get to the church, anyway?"

"Hitched a ride."

"You realize that someone is probably chasing down Bill Shepherd right now to tell him," Gemma says, pulling to the side of the road. "He'll be looking for you in a few minutes."

"I'm tired of hiding, Gemma. I can't hide anymore."

"Okay," Gemma says, and turns the car around. When they pass the church on the way to the cemetery, they notice vehicles lining the side of the road and realize that the funeral service is still in progress. They drive a mile farther and park in a field at the foot of the mountain, deciding to walk the rest of the way to the cemetery. Around them winter trees stand naked and bleak, and gusts of cold wind beat against their faces. Though not as old as the one at Washburn Creek, the cemetery where Mildred will shortly be laid to rest is old and slightly run-down, with no fence or gate marking its boundary. Once past the piney shrubs that surround it, they easily spot the freshly dug grave awaiting Mildred's coffin.

"Well, there it is, the place we'll all end up," Rosalee says, as they stare into the rectangular cavity of half-frozen earth. "They'll bring her up here, lower her down, and cover her up, and that will be that."

Gemma tries to think of something comforting to say to Rosalee, but every word that comes to mind seems trite and untrue. She finally says, "Do you reckon Gilman ever got to the house? If he did, I wonder where he thinks you are."

"I don't know, but I'm not goin to worry about it. Gilman don't need to know everything. Let him wonder."

Gemma begins to feel dizzy and cold from staring into the empty grave. "I'm going to walk around a minute to keep warm. Wanta come with me?"

"No. I'll stay here."

Gemma wanders to the edge of the cemetery, looks down the road to the bottom of the hill, and sees the hearse, followed by the rest of the procession, pulling into the parking lot. As people get out of their cars and walk up the hill, she notices her mother among them, and Bill Shepherd. Gemma looks around at Rosalee and walks back to the grave to be with her. There is nothing more to do but wait for things to happen.

As June Collet nears the cemetery, she sees Gemma standing with Rosalee at the grave site and walks hurriedly around the others in order to get to them first. "Well, there you are," she whispers to Gemma. "I didn't know where you'd gone."

The pastor, a tall man with large bones, a huge head, and lips that twist from side to side as he speaks, steps around to one end of the grave and begins to speak one more time. The people at the grave site barely hear what he says, they are so intently staring at Rosalee with shameless curiosity. As the casket is being lowered into the ground, Bill Shepherd, tall and lean, his shoulders bent, his head lowered, stands inconspicuously at the back of the group with his eyes closed.

When the service is over, a few of the braver souls approach Rosalee armed with appropriate words of sympathy. June and Gemma stand on either side of her. "She was a good person," one woman says. "We wondered where you were all this time," says another.

Rosalee nods and smiles.

Finally everyone is gone except Rosalee, Gemma, June, and Bill Shepherd. Bill shuffles his feet awkwardly and behaves as if he doesn't know in what direction to look.

"Hi, Bill, long time no see. I guess you want to talk," Rosalee goes over to him and says.

"I do."

"Well, let's not talk here. Why don't we go to Gemma's house?"

"That's fine with me," Bill says.

When they arrive at the house, Gilman Lee's truck is parked in the driveway. They enter the kitchen and find him sitting at the table eating a piece of spice cake. "I've been working some of your puzzle, June. This is a damn good cake. Anyone want to join me? You want a piece, Bill? You don't mind Bill having a piece, do you, June?"

"Of course not," June says, taking off her scarf and gloves.

"Well, why don't we go into the living room and talk?" Gilman suggests. "Rosalee, I swear, you gave me the scare of my life when I got here and found you gone. I was so let down, I couldn't do anything except sit down here and start eating."

Once everyone is settled, Gilman looks at Bill Shepherd and says, "I guess you've got the floor, Bill."

Bill looks around at Rosalee. "I think Rosalee ought to be the first one to talk."

June goes into the kitchen to begin cooking while Bill takes out a notepad, preparing to listen to Rosalee tell her story. She tells him about Frank, about the incident in Florida, about hiding out in the house on the hill, and explains her suspicions that Frank killed Mildred. Gemma sits close beside her. It takes Rosalee half an hour to finish the tale; and Bill doesn't interrupt her while she's talking, but he does take quite a few notes.

When she is finished, Gilman looks at Bill and says, "What do you think?"

June, by now, has dinner ready, and she and Gemma bring plates of food to their guests. "You fellers eat," June says. "You can talk about this later."

During the meal, which they eat in the living room because the table is covered with the half-finished jigsaw puzzle, they make a few attempts at small talk, but a real conversation never gets off the ground. Bill stares at his plate, deep in thought, and except for Gilman, no one seems to be very hungry. June and Gemma take the half-full plates back to the kitchen.

"I think we'll just keep things as they are," Bill says.

"What do you mean?" Rosalee asks.

"I mean no one except the people in this room and Tom Jett knows you're staying here with Gemma."

"Ten-Fifteen knows," Gilman interrupts.

"Is he going to tell anyone? Is Tom?"

"No."

"Point is I think you ought to just hide out here, Rosalee, until we find this guy. Everyone at the cemetery saw you with Gemma, but they don't know you're staying with her, and I'll let it be known you're not. I just need some time to ask around. See if I can find this Frank Denton."

"You might wanta ask Wade Miller some questions," Gilman says. "I talked to him the other day, and I think he knows something he's not telling."

Gemma looks up surprised.

Bill turns to Rosalee. "Have you been in contact with Wade since you've been back?"

"No, Wade don't know anything from me." Rosalee gazes past Bill to the window. "I hope you don't spread Frank's name around. If he knows you're looking for him, he'll get away."

"I won't," Bill says.

Gilman nods at Bill. "I'm glad you believed us on this . . . but people are goin to want to know about what happened with Rosalee. They know you saw her at the cemetery, and they know you were goin to question her. I imagine they'll be curious about the outcome."

Bill smiles. "I'm sure they will, but I'm just going to tell them she didn't have anything to do with it."

"They won't be satisfied with that."

"I don't care if they're satisfied or not." Bill gets up and puts on his hat and coat. "I guess I'll be going. I've got some things to look into."

Rosalee walks him to the door and watches him drive away. "I went to high school with that boy," she says, glancing around at Gilman and Gemma, who are sitting side by side on the couch, their shoulders brushing together, their fingers touching.

38
Chapter

With his unshaven face an army-green hue and his eyes circled and dark, Wade Miller sits behind his desk, staring at a nicked place in the wood-grain surface. He heard about Rosalee's appearance at the funeral yesterday from his wife, who was in attendance. He feels as though everything he has worked for all of his life has just been tried and found guilty, and it is becoming increasingly difficult for him to keep his mind on business at the bank. At least Gemma came to work again this morning, he thinks, hoping she can catch up on the backlog that developed while she was out with the flu. Wade's wife informed him that Gemma seemed to be *with* Rosalee yesterday, that she left with her from the service, that she was with her when the body was interred. So far, he hasn't questioned Gemma about her connection with Rosalee; he's been afraid to.

Wade is afraid of everything, including the fact that Gilman suspects he knows more than he's telling, but most of all he is afraid of what Fred Dudley might do next. He wonders if Fred has heard that Rosalee showed up at her mother's funeral. He is almost sure he has. News travels fast in Pick.

Gemma is sitting at her desk behind a stack of accounting that Marcy and Jo Ellen chose to save for her return when Bill Shepherd walks in and asks to speak to Wade.

"Sure, go right in," Gemma says, wondering why Gilman thinks Wade of all people knows something about Frank Denton.

Wade is still staring at his desktop as Bill walks in unannounced. He looks up and feels his stomach ball into a firmer knot.

"Bill!" he says in the friendliest voice he can muster. "What can I do for you?"

"You can answer some questions. Mind if I sit down?"

"No, go ahead." Afraid of what Bill might ask him, Wade tries to create meaningless chatter. "God, what a gloomy-looking day it is!" he says, pointing to the gray, murky weather outside his window. "I hate this kind of weather, don't you? I've been thinking about just leaving everything and taking a trip to Savannah, Georgia. Soak up some sun, you know? I don't know if I can stand another one of these gloomy days. Have you ever vacationed in Savannah, Bill?"

Bill leans back in his chair. "I don't think it would be a good idea for you to go to Georgia just now, Wade."

"Why not? This bank almost runs itself, especially now that I've got Gemma back to work. She's been out sick for a while, but we'll get caught up in no time."

"Rosalee came to Mildred's funeral yesterday, Wade. Did you hear?"

"I heard," Wade says, batting his eyes.

"You've not met anyone lately who asked you for information about Rosalee, have you?"

"No. I mean, just you . . . and Gilman stopped in the other day and asked me if I'd seen or heard from her."

"I'm not talking about me or Gilman. I'm talking about

someone new to town. Has anyone new asked you about Rosalee?"

Wade stands up suddenly and starts pacing the floor. "No,
Bill. Why would they?"

"I have reason to believe that someone from out of town is
looking for her, that's all."

"No one like that has asked me anything, Bill. And, if they
had, I wouldn't have known anything. I'm sure, if you've
talked to Rosalee, she's told you I don't know anything about
her recent activities."

"She did mention something to that effect."

"How is she, by the way? Can you tell me where she's staying? I'd sort of like to see her, offer my condolences. You
know, I think it's just awful the way people started thinking
right off the bat that she had something to do with Mildred's
death. You don't think she did it, do you?"

"I know she didn't do it. And no, I can't tell you where she's
staying. She may not even be in the county anymore." Bill
stands up to go. "Now's not the time to go to Georgia, Wade.
Stick around."

When Bill has gone, Wade sits back down at his desk. He
would never have believed a situation could be so unfair to an
innocent man like himself, and deciding to take his chances
with Gemma's caustic attitude, he calls her into his office to
question her about Rosalee.

"What do you want?" Gemma says when she enters. "Don't
you know I'm busy?"

"Yes," Wade says. "I know you're busy, but I wanted to ask
you about Rosalee. My wife tells me you were with her at the
service yesterday. How's she taking things?"

"Pretty good."

"Do you know where she's staying? Is she at her mother's
old house? I'd like to stop in and see her at a time like this."

"I don't know where she is. I've not seen her since the
funeral."

"My wife tells me you really seemed close to her yesterday. I didn't even realize you knew her."

"I used to be friends with her a long time ago," Gemma says, lying.

"I didn't know that."

"Well, you do now."

"You sure you don't know where she's staying?"

"I'm sure," Gemma says. "And Wade, I really do need to get back to work."

When she leaves his office, Wade tries for a moment to do some work, but finds it impossible. His stomach does a sudden flip-flop, reminiscent of the night he found Mildred, and running to the bathroom, he vomits and vomits until nothing is left.

*F*rank Denton has just ordered his usual morning bowl of oatmeal and toast at the diner in the Blue Mountain Inn when he overhears a conversation about Rosalee's appearance at the funeral. He cancels his usual, orders a cup of coffee to go, buys a newspaper, and goes back to his room, ecstatic—so ecstatic that once in his room he can't sit still, and taking his paper with him, returns to the diner and orders a huge breakfast. That is when Tom Jett walks in and sits down at a nearby table.

"Hello, Tom," Frank says. "Mind if I join you?"

Tom smiles. "Be my guest."

"Have you heard the latest on that murder case? You know, Mildred Wilson? Her daughter showed up at her funeral yesterday."

Tom turns pale. "No, I hadn't heard that."

"Well, she did. I wonder if she's under arrest or anything."

"I don't know," Tom says, and gets up from the table. "Well, I've got to go to work. I'll see you later."

"Aren't you going to have breakfast?"

"Don't have time."

Tom walks out of the diner, intending to drive to Gemma's house, until he sees her car parked on the street in front of the Pick Citizens'. He walks into the bank, straight up to her desk, and says, "I have to talk to you. Let's step outside a minute."

Gemma follows him out, and they stand on the sidewalk in front of the bank.

"What's going on?" Tom asks.

"Nothing."

"I just heard about Rosalee. Is she under arrest?"

"No."

"Where is she?"

"She's still with me."

"I thought they suspected her."

"They did, but we had a talk with the sheriff. Rosalee went to high school with him. He believed her, and he's going to try to find Frank Denton."

"You know, it would be nice if you guys would keep me informed about what's going on so I don't have to find out the latest news by way of gossip."

"I'm sorry," Gemma says, noticing the hurt look in Tom's eyes. "How did you hear about it, anyway?"

"A guy who stays at the Inn. Interesting fellow. Like everyone else, he seems to be fascinated by this case."

Gemma looks closely at Tom. "We need to talk soon. Maybe I'll stop by some evening, soon. Would that be all right?"

Tom can tell by the look in Gemma's eyes that she feels an obligation to give a good-bye speech to him. She wants to tell him what a nice guy he is and that she loves him dearly, but that she doesn't love him in the *right* way. He has an urge to tell her to save her breath, that he already knows how she feels, but he says, "Sure. Whenever."

Gemma goes back inside the bank, and Tom stands there on the sidewalk for a moment before getting into his car.

From the window of the diner at the Blue Mountain Inn, Frank Denton has been observing their conversation, wondering why, after he mentioned Rosalee, Tom left the diner so suddenly. Maybe Tom Jett's little chitchat with the white woman at the bank had nothing to do with Rosalee. Maybe it was just a conversation between lovers, but he isn't convinced.

A few minutes later, he walks across the street and enters the bank. There are no customers inside as he approaches Gemma's desk and says, "I'd like to speak to Wade."

Gemma looks up at the man, recognizing him as being the same one who came to see Wade a couple of months ago. How could she forget those blue-black eyes, the way they tried to look right through her? "Your name?" she asks.

"Fred Dudley. I'm sure he'll see me."

The name doesn't register, but his eyes do. "I'll check," she says.

Gemma knocks on Wade's door and goes inside his office. "Wade?" He is sitting at his desk, sticking a pushpin into the skin around his fingernails. He doesn't appear to have heard her come in. "Wade? There's a man here to see you. A Fred Dudley? Can you see him now, or do you want me to tell him you're busy?"

A look of horror crosses Wade's face, as Frank Denton steps up behind Gemma, looks past her into the office, and says, "Hello, Wade. I told her you'd see me." Gemma moves to the side, and Frank enters the office and closes the door.

Gemma goes back to her desk, thinking that something funny is going on. There's some connection here that I'm not getting, she decides. What in the world is wrong with Wade? He's not been himself for months. I've been so wrapped up in myself that I haven't paid much attention, but something is wrong with him. Why did he look so afraid when I told him Fred Dudley wanted to see him?

In the office, Frank sits down in the chair in front of Wade's desk and scrutinizes him carefully. "Wade, you look terrible.

Just terrible. I hope you're not snorting too much of that co- caine. It can take its toll after a while."

Wade sticks the pushpin through a fingertip and rips off the skin. "What do you want from me? I've not done anything to you except try to help you out. Leave me alone! Just get out of here and leave me alone!"

Frank smiles. "Oh, Wade," he says gleefully, "I'm so excited about Rosalee. I'm sure you've heard about her coming-out, so to speak. Still, no one seems to know much about it. You've not been holding out on me, have you?"

"I don't know anything about it. She was at the funeral— that's all I know."

"You don't know where she is right now?"

"Certainly not. All I know is what my wife told me. She was there at the funeral yesterday. She saw Rosalee with Gemma. The sheriff questioned Rosalee, but he doesn't think she is re- sponsible for . . . what happened." Wade cringes from the con- tinuing smile on Fred's face. "I tell you that's all I know."

Frank taps his fingers on the arm of the chair. "Who's Gemma?"

Wade takes in a deep breath. "Gemma Collet. She works for me . . . right out there. She was the one who led you in here. Surely you must have caught her name before."

"I guess I have, but I wasn't paying much attention before." Frank glances out at the gray fog rolling past the window. "I'm paying attention now. Is she friends with Rosalee or some- thing?"

"Well, I didn't think she was, but she says she is. She doesn't know where Rosalee's staying, though. I've already asked her."

"You shouldn't believe everything you're told, Wade."

Wade is unable to control his emotions a second longer, and he breaks into an eerie growl. "I'm not at fault in any of this. None of it. Do you hear me?"

"Of course not, Wade. You're just a small-town banker try- ing to stay afloat in a piss-poor economy. You deal a little cocaine. And probably a lot of marijuana. God only knows what else you're involved in. I feel for you, Wade. I really do."

"I think they know about you, Fred," Wade blurts out between feral groans and gasps.

Frank sits up straight, all of his senses finely tuned. "You didn't tell them, did you?"

"Tell them? No, I didn't tell them," Wade squeaks. "The sheriff stopped by and asked me some questions. He wanted to know if anyone new to town had asked for information on Rosalee in the past few months. I told him no."

"Why would the sheriff ask you that question? Did he happen to suggest a name for this stranger?"

"No. He didn't seem to have a name for him." Wade shudders. "I don't know why he asked me in particular. Maybe he's asking everyone."

"Maybe Rosalee told him to ask you."

"But why? Rosalee doesn't know that you and I have met. She doesn't even know that you're in town."

"Yes, but I'm sure she suspects I'm here."

Wade remembers the conversation he had recently with Gilman, the day he barged into the office. "Someone else asked me the same thing," he manages to say.

"Who? Asked you what?"

"Just the other day, Gilman Lee came in here and wanted to know if any strangers in town had made inquiries to me about Rosalee."

Frank leans forward in his chair. "Gilman Lee?"

"Yeah, you know. He's the guy Rosalee used to date."

"Yeah, I know." Thoughts race through Frank's head. I should have made Mr. Lee's acquaintance before now, he thinks. She may have been with him all along. "I've got to go," he says, "but I may want to talk to you again later."

He steps out of Wade's office and sees Gemma standing at a file cabinet, her back turned, obviously unaware that he came out of the office. Noting that the other two women are at the teller counter, busy with customers, Frank slips quietly behind Gemma, leans close to the back of her head, and whispers, "Boo!"

She calmly turns around and glares at him. "Can I help you with something else, Mr. Dudley?"

"Not right now, Gemma. Maybe later."

"There is no *later* with me, Mr. Dudley. I'm a *now-or-never* kind of person."

"Is that so? Well, I'm a *now-or-later* kind of person."

"I've found that your kind of people are usually too *late*, period," Gemma says. "If you'll excuse me, I've got to get back to work right *now*." She takes a file out of the cabinet and goes back to her desk.

Frank Denton walks out of the bank and returns to his room at the Blue Mountain Inn, his mind ablaze with new information. It is obvious to him that Gilman Lee and Gemma Collet both know where Rosalee is staying. Perhaps she is even staying with one of them. The fact that his workplace at the mine is in such close proximity to Gemma's house fills him with triumph—it will be so easy to sneak down there and take a peek through the windows. He intends to find out if Rosalee is at Gemma's house no later than tonight.

39
Chapter

Gilman hasn't worked at all today, or shaved, either. He drives down to Gemma's house and visits with Rosalee and June for a while, then he walks to his old house, which is empty again—abandoned and shabbier now that neither Rosalee nor Tom lives there. He steps onto the porch and stands for a moment looking toward the prayer chamber at the edge of the field, imagining Zack sitting in the chamber alone, cold at the table with that ridiculous cap on his head, that stale cigarette in his bony fingers, those hollow eyes. He remembers the last time he visited him, dew streaked like tears down Zack's cheekbones.

Gilman walks out to the chamber, unlocks it, and steps inside to a smell of must with a touch of manure. The bag of defecation the Texan gave him is positioned in a corner in the wheelbarrow, and Zack sits at the table just as he imagined. Gilman takes a pint of Jim Beam out of his coat pocket, takes a swig, and looks at Zack, wanting to tell his old friend about Gemma, about how much he loves her, how miraculous it is that he has met his match, but there is a sadness in the chamber that won't let him speak, that hovers over him like a worried mother who loves her child but believes he is doomed. He can't talk to Zack, doesn't dare touch him for fear the bones will crumble into dust.

After a few awkward moments, Gilman leaves and drives back toward the machine shop while bothersome thoughts creep into his head. The Conroy Coal Company, whose miners are still mining on the hill, continues to steal his coal, and he is painfully aware that he's doing nothing about it. And Tom Jett? Tom has been a friend to him, a good one. He helped rebuild his shop, guarded his house on the hill, even did repairs on the house, and was there for him the night of the sugar attack. "I've done nothing for him, except steal his woman," Gilman mutters as he drives along.

When he gets home, he tries to block out these disturbing thoughts by thinking of Gemma, but that doesn't work because every time he thinks of her, Tom is close behind. He starts to drink, finishing off the rest of the pint and getting another from the cabinets Tom constructed so well. Then he looks around at the paneling Tom nailed to his walls and notes the craftsmanship. He knows he can't go to Tom and say, "Well, Tom, even though me and Gemma love each other, I'm goin to step out of the picture because you're such a nice guy," but at least he figures he should talk to him. Gilman has rarely in his life been the first to make a move in patching up bad feelings between himself and another party. Sitting down on the couch and squaring his shoulders, he takes another drink.

*A*t the bank, Gemma is beginning to get caught up with her backlog, and she's taking a time-out to ponder recent events. Gilman thinks Wade knows something, and Gemma can vouch for the fact that her boss has been acting pretty odd.

She gets a picture of that man—what was his last name?—
Dudley, clearly in her mind. Then she remembers that Rosalee said Frank Denton had strange eyes. Gemma drums her
fingers on the desk, gets up and walks over to the window, and
looks across the street at the Blue Mountain Inn, lost in
thoughts.

Marcy and Jo Ellen look at her and shake their heads. Like
Gemma, they have noticed that mornings, their boss, Wade
Miller, doesn't whir into the office the way he once did.
They've guessed something is on his mind, but can't imagine
what it is. They look from Gemma to the closed door behind
which Wade sits, as if acknowledging that both of their work-
mates have gone around the bend.

Gemma sees Tom Jett pull into the parking lot and get out
of his truck just as the door opens at the Inn and Fred Dudley walks out carrying a lunch pail, obviously on his way to
work. When Tom meets Fred on his way inside, they speak as
if they know each other. Gemma recalls the conversation she
had with Tom this morning, in which he said a man at the Inn
had told him about Rosalee's showing up at the funeral, a man
who was fascinated with the case. She wonders if that man
could be Mr. Dudley. Gemma walks back to her desk and puts
on her coat and grabs her purse, thinking that perhaps this is
as good a time as any to pay her overdue visit to Tom. She not
only needs to make her position regarding Gilman clear to
him, she needs to ask him some questions about Mr. Dudley.

"Did you see that? They's a hour till quitting time. Wish I
could just leave any time I felt like it," Marcy says to Jo Ellen
as the door bangs closed behind Gemma. "Reckon we ought
to tell Wade?"

"What good would it do?" Jo Ellen says, wagging her head
and clicking her tongue on the roof of her mouth. "He's crazier than she is."

Gemma walks across the street to Tom's door and knocks.
"Can I come in?" she asks when he opens up. Tom lets her

in, and she stands awkwardly in the middle of his room.

"Have a seat," Tom says, "I've got to go in here and wash up. I won't be long."

Gemma walks over to the window and sees Wade Miller stumble out of the bank, get into his Cherokee, and drive haphazardly out of town, causing her to wonder if he really is connected somehow to what has happened. She sits at a table in the corner, on which there is a portable typewriter and a pile of typewritten pages.

Tom comes out of the bathroom, gets a couple of beers out of the cooler, and sits down with her at the table. Gemma pops open the beer and takes a sip. "Like your typewriter," she says. "Are you writing something?"

"Something."

"What is it you're writing?"

"I'm not sure yet, but I think it's about a sentence I don't know the meaning of. Now, what do you want to talk to me about?"

Gemma sighs. "I just wish I knew what was going on," she says.

"Really? I thought I was the one who was in the dark."

"I mean about this whole thing with Frank Denton. Is he here or not? And if he is, where is he? Who is he?" She looks across the table at Tom and a small wave of the feeling she had for him surfaces. She nervously picks at her fingers. "Gilman thinks my boss, Wade Miller, knows something. I'm beginning to think so, too."

"Your boss?"

"Yeah, well, he used to go with Rosalee. Something is wrong with him. Marcy and Jo Ellen have noticed it, and I've noticed it, too. He looks like he hasn't slept in a month. He's nervous . . . I don't know. Today, a Fred Dudley came to see him, and he . . . it upset Wade. When he saw the man, I could tell he was scared."

"Fred Dudley?"

"Yeah, I think he lives here at the Inn. I saw you speak to him this evening. Do you know him?"

"Not very well. He works for some mining company and frequents Betty Marker's pretty regularly. The other night we had a few drinks and got into a conversation about Nietzsche."

"Nietzsche? Usually miners aren't real versed in philosophy. Is Fred the one that told you about Rosalee showing up at the funeral?"

"Yeah."

"Well, this makes the second time he's come to see Wade. He came once before, a couple of months ago."

"What are you saying?"

"I don't know. I just know that Gilman asked me if anyone new in town had come into the bank and started an account."

"This new person being Frank Denton?"

"Yeah, I mean Frank is rich, according to Rosalee, and has funny-looking eyes."

"Do you think Fred could be Frank?"

"Maybe."

"But I don't think he has much money. Otherwise, why would he be working at a mine?"

"He didn't start an account at the bank, either."

"You say he's never been to Pick or visited Wade until a couple of months ago?"

"Not that I know of."

"That's interesting," Tom says, "but Fred claims to be from Somerset. He seemed . . . I don't know . . . sincere. We listened to a Robert Johnson tape and discussed . . ."

"Rosalee said he could be real charming at times and softhearted, remember?"

"If there was some way we could be sure. If Rosalee could just get a look at him. The problem is how could she do that without him seeing her."

"I'll tell Gilman about it. See what he comes up with. And

of course I'll ask Wade about it tomorrow." She glances out the window. "Anyway, that's not the only thing I wanted to talk about."

Tom looks away. "What else is there?"

"There's the matter of me and you and Gilman."

"I thought that was a closed case. I heard you that day when we brought Rosalee to your house. You were on the phone with Gilman, and I heard you tell him you loved him. I've known it was over since then."

Gemma frowns. "He goaded me into saying that."

"And you meant every word of it. You may wish you loved me, but it's Gilman you really want. Every woman wants him. They hang around him like parboiled leeks."

"You think I'm a leek?"

"I don't know who or what you are. You're a hard case."

"You're not going to leave, are you? Because I don't want you to leave. I couldn't stand it if you left."

"Oh, God, you're not going to ask me if we can still be friends, are you?"

"Not if you don't want me to."

Tom looks out the window. "This may be hard for you to believe, but you are not the only reason I've stayed here this long. I happen to like this goddamned place. I don't know if I mentioned this to you before, but I'm going to be moving into a cabin. There's a cave behind the place I'd like to show you sometime."

Gemma squeezes Tom's hand. "I'd like that."

They are silent for a moment.

"I guess I'll be going," Gemma says. "Talk to you later."

Tom watches her go, trying to digest what has just happened, then he chucks the analysis and dashes out the door, not fully understanding why he is running to catch up with her, only knowing that he is. When he gets outside, he sees her at the end of the slush-filled parking lot, standing there as if she is preparing to cross the street. All at once, she turns around and walks back toward him, and when they meet, they kiss like lovers in a dark room on a rainy night. They kiss as if they hope the whole town of Pick is watching.

As it happens, the only person watching them is Gilman Lee, who finally decided to come into town and make a conciliatory call on Tom. He stopped at the drugstore first and, leaving his truck parked on the street, decided to walk to the Inn. Coming up the sidewalk, he sees them in the parking lot, holding each other and kissing like Romeo and Juliet. He looks away from them to the sky, shuffles his feet in the slush, starts to walk toward them, changes his mind.

"Amazing," he mutters to himself. "Maybe everyone is right. I ought to just leave them alone." Gilman walks back down the street to his truck, and as he opens the truck door to get inside, he catches a glimpse of his pale face in the side-view mirror. He revs the engine and hot-rods out of Pick like a teenage punk.

40
Chapter

At Gemma Collet's house, Rosalee is getting more restless by the minute. In part, she showed up at Mildred's funeral because she wanted the hiding to be over, wanted to step right out into the open and say, "Here I am." Now things are back where they were—she is undercover and Frank is still out there somewhere, looking for her.

At the same time that Gemma is walking out of the bank to visit Tom at the Blue Mountain Inn, Rosalee puts on her coat and boots and grabs her guitar.

"Where're you goin?" June asks.

"Up to the house," Rosalee says. "I feel a sudden urge to write a song. Do you have paper and a pen?"

"Yeah, but why don't you write it here? I've never seen a person write a song before. I'd like to see it."

"I have to be alone when I write."

"Well, you could go into Gemma's room."

"That's not alone enough. I need to be completely by myself. Where's that paper and pen?"

June pulls open a drawer on the end table and gives Rosalee some writing material. "I don't like the idea of you being up there by yourself. How long are you goin to stay?"

"Till the song is wrote."

"Is they any firewood up there?"

"There's a little electric heater in the closet. It works pretty good. I'll see you later, June."

Rosalee still has a key to the front door of the old house, and when she steps inside, she finds the place much the same as she left it. She takes the heater out of the closet, drags it into the kitchen, and closes the door so the warmth will be trapped inside the room. She sits down at the picnic table and begins working, playing quietly, putting herself into a trance with a repetitive strum. Cold gray light outside the window casts a pale glow in the room. She begins to feel as though from somewhere above she sees herself sitting at the table holding the guitar. A melody comes to her, though not from a conscious attempt at creating one; perhaps it comes from the cold gray light outside the window or from her other self, floating above the table.

The words to Rosalee's song are beginning to materialize, while outside the house, Frank is driving up the road to the mine. "Under the gray skies, ghosts sing the old songs . . ." she sings. "I hear their echoes," she adds.

Frank arrived at work at four o'clock instead of his regular starting time of five because the prospect of finding Rosalee tonight made it impossible for him to stay a minute longer at the Inn. Uncharacteristically, he walks around chitchatting with the other miners. When the majority of the men leave at four-thirty, only Ed Toothacre and Frank are left at the mine.

"Why did you get here so early?" Ed asks Frank. "Do you like this job or something?"

"Nothing better to do," Frank replies.

"If you don't mind my saying so, you ought to get a social life," Ed kids Frank as he locks up his office at five o'clock. In a few minutes, Ed leaves for home, and Frank makes his first inspection of the area around the strip mine. With that done, he returns to the mining shed and pours a cup of coffee from his thermos. He plans to make an excursion down the hill to Gemma's house as soon as it gets dark, and watching for the last trace of sunlight to slip behind the mountain, he waits in the gray light that will soon become darkness. "Why did you leave me, Rosalee?" Frank asks. "What was going through your mind?"

*A*fter the kiss in the parking lot, Gemma decides not to go home right away, knowing she can't think clearly at home with Rosalee and June jabbering in the background. She drives out of town in the opposite direction from her house, continues driving for about fifteen miles. When she finds a roadside diner, she decides to stop and order a meal, sits there picking at a Salisbury steak, not in the least hungry.

Some good-bye kiss, she thinks, remembering Tom's lips on hers, the feeling she'd had of being swept into brightness where everything smelled like freshly washed sheets hanging out to dry. What was that, anyway? Obviously I'm still attracted to him, but still it was a good-bye kiss. That's all it was. Gemma looks around at the other people in the diner, several truck drivers, a young couple, an old man, and in one corner of the room an old-fashioned jukebox. She walks up to it, drops in a quarter, and plays "You Win Again" until it Gilmanizes her.

*H*ot-rodding most of the way home, Gilman slows down before he gets to the shop, not wanting Ten-Fifteen to hear him screech to a halt in front of the shop and worry that something is wrong. He gets out of his truck and stands in front of his friend's trailer with an overwhelming compulsion to peek through the window and see what his buddy is doing, even though he already knows. Ten-Fifteen is watching a movie, probably an old one on a classic movie channel on cable. That's what he always watches this time of evening. Gilman steps up to the window and looks inside. He was right; Ten-Fifteen is sitting on the couch, watching a Western. Gilman catches a glimpse of Gregory Peck in a passionate embrace with Jennifer Jones. "No point in disturbing him," Gilman whispers. "I'll just leave him to his show."

He goes inside the shop and stands in the middle of the floor, looking around. "Well, that was definitely more than your average friendly peck on the cheek. No getting around it," he mutters grumpily. "I reckon I'm goin to have to talk to Miss Gemma. I thought everything was all squared away as far as Tom was concerned, but I guess it ain't." Gilman goes to the cabinet and takes out a fifth of Jim Beam, pours himself a hefty drink, and sits down. He figures it must have been a momentary lapse on her part to have been kissing Tom Jett like that. Still, the incident does not help to alleviate the strange mood he has been in all day and, instead, makes it clear that he is no longer on top of things. "You know, maybe I oughta stir up a ruckus tonight, remind people that I'm still alive."

He thinks of the Conroy Coal Company taking his coal. Inside one of his kitchen cabinets sits the satchel containing a handy pocket-sized detonator, a receiver, a stick of dynamite, and a rope that was given to him by his friend the Texan. He takes his gun from a table drawer and inspects it carefully. He needs the gun to collar the night watchman, the rope to tie him up with. The detonator, receiver, and dynamite speak for themselves. Tonight is as fine a night as any, Gilman thinks.

*I*t is dark when Frank Denton begins walking slowly down the hill toward Gemma Collet's house. Passing near the turnoff to the old house Gilman Lee owns, he hears music— guitar music and singing pure and earthy as the mountain he's standing on. Although he can't make out the words to the song, it is the most beautiful melody he has ever heard, far too lusty and real to exist only in his imagination. Deciding to check out the situation, he slips into the grove of sycamore trees and peeps through their winter branches toward the rear of the house. A light is on. Someone is in there. Suddenly, he knows without a doubt that the voice he hears belongs to Rosalee, and Frank disappears into a kind of ecstatic trance. It is as though the discovery of Rosalee, after months of patient searching, amounts to the apex of his existence, and he stands in one spot for several minutes, trembling with anticipation.

Rosalee puts down her guitar, steps out the front door of the house where the cold damp air feels like rain, walks out to the field, and stands in front of Gilman's prayer chamber, wondering what's in it besides the bag of turds. A time or two while she's been here on the mountain, she's considered breaking into the chamber, but then she remembered the story of Pandora. As a child, she didn't like the story, and to this day she thinks it ought to be against the law to read it to children since it puts a damper on a little person's natural curiosity and makes Pandora come off as being a nosy busybody. Rosalee stands there wondering what, if anything, she would let loose on the world if she broke down the door and went inside. She turns around abruptly when she hears footsteps coming down the side of the hill.

Quickly stepping to the side of the chamber, she peeps her head out an inch, waiting for the person to approach the house, figuring it is possibly Gemma. June was probably worried about me and sent her up here to make sure I'm okay, she thinks. The problem is that the footsteps sound as if they're coming *down* and around the mountain, not *up* and around, which is the direction the sound would be coming from if the footsteps were Gemma's. Rosalee is about to emerge from behind the prayer chamber and yell to whomever it is, when she sees a shadowy form walk deliberately toward the front porch of the house. It isn't Gemma.

It's Frank.

She would recognize his shadow anywhere. Rosalee moves to the back of the chamber and crouches down as he knocks on the door of the house, amazed that he would just walk up and knock on the door like a neighbor stopping by to borrow something. She feels a cold, overwhelming sadness at seeing him standing on her porch. She remembers the good times, how passionately he read poetry, how gentle he could be, how much love Frank could show her (if he were in the right frame of mind). Sometimes it has occurred to her that Frank might not have turned out so bad if he hadn't had an extraordinarily high standard of morals to begin with. She figures it is his great expectations, too great to ever come true, that causes him to want to kill everything he loves. Then she remembers the bad times—her mother, the man in the alley, herself.

"Rosalee?" He calls her name and waits for an answer. He turns the doorknob, and finding the door unlocked, steps inside, while outside Rosalee waits spellbound for him to discover she isn't there. What will he do? She looks behind her toward the trail that leads around the side of the hill, the old road to Harlan, and sprints toward it just as Frank steps back out.

He hears her running through the frosted weeds in the field toward the trail and takes off behind her. "Rosalee? Wait! I just want to talk to you. *Rosaleeeee!*"

*W*hen Gilman pulls into Gemma's driveway, he notices her car is not there. She must still be down at the Blue Mountain Inn, French-kissing Tom. "More power to 'em," he mutters as he walks across the swinging bridge and up the mountain. He intends to go straight to the prayer chamber and pick up the bag of turds, but as he approaches the house, he sees the lights are on. Going inside, he finds Rosalee's guitar propped against the wall in the kitchen as though she just leaned it there a minute ago. He sees the electric heater positioned near the table, but no one is home. Gilman stands still for a moment trying to get his bearings straight. He figures Rosalee probably came up here earlier, forgot the light and heater were on, left her guitar, and didn't lock the door. That would be just like her to do that, he decides, but he doesn't have time to try to second-guess Rosalee because he can't let anything distract him from the task at hand.

The task is to go to that shed and pull out the wheelbarrow containing the bag of turds, place the satchel containing the explosives, etc., in the wheelbarrow, and push it about halfway to the mining site, park it beside a tree momentarily, and go on ahead to scout the situation. Wearing a ski mask to disguise himself, he plans on tying up and gagging the night watchman and placing him inside the mining shed, after which he will come back to the tree where he parked the wheelbarrow, take the explosives to the site, and set the charge.

That done, he plans on getting the night watchman out of the shed and walking him down to the old house, where he will guard him till morning. He intends to wait until Ed Toothacre drives up the road to begin work tomorrow morning before pushing the button. Gilman lightly rubs his hand over the detonator, which he is carrying in the front left pocket of his Levi's jacket, figuring the explosion probably won't destroy every machine on the place, but it will wipe out several and damage the rest. Shit will be flying everywhere if things go as planned. Some of it, he hopes, will land in Ed Toothacre's face.

These are Gilman's plans, but finding the light on in the old house and Rosalee's guitar propped against the wall, the heater on, and no one present has him wondering if he should change his plans to fit these unknown factors that have presented themselves. No, Gilman decides, the only thing I might change is that when I get back down here with the watchman, maybe I'll lock him in the closet and go down to June's house to ask about Rosalee. If she's there, I'll give her a piece of my mind for leaving the light and the heater on in the house. If she's not there, I'll find out where she is.

Gilman goes out of the house to the prayer chamber, unlocks it, and steps inside. It is cold and damp in the shed as he shines his flashlight on Zack's skeleton and winks at him. "Zack, old buddy, I'm goin to do some damage tonight." He moves close enough to touch Zack, but he doesn't because Zack seems too sad to touch. "Zack?" he says. "Would you like to go back to Washburn Creek? Now that I think about it, I was pretty selfish to dig you up and bring you here." He pauses, as if he expects his friend to answer him.

"God, I'm weird. I know I am," Gilman whispers, glancing around the shed as though he's making sure no one is watching him. "I'm gonna take you back to Washburn Creek and let you rest. Looks like I'll be too busy to visit much from here on out. I'll have to give Gemma Collet my undivided attention— a hell of a woman!" Gilman turns from Zack and grabs the wheelbarrow in the corner. He has just gone back outside and is preparing to lock the door when he hears the words, "You were a good man, Gilman," come from inside the shed. He forgets about locking the door, and taking off at a swift clip, he pushes the wheelbarrow up the hill. First of all, I didn't really hear that, Gilman is thinking as he pushes. I'm imagining things. Second of all, I've been called many a thing in my life, but I ain't never been called good.

When he is the right distance from the mine, he shoves the wheelbarrow under a pine tree and slips quietly up to the site, holding his snub-nosed .38 out in front of him. Scouting the perimeters of the mine, he doesn't see or hear a thing and sneaks noiselessly to the miners' shed; the watchman isn't there or anywhere around. Gilman stops still for a moment, pulls his ski mask off, and scratches his head. A light rain begins to fall.

He walks down the other side of the mountain to where the auger is. The watchman isn't there, either. "Fuck it," he says loudly. "Where the fuck is everybody?" He pushes the wheelbarrow down to where the auger is positioned and begins to set the charge, to set it right under the engine so the engine will be blown apart. He strategically places the bag of mixed excrement on top of the charge. Again, as if to make sure it is still there, he puts his hand on the detonator in his front left jacket pocket. When the time comes, all he'll have to do is push the button.

*F*rank Denton has lost Rosalee. She disappeared like a thin trail of smoke, like the sound of his mother's laughter. "Alaine," Frank calls to the darkness and rain, "tell me where she went." He can't hear her anywhere, can't hear her running in any direction. He tries to imagine Rosalee's soft hair and green eyes and pictures himself walking up to her—she extends her hand, he takes it. They smile. Green, they're surrounded by green, and they're both so young, not much more than children, really. Frank stands in the middle of the trail and doesn't move.

Gemma leaves the diner, drives to the machine shop, and knocks on the door. There is no answer. Noticing that Ten-Fifteen's lights are on, she tries to get an answer there.

Ten-Fifteen opens his door. "Well, hello, Gemma, come in."

Gemma has always wondered what the inside of Ten-Fifteen's trailer looks like, and she enters inquisitively, half expecting to see Gilman Lee sitting on the couch with a smile on his face, but he isn't there.

"Ten-Fifteen, do you know where Gilman is?"

"No, I don't. Actually, I've not seen him since this afternoon."

She looks around at the TV. "What're you watching?"

"Ah, nothing." Ten-Fifteen scratches his head. "Gilman was goin to Tom's today. That's the last time I seen him."

"He was going to see Tom?" Gemma sits down on the couch. "Why was he going to see Tom? Do you know?"

"He was goin to try to straighten out their differences."

Gemma sits there for a moment, feeling something akin to pride at Gilman's good intentions. He was going to talk to Tom. Ain't that nice? "What time did he go to see him?" she asks.

"Around three-thirty, I believe."

Around three-thirty, Gemma thinks to herself. I was at Tom's at three-thirty. He certainly didn't show up while I was there. "You mean he left here at that time or got down there at that time?"

"I didn't keep that close a tabs on it, Gemma," Ten-Fifteen says.

"Can I use your phone?"

"Sure."

Gemma dials Tom's number. "Hello, Tom," she says. "It's me."

"I know who it is," Tom says softly. He's been trying to forget that parking-lot kiss ever since it happened. He almost succeeded until the phone rang and he heard her voice again.

"Has Gilman been to see you?"

"No, why?"

"Ten-Fifteen said he was going to see you today."

"He hasn't been here unless he came while I was still at work."

Gemma hangs up the phone and stares at the TV. Something is not right. Something is very wrong; she feels it in her bones. Ten-Fifteen sits opposite her, smiling.

About twenty minutes ago, Rosalee slipped inside a small cave, the opening hidden by a clump of baby spruce pines. She heard Frank's footsteps go past her on the trail and, shortly after, heard them come back. Right now he is standing just outside the cave. As she listens to him breathe, she thinks, this is where it will end, here in this little cave by an old trail that hardly anyone still remembers. My body may never be found. I don't even know why he's doing this.

"Alaine!" Frank calls out his mother's name.

Since Mildred's death, Rosalee has rarely thought of Frank except with hatred, but tonight, seeing him enter Gilman's old house looking for her, and now, also, hearing him call his mother's name, she feels nothing but an overwhelming sadness for him and for all his victims, herself included.

Frank can't sense Rosalee's presence at all. Finally he decides she may have backtracked to the house, may be bolting right now down the hill to the swinging bridge. He turns and beats it back to the house. She isn't there. He stands on the porch, barely breathing, listening for a sound, any sound, and he hears one, a sound of scraping metal coming from the mining site. Walking down the porch steps, he notices tracks on the muddy ground, and they're heading out of the yard and up the side of the mountain.

Frank smiles, walks slowly to the mining site, and after checking out the area around the shed, he slips quietly down the other side of the mountain to the auger and sees Gilman, who has just finished setting the charge, take hold of the wheelbarrow and begin walking away. Frank thinks that if it were daylight he would undoubtedly find the wheelbarrow to be red. He is reminded of the famous poem by William Carlos Williams:

> *so much depends*
> *upon*
>
> *a red wheel*
> *barrow*
>
> *glazed with rain*
> *water*
>
> *beside the white*
> *chickens.*

Frank steps out from behind a tree. "Hi, there," he says to Gilman. "Nice night, isn't it?"

Gilman turns around. "Real nice," he says to the night watchman.

"Except of course for the rain, but then I've always liked rain," Frank says.

"Me too."

"You're Gilman Lee, aren't you? I've heard a lot about you. People around here are always talking about your exploits. Rosalee used to talk about you, too."

A chill runs up the back of Gilman's neck as he sees images

of Mildred neatly tucked into her bed, Rosalee's guitar propped against the wall, and the heater and lights on in the old house. "Frank Denton?" Gilman says.

"The one and only."

"Where's Rosalee?"

"Good question. By the way," Frank continues, "what are you doing up here?"

"I come to blow the place up," Gilman says. "Now answer me something. Why are you looking for Rosalee?"

"I want to take her back to Florida with me."

"She don't want to go." Gilman slowly moves his hand down his jacket toward his pants pocket. The man is standing only ten feet away from him, his face clearly visible here, where the moon has come out from behind a cloud and the rain has stopped for the moment. Gilman can't tell what color his eyes are, but they are cold and powerful—he feels their icy strength pierce the space in front of him. For some reason, he gets an image of Gemma as he and Tom Jett saw her that day, standing naked in the creek, her arms stretched toward the sky. She looks like a song he wishes he had written. Frank Denton is staring into his eyes, causing him to wonder if Gemma could stare down this man and whether Frank sees his hand move toward the handle of the gun that is sticking out of his pocket.

Frank sees Gilman's hand. He waits till it touches the handle before he fires. He shoots Gilman in the stomach, and Gilman just stands there smiling.

"Don't you know that shooting a man in the stomach won't kill him? You should've aimed for the heart, buddy," Gilman says in a slurred voice, as the warm blood spreads over his shirt. He feels a pain that goes deep and takes root as if it plans to stay for a while.

"Thanks for the tip," Frank says and directs the next bullet for the left front pocket of Gilman's Levi's jacket.

He hits the detonator, causing the dynamite to blow and

shit to fly. Gilman falls to the ground and glances up just as a piece of metal flies off the engine and hits Frank Denton square between the eyes, knocking a good-sized hole in his forehead. The piece of metal is followed in a split second by an enormous glob of excrement; Gilman can't tell if it's cow, horse, dog, or human. A ball of fire flies over him in the direction of Ed Toothacre's office. He watches Frank fall and looks up at the sky, where a passing cloud bursts a sheet of water over everything.

Gilman's life swims before him, doing backstrokes and dog paddles. It floats faceup. He sees everything now, the sky on a blue day, sun glinting through green leaves, himself skinny-dipping, swinging from a rope over water, dropping, sinking to the bottom of a clear river. He looks up and sees Zack. Zack says, "Gilman? You heard me while ago, didn't you? When I said you were a good man? Well, I just want you to know that I didn't mean you were a good man in the ordinary sense of the word. I meant in the abnormal sense. I used to not have to explain myself to you. By the way, I liked the bag-of-shit thing. Nice touch."

Gilman Lee smiles. "But what about Gemma?"

"Gemma will be just fine. This don't concern Gemma. This only concerns you. Now, come on, ol' buddy. We got places to go and hell to raise."

"Wait just a minute, asshole," Gilman says. "I ain't through here, yet."

Gilman reaches his hand out, as if he is trying to grab on to something of the earth, but all he can see is Zack standing there, waiting with his arms folded.

*R*osalee hears the explosion and runs out of the cave toward the mining site, a hundred possibilities changing places in her mind. Maybe Frank decided to blow everything up, she thinks, as she reaches the mining area. Rain is pouring like a waterfall over all the equipment, but the mining site seems intact except for a small fire in Ed Toothacre's office. When the rain settles down, she notices an odor and sees smoke coming from an area just over the side of the mountain. She approaches slowly and quietly as she can, not knowing what to expect when she gets there.

The auger and a high lift are smoking, but the rain seems to have quenched almost all the flames. The two men are lying not five feet apart, Frank dead and Gilman bleeding all over the place.

Rosalee freezes in her tracks when she sees Frank's body covered with rain and fecal matter and part of his head missing. She looks at him and feels cold, nothing but cold, until she catches a glimpse of his closed eyelids and remembers when she was so in love with him that she sat for long periods of time just watching him sleep. For an instant, she considers that his spirit is still somewhere around, maybe flying past her at this very moment on its way to God knows where.

"He's dead, Rosalee," Gilman says, a small trickle of blood running out of his mouth. He considers telling her that Frank isn't the only one, that someone else is dead, too, but right now he can't remember who it is.

Rosalee turns around and sees the wound in Gilman's stomach, blood oozing in a steady stream out of the hole in his jacket and mixing with the rainwater on the ground.

"I told him a little stomach wound wouldn't kill a man, but I may have been wrong," Gilman says, arching his eyebrow.

Rosalee begins to shake. "Well, you wouldn't wrong. You're never wrong, asshole! I'm getting you home. Do you hear me? I'm taking you to the house."

"How?" Gilman asks.

Rosalee begins to cry. "In that wheelbarrow there, fool!" She grabs hold of the wheelbarrow, pulls it close as she can to where Gilman is lying, lifts him up as if he is light as a feather, and sets him in it. Gilman closes his eyes and smiles at Zack.

Rosalee screams and grabs hold of his shoulders. "Don't you close your eyes, goddamn it! You're not goin to die, Gilman Lee. You said it yourself. A man won't die from a stomach wound."

She begins pulling the wagon down the hill through the mud, the wet brown leaves, and bomb excrement. The rain lets up some, a whippoorwill starts to sing, and Gilman Lee loses consciousness halfway to the house.

41
Chapter

Rosalee doesn't stop for a second along the way; she just keeps walking straight down the hill toward the old house. When she gets to the front porch, she stops, lets go of the handles, and bends down to say something to Gilman. She wants to tell him that she is going to leave him there, just for a minute, that she's going to run down to Gemma's and call an ambulance, but when she bends over him, she sees from his vacant stare and half-frozen smile that he is unconscious. She doesn't dare leave him for a minute, and picking up the wheelbarrow again, she starts on down the hill toward the swinging bridge, thinking that if she just keeps walking with the wheelbarrow and doesn't stop he won't die. *He won't die.* "He won't die," she says over and over again as she pushes the wheelbarrow.

When Gemma leaves Ten-Fifteen's trailer, she drives straight home. Pulling into her driveway, she sees Gilman Lee's truck parked there, the sight of which brings various speculations to mind. She sits in the car for a moment, looks toward her house, and sees a light on in the kitchen. He must be waiting

for me down there. God, I hope he is. There is so much I want
to tell him. I want to tell him that I've said good-bye to Tom,
that I want him to take me home with him. I wonder what he's
doing down there. Maybe he's sitting at the kitchen table helping Momma work her jigsaw puzzle. Gemma tries to imagine
what life with Gilman might be like. If they move in together,
will they work jigsaw puzzles, watch TV, go to movies? She tries
to picture herself and Gilman just getting home from seeing a
film. Will they discuss its merits and shortcomings like ordinary
people? She doubts it, and so much the better. *Oh, God, what
will it be like if we actually begin to live together?* She is interrupted from these thoughts when she hears someone yelling
nearby. The sound is coming from the direction of the swinging bridge.

Gemma gets out of the car and stands as though she is
glued to the ground, listening to the god-awful wailing, the
gut-wrenching howl. She suspects that something more hor-
rifying than anything she will ever see awaits her if she walks
down the bank to the bridge—she smells it hanging in the air
like something that has seeped out of a grave. Walking slowly
down the bank, she makes out a bulky shadow on the bridge.
The wailing subsides to a whimper, and it is coming from
Rosalee.

"Rosalee?" Gemma yells and runs toward her. She sees
something else. A box? No, a wheelbarrow. Something's in it.
She stops running, looks down at the wheelbarrow, and sees
Gilman lying there not moving a muscle, blood seeping out of
his jacket, the half smile on his face.

She grabs the wheelbarrow from Rosalee's hands. "We've
got to get him to a hospital!"

Rosalee just stands there.

"Come on, Rosalee!"

"Is he dead?" Rosalee whispers. "I can't tell."

"Of course he's not dead. Now help me get him into the
car."

They push the wheelbarrow up the bank to Gemma's car, gently lift Gilman out of the wheelbarrow into the backseat, and jump into the front. Gemma blasts out of the driveway and peels rubber around the curve on the road to Harlan.

"The hospital in Pick is closer," Rosalee says.

"But I'm not sure they know what they're doing. They might let him die. He'll be all right if we can just get him to Harlan," Gemma says, pushing her foot down on the accelerator until the speedometer moves to eighty miles an hour.

"How did this happen?" she asks, her eyes fixed on the highway in front of her.

Rosalee starts to cry.

"I'd sure like to know what happened," Gemma says, "when you can talk."

Rosalee grabs hold of the strap of the seat belt, as if she's hanging on to a lifeline. "It was Frank," she finally gets out. "It happened at the mine. Gilman finally decided to blow it up, I guess. I went to the old house this evening to write a song, and Frank found me. I ran away from him, hid in a cave. After a while I heard the explosion. It come from the mine. When I got there, I found them. Frank was dead."

Gemma cranes her neck around toward the back of the car. "Check on him, Rosalee. Here, I'll turn the inside light on."

Rosalee leans between the bucket seats, and takes a close look at Gilman. "He's all right, I think."

"Take hold of his wrist, Rosalee. See if he's got a pulse."

Rosalee checks. "Yeah, he's got one, but it's real faint."

Gemma presses a little harder on the gas pedal, grips both hands on the steering wheel, and, in her own peculiar way, she prays. If he just gets well, she tells herself, I will never again have a nasty disposition, I will be polite to everyone I meet, I will be so sweet birds will nest in my hair. I'll do penance for the rest of my life—become a monk. I'd make a good monk.

A blur of activity engulfs them when they arrive at the hospital. Doctors and nurses run out of the emergency room, load Gilman onto a cot, and wheel him in for surgery. Rosalee and Gemma sit in the waiting room, fluctuating in personality from manics to depressives during the surgery that lasts for five hours. Rosalee smokes an entire pack of cigarettes while the operation is in process. Gemma talks about Indians for an hour straight. A few times they ride the elevator down to a snack bar where they drink coffee and pop Junior Mints and stare at other people, who, like themselves, are in the kind of shock that only an emergency can produce.

When the operation is over, he is still alive—that's all they care about. He has made it through. A doctor comes out to give them the news, a doctor who appears to have just emerged from hell, still with blood on his smock, holding his gloved hands out in front of him as if they are contagious.

"His heart stopped once, during surgery," the doctor says, "and he almost died. He's lost a lot of blood and is in critical condition."

He goes on for a moment about the details of the surgery—where the bullet was lodged, the risks he had to take to remove it, but Gemma and Rosalee don't digest any of this. All they care to know is that Gilman is alive.

"We've moved him to Intensive Care," the doctor says. "He'll be there for quite some time. If I were you, I'd go on home and get some rest."

Gemma and Rosalee look at the surgeon as if he is a fool, and when he leaves, they sit back down; Rosalee lights a cigarette, Gemma bites her nails. A nurse comes in and leads them to the ICU waiting room, gives them pillows and blankets, and tells them to get some sleep.

The next morning they remember to call people. They call Bill Shepherd, June, Ten-Fifteen, and the desk clerk at the Blue Mountain Inn, whom they ask to inform Tom of what has happened.

Bill Shepherd is the first to arrive.

He was called to the mining site earlier this morning, he tells them. Some of Conroy's equipment was dynamited, and their night watchman found dead.

"Their night watchman?" Rosalee asks.

"Yeah," Bill says. "Fred Dudley was killed in the explosion. We couldn't figure it out. Fred was laying on top of the mountain, dead, but there was a trail of blood going downhill to Gilman's old house and then on down the hill to the swinging bridge. We found the wheelbarrow. Blood was in it.

"I went up to the shop to ask Gilman some questions, but he wasn't there. Ten-Fifteen didn't know where he was. Then we got the calls from you. It's beginning to come a little clearer now."

"Yeah," Rosalee says, "I guess you think you've got it all figured out, but you don't. Because Fred Dudley ain't Fred Dudley. He's Frank Denton, and he was trying to kill me last night."

Bill Shepherd doesn't say a word. He just stares in disbelief.

Rosalee tells him about the events from last night, as far as she knows them. Bill jots down her story in a notepad. "I'll need you to come into town so I can question you further," he says.

"Not right now, Bill," Rosalee responds. "Not until they let us see Gilman. He's in real bad shape. Frank shot him up pretty good, and he may not make it."

Bill stands up. "I've got to get back. Burr County is crawling with state police officers, asking questions all over the place."

Within half an hour after Bill Shepherd leaves, Tom and Ten-Fifteen arrive, scared pale and full of questions. Ten-Fifteen, who can barely talk, his normally bright disposition blown to the ends of the earth, paces in the ICU waiting room like a lion in a cage. "When're they goin to let us see him?" he keeps asking.

Men from Burr County come in droves to donate blood, so many that the hospital is barely able to accommodate them as

they file in with somber faces and dazed eyes. Later, when
Ten-Fifteen finds out about it, he thanks each one for his do-
nation.

A nurse passes by, and Gemma corners her, persuading her
to give them some information about Gilman's progress. A few
minutes later the nurse reappears and tells them that if things
go well they may be able to visit Gilman later this evening.
"But only two can go in at a time," she says, officiously. "And
don't say anything to upset him. He isn't conscious right now,
but he may be conscious by the time you visit him. Still, I
doubt that he'll be fully aware of what's going on for a week,
maybe longer. And he's hooked up to all kinds of machines.
Try not to let that worry you. He needs to be closely moni-
tored. That's what the machines are there for."

At eight o'clock that night, they finally allow Gemma and
Rosalee to visit Gilman. The nurse was right—an array of
monitors lines the wall behind his bed. His face is white as the
sheet spread over him. Gemma stands on one side of the bed,
and Rosalee on the other, and they each take hold of a hand,
finding them to be cold as ice, dry, and limp. His breathing is
labored, his eyes are closed, the smile is gone from his lips,
and he looks old, so old they hardly recognize him. A buzzer
on one of the machines goes off, and Gemma screams. A nurse
hurries in and makes an adjustment. "It's okay," she says. "It
doesn't mean what you're thinking. He's all right."

Gemma starts to shake. She takes hold of his hand again,
and it happens, an event more distinct than anything she has
felt in all her life, a squeeze. He squeezes her hand, just a little, but to Gemma it is as though he grips her hand hard
enough to yank it off.

She laughs between her tears. "He squeezed my hand,
Rosalee. I felt it."

Rosalee looks up at her and smiles. "He squeezed mine,
too."

The nurse comes in and tells them it's time to go, and Tom and Ten-Fifteen are allowed to visit him for a few minutes.

While Gemma and Rosalee wait in the hallway for them to come out, Gemma wants to break down and cry more than she has ever wanted to do anything, but she won't let herself because doing so would mean she doesn't believe he will survive.

"He wouldn't open his eyes," Ten-Fifteen says, when he comes out. "He wouldn't say a word."

"It's the anesthesia," Gemma tells him. "That's all it is."

They walk out to the parking lot, get into their cars, and drive back to Pick to get some sleep and a change of clothes.

42
Chapter

T he next morning Gemma, Ten-Fifteen, and Tom go back to the hospital to be with Gilman. Trying to piece together the events that took place as best they can, the police request that Rosalee stay behind in Pick for questioning. Rosalee tells them about the dynamite and the bag of excrement that Gilman placed over the charge. It doesn't take long for that news to spread around Pick and for people to gather in huddles all over the county talking about it.

Rosalee tells them about Frank Denton, and everyone is amazed that all this time Frank was working at the strip mine and somehow failed to discover that Rosalee was in Gilman's old house just yards down the hill. When Bill contacts Frank's mother in Palm Beach, she agrees to fly up the next day to identify the body and take it back to Florida for burial.

Later, Bill questions Ed Toothacre, who is plenty distraught about the destruction to his equipment and thankful it wasn't worse. Ed figures they will be able to continue work in about three days.

"How did you happen to hire Frank Denton in the first place?" Bill Shepherd finally gets around to asking Ed.

"I told you I didn't know him as Frank. He was Fred. Fred Dudley."

"Well, Fred, then. How did you come to hire him?"

"I don't . . ." Ed tries to remember. Right now it's hard for him to think of anything except the destruction of the auger and high lift and the damage to his office. He is afraid to think how his boss at Conroy will take another setback. Fred Dudley? He manages to remember Fred's first day. Was he a local? No, he was from Somerset, and someone recommended him. Wade. "It was Wade Miller!" Ed says, excitedly. "Wade Miller asked me to do him a favor. He said he had this friend from Somerset who could use the work. Yeah, it was Wade!"

Bill Shepherd smiles and thanks Ed.

*W*ade Miller has been sick since he heard the news this morning, sick in the same way that a person gets sick after going through a terrible time in his life and realizes one day that the worst is over. He has finally let down his defenses. As far as he can see, no one can associate him with Fred or Frank or whatever his name was, especially now that he's dead. Dead! "Thank God," Wade mutters, recalling that Gilman is critically injured also. "Oh, well," he sighs. "That's the way the cookie crumbles. At least I won't have him on my back for a while. I won't have to worry about either of them."

At home now, he yawns, sits back in the recliner in his den, and sleeps for two solid hours before he wakes in a cold sweat and sits upright in his chair, realizing that he has forgotten something, some detail that will connect him to Frank Denton, a detail that was crystal clear in his dream. "Just a dream," he mutters, and he is about to go back to sleep when his wife comes in and nudges him in the ribs.

"Go away," he says. "I'm sleeping."

"Bill Shepherd is here, honey. He wants to ask you some questions."

"Well, I don't want to answer any. Now, tell him to go away."

At that point, Bill Shepherd steps in the room. "I need to talk to you, Wade."

Wade Miller coughs nervously and sits up straight. His wife looks from one man to the other and leaves the room.

"I'm glad you didn't decide to take that vacation to Georgia," Bill says when he takes a seat, "because I need to ask you some questions about Fred Dudley or should I say Frank Denton?"

Wade hunches over and holds his head. It comes back to him in a rush, the connecting detail he forgot to consider. "Who?"

"The guy you recommended to Ed Toothacre that he hire. He was generally known around here as Fred Dudley."

"Oh, him. Yeah, the guy from Somerset. Right?"

"He wasn't from Somerset."

"Really? He told me he was."

"Were you and him friends?"

Wade vigorously shakes his head. "No sir. No, we definitely were not friends."

"Why did you recommend him for the job, then?"

Wade fidgets uncontrollably in his chair as mucus runs from his nostrils down to his upper lip. He walks over to the desk, grabs a tissue, and wipes. "Well, you know, he came in here and asked me if there was any work in the area. Said he was from Somerset, had lost his job, and was looking for work. I thought of that strip mine up there and recommended him. That's all there is to it. All."

Bill Shepherd chuckles. "Are you some kind of employment service, Wade? I mean, I wasn't aware that you are in the habit of finding work for total strangers. Especially if there is nothing for you to gain by it."

Wade sits back down in the swiveling recliner and turns from side to side. "You know, I don't understand why it's so hard to believe that I could help somebody out."

"But why, Wade?"

"I told you why."

Bill Shepherd gets up from his chair, grabs Wade by the throat, lifts him out of the chair, and says, "Now look, you little grubworm, I want to know the truth, and I want to know it now. What were your dealings with Frank Denton? If you don't tell me this minute, I will throw you in jail and you will never see the light of day again. Spit it out!"

Wade Miller begins to cry.

*H*e's not getting any better," Gemma tells Rosalee when she returns from the hospital that night.

"Does he still squeeze your hand?"

"Yeah, but nothing else. He won't open his eyes, won't talk, while I just stand there like a fool."

That night Gemma lies in bed looking out the window at a tree branch swaying. She concentrates until she sees Gilman as he is now, pale and immobile. Then she places him on the tree branch, imagines him with color in his cheeks, sings a lullaby, rocks him to sleep.

The next morning, Rosalee gets up before Gemma and fixes her breakfast. "I want you to do me a favor before you go to the hospital today. I want you to take me up to my mother's house so I can see if her old Chrysler will start. I need my own transportation."

Gemma agrees to drop her off there on her way to Harlan, and in half an hour they are driving up the dirt road to

Mildred's house, which sits like a small white tomb at the head of the hollow among the trees where wind has blown dead leaves and branches all over the porch.

"I guess I ought to move back up here," she tells Gemma when they go inside the house to get the keys to the car. "But I'm just not ready to do that, yet."

"You can stay with us as long as you want to," Gemma says.

As the two of them walk back outside to check the car, they look back at the leaf-strewn porch. "Boy, it sure don't take a place long to go downhill when they ain't no one living in it," Rosalee says.

She unlocks the door to the Chrysler, puts the key in the ignition, and the car starts without a hitch. "They don't make 'em like they used to," Rosalee says.

Opening the door on the passenger's side, Gemma gets inside, too. She is amazed at the good condition of the interior, which Mildred obviously treated with great care. It couldn't be more clean if it were new.

Gemma looks around at Rosalee. "Are you going to come to the hospital with me?"

"Not right away. I need some time to myself."

"Are you all right?"

"I'll make it. I always do."

Gemma gets out of the car. "Well, I've got to go."

"Tell Gilman I'll be over to see him this evening," Rosalee says. "And tell him he'd better be talking when I get there."

When Gemma leaves, Rosalee sits in the car awhile longer. Alaine is supposed to arrive in Pick sometime today, and Rosalee has been fantasizing a meeting between the two of them. She imagines visiting Alaine at the Blue Mountain Inn, where she will more than likely take a room. Alaine is dressed in a mint green chiffon nightgown, and she's wearing green silk house slippers, the kind with heels. She keeps rambling on in her aristocratic Southern accent about how she's going "to sue these . . . these *hicks*" for saying her son killed a woman. In her dainty silk slippers, she paces back and forth, stopping in front of the mirror to brush her honey blond hair. "You wouldn't believe what a horrible year I've had," Rosalee imagines her saying. "First my divorce and now this." Alaine bends closer to the mirror. "My face looks awful. Just awful. I hate it when I get bags under my eyes."

Rosalee pictures herself yanking the brush out of Alaine's hand and beating her over the head with it until she screams, and she can't get this image of Frank's mother out of her mind. She starts the engine and drives down to Pick in hopes of seeing the woman for real.

At the Blue Mountain Inn, she asks the desk clerk if Alaine Morrison has checked in yet; he tells her no. She decides to wait for her in the lobby, sits down on a sofa, and begins leafing through magazines.

An hour passes and Alaine still hasn't arrived. Rosalee gets up from the chair and buys a cup of coffee from a machine. Just as she is walking back to her seat, a woman hurriedly enters the lobby, bumps into her, and coffee flies everywhere.

"Watch where you're going," the woman yells. "You've spilled coffee all over my coat! Idiot!" The woman is wearing a sable jacket with severe shoulder pads. Her dyed black hair is drawn tightly in a bun and thick black eyebrows dominate her box-shaped face.

Looking at Rosalee with disgust, the woman brushes past her and approaches the desk clerk. "I'd like the key to my room," she tells him. "Alaine Morrison is my name. I trust you still have it reserved. That girl back there doesn't work for you, does she? I hope that little mishap is no indication of the service I'll get during my stay."

Rosalee steps outside and waits for Alaine to emerge from the lobby. She watches her get back into her car and pull around to one of the rooms. She waits until Alaine is standing with her suitcase in front of the door with the key in her hand before she walks up behind her and says, "Hello."

"What do you want?" Alaine turns around and says. "Have you come to torment me further?"

"I knew your son," Rosalee says.

"You knew Frank? Well, good for you. I'm glad someone knew him. I never did."

"He killed my mother and a man in Florida."

"That's what they say," Alaine says. "Anything else?"

"No, I guess not," Rosalee mumbles.

"Good, because I've got a lot of things to take care of."

Alaine turns back to the door, unlocks it, and steps inside. Rosalee stands there for a moment feeling reduced to a small, ugly spot on the ground. She knows that in the time it takes to let out a breath she could give in to the rage that is boiling just beneath the surface. She could beat that door down and choke Alaine Morrison until she turns blue—wipe her off of the face of this earth—but what would that prove? Not a thing. Alaine Morrison would be battered, but she'd still be the same person she always was. Rosalee wraps her arms around her waist and takes long, deep breaths. Then she gets into her car and drives toward Harlan to see Gilman.

*A*t the same time that Rosalee is in route to the hospital, Gemma is standing at Gilman's bedside looking down at him. Suddenly his eyes open, and he raises his arms a few inches from the bed, trailing a multitude of tubes. "What is this shit?" he asks. "Where the fuck am I?"

Gemma almost passes out.

He reaches up and grabs hold of the oxygen tubing sticking in his nose. "I feel like I've got a big long booger coming out of my nose. Will someone kindly hand me a Kleenex?"

Gemma bends over him and smiles. "Well, it's about time

you said something. You're in a hospital, Gilman. This is a tube that's giving you oxygen. It's not a booger."

Gilman almost smiles. "Gemma?"

"Yes, it's me."

"Why did you let 'em do this to me? They've got something in my mouth, too. What is this damn thing in my mouth?"

"Another tube. It's got to be there. You'll be all right in a day or two, and they'll take all this stuff away. You've got to put up with it for now."

Gemma bends down and lightly kisses him on the cheek, and he goes back to sleep.

Later in the day when Rosalee, Tom, and Ten-Fifteen visit Gilman, he complains to them also, ordering them to get him out of the hospital right now, and when they tell him they can't, he tries to sit up in bed.

A nurse comes into the room and asks them to leave. She tells them to go home for a while, that it is obviously upsetting Gilman to have visitors right now. She suggests that Gemma call the hospital the next day to see if he is in a calmer mood. "We don't want to do anything to jeopardize his recovery," she says. "He's not out of the woods by any means. He could easily get pneumonia or some other complication."

That night they all go to Gemma's house and spend the night. Ten-Fifteen sleeps on the couch, and Tom on the floor.

In the morning they call the hospital, and the nurse suggests they wait until the next day to visit Gilman. "He's still pretty upset," she says.

"What's he doing?" Gemma asks.

"He keeps trying to unhook himself from the monitors," the nurse says, "and he wants us to give him a beer."

The four of them, together with June, are sitting around talking about the hard time Gilman is obviously giving the staff in the ICU when Bill Shepherd knocks on the door.

"You guys come up the hill with me a minute. I've got

something to show you. June, you stay here," he says. "We'll explain about it later."

They walk across the swinging bridge, where wooden slats are still speckled with Gilman's blood.

"Why did you bring us up here?" Rosalee asks when they reach the field by the old house.

"There's something in that shed I need to find out about," Bill Shepherd says.

Rosalee gasps. "You opened it. You opened Gilman's prayer chamber. How could you do that? Didn't you see the curse over the door? Gilman will kill us all when he finds out."

"I didn't open it. It was already open. Today one of the state police officers was out here snooping around and found it unchained. He found a skeleton in that shed and I'd like to know whose it is and what it's doing there."

"A what?"

"A skeleton."

"I don't believe it," Ten-Fifteen says.

Bill Shepherd stands with them in front of the chamber where the chain is hanging loose, and the door is ajar. "Gilman never wanted anybody to go in there," Ten-Fifteen says, peering conspicuously through the crack left by the slightly ajar door and seeing nothing but darkness.

"I know who opened it," Rosalee says. "Gilman opened it himself. That's where he stored his bag of shit. He must of left the door open that night. I was prob'ly running around the hill there trying to run away from Frank when he come up here to get it."

Ten-Fifteen reads aloud the curse over the door. " 'Anyone who breaks this chain and enters uninvited will lose his or her genitals.' "

Bill Shepherd orders them to open the door and look inside, but they stand precariously in place, with the unlocked door in front of them beckoning. "I wonder if that curse would still apply if anyone just went against half of it. I mean, the chain is already unlocked," Rosalee says.

Tom squares his shoulders. "Personally, I think a person would have to violate the entire mandate for the curse to be effective."

Ten-Fifteen studies on this for a minute. "Yeah, but we wouldn't invited."

"I'm inviting you," Bill Shepherd says.

"You don't count, though," Ten-Fifteen says. "Gilman would have to invite us, and he didn't."

"Perhaps he did," Tom says with authority. "One theory holds that there is a reason for everything a person does. Perhaps Gilman left that door open on purpose, the purpose being that we were invited to go in."

"Maybe we ought to call and ask him," Ten-Fifteen says.

"Gilman's not in any shape to be bothered with this right now," Gemma says.

Bill Shepherd looks at them with exasperation and pulls the door open wide.

Rosalee looks around at the sheriff. "If we all lose our genitals it will be your fault, Bill."

They step inside and find a wooden table, on top of which sits a fifth of Jim Beam and two glasses, one of them half-full. Two chairs are positioned around the table, and one of them is occupied by a skeleton who has an unlit cigarette between two of its fingers. Its mouth is open in such a way that it appears to be smiling, and it's wearing a baseball cap with a single word stitched in bright red over the bill. ZACK, it says.

"Zack?" Tom gasps.

"Morley?" Ten-Fifteen adds.

Gemma and Rosalee look at each other completely bewildered.

4 3
Chapter

The next day, when they go to the hospital, Gilman is in a slightly better mood, but his conversation rambles from one thing to another.

"Did I do any damage up there that night besides the damage to Landon Couch?" he asks her.

"Landon Couch?"

"I mean Frank Denton," Gilman says, confused.

"You blew the auger up, and a high lift, and set Ed Toothacre's office on fire."

The nurse comes in, winks at Gemma, and says, "I wish you'd tell him to leave us nurses alone. I've never seen such a griping man. We're going to move him out of here tomorrow into a private room."

Gilman's eyes sparkle for a second, and then the sparkle fades. "Gemma, is Tom Cat out there?"

"Yes."

"Would you tell him to come in here? I'd like to talk to him, alone."

Gemma kisses him on the forehead and leaves.

Tom Jett walks into Gilman's room and stands close by his bed. "Are you feeling better, Gilman?"

"I guess. They say I'm better, but when you're in the shape I'm in, it's hard to tell."

Tom sits down in a chair.

"I wanted to talk to you alone because I want you to know I apologize for taking Gemma away from you. I apologize for it, but I'm not giving her back unless she wants to go. Do you think she wants to go?" Gilman asks.

Tom smiles. "No, Gilman, I don't."

Gilman extends his hand as far as it will go. "If something does happen to me, I wish you'd take care of her as much as she'll let you."

"Nothing's going to happen to you."

"I'm not so sure about that. By the way, my hand is getting tired. Are you going to shake it or not?"

Tom reaches for his hand and shakes it.

When Ten-Fifteen takes his turn with Gilman, he tells him about the discovery of Zack's skeleton.

"Zack's skeleton? What are you talking about? Where is Zack, anyway? Why ain't he been to see me?"

Ten-Fifteen looks around frightened. "I wouldn't of said anything about it," he says. "But Bill Shepherd woulda told you soon enough." Ten-Fifteen holds up a paper bag. "I brought you a change of clothes, Gilman. It's for when they let you out of here. I'm goin to put them in your nightstand."

"What happened to the clothes I had on when you brought me here?"

"I took 'em home to wash 'em," Ten-Fifteen says, remembering the blood-soaked jacket, shirt, and pants.

That night when visiting hours are over, they drive toward Pick, feeling somewhat guarded about Gilman's condition. Ten-Fifteen and Tom both go home. Gemma and Rosalee fill June in on the patient's progress, and everyone sleeps a restless sleep.

Gemma, especially, tosses and turns. She sees Gilman's pale
face whether her eyes are opened or closed. She hasn't been
to work since the explosion. The board of directors at the
bank contacted her yesterday regarding Wade Miller's position, which is now vacant. Wade was asked to resign, and he
did. They want her to take over as bank manager, at least temporarily, and if things work out, they'd like her to keep the job
permanently. Gemma told them that when Gilman is out of
the hospital, she'll let them know.

The bank's board of directors asked Wade to resign because
of the rumors that have been circulating around town, rumors that he is involved in the distribution of cocaine
throughout the county, and that he knew Frank Denton and
helped him get the job at the mine. People wonder if he knew
beforehand that Frank killed Mildred.

When Bill Shepherd questioned Wade on the day after the
explosion, he was not able to learn the whole truth. All he
could get from Wade was that Frank Denton came into his office, representing himself as Fred Dudley, a boyfriend of
Rosalee's. Wade told Bill that Frank claimed he wanted to
marry Rosalee, but that they had had a fight and Rosalee was
hiding from him. He said he needed a job until he could find
her.

"I still don't understand why you agreed to help him,
though, especially considering that you once had a thing for
her," Bill said.

"I didn't . . ."

"Don't bother denying it, Wade. Now why did you decide
to help find him a job? Is it because he threatened to let your
wife know about Rosalee? Or did he have something else on
you? Maybe Rosalee told Frank about your drug dealing."

Wade gets a sharp pain in his chest. "What! What are you
talking about?"

"The cocaine, Wade. I know you're involved in dealing it. I
just can't prove it. Is that what Frank had on you?"

"I'm not answering any more of your questions, Bill. I'm going to get a lawyer."

"Good idea. I'll talk to you later."

Wade has gotten himself a lawyer, but so far he hasn't been arrested. Bill has not been able to prove anything except that Wade knew Frank. As for the cocaine, Rosalee was able to confirm that Wade supplied her with the drug before she left for Florida and says she knows he was dealing it, but that she can't prove it, either.

In the meantime, Wade is going ahead with plans for his McDonald's franchise.

Gemma is annoyed by the job promotion the board of directors is offering her. If she takes the job, at least she won't have to worry about working with Wade Miller anymore, but the truth is she just doesn't want to be a bank manager. Right now all she can think about is Gilman getting well and if she ever does anything work related again, she wants it to be something that doesn't go against everything she believes herself to be.

*T*he next day they unhook most of the machines that have been connected to Gilman and move him out of Intensive Care into a private room. Gemma begins to have cautious hopes that he will get to come home soon, but the doctors say they are moving him out of ICU only because they need the space for more critical patients. They warn her that Gilman's condition is still serious.

Gemma sits close by Gilman's bedside. He hasn't been griping as much today, and it worries her. "Are you sure you're okay?" she asks him.

"I'm fine," he says, "as frog hair."

"Do you want me to read to you? There's a magazine here."

"No, I want you to sing to me."

"What do you want me to sing?"

"I want you to sing 'Red River Valley.' "

"I don't know the words."

"Just sing the song, Gemma."

"I can't, Gilman. That song is too sad."

"Okay, then. Sing the song about 'Drinking, Drugging, and Watching TV.' "

"Never heard of it."

"Well, just lean down here and give me a kiss, then."

Gemma leans down and gives Gilman a kiss on the mouth. He winks at her and closes his eyes. "Gilman?" she whispers, but he doesn't answer. She puts her hand on his chest to make sure his heart is still beating and after watching him awhile, she decides to go home early and let him sleep.

Gilman is awake. He just pretended to go to sleep so Gemma would leave and now that she is gone, he lies in bed and stares up at the stark white ceiling, looks around at the IV running who-knows-what into his arm. Gemma's suspicions were right. He doesn't feel as well today as yesterday because an infection is growing inside of him. In addition to the regular pain, his skin is itchy and his insides feel as if they're about to burst.

"I've got to get out of here," he growls. "This place is killing me—all this ammonia and tile and aluminum."

For an instant, Gilman wishes he had never stepped between Gemma and Tom. "They'd be happy as rabbits if it wouldn't for me. She'd not be coming over here, having to see me like this." When he remembers that first evening they made love, his noble intentions fly out the window.

Listening to the noise in the hall outside his room, the bottles clattering, the nurses and visitors buzzing around, he figures he'll have a better chance of escaping during visiting hours while people are still wandering the halls, talking and complaining. What time is it, anyway? He looks up at the clock; it is eight, only half an hour before visiting hours are over. Luckily, Gemma closed the door behind her when she left and no one will be able to see him get out of bed and get dressed. He would have considered asking her to help with his escape; but he knew she not only would have refused, she'd have warned the doctors to be on the lookout and suggested they post a guard by the door.

Pushing the button on the side of the bed and raising himself to a sitting position, Gilman deftly begins working to get the IV out of his arm, takes the oxygen tube out of his nose, and scoots himself to the edge of the bed. He holds on to the table beside his bed and stands for several minutes until the dizziness goes away. With his knees weak enough to buckle at any moment, he reaches inside the drawer of the nightstand to see if the clean set of clothes Ten-Fifteen brought him were transferred here during his move from ICU. He finds them in the drawer, and placing one hand on the bed for support, he walks around it to the bathroom, where he throws water on his face and gets dressed.

Gilman's stomach is so swollen that he has no choice but to leave his pants unbuttoned. Keeping his shirttail out for a covering, he steps into his unlaced shoes, walks out of the bathroom, and approaches the door to the hall, feeling better now. He waits a few more minutes, until visiting hours are over and people are leaving. Hearing a group of visitors pass by his room on their way home, he slips out the door and walks with them down the hall to the elevator.

Outside, a block from the hospital, he tries to let out a yell from the sheer joy of his accomplishment. He can't manage more than a groan because of the pain in his stomach, and he sits down on a curb to rest for a few minutes before walking on. After reaching the main drag of Harlan, he stands on a street corner, thumbing drivers stopped for the light, finally getting the attention of a carload of teenagers who arc driving in the direction of Pick. Once inside the car, he turns on the charm, and the youngsters, who have had a few drinks, offer to drive him all the way home.

They let him out of the car at the curve up the road from his house. He thanks them and invites them to a party the next weekend, telling them the drinks will be free and plenty. As they turn their car around and head back to Harlan, Gilman starts walking toward the shop. The pain in his stomach is worse, and the itchy, bloated feeling has come back. He stops to rest a few feet from Ten-Fifteen's trailer, where the lights are out and his friend is sleeping. When he feels a little better, he manages to walk on to the machine shop. Entering his apartment, he turns on the light and looks around, surprised by its appearance, having forgotten for the moment that Tom Jett paneled the walls last summer. He walks to the refrigerator, gets a beer and opens it, moves over to the couch and sits down.

"Home at last," he says, smiling. Then he sees Zack standing in the kitchen area leaning his arms on the counter.

"What're you doin here?" Gilman asks.

"You mean you're not glad to see me? Let's hit the road, buddy. You've stayed too long already."

"But I didn't do what I set out to do. They're still stripping that mountain. I didn't plant enough dynamite."

"It's okay, Gilman. It'll all work out."

Gilman takes another drink of beer and says, "Well, Zack, the other day you said they was some hell to raise. Where's it at?"

Zack smiles and walks around the counter toward him. The house grows quieter than it was before. Outside, the creek stops gurgling, the wind goes to sleep, the birds close their mouths, and for a moment the whole world stops moving in order to let Gilman Lee step off.

44
Chapter

*T*en-Fifteen discovers the body the next morning. Unable to believe his eyes, he sits on a stool at the kitchen counter still as a rock for about an hour before finally calling an ambulance. He can barely talk—can't see or think straight when they come to take Gilman away.

After word gets around, even the people who didn't like Gilman are desolate as shipwrecked sailors. If they were asked to explain their sense of loss, they couldn't, but they feel similar to the way they felt when all the chestnut trees in the area were killed by a blight. They feel as if suddenly no one in the entire county can pick a tune on the guitar, as though an integral piece of what names them who they are is missing.

The men, the regulars, who for years have spent their Saturday nights at Lee's Machine Shop, come to stand out in front of it, talking in hushed voices, their wives having sent with them cakes and pies and sandwiches to give to Ten-Fifteen, as if he is some bereaved, misshapen widow. They don't go inside the shop because it suddenly feels like a church, like a place of worship or a monument of some kind, the Vietnam War Memorial,

maybe. By now they are well acquainted with the events leading
up to and including the explosion at the mine. They know that
Fred Dudley and Frank Denton were one and the same and only
regret that Frank isn't alive so they can kill him. The regulars
stand outside the shop, leaning against the coal-truck bed, scraping the toes of their shoes across the ground, asking each other
how Gilman could have died at the hands of a stranger like that
and why, if Gilman had to die at all, he couldn't have gone suddenly in the explosion. "Why did he have to linger for nearly a
week in the hospital?" they want to know.

They get to talking about how, even though he was almost
dead, Gilman sneaked out of his room and hitched a ride home.
"Ain't no one could keep him in a hospital for long, no matter
what kind of shape he was in," they remark. They remember
the bag of shit that he blasted all over the top of the mountain,
and they shake their heads and laugh. The Texan, collector and
supplier of the explosives and shit, has become a hero to them.
Most of the men who were somewhat leery of him before are
ready to cozy up to him now. "Long Tall," they refer to him, and
they're thinking of chipping in to buy him a big white horse.

So far, Ten-Fifteen is the only one who has ventured inside
the shop. He's been pacing the floor of the apartment ever
since this morning when he made the discovery, intermit-
tently staring at Gilman's guitars leaning against the wall,
striking sour notes on the piano, frying bacon and eggs for
two and eating quickly without taking time to taste, standing
out on the balcony watching the creek run, wondering what
in the world he'll do now.

Gemma takes it the worst. Nothing is left standing inside her.
Her insides have been obliterated by a smart bomb, one that
knew exactly where to hit, one that nosed around until it found
just the right entrance, maneuvered itself through the door,
and exploded. She stands in front of people like a wall of nothing, a white wall on which there is no color variation, no graffiti, no chinks. She doesn't talk coherently or reason, doesn't

even grieve in a way that most people would describe as grief.

She wanders up the mining road to the old house, making her way through guards for the Conroy Coal Company who have cordoned off the area around the strip mine.

"I'm just going to the old house," she manages to tell them. Her voice is hoarse and the words shoot out of her mouth like obscenities. The guards let her go. They seem to know that someone in her condition could not possibly do harm to the mine.

She enters the house and sits in the kitchen. It is cold in the room, but she doesn't notice as she listens to the rain, which comes in gusts and beats against the window, soaking into the nearby trees until they are a rich, dark brown. She gets up and stands by the window, watching puddles form on the ground below the eaves of the house. There is nothing left at this moment but a dead ache. She stands there waiting for something to happen, because surely something must happen to a person when she has reached this state of mind. A person must die or go insane.

Nothing happens.

Rosalee and June are so worried about Gemma that they can barely talk to each other. They certainly found it impossible to talk to her this morning, and now she has gone off somewhere, they presume to the old house, since they saw her walk in that direction. They didn't think of following her; it was so clear that she wanted to be alone.

When it gets dark and Gemma is still gone, June begins wringing her hands. "What is she doing up there?"

"She'll be all right," Rosalee says, not at all convinced.

June turns on the TV, tries but is unable to get interested in a show, and eventually drops off to a restless sleep. Rosalee rocks back and forth in the rocking chair, tired from worrying and grieving all day, and when the knock comes at the door, she almost doesn't answer until she looks out the window and sees Tom Jett.

Rosalee lets him in and throws her arms around his neck. "God, I'm so glad to see you," she says and begins to cry. It is the first time she has allowed herself to cry since early this morning.

Rosalee ushers him into the kitchen, scoots the nearly finished jigsaw puzzle to one end of the table, and makes him a cup of hot chocolate. "Could you stay with us awhile? Just stay with us."

Tom looks around the room. "Where's Gemma?"

"She's up at the old house. Wants to be alone, I reckon."

"Is she goin to stay up there tonight?"

"I don't know. I guess. Did you and Gilman ever patch things up?" she asks him. "I know you saw him several times at the hospital."

Tom smiles. "He apologized for taking Gemma away from me. Actually, that whole apology seems rather ludicrous—not the apology so much as the implication that Gemma is a girl who can be taken, rather than a woman who makes her own decisions. I did, however, accept his apology."

"Well, I'm glad," Rosalee says and pours them both a cup of hot chocolate.

On the hill, Gemma is still waiting for something to happen. Glancing around, she realizes it is dark in the house. She gets up from the table and walks outside and down the mountain. She rips her clothes off and steps into the icy water of the creek, stretches her arms toward the sky and, chanting a requiem black as coal, lets the pain from losing Gilman hit her as hard as it can with every memory it can muster—his smile, the way he walked across a room, the way she felt the last time she kissed him.

Finally, no sound will come out of her mouth and her tears

dry. She puts her clothes back on and walks back up the hill to the house, finds some quilts in a closet, makes herself a bed on the floor, and lies there in the darkness, her eyes open wide as a child's.

"I guess I'm just not lucky in matters of the heart," she says. "Some people are and some aren't. People like me lose the ones they love. Well, forget that shit, then. I don't need to be lucky in love. I'm still here, though, I didn't die, and I didn't go insane, and I must be here for a reason, and, if I'm not here for a reason, I'm going to make a goddamned reason."

*T*he next day the sun comes out and warms the winter day to a temperature in the low fifties. Rosalee, Tom, and June are already up and stirring when Ten-Fifteen knocks on the door.

Ten-Fifteen clears his throat. "I guess we need to talk about the funeral," he says.

Tom and Rosalee exchange dumbfounded looks. This is something neither of them had yet considered—a funeral for Gilman Lee. What kind of funeral could they possibly have for a man like him? The idea that he will need to be put in the ground seems most absurd.

"The funeral?" Tom asks.

"Yeah, I mean, we're goin to have to have one . . . of some kind. I've been thinking about it."

"What?" Rosalee asks. "What have you been thinking?"

"Well, first of all, I went through his papers yesterday to see if he had a burial policy. He had one. He kept this box full of important papers in his kitchen. He told me about it a long time ago. Said that if anything ever happened to him, I ought to look through 'em."

"What was in the box?"

"Well, the funeral policy and a life insurance policy and . . ."

Rosalee looks at Ten-Fifteen with disbelief. "Gilman had a life insurance policy?"

"Yeah, had one for twenty thousand dollars, and he had something else, too. He had a will."

"A will?" Rosalee, Tom, and June all say.

"Yeah, he left everything he had to me."

Tom and Rosalee and June look at each other and shake their heads. It seems strange to them that Gilman Lee could ever do anything so practical as to leave a will. They are pleasantly surprised that he had the good sense to make Ten-Fifteen his beneficiary.

"Anyway, I think we ought to talk about the funeral—what kind we're goin to have, where we're goin to have it and stuff," Ten-Fifteen says.

"Well, I'll be damned," Rosalee mutters, and they all just sit around the table staring at each other.

"Where's Gemma?" Ten-Fifteen asks. "She ought to be in on this conversation, too."

"She's up at the old house. She's been there since yesterday," June says. "I'm pretty worried about her if you want to know."

"Yeah, well, I think she's been up there by herself long enough. Let's go get her," Rosalee says.

June begins to wash the breakfast dishes while the other three walk up the hill to see Gemma.

"What's this?" Gemma asks, when she opens the door and finds them on the porch.

"We just thought we'd take a walk, see how you were doing."

"I'm all right," she says, letting them in.

The discussion of the funeral lasts for a good two hours. They decide to bury Gilman at Washburn Creek and to buy a casket that is large enough to accommodate not only Gilman, but his favorite guitar, and a fifth of good Kentucky bourbon. Ten-Fifteen will say the eulogy. They will invite all the regulars at the machine shop, and a party will ensue, a hell of a party.

The weather remains warm on the day of Gilman's funeral. Ten-Fifteen, deciding not to use the services of a hearse, gets six of the regulars to hoist the coffin into the bed of Gilman's old truck. He opens the lid on the casket and lays Gilman's favorite guitar on top of his body as though he thinks his friend might rise up and pick a good one any minute. Yesterday he asked permission of Zack Morley's remaining relatives to rebury Zack at Washburn Creek. After they assented, he procured the skeleton from the funeral home, where it has been since its discovery. He lays Zack's skeleton on the truck bed beside the coffin. He also throws in an ice cooler filled with beer, some fishing rods and reels, and a fifth of Jim Beam.

The procession takes off for Washburn Creek at ten-thirty in the morning, with Tom and Ten-Fifteen driving Gilman's truck and Gemma and Rosalee following them in Gemma's car. Trailing after Gemma is a motley convoy of vehicles loaded with the Machine Shop Society regulars, their wives, girlfriends, and teenage and adult children. June decides not to go, reasoning that there will be nothing included in Gilman's funeral that she'd want to copy for her own. Each car and truck also carries at least one musical instrument and container of alcohol, ensuring that Gilman Lee's final party will be a measurable one.

When they arrive at the graveyard beside Washburn Creek, they set to work immediately, with some of the men and women tackling Zack Morley's grave, redigging the hole so as to present Zack with a decent grave that is at least six feet in depth, and with the rest of the gang excavating Gilman Lee a grave right beside Zack's. When the work is complete, the men lift Gilman's coffin and Zack's skeleton out of the truck and carry them to the grave sites while everyone gathers around for the ceremony.

Ten-Fifteen stands up to say a few words over Zack's grave before they put him in it. "Most of us knowed Zack Morley as being a hell of a hellraiser, but I think we was all surprised when he rose from the grave, or so it seemed. All we knowed was that we come over here one day and he was gone. As the years passed, the only thing his grave held was poison ivy. It seemed fitting, somehow. We never knowed it was Gilman Lee that stole him until a few days ago. I guess him and Zack just wouldn't through partying. Anyway, now that Gilman has crossed over, I'm sure we all agree that it is time for Zack to get some rest. Of course, I don't know how much rest he'll get if Gilman is anywhere around him."

People nod and smile.

"Well, Zack already had one funeral a few years back," Ten-Fifteen continues, "and a lot of good words was said about him then. I guess this is all I've got to say about him this time around."

When it is clear that Ten-Fifteen is finished, they lower the skeleton into the grave and shovel the dirt in.

Ten-Fifteen opens the lid on Gilman's coffin, and everyone takes a look at their favorite host and musician, his guitar lying over him. Ten-Fifteen previously removed the satin from the lid and sides of the coffin to make room for the guitar, reasoning that Gilman was never partial to satin, anyway. Some of the gang mutter that he looks as though he's sleeping, others say he appears to be playing possum, and everyone agrees that he has a faint smile on his lips. With tears in their eyes, they break out the drinks and partake.

Ten-Fifteen gulps down a couple of stiff ones and stands by the newly dug grave to say the eulogy, his fifteen arm still hanging at twenty.

"I've not made a speech since high school," he starts out by saying, "and now here today I'm saying speeches over two men's graves." He stops for a minute to clear his throat. "At first a lot of people was confused about who exactly killed Gilman. I guess by now everybody knows that Frank Denton pulled the trigger, but I'm still confused about who killed him. I sorta think the Conroy Coal Company had something to do with it." Ten-Fifteen stops to listen to the murmuring of the crowd, some agreeing and others disagreeing.

"Now, I know not everybody seen eye to eye with Gilman's opinions on mining, but Gilman cared a lot about this land around here. You'll have to agree with that, especially if you've ever been out camping or fishing with him. He could sit and stare at a river for hours at a time and be happy as a lark. Or he'd notice some odd rock formation on the side of a hill, and he'd get you to see it in a way you would never have thought of, if he hadn't pointed it out. He'd sit and talk to ants crawling on the ground. I've seen him do it. Anybody else'd do a thing like that, people would say they was crazy, but we all just took it for granted that he'd do things like that. He made us notice things, little things that people are usually too busy to see. Yeah, he loved this place, and he knowed that mining has almost destroyed it."

Gemma looks around at Rosalee and they both begin to cry. They are not the only ones. All through the crowd, eyes are filling to the brim.

Ten-Fifteen continues. "He knowed that mining set food on people's tables and sympathized with that—but any time you're keeping yourself alive by killing something else, it ought to put a bad taste in your mouth, especially if they's a chance of making a living some other way. He said people could think of another way if they'd just put their thinking caps on. I say it, too."

A few people in the crowd give little cheers of approval. Gemma, Tom, and Rosalee let out whoops and yells. Other people, unaccustomed to Ten-Fifteen's being so serious, look at each other as if they don't know what to think. "And they's something else," Ten-Fifteen says. "I know a lot of you'uns like to come to the shop to relax and have a good time. Well, you can keep on coming. Gilman would've wanted it that way. I found out something the other day that surprised me. Gilman had drawed up a will, and he left everything to me: the shop, his land, everything. I'm just here to tell you that things are goin to go on. Maybe they won't be the same with Gilman not here, but you all can keep coming to the shop if you want to. And that's all I have to say on that subject."

Cheers and catcalls rise up from the crowd. Ten-Fifteen glances around at the casket and at the hole in the ground. "Well," he says, "I guess it's time to lay Gilman to rest. I would say something more about him, but he's kinda hard to describe, ain't he? So let's just put him in the ground. He always liked it here at Washburn Creek."

The men lower the coffin into the grave, and everyone takes turns heaping the dirt on.

Later, when the party is in full sway, Gemma has a talk with Ten-Fifteen.

"I just want you to know how much I liked your speech," she tells him. "I agree with every word you said. You know, about the land and everything. I'd like to talk to you more about it sometime."

"Sure," Ten-Fifteen says.

Gemma smiles, puts her arm around him, and says, "Gilman sure would have been proud of you today."

The party continues for several hours with the guests singing, drinking, and dancing on the creek bank. It is completely dark before the funeral procession loads up for the trip back home. After they are all gone, Washburn Creek is silent except for the sound of fish swimming near the top of the water to keep warm and the wind playing like a guitar through the pines.

45
Chapter

For the past week, Rosalee has been working for Ten-Fifteen at the machine shop, helping to clear up the work that was left in the lurch after Gilman's death. She enjoys being a mechanic, has a knack for it. Her original intention was to quit after she had completed the work already in progress, but yesterday Joe Carter brought his truck in for repairs, and she agreed to do the job. Ten-Fifteen says she's just as good a mechanic as Gilman ever was. Tomorrow she is moving into Gilman's apartment at the machine shop. Ten-Fifteen cleaned the place and told her she ought to move in so she can be closer to work.

Still spending her nights in the old house on the hill, Gemma dreams of Gilman regularly, and her dreams of him are so vivid that sometimes she is convinced he is still alive. She talks to him in her dreams; they make love. Having just gotten up this morning, she is looking out the window when she sees a truck going up the road to the strip mine. The truck is hauling an auger. "There they go," she says, throwing her hands up in the air like June. "They don't care that a man died," she shouts at the window, the walls, at nothing.

She considers calling Bill Shepherd to see if there is anything he can do to stop them, but she knows there isn't. Conroy owns the mineral rights. Since they station the auger on Dwight Simpson's land and since he signed the agreement, they're not trespassing. They are legally within their rights to do as they please.

A few hours later, she drives to the machine shop where Ten-Fifteen and Rosalee are giving the Texan's truck a tune-up. "They've started augering into Gilman's vein of coal again," Gemma tells them.

Ten-Fifteen and Rosalee put their tools down and look at each other, not saying a word. Leaning against his truck, the Texan smiles. Finally, Ten-Fifteen says, "Well, we knew they would, didn't we?"

"I think we ought to do something about it," Gemma says.

"You're damn right," Rosalee agrees.

"Well, let's stop and think about this a minute," Ten-Fifteen says, and he stops a minute and thinks.

The Texan props his foot on the bumper of his pickup. "I think you all ought to calm down, take it easy. You don't wanta do anything rash."

"I bet you'd have some more dynamite, wouldn't you?" Gemma says.

"Might."

"Tell me something," Gemma says. "Where do you get that stuff and, more to the point, why?"

"Some people collect stamps . . ." The Texan grins. "Did they hire another night watchman after Frank was killed?"

Gemma considers this for a minute. "Well, until about a week ago, they had all kinds of guards up there, but I've not seen them lately. Maybe they think that since Gilman is safely in the ground there's no need to worry anymore. They probably have a night watchman, though."

"Well, I don't want you fellers to do anything, least not right away. Let me think about it." He turns to Ten-Fifteen. "And buddy, I wish you'd go back to fixing my truck. I need to get home and do some things."

The next day, the Texan knocks on the door of Gilman's old house and tells Gemma it might be a good idea if she were to return to her own house for a while.

"Why?" she asks.

"Because things might heat up pretty soon on this mountain."

"What do you mean?"

"Just do it," the Texan orders and walks away before she can say another word.

Gemma goes back to her mother's house that night.

Two days later she is up early, about 5 A.M., standing in the kitchen looking out the window when the whole top of the mountain blows sky-high.

She looks out toward her driveway and sees the Texan running toward his truck.

Once he pulls away, she walks over to the telephone and calls the fire department. June runs out of her bedroom into the kitchen and on outside, wearing nothing but her nightgown. She keeps yelling at Gemma to come outside and see the fire, but Gemma just pours herself another cup of coffee. "He did it," she says, doing a James Brown twist of her hips. "And I feel good."

By the time the firemen arrive half an hour later, the top of the mountain has burned to a crisp. Much later in the day, after calling up all their reserves, Pick's fire department gets the fire under control before it spreads over the entire mountain. Most of the damage was confined to the top and to an area some distance down the side of the mountain on Dwight

Simpson's land. Gilman's old house wasn't even singed. That evening Sheriff Bill Shepherd finds the night watchman gagged and tied to some beams of wood under the bridge the miners built.

Bill Shepherd's investigation dwindles to nothing. He questions every member of the Machine Shop Society, but they all have alibis and tell him they were partying together the night of the explosion. Bill doesn't question the Texan because he has disappeared. His closest neighbor says he's gone on a trip out West and won't be back till next year.

*O*ne morning when June brings in the mail, she notices a letter from the coal company. Opening it, she finds a check for fifteen hundred dollars.

"Well, looks like we're sure enough rich, now. Right, Momma?" Gemma chimes when June shows her.

The Conroy Coal Company quit their operation on the hill shortly after the explosion. Having already mined a large portion of the coal, they felt resuming the enterprise wouldn't be profitable. They realized that Gilman Lee had a lot of friends in Burr County, friends who would probably continue to wreak havoc.

"Just shut up," June says. "I don't want to hear it. And I've got a question for you, Miss Smarty Pants. When are you goin back to work?"

Gemma leaves and goes down to the Pick Citizens', June's question reminding her of something she's been meaning to do. She walks into the lobby of the bank past Jo Ellen and Marcy to Wade's old office. Bob Foster, a member of the board of directors, has been taking on the duties of bank manager until a permanent manager can be found. He is sitting at Wade's desk when she walks in and says, "I can't take the job you offered me. I can't work anymore at my old job, either. Good luck finding someone, and have a nice life."

She walks back through the lobby, sticks her tongue out at Marcy and Jo Ellen, and drives home.

When she gets to her house, she finds her mother in the living room, sitting on the floor. June has spread newspapers to protect the carpet while she glues the completed jigsaw puzzle to a piece of cardboard. She has intentions of framing the picture—which depicts Buckingham Palace—and hanging it in the living room.

"I've quit my job," Gemma tells her mother.

June throws her hands up. "I knew something like this was going to happen. I just knew it. Well, what in the world are we going to do now?"

Gemma positions herself squarely in front of June and takes hold of her hands. "I don't know what we're going to do, but I can't go back to work there. That job was killing me."

June sits straight back as if she is bracing herself for hard times to come.

"Did you know," Gemma tells June, "that some people actually choose to be dirt poor? They think being poor makes them rich in other ways."

June glares at Gemma. "Is that what you think?"

"Maybe."

June gets up, brushes past Gemma, and goes to the kitchen. "I baked some cookies today."

"What kind?" Gemma asks, following her.

"Chocolate chip." June lifts the cover from a bowl. "Want one?"

"Don't mind if I do."

June sits down at the table. "I just want you to know something. I've been thinking about not cashing that check from that coal company."

"You mean it?"

"That's what I've been thinking."

"Momma, don't do that," Gemma says, taking a bite out of a chocolate chip cookie. "If you do, you'll regret it the rest of your life. Go ahead and take the money. Besides, you'll need it, now that I've quit my job."

"Don't tell me what to do, Gemma."

"Cash the check," Gemma says, taking another bite.

"How did the cookies turn out?" June asks.

"Great, Momma. They turned out great."

Tom Jett, having finished the repairs, moved into the cabin last week. Today he invites Gemma to the cave and shows her the writing on the wall. The two of them sit on the floor of the dark, musty room and stare at the line of words, made visible by torches he has placed on either side. The words rush around them like ghosts scurrying between the past and present, words that sing, whisper, and laugh.

"I've decided I don't want to know the literal translation," Tom tells her.

"Why not?"

"Because as it is now, it could mean anything I want it to mean. It could be something out of this world, something sacred."

Gemma has heard rumors of writings having been found in other caves in eastern Kentucky, writings that language experts claim is Phoenician. How it got there nobody knows. She decides not to tell Tom this bit of information. If the writing were Phoenician that would be pretty exceptional, but Tom imagines it is filled with even more magic than that. Suppose he's on the right track, Gemma speculates. What if those words have been on the wall of this cave since the beginning of time? What if they're something the earth wrote?

"Well, I'm glad you're not having it translated." Gemma looks around at Tom and smiles. "This cave must have been someone's home at one time."

"It must have been."

"Well, it's yours now, and it suits you to a tee. I'd like to come again if that's okay."

"Anytime."

After Gemma has gone home, Tom sits by his fireplace watching sparks fly. He thinks that she is right—this place does suit him. He can't help appreciating the irony that, for someone who was always so concerned with the ineptness of language, he now is so taken with a line of words he chooses not to decipher.

He has begun to entertain several rather farcical meanings for the line. "Don't go to hell before you raise it," he imagines it says, and, "Many, many years ago, when the world was very young, shit happened." Tom creates a meaning for the words every night when he writes. He still doesn't know what he is writing—whether it is a book, a story, a philosophical treatise, or just notes to himself.

Tom feels a kinship with the country around him, and he has begun to wonder if it is possible to bring a class-action suit against the company or companies that came into the area all those years ago and bought the mineral rights for a pittance. Considering this for a moment, he dismisses the idea on the grounds that he is a philosopher, not a political activist, and that if the people did get their mineral rights back, they would mine the coal themselves because they need the money. Gilman Lee often suggested that people ought to go into the pot business, but instead of growing and harvesting the marijuana illegally, which is what a lot of people in the area do when they can't get regular jobs, that a heavy campaign ought to be started to legalize the drug. Tom figures that if marijuana were legalized, huge farms would be developed in other parts of the state where level terrain is more conducive to farming. The people of eastern Kentucky would very likely never see a profit.

Realizing he can't solve the problems around him all in one sitting, he walks out to his porch and inhales deeply while the smell of pine drifts past him down the mountain.

46
Chapter

Gemma wanders the mountain every day, sometimes following the old road all the way to Mildred Wilson's house. She is rediscovering the Indian ghosts from her childhood. She follows them as she walks, and they tell her the history of the hills, of the trees and the rich, dark soil. They teach her their ways—their ways are as simple and complex as the mountain itself.

Today she contemplates the Conroy Coal Company's having stopped their mining operation on her property. She thinks about the fact that she won, that Gilman Lee won, that Tom, Rosalee, Ten-Fifteen, and the Texan all won a battle the minute that the mining was discontinued. Granted, it was a small battle, but its size isn't important to her. What is important is that it is possible to win.

With a sudden desire to talk to Rosalee, to remind her of their victory, she makes her way down the mountain, crosses the swinging bridge, and drives to the machine shop. When she gets there, Rosalee is not among the junky cars and auto parts in the shop, but Gemma can hear her humming and washing dishes in the apartment.

"Hello," she calls out. "Are you in there?"

"Sure am," Rosalee answers her. "Just come on in."

Gemma hasn't been in the apartment since Gilman's death, and she isn't prepared for the emotions that rise to the surface when she steps inside. It all comes back to her in a rush—the night they first got together, the silly beret he wore, the turtleneck sweater. Remembering that first kiss, his gruff mouth on hers, the scent of Old Spice on his face, she sits down on the couch and puts her head in her hands.

Rosalee turns from the sink. "Are you all right, Gemma?"

Gemma takes her hands away from her eyes. "He's still in here. I can feel him. I didn't know he'd still be here."

Rosalee smiles. "He'll always be here, Gemma. He had too many good times in here to leave this place just because he died."

Gemma looks at the Polaroid photographs still hanging on the wall. "I don't think I'll ever get over him."

"I doubt you will," Rosalee says. "I sure hope you don't. A person like Gilman ought not ever be gotten over."

Rosalee walks over to the refrigerator and gets them each a beer. "You know, we ain't been on a singing and drinking binge in a long time. You want to?"

"I don't know," Gemma says, her eyes fixed on the piano where Gilman used to play "You Win Again."

"Sometimes they ain't nothing for it but to get drunk and sing to the top of your lungs."

Gemma takes a drink of beer, and says, "I've not heard you talk much about going to Arizona lately. Are you still thinking about it?"

"Been too busy to think about it. But I still might go if I can ever get away from Ten-Fifteen. He thinks he's got himself a lifetime employee. Acts like a mother, too. The other night I went out with Bill, and he waited up for me till I got home."

"Bill?"

"Yeah, you know, Bill Shepherd."

Gemma grins. "Bill, eh?"

"Why not? Bill's okay."

"I didn't say he wasn't." Gemma looks around at Gilman's guitars leaning against the wall. "Probably the reason Ten-Fifteen was waiting up for you is that he likes you, too. You realize that, don't you?"

"I guess I do."

"Well?"

"Well, I don't know," Rosalee says. "I'm not ready for a serious fling, right now."

"Me either," Gemma says. "Go ahead and play us a tune, Rosalee. Do you know 'Fraulein'?"

Rosalee picks up a guitar and begins to play. "I just had a idea," she says between strums. "Why don't we get everybody over here—Ten-Fifteen, Joe Carter, Tom Jett, the whole gang—and get serious about this thing?"

Gemma smiles and says okay.

Rosalee calls them, and they tell her they'll be there with bells on. She puts the phone down and begins playing the guitar and singing while Gemma gets up from the couch and walks out to the balcony. The creek behind the house is yellow with mud and running a little higher than usual from recent rains. Rosalee's voice carries through the room to the balcony and skips down to the creek, where it gurgles like water over the rocks. Gemma rubs her fingers over the railing and looks out at the mountain across the creek. She considers how many times Gilman must have stood here in this very spot, looking at the same scene.

Rosalee finishes the song just as Ten-Fifteen walks into the apartment and asks, "Where's the party?"

"You've found it," Gemma hears her tell him.

Rosalee looks out at the balcony, where her friend is still standing. "Hey, Gemma," she yells to her. "Me and Ten-Fifteen ain't goin to sit in here and act like fools all by ourselves. We ain't the ones that needs to get drunk, anyway." Rosalee starts picking another tune while she's talking.

Gemma turns away from the creek and looks in at them. Ten-Fifteen is sitting on the piano stool, tapping his toes while Rosalee smiles and holds on to her guitar as if it is part of herself. I will never lose this, she tells herself. Like Gilman, I will always be here no matter what.

"Are you coming?" Rosalee yells.

"Be right there," Gemma says and goes inside.